Jesmyn Ward

Jesmyn Ward

New Critical Essays

Edited by
Sheri-Marie Harrison, Arin Keeble and
Maria Elena Torres-Quevedo

EDINBURGH
University Press

Edinburgh University Press is one of the leading university presses in the UK. We publish academic books and journals in our selected subject areas across the humanities and social sciences, combining cutting-edge scholarship with high editorial and production values to produce academic works of lasting importance. For more information visit our website: edinburghuniversitypress.com

Edinburgh University Press Ltd
13 Infirmary Street, Edinburgh, EH1 1LT

First published in hardback by Edinburgh University Press 2023

Typeset in Sabon and Futura
by Manila Typesetting Company

A CIP record for this book is available from the British Library

ISBN 978 1 3995 1061 5 (hardback)
ISBN 978 1 3995 1062 2 (paperback)
ISBN 978 1 3995 1063 9 (webready PDF)
ISBN 978 1 3995 1064 6 (epub)

Contents

Contributors

Devon Anderson is a doctoral candidate in the Department of English and American Studies at the Paris Lodron University of Salzburg. Her dissertation project examines the role of disnarration in early twentieth-century queer autobiographical writing. Devon holds a bachelor's degree in English Literature from the University of California, Berkeley, a master's degree in English from Brown University, and a master's degree in adolescent education from Hunter College, CUNY. She has taught undergraduate courses on American literature, queer theory, gender theory, theories of reading, critical thinking and non-fiction writing. In addition to her academic research, Devon teaches literature courses at the American International School, Salzburg.

Lucy Arnold is a Lecturer in English Literature (Contemporary) in the Department of English, Media and Culture at the University of Worcester, UK. She is a specialist in contemporary literature with particular research interests in contemporary Gothic, narratives of haunting, contemporary women's writing and psychoanalytic criticism. Her published work to date has concerned the writing of Booker Prize winning novelist Hilary Mantel, including her monograph, *Reading Hilary Mantel: Haunted Decades* (2019). Outside of her research and teaching, she is currently exploring the use of psychodynamic theory in higher education teaching. She is currently working on her second monograph project, *Little Strangers: The Spectral Child in Contemporary Literary Culture*.

Martyn Bone is Associate Professor of American literature at the University of Copenhagen. He was previously Associate Professor of English at the University of Mississippi, and Lecturer in American studies at the University of Nottingham. He is the author of *Where the New World Is: Literature about the U.S. South at Global Scales* (2018) and *The Postsouthern Sense of Place in Contemporary Fiction* (2005). He is the editor of *Perspectives on Barry Hannah* (2007) and co-editor of the University Press of Florida mini-series *Creating Citizenship in the Nineteenth-Century South* (2013), *The American South in the Atlantic World* (2013) and *Creating and Consuming the American South* (2015). His articles have appeared in *American Literature, African American Review, Journal of American Studies, Mississippi Quarterly* and other journals. For the 2022–3 academic year, a monograph fellowship awarded by Denmark's Carlsberg Foundation will support the writing of 'Matters of Black Southern Life and Death: The Writing of Jesmyn Ward'.

Donald Brown is a Postdoctoral Fellow at Brown University in their English Department. He specialises in twentieth-century African American literature and focuses on how the Great Migration impacted the Southern region of the United States.

Candice N. Hale is a Black biracial woman from the Deep South, who has always been keen on highlighting her journey of race in America. She has been teaching English composition and literature for fifteen years now in the South at different colleges and universities. For Hale, literature is both escape from and instruction for society. She holds a PhD in English from Louisiana State University. She specialises in twentieth-century and contemporary African American Literature. She also has a specialised minor in Women's and Gender Studies. She has one daughter, two cocker spaniels and family in Alabama.

Sheri-Marie Harrison is an Associate Dean of Graduate Studies and Faculty Success at the University of Missouri, where she also researches and teaches contemporary literature and mass culture of the African Diaspora, and directs the Individualized Degrees programme. She is the author of *Negotiating Sovereignty in Postcolonial Jamaican Literature* (2014). Among her ongoing projects is an author study of Marlon James and a monograph on genre in contemporary Black fiction. She is also a co-editor for the *Routledge Companion to the Novel* (forthcoming 2024).

Arin Keeble is a Lecturer in Contemporary Literature at Edinburgh Napier University. His most recent book is *Narratives of Hurricane*

Katrina in Context (2019) and his essays can be found in *Journal of American Studies, Critique: Studies in Contemporary Fiction, Parallax, Post45 Contemporaries, Comparative American Studies, European Journal of American Culture, Canadian Review of American Studies* and the *Times Literary Supplement*, and in collections including *The Routledge Companion to Twenty-First Century Literary Fiction, The City in American Literature and Culture* and *The Routledge Companion to Music and Modern Literature.*

Zsuzsanna Lénárt-Muszka teaches at the North American Department of the Institute of English and American Studies, University of Debrecen, Hungary. She received her doctorate from the University of Debrecen (2021); the title of her dissertation is *Mothers in the Wake of Slavery: The Im/possibility of Motherhood in Post-1980 African American Women's Prose.* Her research interests include the portrayals of maternal bodies and subjectivities in contemporary North American literature and visual culture, girlhood studies and Afropessimism.

Apryl Lewis received her PhD from Texas Tech University in 2021 and is an instructor at Fresno City College. Her research interests centre on contemporary African American literature, Black Feminist Studies and trauma studies. Her monograph, *Black Feminism and Traumatic Legacies Within Contemporary African American Literature*, examines select African American novels and applies trauma studies and Black Feminist Studies to advance scholarly discussions about an African American literary tradition that articulates the impact of slavery's traumatic legacy over time.

Christopher Lloyd is a Senior Lecturer in English Literature and Learning and Teaching Specialist at the University of Hertfordshire, and co-editor of the *European Journal of American Culture*. He is the author of *Corporeal Legacies in the US South: Memory and Embodiment in Contemporary Culture* (2018), *Rooting Memory, Rooting Place: Regionalism in the Twenty-First-Century American South* (2015), and numerous special issues, journal articles and book chapters on race and memory in contemporary US culture.

Mary McCampbell is Associate Professor of Humanities at Lee University where she regularly teaches courses on critical theory and fiction, film and philosophy, popular culture, and modernism. Recent academic publications include chapters or articles on contemporary fiction and popular culture in *Isn't it Ironic?: Irony in Contemporary Popular Culture*, *ASAP Journal*, *Spiritual Identities: Literature and the Post-Secular Imagination*, *Sacred and Immoral: on the Writings of Chuck Palahniuk* and The Modern Humanities Research Association's *Yearbook of English Studies*. Her first book, *Imagining Our Neighbors as Ourselves: Empathy, the Arts, and the Religious Imagination* came out in April 2022.

Wendy McMahon is an Associate Professor in the literature and culture of the Americas at the University of East Anglia. She specialises in contemporary Caribbean and African American literatures, legacies of colonialism in contemporary culture, human rights, literature and law, and American Studies, particularly the crises and responses to crises of the twenty-first century.

Chiara Margiotta is a postgraduate researcher at Edinburgh Napier University, looking at the intersections of abjection, class and race in contemporary literature and new critical interpretations of Kristevan abjection theory. Her research is focused on marginalised bodies and, in particular, the maternal body.

Lara Narcisi is a Professor of English with degrees from Yale and New York University. Her areas of specialisation are twentieth- and twenty-first-century American literature, race and gender studies, and literary theory. She has given presentations at the MLA, MELUS and ALA conventions, and at conferences at Oxford University and Kings College, London. Her essays appear in journals such as *MELUS* and *JMMLA*, and her recent book chapters appear in *American Indians and Popular Culture*, *Critical Insights: Kurt Vonnegut*, and *Passing While 'Post-Racial': Performance and Identity Production in Neo-Passing Narratives*. Dr Narcisi teaches such classes as 'Race and Gender in American Culture', 'Freaks and Geeks: The Abnormal in Contemporary Literature', 'Faulkner', 'U.S. Women Writers of Color', 'Contemporary African American Lit' and 'Literature of the Atomic Age'. She was most honoured to receive the Golden Dozen Outstanding Teaching Award (all faculty, university-wide) at New York University, and the 2019–20 Faculty Lecturer of the Year award at Regis.

Melanie Petch is a Senior Lecturer in Design Cultures at De Montfort University in the UK. Her research contributes to the growing interdisciplinary field of material culture and contemporary literary studies. She is interested in the link between the wearing of cloth and the self, and how this is expressed through modern and contemporary literature.

Marco Petrelli is a Research Fellow in Anglo-American literature at the University of Turin, lecturer of Anglo-American literature at the University of Bologna, and literary critic for the Italian newspaper *il manifesto*. He authored *Paradiso in nero* (2020); *Nick Cave. Preghiere di fuoco e ballate assassine* (2021); and several essays dedicated to the literature and culture of the US South, American Gothic fiction, African American literature, geocriticism and graphic narratives. His current research project focuses on the role of ghosts in contemporary African American Gothic narratives.

Cydney Phillip is a UK Arts and Humanities Research Council-funded PhD candidate at Goldsmiths, University of London. Her thesis intervenes in emergent discussions of the Plantationocene by illuminating the patterns of aqueously mediated, racialised violence that underpin it. Engaging with first-hand community responses to the ecologically mediated legacies of the Plantation, her work investigates how expressive cultures of the US South offer alternative epistemologies of the Plantationocene and illuminate the ways in which plantation structures of the past and present are indebted to water.

Jay N. Shelat is an Assistant Professor of English at Ursinus College. His research on contemporary literature and culture has appeared in *TSLL*, *Post45 Contemporaries*, *CEA Critic* and elsewhere. He is currently working on a book about how 9/11 and the War on Terror effect familial and domestic dynamics. You can find him on Twitter @jshelat1.

Beth Beatrice Smith is a full Professor in the English department at SUNY Nassau. She holds a BA in English from Wesleyan University, an MFA in creative writing from The New School and an MA in Literature, Language and Theory from Hunter College. Smith lives in New York City.

Michelle Stork studied English Studies, Moving Cultures, Comparative Literary Studies and History of Art at Goethe University Frankfurt and Universiteit Utrecht. She holds an MA in Moving Cultures – Transcultural Encounters and an MA in History of Art, both from Goethe University Frankfurt. Her PhD project aims at reading road narratives in fiction and film across the anglophone world from a transcultural perspective. Since November 2020, Michelle has held a scholarship with the German Academic Scholarship Foundation. Her research has been published in an edited volume entitled *Mobilizing Narratives: Narrating Injustices of (Im)Mobility* (2021) and in *Postcolonial Interventions* (2022).

Maria Elena Torres-Quevedo is a trade union organiser based in Edinburgh. She received her PhD from Edinburgh University in 2021. Her dissertation focused on contemporary American women's autobiographies and posthumanism.

Leah Van Dyk (she/her) is a doctoral candidate and Killam Laureate in the Department of English at the University of Calgary. She gratefully researches and studies as a settler on the traditional territory of Treaty 7, with her primary research interests located around the environmental humanities and radical revisionings of being in community – both pedagogically and practically – as a model of literary practice. She has recent publications in *English Studies in Canada* and *Research on Diversity in Youth Literature*, is passionate about community projects, and is overly fond of tea. Follow her on Instagram and Twitter @leahvandyk.

Introduction: The Restless Social Vision of Jesmyn Ward

*Sheri-Marie Harrison, Arin Keeble
and Maria Elena Torres-Quevedo*

On 1 September 2020, Jesmyn Ward's essay 'On Witness and Respair: A Personal Tragedy Followed by a Pandemic' was published in a special issue of *Vanity Fair*. It was not Ward's first personal essay, and it is not an entirely unusual example of this increasingly popular form, either.[1] However, this moving account of loss and grief in the contexts of the Covid-19 pandemic, and the global protests against systemic racism that followed the murder of George Floyd, is a vivid example of Ward's unique voice. The craft and clarity of the prose, the balance between control and urgency, and the restless, searching range of its social vision are redolent of the qualities that make the two-time National Book Award-winning author's work so important. Over three short pages, 'On Witness and Respair' also exemplifies the generosity of Ward's writing, in its sharing of the most intimate and private of experiences in order to help better understand and better resist America's present and deep history of systemic racism and state neglect. And, as in Ward's long-form fiction and non-fiction, it connects the imperative to challenge and resist endemic white supremacism in America, to global anti-racist and anti-colonial currents. Indeed, as in her three novels and memoir, 'On Witness and Respair' depicts traumas private and public occurring in the contexts of the slow violence of historic and institutional prejudice. Yet, reading Ward's writing strictly as trauma fiction, or poverty realism would be a mistake and the chapters in this volume focus variously on her depictions of community and kinship, her engagements with the natural world, the historical and intertextual dimensions of her work, and crucially, the possibilities for hope that emerge via gestures of solidarity and care. Trauma is undoubtedly a component of Ward's writing, but the essays here consider a broader matrix of public and private forms of memory, systemic violence and unyielding hope – and show how Ward's writing brings the intersections of these phenomena uniquely into focus.

'On Witness and Respair' begins with an intimate depiction of the days and hours leading to the loss of the author's husband – her 'Beloved' – in January 2020, just before the pandemic swept America and the world (Ward 2020, 104). It is a painful read, particularly for those who have read Ward's memoir, *Men We Reaped* (2013), or who know the story of how she lost her brother, cousin and three close friends in the early 2000s in 'seemingly unrelated' circumstances.[2] Ward describes how she and her husband and their two children all got the flu, but while the rest of the family responded to treatment, her husband did not. And in just the second paragraph of the essay she describes his last hours and death from organ failure and sepsis. But in her account of this tragic and deeply personal moment, there is also a gesture outward. We learn that just before he died, Ward's husband 'panted: *Can't. Breathe*', an expression that has taken on great power and significance since the death of Eric Garner in 2014 (Ward 2020, 104). From this point, in a movement that poetically combines love, defiance, resistance and a will to survive, the essay formally replicates the act of taking a breath: it expands – deeply and purposefully – and then contracts. It moves from this private moment of immeasurable personal loss outward to a stirring account of the protests that exploded after another Black man's life was violently extinguished by a police officer – his own desperate attempts to breathe beneath the officer's knee, captured in a viral video. It expands further, taking in the global scope of this moment of protest from Mississippi to Paris, New Zealand and London and swells further still, framing this moment world-historically:

> I woke to droves of people in Paris, sidewalk to sidewalk, moving like a river down the boulevards. I knew the Mississippi, I knew the plantations on its shores, the movement of enslaved and cotton up and down its eddies. The people marched, and I had never known that there could be rivers such as this, and as protesters chanted and stomped, as they grimaced and shouted and groaned, tears burned my face. (Ward 2020, 105)

Finally, after a closing movement which connects these scenes to the steady '*thump*' of the author's own heartbeat, and after an impassioned refrain that calls readers to 'witness' both the power of protest and the continuing violence of injustice, the essay contracts again (Ward 2020, 105), narrowing back to the painfully personal. In a closing paragraph it returns to the depiction of intensely felt love and loss that it began with, and in doing so it connects this very public, historical moment to an intimate human story.

'On Witness and Respair' is exemplary of the clarity and scope of Ward's social vision as well as the range and diversity of her oeuvre. Not only is it examplary of the ways Ward's writing connects the intimate stories of individuals and families to larger public events and histories, but it is also a potent example of the unique way her writing combines expressions of grief and anger with expressions of love and solidarity. These seemingly contradictory impulses are taken up in one way or another in all the chapters in this volume. For instance, Wendy McMahon emphasises precisely this sense of range in the opening chapter of this book, 'Bois Sauvage as Biotope', an exploration of the fictional inner-coastal Mississippi town in which all of Ward's novels are set. McMahon notes that, '[d]espite the violence that saturates the landscape of Bois Sauvage, all three novels create a life world full of deep relationships between people and the environment' (p. 24). In the next chapter, 'Wayward Kinship and Malleable Intimacies', Jay Shelat also identifies forms of optimism in his analysis of the 'grammar of intimacy' that comes into view in Ward's depiction of families, where despite endemic racism there is an 'ever-budding vulnerability that permits trust, hope, and love' (pp. 27–8).

These ways in which Ward's writing depicts the effects of historical and biopolitical state violence and neglect, while emphasising forms of solidarity and care in communities and families, call to mind one of the theoretical touchstones for the chapters in this volume: Christina Sharpe's *In the Wake: On Blackness and Being* (2015). Sharpe uses various definitions of the term 'wake' – beginning with '*the track left on the water's surface by a ship*', or more precisely, slave ship, and building 'a conceptual framework of and for living blackness in the diaspora in the still unfolding aftermaths of Atlantic chattel slavery' (Sharpe 2015, 1, 3). This term also refers to 'the state of wakefulness; consciousness' and to the idea of keeping watch with the dead (4). Indeed, among the definitions of wake that are deployed in Sharpe's book that bear direct relevance for Ward's work are wake as 'grief, celebration, memory, and those among the living who, through ritual, mourn their passing and celebrate their life in particular the watching of relatives and friends beside the body of the dead person from death to burial and the drinking, feasting, and other observances incidental to this' (10). Sharpe tells us too, that 'death, disaster, *and possibility*' are all present in the wakes of 'the river, the weather, and the drowning' (104, cmphasis added). This potent and multifaceted use of figurative language – which often draws on images of nature and climate – connects to Ward's fiction and non-fiction in some compelling ways. Like Sharpe, Ward addresses affective phenomena and material realities that are sometimes contradictory and complex with language that is suggestively open and multivalently symbolic, but also purposeful and precise. Consider for instance, these lines from the final pages of Ward's memoir, *Men We Reaped*:

> We who still live do what we must. Life is a hurricane, and we board up to save what we can and bow low to the earth to crouch in that small space above the dirt where the wind will not reach. We honor anniversaries of deaths by cleaning graves and sitting next to them before fires, sharing food with those who will not eat again. We raise children and tell them other things about who they can be and what they are worth: to us, everything. We love each other fiercely, while we live and after we die. We survive; we are savages.

This is a stark and moving image of survival under contemporary, racialised neoliberalism. Here, the 'other things' that children are told about 'who they can be' will in some cases be fantasies that briefly obscure the pernicious forces of state violence, or correctives that respond to normative logics and racist stereotypes – or both. There are other evocative ideas at work here, too. Ward does not just express fierce love for those who have passed but insists that 'we love each other fiercely while we live, and after we die', suggesting that the dead can love too. This notion is addressed throughout this collection. For instance, In Chapter 12, 'Releasing the Heavy Repercussions of Black Death in Jesmyn Ward's *Men We Reaped*', Candice N. Hale reads Ward's memoir as a kind of conversation with the five young men whose deaths structure the book. The spiritual and supernatural elements of *Sing, Unburied, Sing*, which followed *Men We Reaped*, are also foreshadowed here, and this is a part of Ward's writing that is taken up directly by Lucy Arnold in Chapter 14, '"Something like praying": Syncretic Spirituality and Racial Justice in Jesmyn Ward's *Sing, Unburied, Sing*' and Mary McCampbell in Chapter 13, 'A Prophetic Tension: Bearing Witness Against Black Nihilism in Jesmyn Ward's *Men We Reaped*'. While Arnold's analysis of the depiction of Haitian and Louisiana Voodou and Hoodoo is very different to McCampbell's discussion of the 'absence and presence' of Christianity, both move away from the focus on traumatic haunting that has been prevalent in Ward scholarship. But if the image of loving 'each other fiercely, while we live and after we die' suggests alternatives to the dominant discourses of psychological trauma (where one is trapped in the frozen moment of incomprehensible violence or loss) or trauma fiction (which seeks to find a way to represent the unrepresentable) then the final declaration of the above passage, 'we are savages' is stark, unadorned and unsentimental. It suggests a state of being where grief, anger, 'fierce' love and the imperative to survive have stripped away pretences and superficiality. Certainly, the word 'savage' feels in some way synonymous with Ward, given that all three of her novels take place in the fictional 'Bois Sauvage' and even in that 'savage' is a letter away from 'salvage', and therefore *Salvage the Bones*.

There is much more to say about this passage from *Men We Reaped* or 'On Witness and Respair', but we begin with these short readings as examples of the qualities of Ward's writing that make it so rich: the balance between the thickly figurative and precisely descriptive, the urgency and control of the prose, and its restless, searching, social vision. The aim of this volume, in broad terms, is to provide a diverse spectrum of approaches to Ward's writing, within its key cultural, political, social and historical contexts, that does justice to this distinct body of work. In some ways this is a unified oeuvre that is characterised by striking continuities and connections. As noted, each of Ward's three novels, *Where the Line Bleeds* (2007), *Salvage the Bones* (2011) and *Sing, Unburied, Sing* (2017) is set in the fictional town of Bois Sauvage, Mississippi, a town that approximates Ward's home town of DeLisle, Mississippi – memorably depicted in *Men We Reaped* (2013). In each of these depictions of Bois Sauvage – and DeLisle – a powerful image of the daily experience of precarity and state neglect or abandonment emerges. This is a community that sustains itself in the absence of any social safety net and where the only institutional interventions are menacing ones.

During Ward's formative years, a period her fiction draws heavily from, the Mississippi Gulf Coast was particularly impacted by the accelerated neoliberalism of the Clinton administration, whose 'Personal Responsibility and Work Opportunity Reconciliation Act' of 1996 represented what Liam Kennedy and Stephen Shapiro have described as a 'concluding blow to the American working class' (Kennedy and Shapiro 2019, 12).[3] This evisceration of the welfare state also coincided with a 'tough on crime' approach designed to appease conservative voters, which inevitably was aggressively meted out on poor Black communities. As Michelle Alexander has shown, this period, which immediately precedes Ward's novels, 'created the current racial undercaste' and resulted in so many citizens being 'locked out ... of mainstream society' (Alexander 2011, 57). This bleak social and economic reality is a constant part of Ward's writing, as are the mechanisms that people in her region rely on to survive: family, community and kinship. Indeed, characters recur across the three Bois Sauvage novels, and Ward's writing consistently explores the meanings of family relationships in this context.

There are other forms of connective tissue across Ward's works, too. Her writing's sustained engagement with the natural world, climate and extraction are discussed in multiple chapters here. In addition to various engagements with climate change and extraction in *Salvage the Bones*, in Chapter 16, 'Experiencing the Environment from the Car: Human and More-than-Human Road Trippers in Jesmyn Ward's *Sing, Unburied, Sing*', Michelle Stork analyses the 'road trip from Bois Sauvage to Parchman prison and back against the backdrop of the Deepwater Horizon oil spill' in *Sing, Unburied Sing*, linking 'historical and ongoing racialised violence to environmental concerns' (p. 254). In 'Carceral Ecologies: Incarceration and Hydrological Haunting in Jesmyn Ward's *Sing, Unburied, Sing*', Cydney Phillip identifies another critically important dimension of this novel, arguing that 'it prompts us to engage with the ways in which water is imbricated in the carceral continuum from slavery to mass incarceration' (p. 290). Another way in which Ward's oeuvre is broadly unified is via its intertextual gestures. This includes the way characters appear across the novels, but also in the patterns of allusion and citation that come into view in each of her long-form works. This feature of Ward's writing has been the subject of some of the most prominent existing scholarly works on the author and several of our chapters build on this scholarship.[4] For example, in Chapter 9, Chiara Margiotta further develops Sinéad Moynihan's argument that *Salvage the Bones* operates via acts of 'literary recycling' and discusses the novel in relation to a 'lineage of Black literary foremothers' (p. 141) citing work by Alice Walker, Gayl Jones, Toni Morrison and Saphire. Similarly, in Chapter 19, Lara Narcisi reads *Sing, Unburied, Sing* in critical conversation with Toni Morrison's *Song of Soloman* (1977) and compares the ways in which both novels 'use physical journeys to initiate historical journeys' (p. 305).

History is, of course, another topic that connects Ward's work and as such it is another central theme in our collection. For instance, Chris Lloyd builds on his theory of 'corporeal legacies', the subject of his 2018 monograph, *Corporeal Legacies in the US South: Memory and Embodiment in Contemporary Culture* (2018), in Chapter 15, 'Ghosts in Mississippi: Jesmyn Ward's *Sing, Unburied, Sing*'. For Lloyd – like other authors here – the novel is 'about giving voice to the dead' but also about forms of 'embodiment' that 'index or register the ongoing and historical subjugations of, and violence done to, Black lives in the US South and beyond' (p. 240). In Chapter 3, Donald Brown positions Ward's body of work as a 'counternarrative to the migration narrative' and theorises this work as exemplars of the contemporary 'standoff narrative', that centre the experience of 'Black Southerners who reused to be moved despite many attempts by Southern white supremacists to disperse and dispossess' them (p. 44).

Yet despite these continuities and connections, and the clear thematic links, each of Ward's novels has its own distinct formal features and genre identifications, meaning that Ward's oeuvre is unified but also diverse and ranging. Her first novel, *Where the Line Bleeds* (2007), is a coming-of-age story about twin brothers, raised by their blind grandmother. As the boys graduate high school and enter adulthood, the severely limited opportunities available to them put pressure on their young lives and their paths diverge. *Salvage the Bones* is, using Susan Fraiman's and Kristen J. Jacobson's definitions, a 'domestic' novel, about the lives of teenage siblings surviving and supporting each other in the face of both everyday precarity and the imminent landfall of Hurricane Katrina.[5] *Sing, Unburied, Sing* (2017) is a road novel that also, as Sheri-Marie Harrison has noted, reworks 'Gothic traditions for the 21st Century' (Harrison 2019). At its heart is Jojo, a young teenager who cares for his toddler-aged sister while their mother grapples with addiction and the trauma of having lost her own brother, Given, whose ghost haunts her throughout the narrative. A fourth novel (October 2023) is a historical narrative set in the mid-nineteenth century, about an 'enslaved woman whose mother is stolen from her and sold south to New Orleans, whose lover is stolen from and her and sold south, who herself is sold south and descends into the hell of chattel slavery in the mid-1800s' (Ward 2020, 104). In addition to these three published novels, the novel in progress and memoir, Ward has also edited a collection of essays, *The Fire This Time* (2015), and has recently published a commencement speech she made at Tulane in 2018 as *Navigate Your Stars* (2020). This is a stunningly diverse body of work, despite the clear thematic links that we have outlined and points to a kind of restlessness: Ward is both focused on the stories of her community in the past and present, but perennially looking for new ways to tell these stories.

Given the ways that Ward's oeuvre is both unified and divergent, as co-editors we puzzled over the most appropriate structure for this book. There are certainly some clear thematic clusters that might have been used to guide its organisation: nature and climate, history and memory, community and family, and intertextuality, for instance.

This was, broadly speaking, our provisional plan and we held two Zoom meetings with our authors to develop these groupings and to foster connections across the chapters. In addition to the sections we initially imagined, a rich set of less obvious echoes and resonances came into view and we became less persuaded by the idea of imposing any kind of thematic order. Ultimately, the least contrived and most satisfying structure emerged by arranging the chapters by text, beginning with essays discussing the body of work as a whole, then moving chronologically from *Where the Line Bleeds* to *Salvage the Bones* to *Men We Reaped*, and finally, to *Sing, Unburied, Sing*. It is worth noting here that many of our authors have gravitated towards Ward's short-form non-fiction, too. Indeed, from Donald Brown's discussions of Ward's 2016 Buzzfeed article, 'This Was the Year America Finally Saw the South' and her recent 'Introduction' to the *Penguin Best American Short Stories* (2021), to Candice N. Hale's citations of 'On Witness and Respair', Ward's short-form writing is in constant conversation with her books.

The first three chapters, by Wendy McMahon, Jay Shelat and Donald Brown, discuss Ward's work in broad terms, focusing in turn – but with many compelling overlaps – on setting, family and community, and history. These are followed by two chapters on *Where the Line Bleeds*, by Martyn Bone and Beth Beatrice Smith, which we believe are the first full scholarly discussions of Ward's overlooked debut novel. Bone reads the novel as an examination of racialised and neoliberalised disposability via the central relationship between twin protagonists Joshua and Christophe, while Smith connects the physical landscape of Bois Sauvage – interrogating notions of the 'dirty South' – to the interior worlds of the twin protagonists. We then move into five diverse chapters on Ward's breakthrough novel, *Salvage the Bones*. Leah Van Dyk discusses the ways in which it 'examines the disproportionate effect of the climate crisis and environmental degradation on marginalised bodies' (p. 95). Following this, Devon Anderson discusses the ways the novel depicts social abandonment alongside 'descriptions of a natural world marked by poverty and neglect' (p. 111). Zsuzsanna Lénárt-Muszka draws on the figurative language of 'the weather' and 'the wake' in a discussion of *Salvage* as a novel that 'juxtaposes the literal and metaphorical meanings' of the weather and climate (p. 126). This is followed by Margiotta's previously mentioned intertextual reading of the novel, and then by an innovative interdisciplinary chapter by Melanie Petch, who focuses on the novel's depiction of cloth and clothing and provides a new understanding of the novel's depiction of material deprivation and its characters' experiences of intimacy and corporeality. We then move into three chapters on *Men We Reaped*. Maria Elena Torres-Quevedo argues that it subverts the ideological components of American autobiography by exposing the biopolitical realities of 'cruel optimism' and via emphasis on community rather than individualism. For Torres-Quevedo, Ward's memoir is a disavowal of the rags-to-riches individualism that typifies the genre. Candice N. Hale then focuses on making visible the connections between the 'seemingly unrelated' deaths of the five young Black men that are a central focus of the memoir. This is followed by Mary McCampbell's analysis of Ward's relationship with Christianity, and the 'presence and absence of God' in *Men We Reaped*.

We conclude with seven diverse approaches to *Sing, Unburied, Sing*. Lucy Arnold's chapter follows nicely on from McCampbell's, in that it also focuses on the spiritual, though rather than Christianity it considers Haitian and Louisianan Hoodoo and Voudou, in an in-depth analysis of the spiritual dimensions of the novel. Further connections emerge in Christopher Lloyd's discussion of history and embodiment, which resonates powerfully alongside the chapters by Petch, and Brown. Michelle Stork's and Cydney Phillip's previously noted environmental readings are nicely complemented by Apryl Lewis's reflexive and probing discussion of the novel's depiction of intergenerational trauma. Finally, we conclude with Lara Narcisi's intertextual reading of the novel alongside Morrison's *Song of Solomon* (1977) and the final chapter, Marco Petrelli's '"I Need the Story to Go": *Sing, Unburied, Sing*, Afropessimism and Black Narratives of Redemption'. Petrelli reads the novel in the context of Ward's wider oeuvre, but looks in depth at this novel's depiction of the supernatural, noting a set of key departures.

Near the end of *Sing, Unburied, Sing*, Leonie, grappling with addiction and the burdens of parenthood, and haunted by the loss of her brother, Given, draws strength from family even as she struggles in her familial roles. In a moving scene she recalls tracing the lines of her father's tattoos as a child:

> a ship; a woman who looked like Mama, clothed in clouds and carrying arrows and a pine branch in her hand; and two cranes: one for me and one for Given. Given's is alight, poised in flight, feet skimming the marsh grass, while mine is beak down in the mud. When I was five, Pop point at mine and told me: *This is the one I got for you: they a sign of luck when you see them, mean everything is in balance, that it's raining good and there's fish and here's things squirming under the marsh mud, that the bayou grass going to be green soon. They a sign of life.* (212–13)

Some of the most distinctive features of Ward's writing are visible in this scene: an emphasis on the power of familial ties, as well as living daily with loss; the beauty, violence and potent symbolism of the natural; and the collapsing of hierarchies of life. We are deeply grateful to Jesmyn Ward for her generative and illuminating work. This collection would not be possible without our contributors, and we thank them for their attention to Ward's writing. Among the things that we are proudest of is that the critical perspectives offered here include an international array of scholars from all strata of the profession. More than representation, this range of perspectives reflect the broad reach of Ward's work. We are pleased to present this volume that explores these and so many other features of Ward's writing through a diverse range of approaches. In our view, these essays confirm Ward's place as a critically important voice in contemporary world literature.

Notes

1. Other notable personal essays include 'Cracking the Code', a *New Yorker* essay that would later feature in *The Fire This Time* (2015); her *Buzzfeed* essay, 'This Was the Year America Finally Saw the South' (2016) and her introduction to the *Penguin Best American Short Stories* (2021), which Ward edited.

2. In the introduction to Ward's memoir, *Men We Reaped* (2013), she describes the deaths her book sets out to discuss: 'From 2000 to 2004, five Black young men I grew up with died, all violently, in seemingly unrelated deaths' (7). The conspicuous part of this short, succinct sentence is the 'seemingly', which tells us that there are in fact connections in the deaths but that it might not be immediately obvious. The connections are systemic inequality, structural racism and the absence of the state, and through the narrative's unique structure, it is able to make these connections visible.

3. In their influential introduction to *Contemporary Literature and Neo-liberalism and Contemporary Literary Culture* (2017), Mitchum Huehls and Rachel Greenwald Smith posit a 'four phases' periodisation of neoliberalism where the 90s is critically important: 'the Clinton-Blair nineties mark a more granular extension' from economic policies and ideological formations into 'previously noneconomic domains of human life' (7).

4. Essays by Sinèad Moynihan (2015) and Benjamin Eldon Stevens (2018) focus respectively on *Salvage the Bones*'s key diegetic intertexts: William Falkner's *As I Lay Dying* (1930) and the Medea myth as it appears in Edith Hamilton's *Mythology* (1942). Other essays by Mary Ruth Marotte (2015) and Holly Cade Brown (2017) discuss Ward's intertextual references to other African American pregnancy narratives such as Toni Morrison's *Beloved* (1987). More recently, a wave of scholarship on *Sing, Unburied, Sing* has identified the

ways that the novel responds to previous iterations of the US 'road novel' and 'Southern Gothic' fiction.

5. Kristin J. Jacobson's recuperation of the term 'domestic fiction' in *Neodomestic American Fictions* (2010) is a useful point of reference here. Jacobson points out that 'domestic literature features a self-consciousness about the home's physical space and the project of homemaking, highlighting domestic instability in positive and negative ways' (3). *Salvage the Bones* certainly emphasises its narrator Esch's obsessions with the precarity of both the physical spaces of the home and her family's well-being. Furthermore, the domesticity of *Salvage the Bones* is also exemplary of some aspects of what Susan Fraiman identifies in *Extreme Domesticity: Voices from the Margins* (2017), which sees the representation of sites of precarious domesticity as potential acts of resistance. Fraiman points to visions of home and homemaking that are characterised by 'economic insecurity' and 'physical vulnerability', perhaps the defining features of the Batiste's family home in *Salvage the Bones*, which they refer to as 'The Pit' (9). Arin Keeble also focuses on domesticity in *Salvage the Bones* in the first chapter of *Narratives of Hurricane Katrina in Context: Literature, Film and Television* (2019).

Works Cited

Alexander, Michelle. 2011. *The New Jim Crow: Mass Incarceration in the Age of Colourblindness*. London: Penguin.

Berlant, Lauren. 2011. *Cruel Optimism*. Durham, NC: Duke University Press.

Cade Brown, Holly. 2017. 'Figuring Giorgio Agamben's "bare Life" in the Post-Katrina Works of Jesmyn Ward and Kara Walker'. *Journal of American Studies* 51, no. 1 (February): 1–19.

Eldon Stevens, Benjamin. 2018. 'Medea in Jesmyn Ward's Salvage the Bones'. *International Journal of the Classical Tradition* 25 (2): 158–77. https://doi:10.1007/s12138-016-0394-6.

Fraiman, Susan. 2017. *Extreme Domesticity: A View from the Margins*. New York: Columbia University Press.

Harrison, Sheri-Marie. 2019. 'Global Horror: An Introduction'. *Post45 Contemporaries*, 4 April. https://post45.org/2019/04/global-horror-an-introduction/.

Huehls, Mitchum, and Rachel Greenwald Smith, eds. 2017. *Neoliberalism and Contemporary Literary Culture*. Baltimore: Johns Hopkins University Press.

Jacobson, Kristen J. 2010. *Neodomestic American Fictions*. Columbus: Ohio State University Press.

Keeble, Arin. 2019. *Narratives of Hurricane Katrina in Context: Literature, Film and Television*. Basingstoke: Palgrave.

Kennedy, Liam, and Stephen Shapiro, eds. 2019. *Neoliberalism and Contemporary American Literature*. Hanover, NH: Dartmouth College Press.

Marotte, Mary Ruth. 2015. 'Pregnancies, Storms and Legacies of Loss in Jesmyn Ward's Salvage the Bones'. In *Ten Years after Katrina: Critical Perspectives of the Storm's Effect on American Culture and Identity*, edited by Mary Ruth Marotte and Glenn Jellenik. Lanham, MD: Lexington Books.

Moynihan, Sinèad. 2015. 'From Disposability to Recycling: William Faulkner and the New Politics of Rewriting in Jesmyn Ward's Salvage the Bones'. *Studies in the Novel* 47, no. 4 (Winter): 550–67.

Sharpe, Christina. 2015. *In the Wake: On Blackness and Being*. Durham, NC: Duke University Press.

Ward, Jesmyn. 2007. *Where the Line Bleeds*. London: Bloomsbury.

—. 2011. *Salvage the Bones*. London: Bloomsbury.

—. 2013. *Men We Reaped*. London: Bloomsbury.

—, ed. 2015. *The Fire This Time*. London: Bloomsbury.

—. 2017. *Sing, Unburied, Sing*. London: Bloomsbury.

—. 2020. 'On Witness and Respair'. *Vanity Fair*, 1 September. https://www.vanityfair.com/culture/2020/08/jesmyn-ward-on-husbands-death-and-grief-during-covid.

—, ed. 2021. *Penguin Best American Short Stories 2021*. London: Penguin.

Chapter 1

Bois Sauvage as Biotope in the Novels of Jesmyn Ward

Wendy McMahon

In an interview in 2014 at the Manchester Literature Festival, Jesmyn Ward underlined the importance of place to her writing when she stated her belief that, 'place determines nearly everything about a writer and about a character'. Ward's three fictional works to date, *Where the Line Bleeds* (2008), *Salvage the Bones* (2011) and *Sing, Unburied, Sing* (2017), take place in the fictional town of Bois Sauvage, Mississippi, broadly based on her home town of DeLisle in the same state and as Kelly McKisson highlights, Ward's novels, 'follow the intimacies of this imagined place, Bois Sauvage, situated at the level and scale of human (and often animal) bodies that make up its community' (McKisson 2021, 279). The natural world is deeply inscribed in the novels in which place, indeed, determines everything. As soon as we enter the fictional world of Bois Sauvage, we are introduced to rivers, bayous, trees, birds, family and community livestock, dogs, the climate, weather events, and the red dirt that is an intimate feature in all her characters' lives. The natural world within the novels is not setting, however; rather, it is as important as the characters – and in many ways, inseparable from them. The influence of William Faulkner's fictional world of Yoknapatawpha on Ward's writing is well rehearsed, with Ward herself remarking that the way his writing captures the American South is something she recognises in her bones. For both writers, the landscape and the history inscribed upon it is the vehicle that drives both character and plot and we see the most intimate synergies between Ward's writing and Faulkner's *As I Lay Dying*, the novel that made Ward hesitate in her own writing.[1] As with Faulkner's novel, the landscape of Ward's world is an agent in the action and the boundary between character and setting is blurred. Ward's literary project moves away from and is distinct from Faulkner's in several ways, however. Most obviously, and most regularly discussed, is that Ward's novels attend to the lives of the Black population of Mississippi, giving life to the Black characters that Faulkner leaves flat, creating for us an alternative South attentive to the history of racial exploitation that has formed the landscape. In doing so Ward's writing of Bois Sauvage moves away from Faulkner in powerful ways. For Faulkner, particularly in *As I Lay Dying*, human beings might well be inseparable from the natural world, but they are in perpetual battle with it and the characters within the world of Yoknapatawpha are driven by self-interest. Conversely, Ward's Bois Sauvage is characterised by strong interpersonal and communal bonds tied to the landscape that dignify the lives of the residents of Bois Sauvage and look to possible emancipatory futures.

This chapter reads the world of Bois Sauvage as a biotope; a habitat where the land, animals, plants and people coexist while simultaneously creating, sustaining and surviving their own life worlds. Landscape Studies scholars, Kolen and Renes, define a 'life world' as the 'dwelt-in world of people and other animals and actors who co-create this world while living together' (Kolen and Renes 2015, 21). To read the novels as biotopes and 'life worlds' moves us further towards an understanding of how the past and the present, the text and history, come together and are deeply inscribed upon the topographical. Landscape, W. J. T. Mitchell insists, 'is a dynamic medium, in which we "live and move and have our being," but also a medium that is itself in motion from place or time to another' (Mitchell 2002, 2), and in Ward's novels to date novelistic time is entangled with historical time, which in turn is entangled with deep time. In the life world of Bois Sauvage, time 'does not consist of a string of discrete "now-moments," but instead past and future are held together in the life world of the present [where] the present retains the past, but also points ahead to what is still to come' (Kolen and Renes 2015, 21). The land, the environment, is not only a place where people live in the now but a place that is a palimpsest of lives that came before. In Ward's texts, history is written and read across the terrain and, importantly, the landscape becomes a way of seeing as it helps communities envisage a future as they navigate the intersections of past and present exploitation.[2]

In this way, landscape is inherently textual; co-scripted by human and natural forces alike with human and ecological experiences inscribed onto the topographical. As Mitchell states in his work on place, it is 'clear that landscapes can be deciphered as textual systems' where '[n]atural features such as trees, stones, water, animals, and dwellings can be read as symbols in religious, psychological, or political allegories; characteristic structures and forms' and 'can be linked with generic and narrative typologies' (Mitchell 2002, 2). What we must pay attention to, he urges, is not what landscape is or means, but rather what it does and 'how it works as a cultural practice' (Mitchell 2002, 3). For Mitchell, landscape is an instrument or, more precisely, an agent of power. Ward's novels explore the dialectical movement between this agent of power and the rest of the biotope of Bois Sauvage. The novels create a complex layered landscape that combines the historical and the geological; tracing the historical record onto the stratigraphy of sediments and buried landscapes exploring the multiple experiences of place to expose the ways that traumatic, violent landscapes naturalise ideologies and oppressive social realities, in order to dignify her characters' lives.

The Biotope of Bois Sauvage

A biotope is a life world for human and non-human subjects where those subjects and the environment create one another in a process of dialectical motion. And, as Kolen and Renes elaborate, landscapes are 'an essential part of human life worlds' that 'have the potential to absorb something of people's loves, works and thoughts', shaping 'life histories on different timescales, imprinted by human existence, affecting personal lives and transcending individual human life cycles' where this 'combination of reciprocity and distinctness creates a strong but complex intertwining of personhood and place' (Kolen and Renes 2015, 21–2). Merleau-Ponty captured this relationship beautifully when he wrote, 'to be a body, is to be tied to a certain world (Merleau-Ponty 2002, 169), and we see this throughout Ward's novels which map the biotopic life world of the characters as one of geographical, geological and historic symbiosis. From the very first page of *Where the Line Bleeds*, for example, we are invited to associate the twin protagonists, Christophe and Joshua, with the topography of Bois Sauvage. The novel opens with a description of the river, moving quickly to include the two main protagonists as part of the terrain, mapping and grounding their place geographically as well as temporally.

> The river was young and small, we are told, at its start it seeped from the red clay earth in the piney woods of Southern Mississippi, and then wound its way, brown and slow, over a bed of tiny gray and ochre pebbles

through the pines, shallow as a hand, deep as three men standing, to the sandy, green lowlands of the gulf of Mexico [. . .] Near the river's end [. . .] two teenage boys, twins [. . .] underneath them, the water of the Wolf River lay dark and deep, feathered by the current.

They were preparing to jump. (Ward [2008] 2018, 1)

This opening of the novel, with its rich description of the river's journey from its source in the 'red clay earth' to where it meets the sea at the Gulf of Mexico, suggests a journey through geological time, too, from the river's beginning to the present, when the twins jump in and swim as they celebrate leaving high school. As noted by Kirsten Dillender in her discussion of *Sing, Unburied, Sing*, but applicable to all three novels set in Bois Sauvage:

Ward imbues the physical landscape with a deep temporality that connects the present of the narrative to the past 'superimposing the past onto the present so that it becomes difficult, or even impossible, to distinguish between them' with 'this temporal conflation connect[ing] the characters' lives with the trauma of those who have come before them and those who will come after'. (Killender 2020, 134, quoting Recker, 26)

The intertwining of past, present and the landscape of Bois Sauvage to form a biotope as life world becomes ever more apparent as *Where the Line Bleeds* progresses. We see the history of the community etched deep into the terrain, with descriptions of its physical elements interwined with personal and community stories of migration that together encapsulate the social history of the region and is helpful to quote at length:

Bois Sauvage dug in small on the back of the bay, isolated. Natural boundaries surrounded it on all three sides. To the south, east, and west, a bayou bordered it, the same bayou that the Wolf River emptied before it pooled into the Bay of Angels and then out to the Gulf of Mexico. There were only two roads that crossed the bayou and led out of Bois Sauvage to St. Catherine, the next town over. To the north, the interstate capped the small town like a ruler, beyond which a thick bristle of pine forest stretched off and away into the horizon. It was beautiful.

Joshua could understand why Ma-mee's and Papa's families had migrated here from New Orleans, had struggled to domesticate the low-lying, sandy earth that reeked of rotten eggs in a dry summer and washed away easily in a wet one. Land had been cheaper along the Mississippi gulf, and black Creoles had spread along the coastline. They'd bargained in broken English and French to buy tens of acres of land. Still, they and their poor white neighbours were dependent on the rich for their liveli-hood just as they had been in New Orleans: they built weekend mansions along the beach for wealthy New Orleans expatriates, cleaned them, did their yard work, and fished, shrimped, and harvested oysters. Yet here, they had space and earth. (Ward [2008] 2018, 6)

This description begins with the named place and ends with the earth, and demonstrates clearly that the communities from which Christophe and Joshua are born are rooted deeply in Bois Sauvage since they 'em-bedded themselves in the red clay and remained' (Ward [2008] 2018, 6). Moreover, the human and built environment are given an intimacy usually preserved for close kin, or evocative of conjuring, with the communities' raising 'small, uneven houses from the red mud' (Ward [2008] 2018, 6). Simultaneously, we see racial and class stratification of the built environment onto the landscape of Bois Sauvage with the 'weekend mansions along the beach' which echo with the descrip-tions in *Salvage the Bones* where we see the natural world revealing the history of slavery: 'there's always a hurricane coming or leaving here', we are told, with each pushing 'its way through the flat Gulf to the twenty-six mile manmade Mississippi beach, where they knock against the old mansions with their slave galleys turned guest houses before running over the bayou, through the pines, to the lose wind, drip rain, and die in the north' (Ward [2011] 2017, 4).

The characters in *Salvage the Bones* and *Sing, Unburied, Sing* have equally intimate relationships with the landscape of Bois Sauvage. The life world depicted is one where the lives of the characters are so intwined that the characters are an extension of the landscape. Across the novels, characters are described in natural terms. Esch's mother was as 'dark as the reaching oak trees' (Ward [2011] 2017, 22); Jojo's grandfather is as 'slim and brown as a young pine tree' (Ward 2017, 1) and the families from both novels share the same in-timacy with the red soil of Bois Sauvage as the family of Christophe and Joshua. Like the land where Christophe and Joshua are rooted, the 'Pit' in *Salvage the Bones* is a historical biography of the family and community. Esch provides us with this history when she tells us:

My mama's mother, Mother Lizabeth, and her daddy, Papa Joseph orig-inally owned all this land: around fifteen acres in all. It was Papa Joseph nicknamed it all the Pit, Papa Joseph who let the white men he work with dig for clay that they used to lay the foundation for houses, let them excavate the side of a hill in a clearing near the back of the property where he used to plant corn for feed. Papa Joseph let them take all the dirt they wanted until their digging had created a cliff over a dry lake in the backyard, and the small stream that had run around and down the hill had diverted and pooled into the dry lake, making it into a pond, and then Papa Joseph thought the earth would give under the water, that the pond would spread and gobble up the property and make it a swamp, so he stopped selling earth for money. (Ward [2011] 2017, 14)

Life stories are etched into the earth alongside the social, cultural and economic histories of an area which threaten to undermine the very place itself.

The presence of history is felt even more keenly in *Sing, Unburied, Sing*, with Pop, Jojo's grandfather, continuously telling him stories. 'That is what Pop does when we are alone, sitting up late at night in the living room or out in the yard or woods' Jojo tells us, 'He tells me stories' (Ward 2017, 17). Whereas *Where the Line Bleeds* opens its narrative with sweeping geological time, *Sing, Unburied, Sing*, begins with the newly teenaged narrator, Jojo, contemplating death as he prepares to help his grandfather slaughter a goat for a celebratory birthday meal. 'I like to think I know what death is', Jojo states in the opening line of the novel, 'I like to think that it's something I could look at straight' (Ward 2017, 1) not only foreshadowing the killing and careful butchery of the goat that immediately follows, but the multiple forms of death and concomitant histories that permeate the novel and come together on the family property at the novel's denouement.

Similarly, the present, the past, and inhabitants of 'the Pit' come together on the first page of *Salvage the Bones*, and throughout the novel we see the characters describe themselves and others as a biotope. The novel opens with Skeet's dog China giving birth, described by our teenaged protagonist, Esch, in visceral terms. The bloody birthing of the puppies is fused with Esch's mother's birthing of her children, and the 'house she bore all of us in, here in this gap in the woods her father cleared and built on' (Ward 2017, 1). As Richard Crownshaw underscores, the people that populate Bois Sauvage in *Salvage the Bones* cannot be separated from the environment within which they live. The characters merge with the 'more-than-human world' and the 'distinction between [the characters'] humanity and the surrounding animal life is blurred' with their subjectivity 'found forever breaking its bounds, oscillating between the world of subjects and objects, the human and the nonhuman, environmentally dispersed, or, more accurately put, ecologically constituted [. . .] This is not a naturalization of African American identity and subjectivity', however, 'but rather Ward's (implicit) registration of the ways in which human and natural, social and environmental, histories, have become catastrophically imbricated' (Crownshaw 2016, 228). Within the biotope of Bois Sauvage, birth, life, the land and death sit together in the present. The death of Esch's mother and the threat of the incoming hurricane rub alongside the birth (and death) of China's pups and the life growing in Esch's womb. If it is the case that through the course of the novel we see the blurring of boundaries between character and environment, by the story's end and in the wake of Hurricane Katrina, it is almost impossible to distinguish between them as they form part of the rubble and detritus of the devasted landscape. While waiting in hope for China to return to the ruins of the Pit, Skeet, we are told, 'is still again: sand seared to rock' (Ward [2011] 2017, 258). The people who populate Bois Sauvage are entirely at one with the environment across the novels. As Christophe tells us in *Where the Line Bleeds*, 'Ma-mee always said we got that blood in us, the kind that knows things, that Bois Sauvage blood. I know she can tell the weather, but I swear, before them clouds came and before I even knew they was on the way, I smelled it in the air' (Ward 2018, 130).

Landscape as History

The relationship between land and history is well understood in Caribbean and Postcolonial Studies, with writers and thinkers such as Wilson Harris urging us to enter into a 'profound dialogue with the landscape' in order to counter the insidious manner in which colonial discourse has effaced that very relationship in order to mystify its own history of violence (Harris 1990, 75, quoted in Deloughrey and Handley 2011, 4). As DeLoughrey and Handley elaborate, 'Historicization has been a primary tool of postcolonial studies and, as Said and Fanon imply, it is central to our understanding of land and, by extension, the earth' and that central to postcolonial and decolonial thought is the acknowledgement that 'place encodes time, suggesting that histories embedded in the land and sea have always provided vital and dynamic methodologies for understanding the transformative impact of empire and the anticolonial epistemologies it tries to suppress' (4). The landscape is an active participant in the historical process, intimately bound with the wider community of the biotope and lifeworld. 'Landscape is a character in this process', according to Édouard Glissant, and 'its deepest meanings need to be understood' (Glissant, 105–6).

Ward's novels rise to the challenges set by these decolonial and postcolonial thinkers by exposing the histories of colonialism and racial capitalism that are scored into and scar the landscape of Mississippi and which connect this locale to those global forces. Bois Sauvage and the lives of the characters within has been shaped, ultimately, by plantation enslavement and its ongoing legacy of violent racial capitalism. As we have already seen, the families and communities in all three novels reside in areas forged from environmental, racial and capitalist violence underpinned by anti-Blackness, functioning on the borders of and in spite of the neoliberal economy which excludes them. The brutality of an economic and social system which treats Black life and the environment as debris is laid bare throughout the novels with characters' choices limited to work in fast-food outlets, dealing drugs, or, as in *Where the Line Bleeds* and *Sing, Unburied, Sing*, working for the oil industry that is a feature of the Mississippi Gulf. Environmental and social destruction cuts through the novels with Hurricane Katrina haunting the narrative of *Where the Line Bleeds* only to devastate Bois Sauvage in *Salvage the Bones* and the Deepwater Horizon disaster that resulted in Michael's unemployment and turn to drugs in *Sing, Unburied, Sing*. 'The concept of progress must be grounded in the idea of catastrophe', Walter Benjamin told us (Benjamin 1999, 473), and this catastrophe is the 'disaster of black subjection' which was and is planned (Sharpe 2016, 5). Ward's novels are explicit in the ways that they show that the 'history of capital is inextricable from the history of Atlantic chattel slavery' (Sharpe 2016, 5) and they are unapologetic in casting this history as the present. The Parchman plantation-cum-prison in *Sing, Unburied, Sing*, and the unfolding story of River's past incarceration there with Richie brings the presence of the past and the present of the past home with force, for example.

River relates to Jojo the story of his own incarceration as a fifteen-year-old boy, charting the Jim Crow-era policies of his youth. Through the telling of his friendship with and protection of the boy, Richie, and Richie's presence as a ghost-narrator within the novel, we see the ways in which these policies reverberate in the present and the ways in which the prison system replicated and continues to replicate the conditions of plantation slavery. This replication is not limited to the prison system but extends to the social and economic world. By excavating the historical and contemporary violence, showing the intimate connections between capital and racial subjugation, all three of the novels highlight the ways in which global forces of colonialism, plantation enslavement and capitalism are etched into the landscape and geography of Bois Sauvage. The landscape here is an active agent of history and place does indeed 'encode time'.

In a 2017 interview published in *The Sydney Morning Herald*, Ward described her hometown as

> a place where family and community are really tightly bound together. It is very poor and working class. It is still segregated in some respects but I think that is because in the past those generations were segregated. It is a place that feels weighted by a lot of history.

We feel this weight of history within the fictional world of all three of Ward's novels where racial violence is etched deeply in the landscape. In their formulation of a postcolonial ecology, Deloughrey and Handley raise important ethical questions about the relationship between writing, the environment and history. 'How can an author recover land that is already ravaged by the violence of history?', they ask, and moreover, how 'can nature be historicized without obscuring its ontological difference from human time?' (2011, 4). They remind us that Harris insisted that 'historical and racial violence is integral to understanding literary representations of geography, particularly because the land is "saturated by traumas of conquest"' (2011, 8). For W. J. T. Mitchell:

> Perhaps the most important of Lefebvre's and de Certeau's insights is the expression of power in the landscape as a manifestation of law, prohibition, regulation, and control – the whole sphere of what Lacan calls 'the Symbolic.' This is Lefebvre's 'conceptualized space,' the administered or shaped space produced by the landscape architect or engineer, the taboo or sacred space declared off-limits by the shaman, or the conquered territory named, claimed, and controlled by the colonial administrator. To this notion of space as the dimension of the Symbolic (as law or negotiation) I would then add the notion of place as the location of the Lacanian Real, the site of trauma or the historical event. (Mitchell 2002, x–xi)

Ward's novels demonstrate a profound understanding of the relationship between the land and history, between land and community, the land and power, with Bois Sauvage as the site of trauma and historical event. In her analysis of *Sing, Unburied, Sing*, Dillender tells us that 'Ward's novel uses the protracted nature of ecological processes layered with recurrent oppression to symbolize a lack of significant social change for black subjects' (Dillender 2020, 134). *Sing, Unburied, Sing* is the novel which most forcefully evokes a topography that is haunted across deep time by 'specters of racialized violence', and where the 'past, present, and future collapse into a single moment in time [. . .] showing readers how neither the land nor its people can escape the denuded futures fostered by racism' (Dillender 2020, 134). The land in the text is infused with intergenerational stories of violence, from Pop's unfolding storytelling of his time at Parchman, through the brutal and senseless murder of Jojo's uncle Given, to the presence of Richie and the story of his horrific lynching. The characters are tied to one another across time by the thread and threat of violence, with this thread tying them to place. 'It's all happening at once. All of it. We're all here at once', Jojo's grandmother tells us, and 'The woods surrounding the family home are "full with ghosts"'. 'Jojo sees that "the branches are full"';

> They are full with ghosts, two or three, all the way up to the top, to the feathered leaves. There are women and men and boys and girls. Some of them near to babies. They crouch, looking at me. Black and brown and the closest near baby, smoke white. None of them reveal their deaths, but I see it in their eyes, their great black eyes. They perch like birds, but look as people. They speak with their eyes: *He raped me and suffocated me until I died I put my hands up and he shot me eight times she locked me in the shed and starved me to death while I listened to my babies playing with her in the yard they came in my cell in the middle of the night and they hung me they found I could read and they dragged me out to the barn and gouged my eyes before they beat me I was sick and he said I was an abomination and Jesus say suffer little children so let her go and he put me under the water and I couldn't breathe.* (Ward 2017, 282–3)

The silent voices and stories of the ghosts merge into one another to form one history that cuts across the ages. 'Their eyes close and then open as one', Jojo states, even though what they wear makes clear that these ghosts lost their lives at different points of time: 'they wear: rags and breeches, T-shirts and tignons, fedoras and hoodies' (Ward 2017, 283). Jojo bears witness to this ongoing racist violence and makes absolutely clear the connection with geological time. 'I stand until there is no sun', Jojo says,

> I stand until I smell pine through the salt and sulphur. I stand until the moon rises and their mouths close and they are a murder of silver crows. I stand until the forest is a black-knuckled multitude. I stand until I bend, find a hollow stick, turn to the house, and whip the air in front of me, away from the dead, to find Pop holding Kayla. They shine bright as the ghosts in the dark. (Ward 2017, 283)

Jojo, Grandma Mam and Leonie can all see things, all have the 'Bois Sauvage blood' that Christophe referred to in *Where the Line*

Bleeds, and throughout the novel we learn that this way of seeing, of knowing, is an important way of bearing witness, of keeping a testimony of historical and present violence in a world where those with power mythologise history. Crownshaw highlights how important testimony is here, because it underscores a 'concept of agency that is truly innovative'. Crownshaw's suggestion that *Salvage the Bones* is a 'form of testimony' is convincing. 'In writing about death and life, oppression and survival, the cumulative burdens of the past and the possibilities of the future, Ward is testifying to agency', he tells us, and 'the novel's chapters count down to the hurricane's landfall, and this concluding testimonial declaration that follows the consequent destruction, suggests that the novel has been, proleptically, from the start testimonial'. For Crownshaw, it is the 'assemblage of the human and non human' where agency is to be found (Crownshaw 2016, 228).

The Life World of Bois Sauvage

It has been noted that racialised experience and disparities in peoples' experience of the environment is often overlooked within ecocritical scholarship. Amongst others, Richard Crownshaw's work has underscored the intimate relationship between racial oppression, the environment and environmental injustice in the South. He reminds us that 'the environment has been coopted in the perpetration of systematic and institutionalized racism, to which black bodies in particular are subjected' (Crownshaw 2016, 229). And as Kirsten Dillender reminds us, '[w]hen ecocriticism does examine the relation between land and blackness, it too readily reduces this relationship to the excruciating labor and violence that black people suffered during chattel slavery' (Dillender, 132). Ward's novels explore the deeply embedded layers of the histories of violence within the landscape of Bois Sauvage, but do so while also 'imagining a black ecological experience that counters antiblack brutality'. In doing so, the relationship between Black experience and the environment becomes a 'transformative engagement in cultural production by people of African descent' that recreates 'legacies of brutality and reveal that those legacies are only one facet of the complex relationship between land and blackness' (Dillender, 132). The relationship characters have with the landscape, the biotope that creates them and a rich life world, imbues their lives, and the novels themselves, with visions and versions of dignified Black lives.

As Esch surveys the destruction caused by Katrina in *Salvage the Bones* we have a moment where a different future presents itself; one where the violence of white power is destroyed by the natural world. 'We reach the end of the road', Esch tells us:

> Here the hurricane has ripped even the road that rimmed the beach away in chunks so there are red clay and oyster shell cliffs. The gas station, the yacht club, and all the old white-columned homes that faced the beach, that made us feel small and dirty and poorer than ever when we came here with Daddy, piled in his truck, for gas or chips or bait on our swimming days are gone. Not ravaged, not rubble, but completely gone. (Ward 2017, 258)

Despite the violence that saturates the landscape of Bois Sauvage, all three novels create a life world full of deep relationships between people and between people and the environment. This world is one rich with possibilities and is entirely rooted in the land that generations of their families have worked, inscribing their stories deep within and through which the younger generations learn to navigate the world. The 'blood of Bois Sauvage' flows through the characters, 'like silt in river water' (Ward 2017, 40) with some, such as Leonie and Grandma Mam passing down a knowledge of the local plants and their healing properties, making clear that the environment is itself a system of knowledge. 'Growing up out here in the country taught me things', Leonie says, 'Taught me that after the first fat flush of life, time eats away at things' (Ward 2017, 46).

Ward's characters create place as place creates them, forming and transforming a dynamic, affirmative life world fusing the long histories of this biotope across time and geological and geographic space. As McKisson states,

> Ward's novels of Bios Sauvage foreground ecological infrastructure by situating embodied experiences within long histories and in relation to larger-scale forces. Aesthetic figurations of subsidence are central to this work, enabling readers not only to attend to the changing environment but also to make connections across space and time to legacies of colonial violences and capitalist expropriations. (McKisson 2021, 491)

Bois Sauvage translates as Wild Woods and in *Men We Reaped* Ward tells us that 'Before DeLisle was named Delisle, after a French Settler, the early settlers called it Wolf Town'. Ward herself reverts to calling it Wolf Town since it 'hints at the wildness at its heart' and she expresses the desire to 'impart something of its wild roots, its early savagery' highlighting the synergy between her hometown and the fictional world that she creates. (Ward [2013] 2018, 9). Through such an exploration of the 'wildness' of Bois Sauvage her writing is an expression of a place which is characterised by resistance to claims of ownership and possession. *Where the Line Bleeds* ends with a powerful image of fish 'dense with the memory of the closed, rich bayou in the marrow of the bones, settled to the bottom of the Gulf of Mexico and turned to black silt on the ancient floor of the sea' (239) and *Sing, Unburied, Sing* ends with the haunting image of the ghosts' refrain, '*Home*, they say. *Home*' (285). When we consider these endings alongside that of *Salvage the Bones* with Esch imagining her future self as a mother, we can understand the ways in which the natural world and the people of Bois Sauvage exist in symbiosis, where the historical record, the present and the future combine to form the sedimentary layers of this landscape creating a biotope, a lifeworld, 'a place that seemed all beginning, a birthplace' (Ward 2018, 10).

Notes

1. Ward has told the story of the time she first read *As I Lay Dying* when she was starting out as a writer. 'Oh god, I should just quit. There's something he's captured about the south that I can't even articulate.' Jesmyn Ward, 'I Wanted to Write about the People of the South.'
2. There are synergies here between my conceptualisation of Bois Sauvage as biotope and Christopher Lloyd's theorisation of corporeal legacies in his chapter, 'Ghosts in Mississippi: Jesmyn Ward's *Sing, Unburied, Sing*', in this volume. Lloyd's reading of embodiment in the novel, specifically of bodies coming apart through various violences highlights how 'contemporary texts set in the US South seem to gesture towards an ongoing and as yet unfinished project of making sense of the past'.

Works Cited

Benjamin, Walter. 1999. *The Arcades Project*. Translated by Howard Eiland and Kevin McLaughlin. Cambridge, MA: Belknap Press.

Crownshaw, Richard. 2016. 'Agency and Environment in the Work of Jesmyn Ward. Response to Anna Harnell, "When Cars Become Churches"'. *Journal of American Studies* 50 (1): 225–30.

DeLoughrey, Elizabeth, and George B. Handley, eds. 2011. *Postcolonial Ecologies: Literatures of the Environment*. Oxford: Oxford University Press.

Dillender, Kirsten. 2020. 'Land and Pessimistic Futures in Contemporary African American Speculative Fiction'. *Extrapolation* 61, nos. 1–2.

Glissant, Édouard. [1989] 1999. *Caribbean Discourse: Selected Essays.* Charlottesville: Caraf Books.

Hwise, Ursula K. 2008. *Sense of Place and Sense of Planet.* Oxford: Oxford University Press.

Kolen, Jan, and Johannes Renes. 2015. 'Landscape Biographies: Key Issues'. In *Landscape Biographies: Geographical, Historical, and Archaeological Perspectives on the Production and Transmission of Landscapes*, edited by Rita Hermans, Jan Kolen and Hans Renes. Amsterdam: Amsterdam University Press.

McKisson, Kelly. 2021. 'The Subsident Gulf: Refiguring Climate Change in Jesmyn Ward's Bois Sauvage'. *American Literature* 93, no. 3 (September): 473–96.

Manchester Literature Festival. 2014. The Manchester Literature Festival Blog. 'We are more than our trauma'. Jesmyn Ward in Conversation. https://blog.manchesterliteraturefestival.co.uk/2018/05/trauma-jesmyn-ward- conversation/.

Merleau-Ponty, Maurice. [1958] 2002. *Phenomenology of Perception.* London and New York: Routledge.

Mitchell, W. T. J., ed. 2002. *Landscape and Power.* 2nd ed. Chicago: University of Chicago Press.

Sharpe, Christina Elizabeth. 2016. *In the Wake: On Blackness and Being.* Durham, NC: Duke University Press.

The Sydney Morning Herald. 2017. Jesmyn Ward interview: 'My ghosts were once people, and I cannot forget that'. 16 October.

Ward, Jesmyn. 2011. 'I Wanted to Write about the People of the South', interview by Emma Brockes. *The Guardian*, 1 December. https://www.theguardian.com/books/2011/ dec/01/jesmyn-ward-national-book-award.

—. [2011] 2017. *Salvage the Bones.* London: Bloomsbury.

—. 2017. *Sing, Unburied, Sing.* London: Bloomsbury.

—. [2008] 2018. *Where the Line Bleeds.* London: Bloomsbury.

—. [2013] 2018. *The Men We Reaped.* London: Bloomsbury.

Chapter 2

Wayward Kinship and Malleable Intimacies

Jay N. Shelat

Here, family has always been a mutable concept. Sometimes it encompasses an entire community . . .

This was like walking into a storm surge: a cycle of futility. Maybe he looked at those who still lived and those who'd died, and didn't see much difference between the two; pinioned beneath poverty and history and racism, we were all dying inside. . . . he saw no American dream, no fairy-tale ending, no hope.

Jesmyn Ward, Men We Reaped (2013)

Jesmyn Ward's fiction emerges from her reality. Writing for and about the community she hails from, DeLisle, Mississippi, her stories depict families beset by systemic racism and inequality – in other words, anti-Blackness – endemic to the United States. Death pervades her work as she portrays contemporary, poor, Southern Black experiences. Yet, her works remain somewhat optimistic, tinged with a sad hopefulness, and buoyed by the luck of survival. This chapter examines how Ward's fiction is defined by radical forms of kinship – moulded by family and community – and how revitalised understandings of intimacy necessarily fortify the contemporary Black experience in the face of institutional racism and historic injustice and sociopolitical inequality. These forms of oppression, moreover, leak into private spheres and impel new visions of intimacy and familial practice. Studying these wayward and savage intimacies ultimately explicates the state's tactics to erase the beating heart of Black life, those kith and kin relations forged despite abominable odds.

The nuclear and found kinship units in Ward's works operate less like a noun and more like a verb, demanding action and effort. Through such grammars of intimacy, Ward's work maintains that kinship requires an ever-budding vulnerability that permits trust, hope and love. This chapter centres on Ward's 2011 novel *Salvage the Bones* (*Salvage*) and concludes with a reading of her 2017 novel, *Sing, Unburied, Sing* (*Sing*). I concentrate on how race, class and gender inform familial constructions and how the Black American South is contingent upon complex intimacies. I want to suggest that family is the hinge in all of Ward's work, propelling characterisation as well as plot, stylistic choices as well as thematic concerns. These familial relations forged, lost and strengthened put in stark relief the political resonances of intimacy. I argue that Ward's treatment of intimacy underscores the necessary dynamic conditions of family and community, especially for poor Black people. That is, I posit that Ward's works broaden definitions of family and community – forms of intimacy – primarily as measures of and resources towards survival. Finding family in neighbours, the characters in Ward's imaginary but all too real Bois Sauvage cannot depend on state-provided support; instead, they must rely on fellow community members and even non-human figures to ensure survival, thereby extending the definitional qualities of kinship and the nuclear family. In essence, the family replaces the state by providing networks of both emotional and material care, demonstrating how such intimacies uplift, whereas the state's neglect devalues Black life. The relationships created because of a shared lived experience of institutional and social neglect resist the very sociocultural and sociopolitical nexuses that seek to disenfranchise and further marginalise poor Black communities. Characters find affinity with the natural and animalistic world, cultivating *otherwise* familial constructions: intimate collectives that resist white-imposed definitions of nuclear family. Here, I follow Saidiya Hartman who avows that Black radicalism arises from and against the institutional racism that defines, undergirds and drives the United States: 'The acts of the wayward . . . redistributed the balance of need and want and sought a line of escape from debt and duty in the attempt to create a path elsewhere' (Hartman 2019, 237). Ultimately, I contend that Ward deploys such wayward and radical forms of Black intimacy to depict and understand how the ethos of kith and kin relations resist the mandates of supremacist ideologies. Such forged intimacies are unrelenting in their power to carve new paths of survival.

Savage Family in *Salvage the Bones*

There's a savage intensity to salvaging: searching for and rescuing what was thought to be lost by '[s]ubverting the racist history of the savage' (Henry 2019, 75). For Ward, the family – what remains dynamic with its additions and losses – is both savage and salvaged, victim to the cruelties of institutional neglect and profound loss. Ward's novel tells the story of a family victim to a cycle of loss. The Batiste family is poor and lives in Bois Sauvage, next to the Pit, a massive hole where the ground collapsed after white people exhausted the earth by extracting dirt for years.[1] Tinged with the loss of matriarch Rose, the family represents close- knit, intimate bonds necessary to survive. Moreover, these familial tethers are concretised by the intimacies shared between the four Batiste children. Yet, as I show below, these intimate relations also extend beyond the nuclear family to incorporate the community. Candice M. Jenkins's theorising of Black intimacy is particularly instructive here because it recognises how civility structures social understandings of blackness and Black intimacy in particular. She writes that Black people's relationship to 'the exposure of intimacy' is complex 'because of the vulnerability that many blacks already experience through racial identity and its associated dangers' (Jenkins 2007, 4). She continues, claiming that 'part of this racial vulnerability has to do with the manner in which African American sexual and familial character has traditionally been stigmatized as *un*civilized in the United States, from the days of slavery onward' (Jenkins 2007, 4). That is, Black intimacy is seen as improper and against the norms established by the white ruling class to stifle and control Black private lives. When read in these terms, *Salvage*, and indeed all of Ward's books, can be seen as rewriting the norms of civility via examples of communal and familial intimacy that always ensures survival. Thus, while this chapter treats waywardness as a resistant behaviour 'inimical to those [ways] deemed proper and respectable' and 'the avid longing for a world not ruled by master, man or police', as Hartman postulates, it also considers this errant behaviour and attitude as a communal, forward-looking methodology that ensures togetherness, survival, futurity (Hartman 2019, 227). Doing so uncovers how kith and kin relations in Ward's works are legitimate lifelines that come to be in part because of institutional abandonment.

Ward extends these intimacies to nature to create a shared splendour that ties both the organic and material worlds – a 'more-than-human environment' (Bares 2019, 31). These intimate relations, therefore, carry important weight for Esch, whose narration and perspective are replete with instances of wonder and beauty in the most mundane and painful aspects of life in Bois Sauvage. This natural world merges with the familial and domestic spheres too where home is not local: it encapsulates the world, reflective of the idea that family itself is mutable. For example, early in the novel when describing the youngest Batiste sibling Junior's birth and her mother's subsequent death, Esch recalls,

> Mama had all of us in her bed, under her own bare burning bulb, so when it was time for Junior, she thought she could do the same. It didn't work that way. Mama squatted, screamed toward the end. Junior came out purple and blue as a hydrangea: Mama's last flower. She touched Junior just like that when Daddy held him over her: lightly with her fingertips, like she was afraid she'd knock the pollen from him, spoil the bloom. (2)

The familiarity of the bed comforts Rose; the domestic sphere is a trusted space in which the most intimate connections of her life can bloom, where the family has lived for generations and 'they been all right' (220). This dependency and trust of and within the home, moreover, is echoed by the alliteration in 'bare burning bulb', which pairs the natural and human world. Ward yokes ordinary objects of both the physical and natural world (a lightbulb and a flower) to signal the organic beauty of the act of mothering in the domestic space. Yet while life indeed blooms, the beauty of the flowering is marked by pain: Junior chokes and Rose dies from complications in the pregnancy. In this moment, the family both gains and loses a member, and Ward's lyrical prose ironises the moment of pain with beauty. Through Esch's voice, the prose in *Salvage* also indicates how forms of kindred intimacy with the natural world untiringly urges survival. Yet still, that very natural world that provides the pomp and majesty of flowers, can be savage, as Hurricane Katrina represents. Described as a cruel mother, the storm sheds light on the intensity of the bonds that structure the Batiste family. The force of the natural world in *Salvage* thus leads to a re-evaluation of the very word 'savage'. Rather than a term that reiterates an otherness or deviant quality in the lives of this Black family, 'savage' shows that, in Ward's own words:

> Even in the face of this, of the . . . pressure of racism, the pressure of the history of racism, of economic inequality, of a popular culture that constantly tells you that you're worth less. Even in the face of all that, we still survive and we still claim for ourselves a certain sense of dignity or humanity. (Hartnell 2016, 212)

Thus, intimate kinship with the quotidian, savage natural world is as life-giving as the relations forged with others.

Indeed, Ward destroys the notion of the nuclear family in *Salvage* because the Batistes find kindred affinity with *every* aspect of

Bois Sauvage. As Christopher Lloyd argues, 'Intimately connected to the natural world around them . . . Ward's southerners are deeply connected to other forms of life in the South even while their own are rendered precarious' (Lloyd 2016, 246–7). Ward makes this animal intimacy clear as sunlight when she describes the Batiste family children as not only part of but reflective of the natural landscape of the city. Esch notes, 'Maintenance workers, usually county convicts in green-and-white striped jumpsuits, come out once a year and half-heartedly try to trim back the encroaching wood, mow the grass set to bloom, the pine seedlings. The wild things of Bois Sauvage ignore them; we are left to seed another year' (117). Using 'we' to align family with the wood, grass and seedlings, Esch perceives herself and her relations as such to oppose the social and cultural recognition of Black people as expendable.[2] The family is inextricable from where they hail; so much so, in fact, that they mirror the world around them: similarly neglected by institutional support. Consider how the Catholic church, cemetery and park '[strive] to impose some order, some civility to Bois' but '[fail]' in their collective mission (117). Little to no social support systems exist to aid this poor community, further marginalising, imperilling and disenfranchising the Black families who want to survive.

As victims of systemic institutional and infrastructural racism, moreover, these families understand themselves in terms of the natural, ungovernable environment.[3] This intimacy with the natural world, presented and understood as a familial and domestic relationship through lyrical prose, suggests that despite the precarious infrastructure maintained 'halfheartedly' by the state, the wild things are ever-encroaching, unable to be controlled.[4] The poetic bridges Ward builds between the Batiste family and Bois Sauvage presents the poor Black quotidian life as not all fraught. While moments of pain and trauma are certainly ubiquitous, beauty and togetherness, sentimental intimacy, also persist. Despite this institutional desertion, the Batiste family and their surrounding Bois Sauvage community practise intimacy that denounces the 'fend for yourselves' attitude of the state. Rather, the intimacies forged – kinship, friendship, community – allow the various characters to quite simply survive.[5] When Skeetah suggests that he will eat dog food to stave off hunger during Hurricane Katrina, Big Henry, a close family friend, immediately interjects with a call to communal arms, suggesting that in times of need, their Bois Sauvage neighbours will spare what they can: 'Man, [Me and Mama] got a little extra. . . . Sure Marquise got some extra . . . Skeetah, you ain't got to eat dog food' (193). Similar to other instances of communal support, which I address below, such community response and provision replaces the state's inaction and resists and unmakes the resounding social stigma arising from respectability politics that claim poor Black communities are nefariously deviant.[6] In other words, the communal support Ward writes in *Salvage* expands definitions and understandings of intimate relations beyond the nuclear family; the novel purports a recognition of communal intimacy, a togetherness and solidarity that forms around survival.

Radical Motherhood

Throughout the novel, oppositions like beauty and pain and loneliness and togetherness are compounded by a similar duality in motherhood. Images of mothers abound in the novel. From China the family dog giving birth on the first page and the myth of Medea, to the analeptic portions that flash us back to when Rose was alive, mothers are present in absence in Esch's life. That is, to fill the void of her own missing mother, Esch narrates the novel paying particular attention to maternal figures. Both powerfully unifying and destructive, motherhood appears throughout the novel as a kind of mythological force. In so doing, Ward illuminates the paradoxes of motherhood in the economically ravaged and socially ostracised community of Bois Sauvage. On the one hand, motherhood, as Rose represents, is beautiful. Couched in lyrical prose that aligns it with flowers blooming, motherhood is a gift of nature. On the other hand, motherhood is often cruel, not only taking Rose away from her children, but, to Esch, it is also murderous. Consider, for instance, how Hurricane Katrina is described as 'the murderous mother who cut us to the bone but left us alive, left us naked and bewildered as wrinkled newborn babies . . . She left us to salvage. Katrina is the mother we will remember until the next mother with large, merciless hands, committed to blood, comes' (255).

Katrina's violent intimacy reiterates the harsh realities of Black life in Bois Sauvage: like a hurricane itself, cruelty in Black life is cyclical, continuously swirling and dealing the worst blows – a Charybdis of state-sponsored, ecological and social censure. Yet, as I show below, motherhood remains a powerful tool towards self-realisation and radical kinship reformulations. For now, however, I want to claim that such dichotomous descriptions of motherhood throughout *Salvage* reveal how the family structure is often at the mercy of the state and nature, and it highlights the 'limitations of the normative language used for describing complex relations of racialized kinship' (Fielder 2020, 126). Ward thus makes clear that Black motherhood as a central force of kinship (whether nuclear or constructed) faces continuous, repetitive vulnerabilities and that the identity marker of 'mother' itself is not fixed within a social structure of normative kinship.

This resistance to normative family constructions extends from Esch's rapport with the feminine community after Katrina leaves them 'as human debris in the middle of all the rest of it' (237). One mother takes another mother when floods during the storm carry China away, and the novel concludes with a cautious hopefulness that the dog will return. Ward shifts to the future tense in the final two paragraphs of the novel to indicate this hopeful yet circumspect futurity that inaugurates not only a new post-Katrina era but also a new Esch who recognises herself as a mother.[7] Esch concretises this salvaged identity after the hurricane by creating kinship and finding affinity with China:

> China will bark and call me sister. In the star-suffocated sky, there is a great waiting silence.
>
> She will know that I am a mother. (258)

The shared demands of motherhood bind the two further into family.[8] This shared understanding of their place both as mothers reiterates the hopefulness that survival engenders, and it also highlights that this deviation from a normative nuclear family construction does not destroy Esch or her family. Instead, this non-nuclear familial intimacy with China underscores how resisting respectability politics founded and buttressed by white supremacist understandings of intimacy and family is a liberating act.

In this way and through the grammars of self-recognition and intimacies, too, *Salvage* undoes the bind that Susana Morris suggests is evident in many Black women's writing about family: 'young Black women eschew non-normative family politics in favor of the seeming security and safety of traditional notions of familial respectability', yet their 'ambivalent sense of self and family underscores how ultimately isolating and destructive these choices can be for these Black women and their peers' (Morris 2014, 7). Indeed, Ward's novel concludes with the antithesis of this very notion. Rather than be ambivalent about her sense of self and family, Esch has never been surer of herself and the community she belongs to, evinced by the perfectly balanced sentence that concludes the novel. 'She will know that I am a mother' puts China and Esch on level ground, matched by the simple sentences that flank the conjunction 'that'. At the same time, the lineal separation of the final sentence recognises the limits of interspecies kinship while also acknowledging the profound emotional connection between Esch and China.[9] This powerful evocation of feminine, maternal solidarity between woman and dog signifies how Black kinship lines, drawn by necessary expanded definitions of intimacy, betray and refuse white-constructed social norms, thereby confirming possibility and survival.

On top of this established solidarity with China to push the boundaries of family, Ward also concludes the novel with a Black feminist rectification of the father-mother relationship. When Esch and Manny (the baby's father) have a mythologically powerful falling out about the baby, she realises that the latter is not equipped for fatherhood and that her child will not consider him as such. The altercation reveals how, like affection, violence is a form of intimacy: 'I loved you!' This is Medea wielding the knife. This is Medea cutting. 'I rake my fingernails across his face, leave pink scratches that turn red, fill with blood' (204). Esch, in realising that loving Manny is futile and that his sexism and denial clouds his ability to be a father, channels ancient mythology and thereby denies the traditional patriarchal figure for her budding family. Unlike Medea, however, Esch does not destroy her child. The scene is not of infanticide but of a sort of mariticide: killing one's partner. While they do not date, Manny and Esch do have a sexual relationship, and Esch-cum-Medea metaphorically killing him and asserting her dominance signals the emergence of her self-identity as a matriarch who does not depend on the patriarch. This female rage and violence work to help birth a new self: 'She uses her body, and his body, as tools – his body, his blood fertilizes the (re)creation of her identity' (Friedman 1996, 71). Esch, in casting Manny from the patriarchal figuration of the family structure, acknowledges her new identity. To that end, through radical forms of kinship practice that eschew normative familial make-ups, Esch rewrites the familiar myth for the contemporary Black woman, declaring her authority and inserting herself within a mythological and maternal tradition largely denied to Black people.[10]

While it is easy to see that Ward's protagonist-narrator in *Salvage* '*deconstructs* a black family romance, and represents unequivocally the ways in which "traditional" – and traditionally idealized – family structures can endanger black women both physically and psychically, largely because of the patriarchal power that such structures grant to black men', I want to argue that this familial revision also occurs through the addition of *many* fathers, rather than one father (Jenkins 2007, 92, emphasis in original). In a stunning reworking of the absent father stereotype, the other men who populate Esch's life fill the void Manny leaves. It is a community-oriented fatherhood for the baby and yet another instance in which Ward radically alters the construction of the Black nuclear family by abdicating norms legislated by the tyranny of white-dictated social strictures and structures.[11] Esch and Big Henry salvage the bones of Bois Sauvage after Hurricane Katrina rips through when the latter asks the girl who the baby's father is. 'It don't have a daddy', Esch replies; Big Henry's quick retort reiterates the communal intimacies that define expanded understandings of family: 'You wrong. . . . This baby got a daddy, Esch. . . . This baby got plenty daddies' (255). The community becomes the family, reiterating how 'Community, an expressed connection between human beings, is vital to the institution of home' (Sweeney Prince 2004, 24). In other words, Bois Sauvage's position as *home* is contingent upon these radical forms of togetherness. As I claim above, drawing Manny's blood is an act of violent intimacy that concretises Esch's self-identification as a maternal figure, but in recognising the multiple fathers and renegotiating the terms of family, Esch still remains at the centre. That is, what is radical is that while the patriarchal figure remains in the family – Esch's brothers, Big Henry and members of the Bois Sauvage community – he is no longer the nucleus of the family: Esch is. This Black feminist insurgent and errant method of motherhood and familial practice powerfully responds to the institutional neglect Esch and her family are subject to. It is radical kinship that imagines new possibilities towards survival.

Found Kinship as Wake Work in *Sing, Unburied, Sing*

The future of Bois Sauvage is bleak, made even bleaker with the knowledge of the future hurricanes that hit the Gulf Coast. Ward literalises this with the future tense, making ambivalent what is to come for the family and the Bois Sauvage community. Yet, in keeping with a theme that saturates Ward's work, hope remains. I reiterate this point to consider how the reformulations of family in *Salvage* encourage a future beyond the white, heteronormative structures that undergird social and cultural dictates. How wayward constructions of family – constrained by the confines of white heteronormative bourgeois ideologies – are uphill battles towards liberation and survival. Moreover, these forms of recalcitrant intimacy, whether the nuclear family, larger communities or found families, speak to the longitudinal histories of racialised violence the nation enacts against Black people. Indeed, as Hortense Spillers has poignantly articulated, enslaved Black people often practised moving beyond and changing the norms of the Black nuclear family because of the cruel familial separation routine in the plantation economy: 'In this movement outward from a nuclear centrality, "family" becomes an extension and inclusion – anyone who preserves life and its callings becomes a member of the family, whose patterns of kinship and resemblance fall into disguise' (249). Ward's reworking of the family formula arises from a long history of altering the course and meaning of intimacy.

Thus this ultimate reorientation – or, following Jenkins, queering – of the family away from the patriarch and incorporating community-as-kin in *Salvage* signals how Black communities continue to face racist social and legal constrictions as hallmarks of slavery's aftermath – what Christina Sharpe calls *in the wake*. In this way, these intimate relations, through an ethos of love, care, support and sacrifice despite the white-created and ordained norms, follow Sharpe's conceptualisation of 'wake work'. With wake work, Sharpe is interested 'in ways of seeing and imagining responses to terror in the varied and various ways that [. . .] Black lives are lived under occupation; ways that attest to the modalities of Black life lived in, as, under, and despite Black death' and how such 'imagining calls forth, to think through what it calls on "us" to do, think, feel in the wake of slavery – which is to say in the ongoing present of subjection and resistance' (Sharpe 2016, 20). While this act of resistance – wake work – is clear via the familial revisions brought on by infrastructural racism and socio-economic vulnerabilities in *Salvage*, I want to move, by way of conclusion, to Ward's latest novel, *Sing, Unburied, Sing*, and how familial renovation is wake work. Whereas the revised familial intimacy I emphasise in *Salvage* incorporates the whole community, in *Sing* Ward scales back created kinship by focusing on two characters whose need for intimacy arises from callous carcerality. This trajectory, from *Salvage* to *Sing*, reveals not only how Ward renders family untenable and highlights the necessary re-evaluation of Black intimacy because of white supremacist tactics that confine Black life, but tracing this arc in Ward's more recent fiction also illustrates how kinship is an ethos and practice that staves off Black death for as long as possible. Ultimately, however, the revised familial dynamics in *Sing* are not enough to fend the horrors of anti-Blackness.

Sing heartbreakingly depicts familial wake work through River, who, at fifteen years old, was wrongly imprisoned in the cruel labour prison Parchman, also known as the Mississippi State Penitentiary. As Christopher Lloyd argues in his chapter in this collection, Ward blatantly depicts carceral punishment as the logical extension of slavery and Jim Crow era ethics:

> '*even though White people couldn't get your work for free, they did everything they could to avoid hiring you and paying for it . . . Damn near fifty thousand acres*' with '*[m]en strung out across the fields, the trust shooters stalking the edge . . . I knew what that was, to be made an animal*'. (21, 69, italics in original)

Against these horrific conditions that embody the nation's anti-Black ideologies and illuminate the legacies of slavery, River befriends Richie, a twelve-year-old boy who was arrested for stealing food for his starving family. At Parchman, River protects and helps young Richie whenever possible, establishing the familial ties that reflect the paternal-fraternal relationship protagonist Jojo (River's grandson) has with his little sister Kayla. Richie considers River both a father and a brother, ascribing him into a life-giving found kinship against the backdrop of the denigrating, dehumanising conditions of the confining prison system. One of *Sing*'s narrators, Richie (as a ghost) proclaims the power of his relationship with River: 'You was the only daddy I ever knew' (222). Unfastening stereotypes about intimate Black masculinity, such a relation also rewrites Richie's definition of home. As a poor Black child whose only family is found in River, Richie finds home in another person. Ward scrambles the definition of home once again: like the woods in *Salvage* that extend the domestic sphere, here the home is rewritten to be just River. Ward takes the power of River and Richie's relationship to supernatural heights when Richie's ghost says he will follow Jojo from Parchman to reunite with the now elderly River and to learn of his own death: '*I will follow*', Richie's ghost says, 'I hope he can hear me. I say: *I'm coming home*' (191). This search for answers framed through home corroborates Valerie Sweeney Prince's argument that 'the search for justice, opportunity, and liberty' for Black people 'can be described as a quest for home' (Sweeney Prince 2004, xii).[12]

The shift in familial dynamics brought on by anti-Black carcerality is an example of what Sharpe calls aspiration. This form of wake work questions how 'in the midst of the singularity, the virulent anti-blackness everywhere and always remotivated, to keep breath in the

Black body. What ruttier, internalized, is necessary now to . . . [keep] breath in the Black body?' (109). When the overseer at Parchman brutally whips Richie, rendering the boy's 'lungs useless', it is River, the father-brother protector, who aids him:

> I could feel him there, knew that he would carry me after they
>
> let me loose from the earth. . . . The way he carried me to my cot, the way he bent over me, made something soft and fluttery as a jellyfish pulse in my chest. That was my heart. Him my big brother. Him, my father. (135)

The familial ethos here shows how pervasive anti-Blackness, in one of its many forms, compels familial emendation. River makes Richie's heart beat and lungs aspire. Moreover, in having River save and give life to Richie, Ward suggests that familial overhaul, where brother and father merge, is necessary work for protecting Black lives. Kinship practices, in other words, are resources that safeguard against social and institutional white supremacy. Ultimately, then, Ward's insistence on new wayward forms of kinship and intimacy throughout her work is just one way in which 'we must continue to think and imagine laterally, across a series of relations in the hold, in multiple Black everydays of the wake' (Sharpe 2016, 113).

Furthermore, as both sibling and parent, River grants us 'particular ways of re/seeing, re/inhabiting, and re/imagining the world' to protect Black life and in conceptualising 'a *beautiful experiment* in how-to-live', yet Ward makes clear that such protection is sometimes futile in the wake (Sharpe 2016, 22; Hartman 2019, 228, emphasis in original). *Sing* makes its most tragic political stance when the brother-father figure must kill the son-brother. River stabs Richie to protect him from oncoming lynchers, from becoming another Black boy murdered at the hands of angry white men. In other words, as Sethe does in Toni Morrison's *Beloved*, River murders Richie in *Sing* as an act of familial love and care. While the radical familial reworking is indeed wake work, the heart-rending collapse of River and Richie's relationship ultimately gestures towards the ongoing pervasive legacies of slavery and white supremacy. As Sheri-Marie Harrison writes, such an 'incomplete abolition' in *Sing* 'demonstrates how we have not yet figured out how to reckon with – or, more accurately, have in fact repressed – global histories of violence, such as that of the transatlantic slave trade' (Harrison 2020). Ward suggests that the revised family River and Richie represent is not enough to carry the weight of history. Such a conclusion reveals 'the realities of our time and their roots in systems that depend on the criminalization and disen-franchisement of black people' (Harrison 2018). Thus, while family in the community Ward writes about is malleable as gold, it is some-times not enough to combat the continuous repression and oppres-sion of Black life. *Sing*'s conclusion reminds us that the vocabularies and methodologies of resisting white supremacy are continuously developing, works in progress as dynamic as familial constructions are and should be.

Conclusion

Tracking the thematic development of family in Jesmyn Ward's work simultaneously unveils how historic, infrastructural and sociocul-tural negligence compels the creation of new forms of intimacy, and it recognises how state-sponsored acts of anti-Black violence enter and upturn intimate spheres. Moreover, Ward chronicles through-out her oeuvre how Black life and Black kith and kinship practices are forged from the oppressive pressure of systemic racism. As such, the otherwise familial constructions in *Salvage the Bones* and *Sing, Unburied, Sing* illuminate the methods the state enacts to erase the heart of Black life: its resilient and radical forms of community and family. The juxtaposition of wayward familial intimacy and state-orchestrated horror spotlight a national yet universal, contemporary yet perennial, struggle for existence in a world determined to erase Black lives. At the same time, however, these families ensure a future of life is possible, as Ward notes about mutable intimacies in *Men We Reaped*: 'We love each other fiercely, while we live and after we die. We survive; we are savages' (250).

Notes

1. The name 'Bois Sauvage' translates to 'savage wood'. Not only does Ward create savage intimacies within the family units, but she also cre-ates a world in which savage intensity defines everything.
2. Ward's first novel, *Where the Line Bleeds* (2008), also poignantly mir-rors the 'little savages' of Bois Sauvage to the natural world by conclud-ing the narrative with twins Christophe and Joshua finding affinity with fish that 'would survive, battered and cunning' (238–9). This novel yokes familial dynamics and economic position to show their symbiotic relationship, as Martyn Bone argues in his chapter.

3. Sarah Wasserman defines 'infrastructural racism' as 'the racist social forms embedded in the built environment . . . Infrastructural racism reminds us that historically contingent racism and resistance comingle in the same spaces' (Wasserman 2020, 531–2). This appears in Ward's work as the profound economic disparity in Bois Sauvage and as infrastructural damage to sites of social engagement; the resistance, therefore, is in the expansion of familial and kinship intimacies despite the infrastructural racism.

4. Hartnell writes that reading Ward 'is not exactly that of a fall from innocence, but it does usher us into a disenchanted America' (Hartnell 2016, 206). Similarly, Arin Keeble writes that Esch's description of her family as 'wild things' and bereft of parental and state support 'speaks to and reverberates against the allegorical narrative of abandonment' seen throughout post-9/11 novels (Keeble 2020, 42).

5. Scholars such as Hartnell and Lloyd have noted the persistence of Black survival in Ward's work, but some suggest that the characters in *Salvage* remain precariously hopeless. For instance, Brian Railsback argues that the 'measure of hope for the future' in John Steinbeck's *The Grapes of Wrath* is missing from *Salvage* (187). While the precarity rooted in economic disparity and pervasive white supremacy that define Bois Sauvage both point Ward's book towards hopelessness, the simple fact that the family survives Katrina and imagines a future of togetherness suggests that the novel is indeed about hope and survival.

6. Following Patrick Moynihan's influential study, *The Negro Family: The Case for National Action*, Susana M. Morris writes that 'the term low-income family and its attendant characteristics . . . have been code for the (mis)perceptions of Black families generally in the public imaginary' (Morris 2014, 1). I follow Morris's definition of respectability politics, which she defines as 'a strategy for navigating a hostile society that characterizes Blackness as the definition of deviance . . . it makes bettering one's life chances depend on adhering to a set of mainstream ideals regarding behavior, and it takes place where the public sphere meets the private' (2014, 5).

7. For more on this particular relationship, see Leah Van Dyk's contribution to this collection.

8. Henry affirms that in the maternal solidarity between Esch and China, 'Ward taps into the mythological world's coexistence of gods, talking animals, the winds, the seas, creatures, and humans equally participating in shaping the world. . . . The human-nonhuman divide . . . does not apply in Ward's mythology' (Henry 2019: 82).

9. I want to thank Rose Casey for this astute observation.

10. Similarly, Anna Bares notes that *Salvage* 'resists racist stereotypes associated with black adolescent motherhood that became particularly salient in the media coverage and political discourse that conflated

the racially marked spectacle of Hurricane Katrina and its aftermath with the racially marked spectacle of teenage pregnancy' (Bares 2019: 27).

11. As Henry points out, the multiple fathers are akin to Carole Stack's idea of othermothers.

12. Sweeney Prince's argument examines twentieth-century literature, but this 'quest for home', I argue, extends into the twenty-first century as well, namely because much, if not all, of the sociopolitical issues surrounding race remain in the contemporary era. In other words, W. E. B. Du Bois's famous claim that the problem of the twentieth century would be the colour line remains true in the twenty-first.

Works Cited

Bares, Annie. 2019. '"Each Unbearable Day": Narrative Ruthlessness and Environmental and Reproductive Injustice in Jesmyn Ward's *Salvage the Bones*'. *MELUS* 44 (3): 2–40.

Fielder, Brigitte. 2020. *Relative Races: Genealogies of Interracial Kinship in Nineteenth-Century America*. Durham, NC: Duke University Press.

Friedman, Vanessa. 1996. 'Over His Dead Body: Female Murderers, Female Rage, and Western Culture'. In *States of Rage: On Cultural Emotion and Social Change*, edited by Renée R. Curry and Terry L. Allison, 62–73. New York: New York University Press.

Harrison, Sheri-Marie. 2018. 'New Black Gothic'. *Los Angeles Review of Books*, 23 June. https://lareviewofbooks.org/article/new-black-gothic/.

—. 2020. '"It's All Happening at Once": Jesmyn Ward's Post-National Black Fiction'. *Humanity Journal*, 13 November. http://humanityjournal.org/blog/its-all-happening-at-once/.

Hartman, Saidiya. 2019. *Wayward Lives, Beautiful Experiments: Intimate Histories of Riotous Black Girls, Troublesome Women, and Queer Radicals*. New York: Norton.

Hartnell, Anna. 2016. 'When Cars Become Churches: Jesmyn Ward's Disenchanted America. An Interview'. *Journal of American Studies* 50 (1): 205–18.

Henry, Alvin. 2019. 'Jesmyn Ward's Post-Katrina Black Feminism: Memory and Myth through Salvaging'. *English Language Notes* 57 (2): 71–85.

Jenkins, Candice M. 2007. *Private Lives, Proper Relations: Regulating Black Intimacy*. Minneapolis: University of Minnesota Press.

Keeble, Arin. 2020. 'Siblings, Kinship and Allegory in Jesmyn Ward's Fiction and Nonfiction'. *Critique* 61 (1): 40–51.

Lloyd, Christopher. 2016. 'Creaturely, Throwaway Life After Katrina: Salvage the Bones and Beasts of the Southern Wild'. *South: A Scholarly Journal* 48 (2): 246–64.

Morris, Susan M. 2014. *Close Kin and Distant Relatives: The Paradox of Respectability in Black Women's Literature*. Charlottesville: University of Virginia Press.

Railsback, Brian. 2016. 'A Twenty-First-Century Grapes of Wrath: Jesmyn Ward's *Salvage the Bones*'. *Steinbeck Review* 13 (2): 179–95.

Sharpe, Christina. 2016. *In the Wake: On Blackness and Being*. Durham, NC: Duke University Press.

Spillers, Hortense. 2003. *Black, White, and in Color: Essays on American Literature and Culture*. Chicago: University of Chicago Press.

Sweeney Prince, Valerie. 2004. *Burnin' Down the House: Home in African American Literature*. New York: Columbia University Press.

Ward, Jesmyn. 2013. *Men We Reaped*. New York: Bloomsbury.

—. 2011. *Salvage the Bones*. New York: Bloomsbury.

—. 2017. *Sing, Unburied, Sing*. New York: Scribner.

—. 2008. *Where the Line Bleeds*. New York: Scribner.

Wasserman, Sarah. 2020. 'Ralph Ellison, Chester Himes, and the Persistence of Urban Forms'. *PMLA* 135 (3): 530–45.

Chapter 3

Determination in the Wake of Dispossession: Jesmyn Ward's Literary Depiction of Black Resistance to Outmigration

Donald Brown

Introduction

Jesmyn Ward is perhaps the leader of the contemporary Black Southern literary renaissance. Her 2016 Buzzfeed article, 'This Was the Year America Finally Saw the South', is the rallying cry for her generation. Ward begins this article by contrasting her grandmother's life with her 'grandaunt Jane', who 'migrated to Chicago' in the 1950s. Her grandmother 'did not accept the invitation' to join her sister in Chicago: 'she remained, and she bore and raised all of her seven children' on the Gulf Coast of Mississippi (Ward 2016). In that article, Ward defines Southern Black literature as a regional genre produced by a people who believed in the power of Southern land, stayed put on that land and forged robust communities that enabled joy and purpose to thrive despite the terrors of Jim Crow. Ward further explains this in her introduction to *Best American Short Stories, 2021* (2021), by providing details of her family history. Her 'great-great-grandfather built a one-room schoolhouse to educate black children in 1940'. He also 'owned acres of land, granted them in perpetuity', because he was 'determined to parcel out all he had to his children so that they might own some piece of this red-sanded, green-fringed, singing earth when he was gone' (Ward 2021, xiv). Two generations later, her grandmother inherited that legacy and became 'the first person who taught [her] something of the power of narrative' (xiv) through her powerful stories at family gatherings (xii–xx). Furthermore, as Ward matured, she was exposed to Southern Black literature produced by women, such as *Their Eyes Were Watching God* (1937) by Zora Neale Hurston and *The Color Purple* (1982) by Alice Walker. Ward 'read and reread' those two novels while searching for 'anything else I could get by the two brilliant Southern women' (Ward 2016).

Following in Hurston's and Walker's tradition, Ward began to write. She did not see anybody else doing what Hurston and Walker did for her generation, namely, 'writing about ordinary black Southerners'. She felt compelled to continue in their tradition and 'write stories that affirmed my existence, that showed black Southerners to the larger American culture. That posited this: *We are here. We are human beings. We live*' (Ward 2016). Though a diverse array of articles has been written on Jesmyn Ward's literature, very few emphasise her depiction of Black farmers, landownership, and its intersection with the Great Migration and the unfinished work of the civil rights movement. Nonetheless, Black farmers' belief in the land inspired many rural Black Southerners to resist outmigration to destination centres of the Northeast, Midwest and West and assert their right to stay home and take advantage of civil rights gains (Coleman 2009). There is a rich history of Black freedom farm dreams in the Mississippi Gulf Coast, Ward's home region within the state. Like hundreds of thousands of others elsewhere throughout the state, perhaps most famously Fannie Lou Hamer and Medgar Evers, some Black Mississippians on the Gulf Coast refused to leave their Mississippi home during intense periods of racial hostility. In the words of Jesmyn Ward, they insisted, 'We are here. We are human beings. We live.' This simple, profound truth undergirds her whole oeuvre: to affirm the ambitions of intergenerational Black families that continue to live in Mississippi. They refused to be pushed out of the state during the Great Migration or post-Hurricane Katrina. In this chapter, I argue that Ward's oeuvre exists as a counternarrative to the migration narrative, as identified by Farrah Jasmine Griffin and Lawrence Rodgers. Her literature is a part of a distinctly alternative narrative I call the stand-off narrative. This narrative centres on Black Southerners who refused to be moved despite many attempts by Southern white supremacists to disperse and dispossess the large Black population in the Deep American South and decrease the power of their vote. It is a consistent feature in her works that ties together her movement from genre to genre, which includes coming of age, disaster, road, Gothic and memoir.

Formally, each stand-off narrative praises characters who decide not to leave. In order to do so, Ward reveals the conditions that would have made it more expedient for the character to forsake their home and the freedom dreams imagined there. In Ward's literary worlds, she details the agency in staying and suggests it requires just as much, if not more, courage to stay, especially in times of planned dispossession by those in power. Ward recognises the ambitions of non-migrants on the land and considers them the key to a more just future. Just as importantly, they are a model of why the right to stay home in the wake of state violence, extralegal violence, agribusiness, gentrification, 'replacement theories' and more is a crucial component to any liberation movement and a more sustainable environment.

I will begin by outlining the Mississippi Gulf Coast land itself and the Black American migration to the region from New Orleans post-emancipation. These newly emancipated people sought to steward the land, not for profit, but for small-scale subsistence. They sought to live on land they could call their own, free from the white gaze and terror. I will then outline how Ward's literary framework stands in contrast to literature that centres on those who left the land. Though there is a body of literature that provides robust language to explain the courage, motivations and struggles of Black Southerners who left during the Great Migration (1910–70), Ward's writing suggests those who remained in place were just as complex and brave. Lastly, I will conclude with reflections on her representation of young adult post-Katrina Black Mississippians, descendants of Black Mississippians who remained in place during the Great Migration. They find the strength to stay on the Mississippi Gulf Coast and properly steward the land post-Katrina.

The Development of the Mississippi Gulf Coast Post-Emancipation

In all of Ward's novels, she proudly represents strong, loving inter-generational rural Black Southern communities. Despite the genre, Ward always sets the scene by establishing the history of a Black Southern family that has asserted their right to stay home on the Mississippi Gulf Coast. In her memoir, *Men We Reaped* (2013), she details the history of Black families like hers who believed in the potential of land on the Gulf Coast: 'Most of the Black families in DeLisle have lived there as far back as they can remember, including mine, in houses many of them built themselves' (Ward 2013, 6). She dates her family's presence – and that of many other Black families – on the Gulf Coast back to the early twentieth century. They built 'houses, small shotguns and A frames . . . in waves, the oldest in the thirties by our great-grandparents, the next in the fifties by our grandparents, the next in the seventies and eighties by our parents, who used contractors' (Ward 2013, 6).

In Ward's first novel, *Where the Line Bleeds* (2008), she uses the history of Black residents of DeLisle to create the fictional world of Bois Sauvage, which Ward bases on her home town. In its opening pages, she describes Bois Sauvage as a small town with 'natural boundaries surrounding it on three sides'. The narrator proceeds to explain how a main character, Joshua, 'could understand why Ma-mee's and Papa's families had migrated here from New Orleans'. Ward continues:

> Land had been cheaper along the Mississippi gulf. [T]hey built weekend mansions along the beach for wealthy New Orleans expatriates, cleaned them, did their yard work, and fished, shrimped, and harvested oysters. Yet here, they had space and earth. (Ward 2008, 14)

Salvage the Bones opens similarly, with references to 'slave galleys' that were converted into coastal 'summer mansions' built along the 'twenty-six-mile manmade Mississippi beach' (Ward 2011, 17).

In *Where the Line Bleeds*, Ward's history of the development of the region mirrors the history told by Andrew Kahrl in *The Land Was Ours: How Black Beaches Became White Wealth in the Coastal South* (2012). Newly emancipated Blacks, alongside whites from New Orleans, flocked to the Gulf Coast. The completion of the railroad line 'linking New Orleans to the coast in 1869' made the Mississippi Gulf Coast a prime spot for former Confederate soldiers. By 1920, approximately 'thirty millionaires, mostly from New Orleans, owned summer homes along the coast, ranging in value from $15,000 to $100,000' (Kahrl 2012, 57). Visits to the Mississippi Gulf Coast for white Southerners became a holy retreat for Confederate veterans and their descendants.

However, the beauty and respite many Southern whites find on the Coast during summer vacations come at the expense of the Black residents who live there all year long. Nonetheless, Ward's family and many other Black families decided to stay there. As she continued in the first chapter of *Where the Line Bleeds*, generations of Southern Black communities on the Gulf Coast refused to leave the land they flocked to post-emancipation: 'They developed their own small, self-contained communities' due to the ability to buy land and farm it (14). Ward continues: 'They planted and harvested small crops. They kept horses and chickens and pigs ... They parceled out their acres to their children, to their passels of seven and twelve' (Ward 2008, 14).

She proceeds to discuss how each family built 'small, uneven houses, married at seventeen and fourteen, and started families' whose posterity eventually saw school desegregation. Therefore, 'they sent them to the public schools in St. Catherine to sit for the first time next to White people'. They also witnessed desegregation of public property: 'their children's children could walk along the beaches, could walk through the park in St. Catherine without the caretakers chasing them away, hollering nigger'. Most importantly, Ward notes that Black families '*stayed* . . . embedded themselves in the red clay and *remained*' (emphasis added). Ward makes a point of mentioning that this is a novel about Black characters – the main two characters are twins named Joshua and Christophe – who love their home town and do not desire to move elsewhere: 'When Joshua and Christophe talked about what they wanted to do with their lives, it never included leaving Bois Sauvage, even though they could have joined their mother, Cille, who lived in Atlanta' (Ward 2008, 14–15).

In a few pages, Ward's sweeping history of multiple generations of Black families with a mind to stay in Bois Sauvage alludes to real-world watershed moments such as the wade-ins that occurred along the Mississippi Gulf Coast. Though it is common knowledge that Black Americans across the South participated in sit-ins to desegregate lunch counters, the wade-ins are less well known. Nonetheless, there was a heated contestation over 'Mississippi's twenty-six miles of white sandy beaches along the Gulf of Mexico'. The beach was fortified by the US Army Corps of Engineers, stands as the 'largest and longest artificial beach in the United States' (Eubanks 2021, 25), and was the site of what the *New York Times* called 'the worst race riot in Mississippi history'. The riot occurred as a response to Black Mississippians on the Gulf Coast asserting their right to unlawfully segregated land that relegated black beachgoers 'to small and less well-maintained parts of this long stretch of sand'. Led by NAACP leader Dr Gilbert Mason (Eubaks 2021, 25), Black residents of the Mississippi Gulf Coast peacefully protested on the portions of the beach they were not allowed to inhabit and eventually gained full access to the beach.

Ward's inclusion of such historical details in her writing serves as the foundation for her understanding of what makes Black Southern history distinct. Like many other Southern Black writers, Ward eschews models of resistance to white supremacy that emphasise mobility. Rather, Ward praises the power of collective non-mobility and forces readers to reckon with the freedom dreams of Black Southerners who refused to leave their home region. Instead of migrating, they worked towards an alternative economic and land development course that would make migration truly a voluntary choice. That work continues in the present day as younger generations continue to reckon with the unrealised freedom dreams of their elders and ancestors as they struggle to reap the material benefits of civil rights legislation.

Coastal Freedom Dreams: Black Farmers Vision for the Region

Many Black Americans in the South, especially during the second wave of the Great Migration (1940–70), felt staying in the South was key to freedom, yet historical scholarship rarely addresses this reality.[1] Understanding that demographic power would mean political power following the Voting Rights Act, Black Southerners in majority or near majority Black states like Mississippi felt it crucial to remain in place in response to white politicians seeking to relocate them to states where they would have no political power. As Mississippi's Wilkinson County NAACP president James Joliff, Jr, stated in 1968:

> We must realize that the real answer is to stay here and to make things better . . . Most Negroes run off to Chicago . . . But I wouldn't trade Mississippi for all the tea in China. Sure, there's guys pushing you here, but you just got to push back. (De Jong 2016, 47)

Many Black Mississippians resisted relocation because they had bought considerable amounts of land in the state just a few generations ago. At the turn of the twentieth century, Black land ownership was on the rise and continued to do so until 1910, when it peaked at 2.2 million acres. Black Mississippians' vision for the land differed significantly from their white counterparts. Instead of viewing the land as a site for profit by any means necessary, they saw themselves as stewards of the land they could use for sustenance and collective empowerment. The most prominent example of collective empowerment on Mississippi's Gulf Coast is the Gulfside Assembly. Founded in Waveland by Bishop Robert E. Jones of the African Episcopal Methodist Church in the tradition of Booker T. Washington, Jones believed in the power of agriculture as a means to achieve racial upliftment and empowerment. As Andrew Kahrl writes, Jones 'purchased more than three hundred acres of mostly undeveloped coastal property from several landowners' in the summer of 1923 (Kahrl 2017).

It was supposed to function as a Black resort, orphan home, vocational school and 'working farm' for at-risk youth (Kahrl 2012, 60–1). One pamphlet called it the 'biggest venture ever started for and by colored people' (Kahrl 2017). However, the original plans of the Gulfside Assembly were diverted because they depended upon funding from white donors and support from the state of Mississippi (Kahrl 2012).[2] As Cydney Phillip notes in her chapter in this volume, 'Carceral Ecologies: Incarceration and Hydrological Haunting in Jesmyn Ward's *Sing, Unburied, Sing*', state politicians had other plans for the Black people who lived near the prized coastal waters. White men in power were more interested in punishing and profiting off Black bodies as displayed by the conditions and demographics of Mississippi's notorious prison known as Parchman Farm, the setting of Ward's third novel, *Sing, Unburied, Sing* (2017). In particular, 'water-based violence' continued to resurface as young Black Mississippians post-Reconstruction were imprisoned and forced to labour in cotton fields. In fact, 'water deprivation and contamination is an underlying issue at the Mississippi State Penitentiary' that persists today. However, to remember what the land could have been, once was, and could still provide for its residents in the future, Ward names the fictional representation of her home town in her novels, 'Bois Sauvage', which is French for 'wild roots'. As she writes in *Men We Reaped*:

> When people ask me about my hometown, I tell them it was named after a wolf before it was partially tamed and settled. I want to impart something of its wild roots, its early savagery. Calling it Wolf Town hints at the wildness at the heart of it. (Ward 2013, 9)[3]

Ward's mother was among those who stayed and fought to implement new power relations on the land her ancestors had bought for their posterity generations earlier. Ward discusses her mother's decision to commit herself to Mississippi though she had the opportunity to settle down in Oakland, California in her memoir. Her mom's work in the South helped a 'transplanted people [who] survived a holocaust and slavery. This is how Black people in the South organized a vote under the shadow of terrorism and the noose. This is how human beings sleep and wake and fight and survive' (Ward 2013, 250). Despite the courage of the civil rights work of Ward's mother's generation, Ward suggests that work is incomplete. Her sweeping historical narration of intergenerational Black family life on the Mississippi Gulf Coast in *Where the Line Bleeds* ends by narrowing in on the life of post-civil rights twin youths, Joshua and Christophe,

Black high school graduates who don't go to college and struggle to make ends meet. As stated earlier, she discusses how 'the government desegregated the schools', which allowed Black Southerners of the civil rights movement to send their children to 'public schools in St. Catherine to sit for the first time next to White people'. However, Ward's recounting of the desegregation is not glorious. The understated nature of the sentence suggests that all Black children got out of desegregation was the opportunity to sit next to white people, but not better education and more access to healthy choices. Similarly, in Ward's narration of the desegregation of public places like the beaches, she once again resists romanticisation: 'their children's children could walk along the beaches, could walk through the park in St. Catherine without the caretakers chasing them away, hollering nigger'. She suggests the only change was superficial: not being called 'nigger'. Nonetheless, at the same time as these momentous civil rights bills were passed and eventually enforced, various entities from banks and nightriders to the government dispossessed Black Southerners and continued structural inequities (Hartman 2007, 10; see also Pete Daniel [2013]).

As many Black Southerners were pushed out of the South, they forfeited land they had fought to own and establish as the foundation of a healthy ecosystem. In 1910, at the onset of the Great Migration, Black farmers owned approximately 18 million acres of land. By 1997, that total had decreased to 1.5 million. The greatest amount of land loss, and Black outmigration, ironically enough, occurred during the two decades of the civil rights movement: the 1950s and 1960s. In the 1960s alone, 'the number of Black farmers declined from 74,132 to 45,428' (Williams 2020, 434).[4] Though US Congress passed civil rights bills, mass outmigration and dispossession limited the bills' impact on the material reality of Black Southerners who stayed put. Leading civil rights activists – such as Malcolm X in 'The Message to the Grassroots' (1963) and Martin Luther King, Jr in 'The Other America' (1967) – brought attention to this crisis of land loss. However, their critiques of agrarian white supremacy have largely been erased from histories of the civil rights movement era. The loss of land led many Black Southerners to leave and decreased the potential of those who stayed to determine their future on the land (Malcolm X 2009, 379–88; King 1967). Today, majority-Black Southern communities are the country's poorest and most food-insecure areas due to a lack of sustainable agriculture and food systems (Brown 2011; Champagne et al. 2007, 1886–94; Ralston et al. 2019, 10–104). The logic of Ward's novels implies that racial capitalism persists today, and perhaps most prominently via continued land loss and the unrealised hydrologic visions of projects like the Gulfside Assembly.[5]

Ward's literary representation of the post-civil rights American South confirms points made by contemporary historians and journalists. As Vann Newkirk stated:

> These cases of dispossession can only be called theft. While the civil-rights era is remembered as a time of victories against disenfranchisement and segregation, many realities never changed. The engine of white wealth built on kleptocracy – which powered both Jim Crow and its slave-state precursor – continued to run. The black population in Mississippi declined by almost one-fifth from 1950 to 1970, as the white population increased by the exact same percentage. Farmers slipped away one by one into the night, appearing later as laborers in Chicago and Detroit. By the time black people truly gained the ballot in Mississippi, they were a clear minority, held in thrall to a white conservative supermajority. (Newkirk 2019)

As historian Andrew Kahrl notes, Black land loss on the Mississippi Gulf Coast was a product of 'coastal capitalism'. Post World War II, beaches became highly commodified, gated, commercial assets designed for 'White and upper-class retirees and vacationers', which led to 'the transfer of public lands to private entities' (Kahrl 2012, 257–8). African American land ownership in rural and sparsely populated coastal and waterfront areas steeply declined in the second half of the twentieth century, and that decline continues now. Given this reality, Kahrl calls for a reconsideration of 'America's triumph over segregation, its achievement of civil rights' (Kahrl 2012, 4–6). Like Michelle Alexander and other critical race theorists, Kahrl argues that a new form of racial discrimination emerged as Jim Crow was being dismantled. Whereas Michele Alexander focuses on the war on drugs, Kahrl focuses on the battle over land development that came at the expense of rural Black coastal farmers Ward centres in her novels. In addition, this anti-Black racism intersects with ecological devastation. Ward documents these intersections in all of her novels, particularly with the highly volatile nature of Hurricane Katrina and its disproportionate impact on communities of colour.[6]

New Literary Framework: African American Stand-off Narrative

Ward's literature critiques coastal capitalism and must be read as a response to the Black literary canon's emphasis on Black American literature set in destination centres of the Northeast, Midwest and West. Ward's novels are *stand-off* narratives, a juxtaposing frame of reference from the *migration* narrative identified by numerous literary scholars. By using the language of stand-off, attention is brought to the battle over land, water and resources between primarily whites and Blacks in the American South in the twentieth century. Contrary to popular belief, the American South was not a place that Black people were willing to simply give to white people because they did not want to be there. Furthermore, those who stayed were not more passive, accommodationist and less ambitious.[7] Instead, there was a fight over how the region should be shared equitably, and many Black Southerners were willing to die in a stand-off with white supremacists over the right to stay home. Though a surplus of sociological and literary criticism on Black migrants and Black migrant protagonists exists, minimal theoretical language exists to describe the agency of Black Southerners intent on resisting migration. As Farrah Griffin rightly argues in *Who Set You Flowin'* (1995), Black migrant writers and blues musicians often led the 'call for urban migration' and 'were oracles of their generation' (Griffin 1995, 20). The recurring motif of railroads and trains testify to Black literature and blues music's theme of 'black wanderers exercising the newly granted right of mobility' (Cobb 2007, 25). Also, in *Freedom Dreams: The Black Radical Imagination*, Robin D. G. Kelley rightly asserts that Black American history has been filled with 'movement – real and imagined' (Kelley 2002, 16). Black Americans have often looked to the Israelites' flight out of Egypt in 'the biblical story of Exodus' as an inspirational source that suggests migration will lead to nationhood on their own terms (Kelley 2002, 17).

While all of this is true, there is also a long history of Black Americans not wanting to have to move again. There is a history of Black Southerners' freedom dreaming of the right to stay home. Therefore, Ward writes against the grain of this hegemonic narrative with non-mobility freedom narratives and represents Black Americans who stayed in the South as determined, passionate, ambitious freedom fighters who refused to be forced to leave the land they and their ancestors had laboured on for generations. Instead of leading a movement to leave the land, Jesmyn Ward is leading a call to stay on rich, fertile Southern land, reorganise what is produced on it and restructure how to share that produce more equitably. Ward's Black freedom narratives of non-mobility celebrate Black Southerners who, as opposed to migrating, sit in (or wade in), literally and metaphorically.

For example, like her first novel *Where the Line Bleeds*, her third novel *Sing, Unburied, Sing* is a stand-off narrative. It details the difficult decisions made by a Black family in Bois Sauvage to stay put on the Mississippi Gulf Coast. The grandfather, Pop, runs the family farm, which consists of plants, goats and other animals.[8] Pop refused to leave the South even when he had an opportunity to do so post-incarceration during the height of the Great Migration. In a flashback near the middle of the novel, the Sunshine Woman, a friend of Pop, tells him the recent news of a Black man getting lynched in Mississippi. She tells Pop to follow her to Chicago once released from prison: 'A person ain't safe', she tells Pop, 'and that's why this is the last you seeing of me around here. I'm heading north to Chicago with my auntie and uncle, and you'd be a fool if you don't come north when you get out' (Ward 2017, 149).

The lynching does not convince Pop, however, to migrate to Chicago. It only leads him to think about making home safer for Black residents. After hearing of the lynching, he even tries to convince one of the inmates who wanted to migrate to Chicago to visit him down on the Gulf Coast. He describes the beauty of the natural environment to his friend, Richie:

> We got so much water where I'm from. It come down from the north in rivers. Pool in bayous. Rush out to the ocean, and that stretch to the ends of the earth that you can see. It changes colors like a little lizard. Sometimes stormy blue. Sometimes cool gray. In the early mornings, silver. You could look at that and know there's a God. (Ward 2017, 150–1)

Pop, not coincidentally also known as River, has a different relationship to water back home on the Gulf Coast. Back home, the abundance of water is a sign of a benevolent divine presence. Therefore, Pop is not 'hydrologically haunted', the phrase Cydney Phillip astutely uses to conceptualise the historic link between the Middle Passage slave ship and the Mississippi State Penitentiary. Rather, the hydrology at work back home on the Gulf Coast is heavenly. Nostalgia for that hydrologic home only increases while Pop is at Parchman, which is a stark contrast to his relationship with water back home.

Ward's juxtaposition of the Black freedom farm dreams on the Gulf Coast with state-sanctioned white supremacist, agrarian capitalism on the notorious prison grounds of Parchman Farm in the Mississippi Delta is a productive way of reading the novel. In the early 1900s, the Mississippi government bought land formerly inhabited by indigenous Americans who were forcibly removed just a few generations ago and started to incarcerate Black men at a disproportionate rate. While incarcerated, the state forced those Black inmates to clear trees from the land, then turn the land into a monocultural cotton farm, and ultimately create inordinate profits for white citizens in Mississippi post-Reconstruction in an era known as 'worse than slavery' or 'slavery by another name' (Blackmon 2008; Oshinsky 1997). In fact, in Chapter 9 of *Sing, Unburied, Sing*, Ward's dream sequence highlights the transformation of the Mississippi Delta landscape over various historical epochs. Ward's decision to centre the land, even above the characters, attends to what some in the environmental humanities have called the 'plantationocene', or a 'way of conceptualizing the current era otherwise nominated as the Anthropocene, Capitalocene, or the Chthulucene', and helps to focus on how the 'current ecological crisis is rooted in logics of environmental modernization, homogeneity, and control, which were developed on historical plantations'. Chapter 9's dream sequence forces readers to imagine alternative realities from the past, denormalise present political ecologies and bring about a more just future (Davis et al. 2019).

Ultimately, Pop's experience on Parchman Farm drove him to understand the potential of the Mississippi Gulf Coast. Being a victim of extreme exploitation on fertile farmland – and as Cydney Phillip notes, water deprivation – in the Mississippi Delta motivates Pop to return to the Gulf Coast and steward his parcel of land differently. Pop and Mam's posterity benefits from their sustenance farming, which provides food and herbal medicine for their family.

How to *Salvage the Bones*: Asserting the Right to Stay Home Post-Dispossession

Salvage the Bones, Ward's second novel, is another story of Black Southern determination in the aftermath of dispossession post-Great Migration, post-civil rights movement and post-Katrina, three intersecting watershed historical periods in the history of the American South. The Batiste family has owned land on the Coast for at least three generations, and readers can see at whose expense the coast was developed through The Pit, the name the Batiste family gives to their land. Esch, the teenage girl protagonist, narrates her family's history of Black farmland loss in the first chapter. Her maternal grandfather, Papa Joseph, once owned all fifteen acres of land on which the Batistes live:

> Papa Joseph who let the white men he work with dig for clay that they used to lay the foundation for houses, let them excavate the side of a hill in a clearing near the back of the property where he used to plant corn for feed. (Ward 2011, 27)[9]

Esch's narration illuminates the various economic pressures that forced Black farmers to make costly trade-offs at the expense of the natural environment and future generations of Southern Blacks.

As a result, the land was no longer farmable. In the place of the former cornfield emerged:

> a cliff over a dry lake in the backyard and the small stream that had run around and down the hill had diverted and pooled into the dry lake, making it into a pond, and then Papa Joseph thought the earth would give under the water, that the pond would spread and gobble up the property and make it a swamp, so he stopped selling earth for money. (Ward 2011, 27)

As Annie Bares puts it, the Pit is now 'part farm, part storage area, and part swimming hole' (Bares 2019, 25). In Bares's article, she connects its present dilapidated condition 'to a genealogy of racialized environmental slow violence' (Bares 2019, 26). The Pit, once fertile land that cultivated and sustained life of all forms – livestock, plants and the Black community's dietary needs – is now desolate, and their house is a junkyard 'nearly invisible under the oaks and behind the rubbish, lopsided' (Ward 2011, 116). The setting of The Pit exists as a regional, racialised, environmental symbol Ward deploys to contrast the potential of the land with its present impoverished condition. Therefore, as Molly Travis notes, *Salvage the Bones* does not argue that the hurricane disrupts their everyday lives. The novel takes place over twelve days – each day getting a chapter – and the storm does not come until Day 11. Ward places the storm alongside the quotidian violence and damage that visit poor, rural Black Mississippians on the Gulf Coast every day pre- and post-Katrina (Travis 2016; see also Trethewey 2010). As Ward writes in the conclusion to her memoir: 'Life is a hurricane and we board up to save what we can and bow low to the earth to crouch in that small space above the dirt where the wind will not reach' (Ward 2013, 250). With the metaphor of life as a hurricane, Ward contends that rural Black Mississippians on the Gulf Coast withstand the struggles of life in the same way they withstand the strength of hurricanes.

They stand their ground. Ultimately, *Salvage the Bones* is a love story to those Black families on the Mississippi Gulf Coast who stayed not just during the hurricane, but stayed on that land even through the Great Migration and beyond, like Ward's grandmother, Dorothy.

On the day of the hurricane, the protagonist, Esch Batiste, reflects on a conversation she had with her now-deceased mother, who first explained to her what a hurricane was. At that time, Esch thought that all the animals migrated once they sensed the impending doom. However, on the day of Hurricane Katrina, Esch rethinks her original assumption. Though Esch still thinks 'the bigger animals' leave, she now wonders if the small animals, such as squirrels and rabbits, actually stay put and hunker down during the storm: 'Maybe the small don't run. Maybe the small pause on their branches, the pine-lined earth, nose up, catch that coming storm air that would smell like salt to them, like salt and clean burning fire, and they prepare like us' (Ward 2011, 215).

The rich imagery Ward uses to describe the savvy, courageous actions of squirrels and rabbits not only highlights the beautiful quiet strength of the animals who refuse to leave during the hurricane. It also speaks to the similar fortitude displayed by poor rural Black families, such as the Batistes, who try to find a way out of a bad situation and struggle to ward off death.Though various media stations and stories characterised families like the Batistes, and Ward's own, as foolishly stubborn for refusing to evacuate, Ward tells another narrative.[10] For Ward, strong, loving community itself is a form of resistance to the hurricane of life, and the impetus that led many Black families to not migrate elsewhere. As she writes in *Men We Reaped*: 'We raise children and tell them other things about who they can be and what they are worth to us, everything. We love each other fiercely, while we live and after we die' (Ward 2013, 250).

On Day 12 of *Salvage the Bones*, the only day in the novel post-Katrina, Ward depicts the ruins in the aftermath of Hurricane Katrina (Ward 2011, 262–3). At the conclusion of her depiction of the town in ruins, she writes: 'People stand in clusters at what used to be intersections, the street signs vanished, all they own in a plastic bag at their feet, waiting for someone to pick them up. No one is coming' (Ward 2011, 263). The question at the end of the novel is: how will the Batistes remain and rebuild? One major factor to consider in answering that question is Esch's pregnancy – and the fact that her baby's father wants nothing to do with their child. Once again, the impact of Hurricane Katrina is just one of Ward's character's problems. Esch worries because the baby 'don't have a daddy', she tells her friend from the neighbourhood, Big Henry. However, Big Henry disagrees. Big Henry suggests that the community surrounding her in the wake of catastrophe will provide necessary love and support to rebuild and thrive in Bois Sauvage. Therefore, Big Henry replies: 'You wrong' as 'he looks away when he says it, out to the Gray Gulf'. He proceeds to claim: 'This baby got a daddy, Esch . . . This baby got plenty of daddies' (Ward 2011, 267). Big Henry's assertion of 'you wrong' holds at least two intersecting meanings. For one, he is not going to allow Esch to have the last pessimistic word concerning her future and the future of her child. The community will provide support. Even further, however, it is important to note Big Henry states, 'you wrong' while looking 'out to the Gray Gulf' that produced Katrina. He will not let Katrina have the last word either: about what life will be like in its wake and about who can rebuild and enjoy life there in its wake.

As Ward has stated in numerous interviews, life for Black Mississippians on the Gulf Coast after Katrina is as difficult as ever. For one, gentrification has become a problem as house prices sky-rocket.[11] Secondly, FEMA relocated many people from her lower-class Black community, and others 'left because they felt like they would have more opportunities elsewhere' (Ifill 2015). Employment options have only narrowed as casinos built post-Katrina have become the 'only source of employment' for many who need more options (Ifill 2015). The storm, for Ward, 'unmade the community', just like the Great Migration did for former generations of Black Mississippians on the Gulf Coast.[12]

Despite these difficulties, many scattered Black Mississippians from the Gulf Coast who relocated to Atlanta, Houston and elsewhere have begun the hard work of rebuilding and reclaiming their lives on the Coast. As Ward told *PBS NewsHour*, Black Mississippians came back 'because they missed home. Because they were from this place where they really felt like they were part of this community and large extended families, so they wanted to live in a place like that' (Ifill 2015). Ward captures this spirit of resiliency and asserts the right for people from her Mississippi coastal community to return and stay home. Since the turn of the twentieth century, Black Mississippians on the Gulf Coast have been there and Ward does not feel they should be forced out by structural inequalities (Ifill 2015).

In conclusion, Ward uses the Gulf Coast of Mississippi as a metaphor for the rest of the state and region. As literary critic Ralph Eubanks has stated, 'The coast is a place associated with the names of two powerful storms that felt like an ending: Camille and Katrina. Yet the highway's terminus at the Gulf of Mexico actually marks the beginning of Mississippi rather than the end.' Only by making sense of those 'life-altering storms on the Gulf Coast', Eubanks writes, can one realise that Mississippi is not stuck in time. Rather, the state is constantly being 'remade, reshaped, and transformed. Reinvention is built into the social fabric of the Gulf Coast', as it is with the rest of the state and region (Eubanks 2021, 27). There is a steady influx of people moving in and out of Mississippi and the Deep South. Some of those people were forcibly removed from the land (i.e. the indigenous). Others have been forced to move down south to labour on the land (the enslaved). Migration in and out of the state will continue to impact the state's future. However, just as importantly will be the fight for the right to remain home, as Ward depicts through a masterful trilogy of novels set in the fictional Bois Sauvage.

Notes

1. See Harrison (2021); De Jong (2016, 44–61); De Jong (2005, 387–409); Webb (2004, 249–71).
2. Gulfside Assembly, in various phases and iterations, continued in some form until 2005: when Hurricane Katrina struck the Gulf Coast. However, they struggled with funding beginning with the Great Depression and continually had to accommodate white funders who had conflicting ideas for the land.
3. For a brief history of Gulf Coast Mississippi, literary representations of it, and Jesmyn Ward's relationship to her hometown of DeLisle, see Ralph Eubanks, *A Place Like Mississippi.*
4. Valerie Grim provides more startling statistics over Black land loss over the twentieth century: 'Faced with these new developments in agriculture, the majority of black farm families in the rural south could not compete. Between 1920 and 1950, the number of black farmers in the 11 southern states fell from 882,000 to 536,000, of whom 195,000 were sharecroppers. After 1950, the exodus of black farmers from the South was so great that by 1978 only 55,995 black farmers remained and those on farms with sales of $2,000 or more numbered a mere 20,272' (170–1). See Grim (1994, 169–84); Daniel (2013).
5. For example, Regina Bradley explores Jesmyn Ward's post-civil rights literary representation of the American South in Chapter 4, 'Still Ain't Forgave Myself' of her book, *Chronicling Stankonia.* She interrogates 'the southern hip-hop space, "the trap" using the music of Clifford "T.I." Harris and the Mississippi author Jesmyn Ward's books *Where the Line Bleeds* and *Men We Reaped.* In southern hip-hop, the trap signifies not only an illicit but nihilistically masculine space. It sonically and lyrically reflects the socio-economic disparities that plague working-class Atlanta

communities. Specifically, I use Ward's writing and Harris's complex narration of trap rap – that is, the fragmentation of his performance personas as the polished and Hollywood ready "T.I." and the other his drug-dealer persona T.I.P. – to position the trap as a mourning space where young southern black men's grief is made legible' (Bradley 2021, 17).

6. For more, see: Center for Climate and Energy Solutions, 'Hurricanes and Climate Change', https://www.c2es.org/content/hurricanes-and-climate-change/; Union of Concerned Scientists, 'Hurricanes and Climate Change', https://www.ucsusa.org/resources/hurricanes-and-climate-change; Environmental Defense Fund, 'How climate change makes hurricanes more destructive', https://www.edf.org/climate/how-climate-change-makes-hurricanes-more-destructive; Buis (2020); Hersher (2021).

7. For two books that document African American writers or theorists, and that suggest Black Americans who left the South were more ambitious, upwardly mobile and righteously discontent from their counterparts who stayed, see Griffin (1995) and Wilkerson (2010). Ward is among a group of writers who writes against this dominant narrative. Another one worth noting is Akinyele Umoja. In an interview with New York University Press, Umoja states he 'wanted to write this book [*We Will Shoot Back: Armed Resistance in the Mississippi Freedom Movement*] to contribute to a new narrative on the Southern movement and understanding of Southern Black folks in particular' to disabuse the broader Black community of 'stereotypes and myths about the movement being exclusively nonviolent, and myths about Southern Black folks'. Many Black Americans who migrated to the North and West thought that Black Southerners were more passive than them, and '*We Will Shoot Back* really counters that narrative . . . The thought is that everybody just sat back and took it, so I really wanted to change that narrative.' See: NYU Press, 'Prof. Umoja discusses why he wrote *We Will Shoot Back*.' YouTube. Historian Neil McMillen makes a similar point to Umoja. Many believe non-migrants to be 'somehow more complacent, less aspiring, less discontent than those who went . . . Too many have assumed that [the Great Migration] drained the state of its best black stock, its most capable and intelligent black role models and community leaders' (87). Such assumptions are highly misguided and dehumanise the courage of those who decided to stay home. Those who stayed sacrificed, took risks, hated white supremacy and had ambition. Though census records do prove that the mass exodus 'left behind disproportionate members of the young, the old, the poorly educated, it does not follow that those who stayed were somehow more complacent or less ambitious than those who went'. Though many whites hoped it would act as 'a racial safety valve, if it siphoned off the most malcontented, aspiring, and protest-minded blacks, it did so imperfectly' (McMillen 1989, 88).

8. Goat farming is quite common in South Mississippi. It features in two of Ward's three novels. For example, in *Where the Line Bleeds*, Joshua and Christophe go with Paul to a 'farm further up in the country to

pick out a goat to barbecue for the fourth' (149–50). *Sing, Unburied, Sing*, of course, begins with Pop killing one of their goats for Jojo's thirteenth birthday celebration. For more on goat farming in Mississippi, see Susan M. Collins-Smith, 'Dairy goats gain popularity with small farmers, 4-Hers', *Mississippi State University Extension*, 10 June 2021, http://extension.msstate.edu/news/feature-story/2021/dairy-goats-gain-popularity-small-farmers-4-hers; and David Elliot, 'Raising baby goats on a South Mississippi goat farm', *WLOX*, 26 April 2019, https://www.wlox.com/2019/04/26/raising-baby-goats-south-mississippi-goat-farm/.

9. Such a narrative is rooted in her own family history in Mississippi. As she writes in the introduction to the *Best American Short Stories, 2021*, her 'great-great grandfather built a one-room schoolhouse to educate black children in 1940 . . . he owned acres of land, granted them in perpetuity, a man who was determined to parcel out all he had to his children so that they might own some piece of this red-sanded, green-fringed, singing earth when he was gone' (Ward 2021, xiv).

10. See: *AtlanticLIVE*. 'A Sense of Place / New Orleans: Ten Years Later'. YouTube, 26 August 2015.

11. See: *AtlanticLIVE*. 'A Sense of Place / New Orleans: Ten Years Later'. YouTube, 26 August 2015. See also Gwen Ifill (2015).

12. *AtlanticLIVE*. 'A Sense of Place / New Orleans: Ten Years Later'.

Works Cited

Bares, Annie. 2019. '"Each Unbearable Day": Narrative Ruthlessness and Environmental and Reproductive Injustice in Jesmyn Ward's *Salvage the Bones*'. *Melus* 44, no. 3 (Fall 2019): 21–40.

Blackmon, Douglass. 2008. *Slavery by Another Name: The Re-enslavement of Black Americans from the Civil War to World War Two*. New York: Anchor Books.

Bradley, Regina. 2021. *Chronicling Stankonia: The Rise of the Hip-Hop South*. Chapel Hill: University of North Carolina Press.

Brown, Novelette L. 2011. 'Starved: Food Deserts in the Mississippi Delta'. University of Mississippi, Master's thesis. *Electronic Theses and Dissertations*. https://egrove.olemis.edu/etd/65.

Buis, Alan. 2020. 'How Climate Change May Be Impacting Storms Over Earth's Tropical Oceans', 10 March. *Global Climate Change: Vital Signs of the Planet*. https://climate.nasa.gov/ask-nasa-climate/2956/how-climate-change-may-be-impacting-storms-over-earths-tropical-oceans/.

Champagne, Catherine M., et al. 2007. 'Poverty and Food Intake in Rural America: Diet Quality is Lower in Food Insecure Adults in the Mississippi Delta'. *Journal of the American Dietetic Association* 107, no. 11 (November): 1886–94. doi:10.1016/j.jada.2007.08.003.

Cobb, William Jelani. 2007. *To the Break of Dawn: A Freestyle on the Hip Hop Aesthetic*. New York: NYU Press.

Coleman, Mary DeLorse. 2009. 'The Rural Poor in the American South: Case Studies of Exits from 20th Century Poverty'. *Poverty & Public Policy* 1, no. 1, Article 5.

Daniel, Pete. 2013. *Dispossession: Discrimination against African American Farmers in the Age of Civil Rights*. Chapel Hill: University of North Carolina Press.

Davis, Janae, Alex A. Moulton, Levi Van Sant and Brian Williams. 2019. 'Anthropocene, Capitalocene, . . . Plantationocene?: A Manifesto for Ecological Justice in an Age of Global Crises'. *Geography Compass* 13, no. 5 (May): 1–15.

Eubanks, W. Ralph. 2021. *A Place Like Mississippi: A Journey Through a Real and Imagined Literary Landscape*. Portland: Timber Press.

Griffin, Farah Jasmine. 1995. *Who Set You Flowin': The African American Migration Novel*. New York: Oxford University Press.

Grim, Valerie. 1994. 'The Impact of Mechanized Farming on Black Farm Families in the Rural South: A Study of Farm Life in the Brooks Farm Community, 1940–1970'. *Agricultural History* 68, no. 2 (Spring 1994): 169–84.

Harrison, Alferdteen. 2001. *Those Who Stayed Home*. Jackson, MS: Town Square Books.

Hartman, Saidiya. 2007. *Lose Your Mother: A Journey Along the Atlantic Slave Route*. New York: Farrar, Straus & Giroux.

Hersher, Rebecca. 2021. 'How Climate Change Is Fueling Hurricanes Like Ida'. *NPR: All Things Considered*.

Ifill, Gwen. 2015. 'Writer Jesmyn Ward reflects on survival since Katrina'. *PBS NewsHour*, 24 August.

Jong, Greta de. 2005. 'Staying in Place: Black Migration, the Civil Rights Movement, and the War on Poverty in the Rural South'. *The Journal of African American History* 90, no. 4 (Fall 2005): 387–409.

—. 2016. 'This is Home: Black Workers' Responses to Displacement and Out-Migration'. In *You Can't Eat Freedom*, 44–61. Chapel Hill: University of North Carolina Press.

Kahrl, Andrew. 2012. *The Land Was Ours: How Black Beaches Became White Wealth in the Coastal South*. Chapel Hill: University of North Carolina Press.

—. 2017. 'Gulfside Assembly'. *Mississippi Encyclopedia*, 11 July.

Kelley, Robin D. G. 2002. *Freedom Dreams: The Black Radical Imagination*. Boston: Beacon Press.

King, Martin Luther. 1967. 'The Other America', *Veterans of the Civil Rights Movement*, 4 April. https://www.crmvet.org/docs/otheram.htm.

McMillen, Neil. 1989. *Dark Journey: Black Mississippians in the Age of Jim Crow*. Champlain: University of Illinois Press.

Malcolm X. 2009. 'Message to the Grassroots'. *Words of a Century: The Top 100 Speeches, 1900–1999*, edited by Stephen E. Lucas and Martin J. Medhurst, 379–88. New York: Oxford University Press.

Newkirk, Vann. 2019. 'The Great Land Robbery'. *The Atlantic*, September. https://www.theatlantic.com/magazine/archive/2019/09/this-land-was-our-land/594742/.

NYU Press. 2013. 'Prof. Umoja discusses why he wrote *We Will Shoot Back*'. YouTube, 18 April.

Oshinsky, David. 1997. *Worse than Slavery: Parchman Farm and the Ordeal of Jim Crow*. New York: Free Press.

Ralston, Margaret, Kecia Johnson, Leslie Hossfeld and Bettina Beach. 2019. 'Examining the Nexus of Obesity, Mental Health and Rural County Food Access: Testing the Enduring Role of Persistent Poverty'. *Journal of Sociology and Social Welfare* 46, no. 2 (June): 10–104.

Rodgers, Lawrence. 1997. *Canaan Bound: The African American Great Migration Novel*. Champaign: University of Illinois Press.

Travis, Molly. 2016. 'We Are Here: Jesmyn Ward's Survival Narratives. Response to Anna Hartnell, "When Cars Become Churches"'. *Journal of American Studies* 50 (1): 219–24.

Trethewey, Natasha. 2010. *Beyond Katrina: A Meditation on the Mississippi Gulf Coast*. Athens: University of Georgia Press.

Ward, Jesmyn. 2008. *Where the Line Bleeds*. Evanston, IL: Agate Publishing.

—. 2011. *Salvage the Bones*. London: Bloomsbury.

—. 2013. *Men We Reaped*. London: Bloomsbury.

—. 2016. 'This Was the Year America Finally Saw the South'.

—. 2017. *Sing, Unburied, Sing*. New York: Scribner.

—. 2021. 'Introduction', *The Best American Short Stories 2021*, edited by Heidi Pitlor and Jesmyn Ward, xii–xx. New York: HarperCollins.

Webb, Clive. 2004. '"A Cheap Trafficking in Human Misery": The Reverse Freedom Rides of 1962'. *Journal of American Studies* 38, no. 2 (August): 249–71.

Wilkerson, Isabel. 2010. *The Warmth of Other Suns: The Epic Story of America's Great Migration*. New York: Random House.

Williams, Brian. 2020. '"The Fabric of Our Lives"?: Cotton, Pesticides, and Agrarian Racial Regimes in the U.S. South'. *Annals of the American Association of Geographers* 111, no. 2 (August): 422–39.

Chapter 4

Local and Global Scales of Racial Neoliberalism in *Where the Line Bleeds*

Martyn Bone

Notwithstanding burgeoning scholarly attention to Jesmyn Ward's writing – epitomised by this edited collection – *Where the Line Bleeds* (2008) remains oddly overlooked.[1] This is a regrettable lacuna, and not only because Ward's debut introduced readers to Bois Sauvage, Mississippi, the majority-Black town – based partly on the author's home town of DeLisle – that recurs so powerfully in her National Book Award-winning second and third novels, *Salvage the Bones* (2011) and *Sing, Unburied, Sing* (2017). In this essay, I hope to demonstrate that *Where the Line Bleeds* is particularly valuable for its precocious attention to the intersection of forms of racialised exploitation long associated with the US South and the more contemporary reality of economic globalisation. The novel dramatises how these overlapping social and economic forces, operating across temporal and geographic scales, impact upon the poor Black denizens of Bois Sauvage.

Where the Line Bleeds opens in the summer of 2005 with the eighteen-year-old twin protagonists, Joshua and Christophe DeLisle, graduating from high school and preparing to enter adulthood and the working world.[2] Over the course of the novel, the twins' experiences anatomise the formation of this world by both a regional history of racialised labour and the contemporary global expansion of neoliberalism. While *Where the Line Bleeds* takes place almost entirely at the local scale of the Gulf Coast of Mississippi, Ward dramatises Michelle Alexander's point that a 'new global economy' has 'deemed disposable' young Black men like the DeLisles (Alexander 2012, 18). If such disposability is disturbingly resonant of slavery and its legacies in the US South, it results too from the recent outsourcing overseas of blue-collar jobs. Facing few legitimate options in a coastal economy largely evacuated of industry and increasingly reliant on poorly salaried service-sector positions at fast-food franchises (McDonald's, Burger King) and box-store behemoths (Wal-Mart), young Black citizens have little choice but to begin dealing drugs to friends and neighbours.

Where the Line Bleeds examines this racialised and neoliberalised disposability at the intimate scale of the twins' interpersonal relationship. Joshua secures one of the Mississippi Gulf Coast's few remaining blue-collar positions while Christophe, unsuccessful in seeking legal work, begins to deal weed and then crack cocaine. Their close bond becomes riven by the language of 'choice' – a loaded word within the novel's drama (is dealing drugs an option or a necessity for Christophe?) and, as David Harvey and Wendy Brown have demonstrated, within neoliberal discourse. Furthermore, the twins are shadowed throughout the narrative by the reappearance of their long absent father Samuel, an unemployed drug addict known locally as Sandman. Sandman is repeatedly associated with dirt and waste, again recalling the regional history of black labouring lives and bodies being exploited and dispensed with – what Achille Mbembe terms necropolitics – as well as the 'biopolitics of disposability' circa Hurricane Katrina that critics such as Henry Giroux have attributed to neoliberalism.

Plight of the Stationary Displaced' and the Neoliberal Fallacy of 'Choice'

Where the Line Bleeds opens with a prologue in which the DeLisle twins go swimming in the Wolf River, which 'seeped from the red clay earth in the piney woods of southern Mississippi'; the suitably sinuous opening sentence ends by remarking that the river 'wound its way' into 'the gulf of Mexico' (Ward 2018, 1). Such aquatic imagery complements the opening chapter's emphasis on demographic flows as part of its potted history of Bois Sauvage.[3] The community emerged as New Orleans' 'black Creoles had spread along the coastline' of Mississippi; after the settlers 'raised small, uneven houses from the red mud', their descendants 'embedded themselves in the red clay and remained' (Ward 2018, 6–7). Yet for all this emphasis on black migratory agency and roots in the physical landscape, the narrative stresses too how racial and economic realities have shaped Bois Sauvage. Black settlers 'were dependent on the rich for their livelihood . . . they built weekend mansions along the beach for wealthy New Orleans expatriates, cleaned them, did their yard work'

(Ward 2018, 6). This history of residential segregation and racialised labour relations resonates down to the narrative present. In the prologue, poised to jump into the river, Joshua is distracted by a white house that reminds both twins of how just such domestic labour was performed not so long ago by their grandmother Lillian ('Ma-mee'). Joshua remarks to Christophe that the house '[l]ooks like the one Ma-mee used to work at, huh?'; in turn Christophe is acutely aware that such houses 'made him feel poor. They made him think of Ma-mee . . . scrubbing the dirt out of white people's floors for forty years' (Ward 2018, 3). Even the DeLisles' own domestic space is inextricable from such (in both senses of the word) white houses: the twins' grandfather Lucien, Lillian's deceased husband, 'bought the land' and 'built the house' by 'sav[ing] up working carpentry and yard jobs for vacationing white families who owned beach homes, mansions really, on the shore' (Ward 2018, 63).

So, while Bois Sauvage provides 'space and earth' (Ward 2018, 6), the elemental landscape of river, bayou and clay offers no organic sanctuary from the historical continuities of place, race and labour. The twins are not 'embedded' in Bois Sauvage because of some romantic, autochthonous link to the land: they remain because they feel indebted to Ma-mee for having supported their upbringing through her domestic work – especially after their mother Cille 'decided to go to Atlanta to make something of herself when the boys were five' (Ward 2018, 7). Christophe ponders that '[t]he only way he could ever consider leaving Bois Sauvage to work was . . . if Ma-mee was gone'; like Joshua, he is conscious that Ma-mee 'spent her entire life working for one rich white household or another to earn money to feed them'. When fellow high school graduate Fabian tells Christophe that he is 'going offshore' to work on an oil rig – as *Sing Unburied Sing* elaborates, one of the blue-collar jobs still available to working-class Mississippians on or off the Gulf Coast – Christophe muses that he and Joshua cannot leave because 'it was their turn' to look after Ma-mee (Ward 2018, 20). In 2009, interviewer Nico Barry observed that leaving Bois Sauvage 'doesn't seem to even really be an option' for the DeLisle brothers; Ward responded that 'For a lot of people here [DeLisle, Bois Sauvage's real-life analogue] that's how it is. Leaving's not an option' (Barry 2009).

Where the Line Bleeds elaborates on how this entanglement of tight family ties with racial and economic factors constrains the central characters' 'options'. The DeLisle twins experience what Rob Nixon calls 'the plight of the stationary displaced'. In *Slow Violence and the Environmentalism of the Poor* (2011), Nixon employs this phrase to define the experience of being both 'ecologically under-mined' and economically 'abandoned' by the 'neoliberal ideology' of globalisation (Nixon 2011, 42). Ward's next novel, *Salvage the Bones*, dramatises this fate in its portrayal of the Batiste family – including Skeetah, who first appears in *Where the Line Bleeds* – before and during Hurricane Katrina. The tour de force eleventh section of *Salvage* starkly renders the Batiste family home, the Pit, being 'ecologically undermined' by the double whammy of hurricane winds and flood waters, a simultaneously natural and anthropogenic disaster. Yet the preceding ten sections reveal how, as poor Black Mississippians, the Batistes already have been rendered expendable by neoliberalism – 'human debris in the middle of all of the rest of it', as narrator Esch memorably observes (Ward 2012, 237). Esch re-calls how, before the hurricane hits, the Mississippi state government issues an automated phone call declaring that '*If you choose to stay in your home and have not evacuated by this time, we are not respon-sible*' (Ward 2012, 217). As Sinéad Moynihan has sharply observed, the robo-call exemplifies a 'neoliberal discourse of choice' in which an inability to evacuate and thereby escape the hurricane's path is 'construed as a "bad choice" on the part of the Batistes, rather than an effect of poverty, lack of transportation, and no access to alter-native accommodations elsewhere' (Moynihan 2015, 555). Scholars have not yet noted, however, that this dubious discourse of choice is already evident in *Where the Line Bleeds*. Relatedly, when Nixon asks 'What does it mean for people declared disposable by some "new" economy to find themselves existing out of place in place . . .?' (Nixon 2011, 19) we can turn to Ward's debut for answers. Anticipating Ward's later work, *Where the Line Bleeds* portrays how the intersection of racialised exploitation (as an afterlife of slavery and Jim Crow) with neoliberal globalisation leaves young black men like the DeLisle twins doubly 'displaced' and 'disposable' at the local scale of their own home town.

Even while the graduation ceremony is still underway, Christophe 'began to make a list in his head of where he and Joshua could go to look for jobs: Wal-Mart, the grocery store in St. Catherine, the McDonald's' (Ward 2018, 22). The second chapter begins with the twins submitting applications to fast-food franchises and gas sta-tions while pondering their 'dull litany of choices: McDonald's, Burger King, Sonic, Dairy Queen, Piggly Wiggly, Circle K, Chevron, Wal-Mart, K-Mart, the dockyard and the shipyard'. The DeLisles are well aware that '[n]one of their options were in Bois Sauvage', and that '[t]hey needed a car to get to all of the places they were putting in applications, because they were all at least two towns over in each direction along the coast' (Ward 2018, 30). We see here what Alexander in *The New Jim Crow* refers to as 'the "spatial mismatch" between . . . residence and employment opportunities' for young Black men, especially those without 'access to a car' (Alexander 2012, 150). It is only because Cille sends money for a second-hand car as a graduation present that the twins secure transportation at all. What Anna Hartnell has remarked about Ward's memoir *Men We Reaped* is already apparent in *Where the Line Bleeds*: 'cars are essential to daily survival' for Black people in rural Mississippi 'exposed to the rough end of American racism and a globalised, neoliberal economy that brands large numbers of US citizens "disposable"' (Hartnell 2016, 205).

It is telling too that in the twins' 'litany of choices', the dockyard and shipyard appear last: vestiges of blue-collar employment once more widely available to working-class black Mississippians otherwise exploited and discriminated against. What the twins do not yet understand, but which the narrative subtly reveals, is that these 'choices' have been reduced by economic globalisation. As Alexander notes, '[n]ot long ago, young, unskilled men could find decent, well-paying jobs at large factories' but 'due to globalization and deindustrialization, that is no longer the case' (Alexander 2012, 150).[4] In *Men We Reaped*, Ward recalls how 'factory jobs like the one my father had once supported a family on were becoming a rarity while only dead-end service jobs remained' following the 'hemorrhaging [of] blue-collar jobs overseas' (Ward 2013, 219–20). Those 'dead-end service jobs' constitute most of the twins' 'choices' in *Where the Line Bleeds*. Though Joshua secures 'hard, backbreaking work' at the dockyard (Ward 2018, 36), Christophe's multiple job applications receive no response, and the ensuing 'hurt and love and jealousy' (Ward 2018, 48) begins to alienate him from his brother. Because Christophe stubbornly 'refused to live like he was poor' (Ward 2018, 44), his cousin Dunny, who juggles dealing weed with a part-time job at the power plant (Ward 2018, 100), offers to 'put [Christophe] onto my hustle'. Until this point, Christophe had vaguely 'assumed . . . that there existed steps to his life: a job at the dockyard or the shipyard where he could learn a trade, pay raises, stacking money'. He had 'dismissed dealing because he saw where it led': 'For most drug dealers, jail and hustling became a job' (Ward 2018, 55–6). Now, however, the bleak reality underlying his supposed 'choices' is apparent. Not only are 'steps' to skilled manual labour – never widely available to black male Mississippians – scarcer than ever, but, as Dunny puts it,

'Everybody and they mama want a job at the pier and the shipyard' because the service-sector alternatives are so unappealing: 'Do you know what niggas start out making at Wal-Mart? Six-fifty an hour, Chris' (Ward 2018, 57). As Tara McPherson has noted, Wal-Mart's business practices are simultaneously 'southern' and 'a key part of a global franchise economy'. Arkansas-based Wal-Mart 'pioneered an approach of opening its stores in rural areas that weren't being served by other stores' even as it 'capitaliz[ed] on the South's long-standing, business-friendly, antilabor policies' (McPherson 2006, 696). This approach allowed the company to pay meagre salaries to young locals like Marquise, who 'worked at Wal-Mart as a stock boy' (Ward 2018, 111). Meanwhile Wal-Mart imports on a mass scale goods once produced in factories across the US South but now closed because production has been 'outsourced to other countries' in Latin America and Asia (McPherson 2006, 696): precisely the 'hemorrhaging [of] blue-collar jobs overseas' that Ward in *Men We Reaped* identifies with the increased disposability of working-class Blacks in a service-centred Southern economy. Moreover, *Where the Line Bleeds* (like Ward's later memoir) emphasises Alexander's point that the crack epidemic exploded even as American '[m]anufacturing jobs were transferred by multinational corporations' via globalisation to countries with lower wages and without unions. Even as 'blue-collar workers often found themselves displaced in the sudden transition from an industrial to a service economy', drugs – and the government's War on Drugs – devastated poor Black communities (Alexander 2012, 50).[5] As a high school graduate circa 2005, Christophe is part of the next generation: his experiences capture the ongoing plight of being 'displaced' on native ground as the drug economy fills the void left by the outsourcing of jobs. Yet Christophe's wounded pride is such that he insists to Joshua that though he cannot find legal work and 'ain't got no more money left', 'I got options' (Ward 2018, 84). In actuality, those 'options' are singular – selling weed for Dunny – and increasingly dealing is no 'choice' at all. When Dunny later asks 'You sure you want to do this?', Christophe answers 'I got to' (Ward 2018, 103).

Excluded from 'honest' employment and increasingly mired in dealing drugs, Christophe at first 'told himself that this was not what he was' (Ward 2018, 127). Having seen how 'hustling became a job' for people he knows, Christophe now attempts to normalise dealing as 'his work' (Ward 2018, 179). But after Javon, 'the main carrier of cocaine in Bois Sauvage' (Ward 2018, 110), manipulates him into selling crack as well as weed, Christophe privately acknowledges that '[h]e did not know who he was' anymore. This rueful realisation emerges partly via a vivid sense of dissociation from his body as 'he watched his hands clenching and pinching and pulling and tying' the small sacks of weed (Ward 2018, 201). This image of alienation from one's own labour eerily echoes slavery in the US South; the subsequent image of Christophe drowsily imagining 'the baggies blossoming in rows around him' pushes the connection further (Ward 2018, 219).[6] Yet Christophe's circumstances more immediately capture the contemporary socio-economic reality of neoliberalism. In *A Brief History of Neoliberalism* (2005), David Harvey remarks that a key component of the neoliberal stress on 'personal responsibility' is the insistence that individuals who 'fail' do so 'for personal and cultural reasons', not because of systemic inequalities (Harvey 2005, 76, 157). Just such ideology perniciously compounds Christophe's sense of failing his family, especially in contrast with Joshua's success in finding a legitimate job. Moreover, for all neoliberalism's insistence that 'individuals are . . . free to choose' (Harvey 2005, 69), for Christophe hustling has become less an 'option' than a necessity:

> He did not want to go to Javon's house again, did not want to see him or hand out nuggets of crack, but he knew he would. After only four or five days of selling, he had made so much he could slip all of the help-money into Ma-mee's purse himself. (Ward 2018, 201)

As Alexander notes, '[t]he temptation is to insist that black men "choose" to be criminals', but this 'myth of choice' obscures how, for young men like Christophe, 'drug sales – though rarely lucrative – are often a means of survival, a means of helping to feed and clothe themselves and their families' (Alexander 2012, 197, 209).

Christophe's increasing immersion in dealing harder drugs does though deepen his distance from Joshua, who disapproves. When Cille visits from Atlanta, Christophe senses that his mother values him less because 'I ain't the one with the job and the girlfriend.' Joshua responds unsympathetically: 'You chose . . . Every day, you choose' (Ward 2018, 196). Here Joshua recapitulates the neoliberal discourse of individual 'choice', not least what Wendy Brown identifies as a disingenuous stress on 'moral responsibility': neoliberalism's insistence that because the '"free" subject . . . makes choices', that subject then is entirely responsible 'for the consequences of these choices'. Even though Joshua knows better than anyone, even Ma-mee, how difficult it has been for his brother to secure legitimate work, he espouses the neoliberal logic that Christophe 'bears full responsibility for the consequences of his . . . action no matter how severe the constraints on this action' – as if his twin simply chose a 'mismanaged life' (Brown 2005, 43, 42).

In the immediate aftermath of this confrontation, Joshua is 'defiantly glad to have a job' (Ward 2018, 197). Yet much as Christophe is alienated from the 'work' of dealing, Joshua too feels debased by his 'stupid, hard job' at the dockyard (Ward 2018, 92). The wearing repetition of 'lifting and throwing bags of chickens and crates of bananas' (Ward 2018, 131) leaves Joshua so exhausted that he 'fell like a downed animal to the bed' (Ward 2018, 189) each evening. The precariousness of both twins' financial circumstances becomes starkly apparent when Joshua suffers a serious injury at the dockyard while worrying about a cut on Christophe's tongue (caused by tasting cocaine on a razor blade proffered by Javon): 'Joshua's hands felt squeezed, smashed, and he lurched away from the boxes and fell to the pavement.' Echoing Christophe's disembodied separation from his hands while packing the weed, Joshua experiences his injuries at a cognitive distance from the corporeality of his labour: he 'saw that the skin had been slashed; it hung in petal-pink strips from the root of his pinkies to his wrists' (Ward 2018, 211). In the aftermath of Joshua's injury, Christophe is quick to recognise the economic implications: 'Joshua's accident had scared him: What if his brother's hands had been crushed? What if he had to support the family?' (Ward 2018, 219).

Whether working at the docks or dealing drugs, each twin experiences an uncanny sense of spatial and temporal dislocation that evokes Nixon's 'plight of the stationary displaced', of 'existing out of place in place'. Driven from the family home by jealousy of Joshua and by Cille asking 'constant questions about where he had applied' for jobs (Ward 2018, 205), Christophe 'thought longingly of the privacy of his park bench' – the public space from which he deals – because it is 'the closest thing he could get to his own place' (Ward 2018, 179). Yet Christophe also yearns to reverse a sense of temporal rupture, to 'pull him [Joshua] up and away . . . back two months into their world' (Ward 2018, 154): Christophe is nostalgic for a time and place before his brother began working at the dockyard and he began dealing. Similarly, Joshua 'wished for it to never stop raining, for the rain to become a biblical flood so that it would wash him not only through space, but through time, away and back to that day in the beginning of his world' (Ward 2018, 129). Given that the temporal frame of the novel is the summer before Hurricane Katrina hit the Mississippi Gulf Coast – as we shall see, the novel's final pages gesture ominously to the imminent impact of Katrina –

such 'biblical' fantasies of renewal after the flood are ambiguous at best. Esch Batiste in *Salvage the Bones* is similarly seduced, the day before Katrina strikes, by the hope that '*Tomorrow . . . everything will be washed clean*' (Ward 2012, 205, emphasis original). Instead, Esch's first-hand account reveals how Katrina's destruction exposes and amplifies the pre-existing precarity of Black Southern life already subject to a perfect storm of regional racism and global neoliberalism: a storm that Ward began to render in *Where the Line Bleeds*.

Dirt, Waste, and the Disposability of Black Southern Lives

While Joshua wishes for aquatic purification and regeneration, Christophe is increasingly associated (and associates himself) with dirt. During a visit to Dunny's parents' home, the twins' aunt Rita (Cille's sister) remarks that they 'smell like animal' before asking Joshua if 'you got that money you said you was putting in on the food' for the family's Fourth of July celebrations. For Christophe, this combined reference to their odour and Joshua's ability to contribute financially engenders shame that '[e]verything was dirty about him: his body, his money. In the dim house, even Joshua's shirt seemed brighter than his' (Ward 2018, 143). Soon, involved in dealing crack as well as weed, Christophe no longer 'see[s] the sense in taking a bath when he was living so grimily' (Ward 2018, 219).

If such imagery indexes Christophe's shame at dealing drugs, it also intones the discursive association of Blackness with dirt through-out US history. In *Clean and White: A History of Environmental Racism* (2015), Carl Zimring traces how '[t]he conflation of non-white skin with dirt formalized spatial relationships in American so-ciety'. Black labourers became associated with '"dirty" jobs such as laundry, waste hauling . . . and other sanitary services'; especially '[i]n the South, domestic cleaning work was almost monolithically the responsibility of African American women from the end of the Civil War onward' (Zimring 2015, 137, 5, 119). We have already seen how in *Where the Line Bleeds* the twins feel indebted to Ma-mee 'scrubbing the dirt out of white people's floors for forty years'. In the novel's early twenty-first-century present, the association between Blackness and dirt constitutes a changing same: the disappearance of blue-collar jobs (however exploitative they may have been) and the related emergence of the illicit drug economy means that a young man like Christophe figures himself as dirt(y) even more acutely. In anthropologist Mary Douglas's classic formulation, dirt is 'matter that is out of place' (quoted in Zimring 2015, 1). Christophe's sense that 'everything was dirty about him' vividly expresses his sense of being (in Nixon's phrase) 'out of place in place'. Involvement in dealing – already conflated with Blackness in the stereotype of the 'criminal blackman' (Alexander 2012, 107) – leaves Christophe feeling alienated within his own home town, and especially the domestic sphere of his family's homes. Besides Joshua, Christophe also compares himself unfavourably to his friend Franco, whose mother and father hold down jobs as a nurse and power-plant worker respectively, so that Franco 'was always clean' and 'pretty and well dressed'. Ruefully Christophe 'remembered his own days of being fresh, of being clean, of smelling good' (Ward 2018, 151).

The twins recover a fragile unity with the distressing return to town of their addict father Samuel, or Sandman. Sandman's reappearance also triangulates between father and sons the associations with dirt and, relatedly, waste. Ma-mee is the first to re-encounter Sandman, as he turns up on her porch while both twins are elsewhere: 'all spindly arms and legs; a naked bush', Sandman 'made her feel dirty' (Ward 2018, 89). Ma-mee's response foreshadows Christophe's later encounter with his father in the kitchen at Javon's house, at which point Sandman has been reduced to raking leaves in the dealer's yard in exchange for drugs. To Christophe, Sandman 'looked especially small and dirty next to the cream front of the refrigerator door' (Ward 2018, 161). By this juncture, however, Christophe himself feels dirtied by dealing drugs for Javon; given that Christophe soon moves from selling to sampling Javon's cocaine (Ward 2018, 207), the dirt association signals the distinct possibility that the son is in danger of following the father's path to addiction. Indeed, Sandman's remark that 'I'm just trying to make a living – just like you' (Ward 2018, 161) suggests that he and Christophe are linked not merely via their relationship to the drug trade, but also the precariousness of their labour, even their lives, as 'to make a living' takes on a double meaning: to earn money, and to avoid dying.

The narrative also dramatises Sandman's marginality and disposability through his repeated association with waste. Driving along the highway, both twins witness their father cycling along the roadside: 'He stopped and scanned the sand and grass at the side of the road . . . They saw him stoop in the sand with his mouth open, and dig. When he pulled out a can, sand sprayed from the dirt-logged aluminum' (Ward 2018, 185). Moynihan has argued persuasively that in *Salvage the Bones*, the Batiste family's practice of salvaging material objects 'call[s] into question the status of that which Esch herself calls "rubbish," "refuse," and "detritus"' (Moynihan 2015, 565) – including the Batistes themselves, the 'human debris in the middle of all the rest of it' (Ward 2012, 232). In *Where the Line Bleeds*, however, Sandman's recycling of 'dirt-logged' discarded cans for cash to feed his crack habit serves to confirm his own status as not merely wasted (by drugs) but waste, a disposable figure barely functioning within either the legal or illegal economies. Later, watching his father return to Javon's house, Christophe 'wondered if Sandman had sold that paltry bag of sandlogged cans to pay for what he had just bought [crack], or if he was hoarding the cans like a skinny gray squirrel hoards acorns' (Ward 2018, 191).

Yet Sandman's association with and status as dirty waste is but an extreme example of more widespread ways in which workingclass Blacks have been, as Alexander dubs it, 'deemed disposable' by the 'new global economy'. Like Alexander, Achille Mbembe in *Necropolitics* (2019) connects this 'capacity to define who matters and who does not, who is *disposable* and who is not' to the interwined histories of slavery and capitalism, which have involved 'separating what is useful from waste, from the detrituses'. Even as Black labour during and after slavery generated massive wealth for whites, 'black life' faced not only 'what some have called "social death"' but also 'this matter of waste'. Mbembe notes that the experience of plantation slavery in the US South and elsewhere involved '[t]he Sisyphus-like effort to resist being turned into waste' (Mbembe 2019, 80, 158, 159). In similar fashion, sociologist Zygmunt Bauman diagnoses 'wasted lives' as a consequence of contemporary globalisation. In Bauman's analysis, neoliberal capitalism has sloughed off 'human waste or wasted humans' (Bauman 2004, 6): those people whom, in a deindustrialised and globalised economy, no longer have residual value as part of the potential labour pool. Bauman's 'wasted human' here dovetails with Mbembe's 'depth negro', 'a subaltern category of humanity . . . a superfluous and almost excessive part for which capital has no use' and so 'destined for zoning and expulsion' (Mbembe 2019, 178). Much as Bauman writes that '[t]o be declared redundant means to have been disposed of . . . "Redundancy" shares its semantic space with "rejects," "wastrels," "garbage," "refuse" – with *waste*' (Bauman 2004, 12), Mbembe remarks on how 'that which is deemed valueless is made redundant' (Mbembe 2019, 158). Mbembe's 'depth negro' reminds us, however, that as under earlier phases of capitalism, so under neoliberalism the 'wasted human' remains racialised.

In *Stormy Weather* (2006), Henry Giroux builds on both Bauman's wasted lives and Nbembe's necropolitics with specific reference to the 'biopolitics of disposability' exposed by Hurricane Katrina:

> Under the logic of . . . neoliberalism . . . the category 'waste' includes no longer simply material goods but also human beings, particularly those rendered redundant in the new global economy – that is, those who are no longer capable of making a living, who are unable to consume goods, and who depend upon others for the most basic needs . . . those populations . . . are increasingly viewed as an unwarranted burden to neoliberal society and left unprotected. (Giroux 2006, 27)

Moynihan relates Giroux's 'biopolitics of disposability' to *Salvage the Bones*, with its powerful rendition of how Hurricane Katrina exposes neoliberalism's 'systematic assault on the welfare state' as a support system for people otherwise rendered expendable (Moynihan 2015, 555). But already in *Where the Line Bleeds*, Sandman embodies the 'human waste' disposed of by neoliberalism; despite his earlier defiant observation to Christophe, he is barely (as Giroux also puts it) 'making a living', reduced to salvaging consumer waste to stay wasted, a form of social death. Like Christophe and many others in and beyond Bois Sauvage, Sandman is unable to find regular work because 'deindustrialization, disinvestment, outsourcing, and downsizing have created a disposable population of black men' (Giroux 2006, 54). Indeed, Sandman's dependency on Javon for his 'most basic needs' (no longer food and shelter but crack) and the illegal dealer's easy dismissal of those needs – 'Yeah, I got it and I told you I ain't giving it to you!' (Ward 2018, 223) – eerily resembles the callous neoliberal view of wasted humans as an 'unprotected' and 'unwarranted burden' who do not merit social welfare.

It is striking too that both of Sandman's sons also appear physically wasted at different points in the narrative. Driving alone, Joshua again sees his father 'pedaling his way slowly down the road', but now notices that Sandman's 'back was thin and narrow as Christophe's . . . for a moment he thought he saw his brother' (Ward 2018, 210). In turn, Christophe is struck that the sheer physical toll of working at the dockyard leaves Joshua looking 'hollow[ed] out' (Ward 2018, 97) like his addict dad: 'his brother looked more like his father now that he was skinnier' (Ward 2018, 192). This series of associations and tensions between father and sons culminates in a violent confrontation at Javon's house. With Katrina incoming off the coast, Sandman takes on further menial work for Javon: gathering plywood to protect the windows of the dealer's house from the hurricane. When Sandman asks, 'You got a dime?' (a dire echo of the Depression-era standard 'Brother Can You Spare Me a Dime?', but referring now to a dime-sack of crack), Javon spits 'You don't get paid for work you ain't did yet, mothafucka' (Ward 2018, 222). The dealer's declaration brutally exposes again the precarious nature of Sandman's marginal status and menial labour within the regular and drug economies. Javon subsequently assaults Sandman, and when Christophe intervenes, Joshua in turn tries to break up the fight between Christophe and Javon; Christophe inadvertently punches Joshua before Sandman, deliberately or not, stabs Christophe with a glass shard. The emergency reconciles the estranged twins as Joshua saves his brother by rushing him to hospital and then covering up the incident. By contrast, rumours about Sandman's whereabouts reconfirm his status as disposable waste: also seriously injured during the confrontation at Javon's, Sandman is 'missing' or has 'disappeared' altogether (Ward 2018, 232). It is a bleakly apt fate given that such wasted humans are 'already seen as dead within the global economic/ political framework' of neoliberalism (Giroux 2006, 22).

The novel's final scene echoes the prologue by taking place in an aquatic landscape and recurring to the core familial trio of Joshua, Christophe and Dunny. Fishing in the bayou, Joshua catches a mullet, and 'Christophe could see a faint line of blood on the metal' (Ward 2018, 236): the image gestures to both the novel's title and the moment when Christophe tasted cocaine for the first time. As Joshua returns the fish to the water, Christophe wonders aloud whether 'it do any good to throw them back' and whether the mullet 'will survive'. Dunny replies: 'Don't think just 'cause they little now, they ain't about shit. Them some little savages.' Christophe falls into a reverie in which he 'imagine[s] the mullet sliding into the obscure, mulch-ridden water . . . They would survive, battered and cunning' (Ward 2018, 238–9). Christophe's vision of the mullet suggests a parallel with the twins – and Bois Sauvage's Black population at large – as 'savage' survivors, despite the precarity and disposability of their lives.[7]

Yet if such imagery of endurance seems to sound a hopeful note, the final scene also stresses an ongoing sense of economic and environmental contingency. Dunny observes that 'they got openings down at the shipyard again – working on government contracts and shit'. Christophe responds 'Who knows? . . . I could get lucky, right?'; the next time Joshua speaks, it is to declare that '[w]e need some rain' (Ward 2018, 237). While this may recall Joshua's own earlier yearning for 'it to never stop raining, for the rain to become a biblical flood' of regeneration, both observations are freighted with dramatic irony given that, out in the Gulf, 'the storm was coming' (Ward 2018, 236). Katrina looms on the horizon, poised to expose and exacerbate the pre-existing realities of environmental racism and economic injustice that Ward will depict in *Salvage the Bones*. Before that breakthrough second novel, though, *Where the Line Bleeds* demonstrates that it need not take a spectacular environmental disaster to reveal the biopolitics of disposability that permeate a region long characterised by racialised exploitation – now buffeted too by the turbulence of neoliberal globalisation.

Notes

My thanks to Sophie Helene Blendstrup for feedback on a draft of this chapter.

1. For example, see the reference to *Salvage the Bones* as Ward's 'first book' in Aikens et al.'s otherwise valuable 2019 article 'South to the Plantationocene'.
2. The twins' surname is also the name of Ward's home town; Joshua is evidently named in tribute to Jesmyn's late brother Joshua, to whom the novel is dedicated.
3. For a reading of the relationship between waterways and the characters' 'interior worlds', see Beth Beatrice Smith's chapter 'Mapping the "Ungeographic" in Jesmyn Ward's *Where the Line Bleeds*', also in this volume.
4. Alexander is referring to 'major Northern cities', but the point extends to the rural and small-town South. Alexander also stresses that African Americans have been far more impacted than whites by 'deindustrialization, globalization, and technological advancement' plus the shift 'to a service economy' (Alexander 2012, 218).
5. With reference to 'the frantic accusations of genocide by poor blacks in the early years of the War on Drugs', Alexander relates it to a widespread sense 'that they had suddenly become disposable [which] was rooted in real changes in the economy' (Alexander 2012, 219).
6. Critical debates continue as to whether or not historical racial slavery can or should be compared with contemporary forms of immiseration, not least the role of 'modern slavery' within a globalised, neoliberal economy. A notable intervention here has been the Afro-pessimist perspective of Frank B. Wilderson: that analogies between African American slavery and other forms of oppression (past and present) are 'irreconcilable' because 'the Black, [is] a subject who is always already positioned as Slave' (Wilderson 2010, 7, 37). An Afro-pessimist perspective might then stress that as a young Black man from Mississippi,

Christophe was 'always already positioned as Slave' even before finding himself surrounded by baggies like cotton bolls. My own position aligns more with Yogita Goyal's recent suggestion that 'slavery as an analytic invites claims to particularity *and* authorizes connections' with other forms of immiseration: what Goyal calls 'an enabling contradiction' (Goyal 2019, 10). Hence my argument that *Where the Line Bleeds* identifies intersections and continuities – rather than reductive analogies or equivalences – between the regional history of racialised labour exploitation in the US South, and the disposability of (still racialised) labour under neoliberal globalisation.

7. Ward pursues this vision of Black Southern 'savage' survival in *Salvage the Bones*.

Works Cited

Aikens, Natalie, Amy Clukey, Amy King and Isadora Wagner. 2019. 'South to the Plantationocene'. *ASAP Journal*, 17 October 2019. http://asap-journal.com/south-to-the-plantationocene-natalie-aikens-amy-clukey-amy-k-king-and-isadora-wagner.

Alexander, Michelle. 2012. *The New Jim Crow: Mass Incarceration in the Age of Colorblindness: Revised Edition*. New York: The New Press.

Barry, Nico. 2009. 'Getting the South Right: An Interview with Jesmyn Ward'. *Fiction Writers Review*, 19 August. https://fictionwritersreview. com/interview/getting-the-south-right-an-interview-with-jesmyn-ward.

Bauman, Zygmunt. 2004. *Wasted Lives: Modernity and its Outcasts*. Cambridge: Polity.

Brown, Wendy. 2005. *Edgework: Critical Essays on Knowledge and Politics*. Princeton: Princeton University Press.

Giroux, Henry A. 2006. *Stormy Weather: Katrina and the Politics of Disposability*. Boulder, CO: Paradigm.

Goyal, Yogita. 2019. *Runaway Genres: The Global Afterlives of Slavery*. New York: New York University Press.

Hartnell, Anna, 2016. 'When Cars Become Churches: Jesmyn Ward's Disenchanted America: An Interview'. *Journal of American Studies* 50 (1): 205–18.

Harvey, David. 2005. *A Brief History of Neoliberalism*. New York: Oxford University Press.

McPherson, Tara. 2006. 'On Wal-Mart and Southern Studies'. *American Literature* 78 (4): 695–8.

Mbembe, Achille. 2019. *Necropolitics*. Durham, NC: Duke University Press.

Moynihan, Sinéad. 2015. 'From Disposability to Recycling: William Faulkner and the New Politics of Rewriting in Jesmyn Ward's *Salvage the Bones*'. *Studies in the Novel* 47 (4): 550–67.

Nixon, Rob. 2011. *Slow Violence and the Environmentalism of the Poor.* Cambridge, MA: Harvard University Press.

Ward, Jesmyn. 2012. *Salvage the Bones.* New York: Bloomsbury.

—. 2013. *Men We Reaped: A Memoir.* New York: Bloomsbury.

—. 2018. *Where the Line Bleeds.* New York: Scribner.

Wilderson, Frank. 2010. *Red, White, and Black: Cinema and the Structure of U.S. Antagonisms.* Durham, NC: Duke University Press.

Zimring, Carl. 2015. *Clean and White: A History of Environmental Racism in the United States.* New York: New York University Press.

Chapter 5

Mapping the 'Ungeographic' in Jesmyn Ward's *Where the Line Bleeds*

Beth Beatrice Smith

Where the Line Bleeds recognises the wounded and their attempts to address their scars, often casting these scars and the path to healing in physical and spatial terms of the landscape. In her work, Ward redresses the notion of the Black community, and more specifically, the Black family as pathological and broken in the wake of slavery, by pointing to alternative configurations of familial relations. In a 2021 interview with Kiese Laymon, in which the authors discuss their connection to the Dirty South and its place in their work, Ward shared her motivation: 'I want to tell stories that transport people . . . It may not always feel comfortable . . . I think there's worth in that' (Layman and Ward, 2021). The inward gaze and the sharing of memory are crucial elements in uncovering and addressing the 'dirtiness' of hidden and untold stories. This chapter investigates how Ward juxtaposes elements of the old South with a newer South, one that seeks to address oppression and inequality, and suggests methods of survival and healing from poverty, trauma, familial stresses and lack of opportunities for her protagonists. Ward's respatialisation of Bois Sauvage shares the texture of the unfolding chronology of Christina Sharpe's 'wake work' (Sharpe 2016, 13) undertaking the 'unfinished project of emancipation' (5).

Ward introduces her reader to the 'ungeographic', spaces where the social lives of Black subjects have been displaced, bringing them into focus through her use of the interior or psychic worlds of her characters, as these geographical spaces are the places where her characters are most comfortable. These are the spaces where they feel safe as they work through their emotions, communicate in a language and style of their own, develop and grow. The reader witnesses the slow awakening of the characters' unfolding in carefully crafted interior monologues which introduce the reader to interior worlds as rich as the physical landscape. By reframing the landscape of the South, just as Kathryn Yusoff (2018) reframes the impact of conquest and extraction during the Anthropocene, Ward brings untold stories to the surface. Laying unknown stories alongside familiar ones opens the landscape and allows for a new freedom for Black bodies. I argue that, using the interior geography of her characters, Ward respatialises the old South and creates a place where the old and the new collide; by mapping the richness of the 'ungeographic', Ward reveals redrawn territories where her characters thrive.

The Southern Landscape and the 'Ungeographic'

Set in Bois Sauvage, Mississippi, a fictionalised version of Ward's home town of DeLisle, *Where the Line Bleeds* is a coming-of-age story following fraternal twins Joshua and Christophe. Twins 'figure in ancient foundation myths and cosmogonies, frequently articulating an originary antagonism or ambivalence, a dialectic of eros and strife, light and darkness' (Gross 2003, 22). Twins are often found in origin stories as they easily allow for a discussion of the oppositions one may find in society, especially that of good and evil. The topic of twins and doubles 'appears made to order for a psychological reading' including the 'exteriorization of inner conflict' (De Nooy 2005, 2). The psychological struggles of the twins reveal an interior world in which Ward's twins work together to find solutions. Without prioritizing one twin's experience over the other, Ward presents the multifaceted experiences of Joshua and Christophe as a collective story one must accept all parts of to understand what she reveals about the Southern landscape.

The first epigraph of *Where the Line Bleeds* is a quote from the Judeo-Christian origin story of Genesis. Genesis 25 tells the story of Rebekah, who is barren. When her husband Isaac prays for children, God grants his prayer and Rebekah conceives. While pregnant, Rebekah feels a struggle within her. Confused, she asks God why. God explains: 'two manner of people shall be separated from thy bowels . . .' (Ward, epigraph). Genesis is a creation story revealing the birth of mankind. What Rebekah's story teaches us is that different beings, different personalities and different sensibilities can be born from the same womb. The second epigraph of the novel turns to Pastor Troy's rap 'Vice Versa'. In the lines, the speaker cautions the reader/listener to question what they see because we live in a world of twisted representation. It reveals the tension of someone who implores the devil to 'protect me' because 'the Lord is trying to kill me' and fears that God, who 'so loved the world' has blessed the 'thug' with 'rock' (epigraph). This is a God who inflicts fear and creates burden. Ward wants us to imagine living in a world where things are upside down, where the devil is God and vice versa. Ward is showing her reader how to (re)frame the brothers' experiences through the story Pastor Troy tells. Before the reader even turns to the first page of the novel, they encounter and must contemplate the conflicts of the epigraphs. Even the title of the novel itself suggests two sides. Where the line bleeds is where we find the interdependence of the twins that is critical to both their growth and their survival. Their entanglement is mirrored in the way the past and present co-mingle and the way the physical and internal worlds of the novel coincide. The epigraphs also speak to the possible fate of the brothers. They suggest that one can work against a perceived fate as the ability to change our perception alters our reading of fate. The importance of perception is clear in the scene in which Joshua and his friend, Leo, observe seagulls. While Leo sees the seagulls as flying rats, Joshua recognises what lies beneath their aggressive, group movement: 'They were just scrabbling and hungry, like everything else' (93). Joshua's inner thoughts reveal a perspective that penetrates the surface and considers underlying or unforeseen factors. Joshua models for the reader one way of seeing the world which considers the feelings and emotions behind an action. This is what Ward asks her readers to recognise as well.

The Dirty South is a Southern hip-hop style, a spatio-musical concept as well as a geographical imaginary, which according to scholar Matt Miller was 'forged in conversation with older or alternate modes of imagining the South' (Miller 2008). Like the old South, the Dirty South, comprised of former slave-holding states, is subject to anti-Blackness and the 'dehumanization of the poor for its growth and support' (Stallings 2020, 1). However, it also 'celebrates, examines, and highlights the various modes that resistance has taken and the possible future directions it may take' (2). The resistance modelled by the brothers includes an emotional intelligence which the brothers develop through their ability to communicate and function in a psychic world of their own. Ward's novel uncovers one of the many hidden stories of the South, with the twins representing what Katherine McKittrick refers to as a 'black absented presence' (McKittrick 2006, 33), those who are forgotten but who have contributed the production of space. Ward says, 'My idea of the Dirty South is that there's a certain rawness to the art that comes out of it. A certain honesty. A willingness to bring secrets and despair and hope and all those other messy human emotions to life' (Taylor 2016, 267).

The novel explores all of those 'messy' human emotions including fear, anger and love, paying particular attention to the way in which the twins of the novel navigate these feelings. The Dirty South is not a replacement of the old South; it is a new way of looking at the same geographical space.

At first glance, the twins' family appears to be the Black family, once cast as dysfunctional by what is commonly known as 'The Moynihan Report', as burdened by an absent father and disconnected mother. In the report, Patrick Moynihan concludes that 'At the heart of the deterioration of the fabric of Negro society is the deterioration of the Negro family' (Moynihan 1965, 9). This view of the Black family advances a predetermined, heteronormative structure as the standard rather than recognising the variety of legitimate, existing family structures. Ward's fiction breaks this pattern of thought by showing her readers a way to reframe what they see. Ward's family is not trapped in this 'tangle of pathology' (Spillers 1987, 66) but rather demonstrates a formulation not considered in the Moynihan stereotype, one which offers a depth not seen or considered prior.

The private thoughts of Ward's characters create a map of interior worlds as intricate as the map of the South along the Mississippi – winding waterways, deep pools, rugged terrain and imaginary lines demarcating the safe areas from the dangerous spaces. Reconstructing 'past interior lives of black people in the diaspora is an important geographic act' (McKittrick 2006, 34). The importance of this act is bringing 'to life new ethnicities and different senses of place by humanizing black subjects who are otherwise bound to the historio-racial schema' and to allow 'past and present black geographies to be believable' (34). Ward is doing this work. By recognising the individual lives of her characters, the reader understands that the family structure presented in *Where the Line Bleeds* defines the Black family in a way that could not have been recognised by Moynihan and the like. The functional Black family is as varied today as Southern culture. Storytelling serves as a vehicle of exploration of one's own displacement and a path to visibility for Black subjects. Ward illuminates the 'unseeable' (McKittrick 2006, xxx) with her stories of characters whose lives have been overshadowed by familiar tropes and representations of the old South. The connection between geography and Blackness is 'crucial to identifying some of the conditions under which race/racism are necessary to the production of space' (12). Black subjects have and continue to participate in placemaking, creating places out of necessity, often in response to societal challenges based on race/racism. After the Great Migration, those who remained in the South continued to live under the threat of lynching, unequal access to education and unfair judicial practices. Those who remained, or returned, created their own spaces within a place suspended in time. This is the South that Ward conjures with references to 'Confederate emblems' (126); however, as she peels back the layers of history and memory, she focuses on the consciousness of her characters, their lived experiences, and the antagonistic relationship between the pull of the past and the push towards a future of change.

At times in the novel, Joshua and Christophe are described as opposites. In the opening scene, Joshua and Christophe choose to mark a moment of transition, their coming-of-age, with a dive into the water. Christophe is thin and muscular while Joshua is taller and heavier. Additionally, one notices that the brothers are already thinking along different lines – one focuses his thoughts on the cold and the other on the heat. There is a nervousness behind Christophe's movements and reactions while Joshua's body language demonstrates greater confidence. However, later in the novel, Ward describes Joshua as an 'inverse shadow' (27) of Christophe and tells us that the brothers 'traded skin like any other set of twins' (69). Their ability to see the world through the eyes of the other is one that Ward trusts her reader will have as well as she leads us through the terrain of the South. The opening water scene marks the start of the twins' journey to manhood and introduces the reader to another aspect of Ward's origin story – the illuminator of interior worlds. Ward's (re)focus on the internal interconnectedness that links generations of African Americans to one another opens an untapped world of knowledge and experience to her reader. Just as African American history has been cobbled together over time with forgotten story after forgotten story, revealed through revisiting and revising, Ward makes the 'unseeable' (McKittrick 2006, xxx) visible.

The reader is introduced to Joshua's attachment to the land early on in the novel. Joshua sees Bois Sauvage as special particularly because he identifies with the land in ways that an outsider would not be able to. For Ward, this insider status is an important element in reintroducing the South to her reader:

> [Joshua] knew that there shouldn't be anything special about Bois Sauvage, but there was: he knew every copse of trees, every stray dog, every bend of every half-paved road, every uneven plane of each warped, dilapidated house, every hidden swimming hole . . . It was beautiful. (Ward 2008, 5–6)

The borders of the land both trap and protect the people. Isolated and largely untouched, Bois Sauvage boasts three natural borders. To the south, east and west, the bayou forms a naturally flowing or moving border. Multiple bodies of water flowing to the Gulf carry stories and histories from the swimming holes of various communities along the Mississippi. The town is small and will offer few economic opportunities for the young men at the centre of the story.

Most importantly, in the passage above, Ward shows us the beauty of this place and the hold that it has on Joshua. Bois Sauvage is where Joshua feels a sense of belonging. Christophe is also influenced by the land, as he marvels at the sights and sounds of Bois Sauvage; however, Ward also uses the landscape to highlight Christophe's fears. This is one of many passages in which the reader is granted access to the interior world of the characters. The juxtaposition of the physical and the interior worlds of the twins helps the reader to see the antagonisms of the landscape. Christophe experiences something dark as the brothers endure the heat of the day and search nervously for jobs:

> The air was already difficult to breathe . . . He could see the barrier islands floating on the horizon of the water, appearing like bristling shadows of elongated reeds as they siphoned the current and blocked the clean blue-green wash of the Gulf of Mexico, blocked the water that swept up from the Caribbean, and impacted the beach that he saw with silt, with mud, with runty, dirty waves . . . He hated those islands. (34)

Christophe's reflections demonstrate an awareness of the world around him and of the limitations of the geography. He focuses on a space marked by the damaging effects of the interactions among the natural elements. The vocabulary of the passage offers an ominous tone. But while the natural world seems dark, Christophe is calm. He seems at peace. For example, as the twins look for work, Christophe reassures his brother by saying, 'We'll find something' (34). In the face of permanent blockages or confinement, he can keep his focus on his plan. Elements of Bois Sauvage which reflect the history of the old South persist as obstacles throughout the text. Christophe demonstrates that those obstacles will not keep him from appreciating what the land gives.

Ward uses the rich history of Bois Sauvage as her foundation and makes plain how place factors into the intertwined narratives of the novel. The name Bois Sauvage translates from the French as 'wild wood', the word 'wild' meaning something or someone untamed or, in essence, free. This is the place where the twins' grandparents settled after searching for a place with like-minded folks, away from their jobs in the homes of the rich along the water. This is also where the brothers feel free to be themselves. The historical reminders of oppression appear on the landscape in the form of 'confederate emblems' placed 'like prayer flags' (126) and home-made billboards recalling Klan leader and former governor of Louisiana, David Duke. Placing the events of the novel on land peppered with lingering prejudice, and perhaps once inhabited by slaves, Ward emphasises not only the modern-day restraints on these characters but also their methods of freeing themselves from those restraints. The reader sees Bois Sauvage through the twins' eyes and notes the details that make this land 'special' to them. Using the vocabulary of the distressed and incomplete, one envisions a place not fully recognised, realised or validated. They see 'stray' dogs, 'half-paved' roads, 'uneven' planes, 'warped, dilapidated' houses and 'hidden swimming hole[s]' (5). While the language describing Bois Sauvage suggests something broken or neglected, this environment is where Joshua and Christophe feel most connected and where their family was first cradled by the land.

Ward looks to the people of the Southern landscape as a source of inspiration. In the face of what she calls 'a dearth of stories about people like me' (Taylor 2016, 267) she began to write about these same people again and again. She asks important questions: How does history 'bear in the present? How does the past bear fruit?' (267). Exploring those questions with different sets of characters has become her method. In her 2013 memoir *Men We Reaped*, one finds the non-fiction stories on which the novel *Where the Line Bleeds* is based. Ward draws on a cultural history as well as a personal one. Interestingly, one learns in the memoir that Joshua is named for Ward's beloved deceased brother, Joshua Adam Dedeaux, and that the twins' family name is that of Ward's home town of DeLisle. Uncovering obscured stories, Ward writes into existence the missing narratives of a hidden people in what Katherine McKittrick calls 'ungeographical' spaces (x).

The 'ungeographic' refers to the people, the lives and the stories not visible when scanning the landscape with an eye only towards to the images of the old South. McKittrick writes that 'the relationship between black populations and geography . . . allows us to engage with a narrative that locates and draws on black histories and black subjects to make visible social lives which are often displaced, rendered ungeographic' (x). The label 'The South' brings with it stereotypes born in antebellum days, when Black men, women and children were not counted among the people of plantations but rather the items for use and sale. McKittrick explores the interaction

between 'geographies of domination' (x) and geographies of the enslaved. In doing so, she emphasises the 'formation of oppositional
geography' (xi), such as the slave ship, which becomes at once the
location of Black subjectivity as well as resistance. Opening a landscape to (re)examination is central to Kathryn Yusoff's *A Billion
Black Anthropocenes or None*, in which she considers geology as the
'hinge that joins indigenous genocide, slavery, and settler colonialism through an indifferent structure of extraction' (Yusoff 2018, xii)
and reveals a long history of entanglement between the need for resources and the action of conquest. In taking her discussion down
to the literal dust of the earth, Yusoff discusses how during colonisa-
tion, the impact of extraction on people is ignored. She writes, 'The
proximity of black and brown bodies to harm in this intimacy with
the inhuman is what I am calling the *Black Anthropocene*' (xii). In
her text, geology 'can finally be recognized as a regime for producing
subjects and regulating subjective lives' (13). What Yusoff's study
offers is a reading of living beings affecting and affected by the earth
rather than human beings as just working bodies. Ward breaks the
surface of the accumulation of history on the land and waterways
of Bois Sauvage, looking beyond the physical labours of the twins to
study the impact of said history below the skin and in the minds of
these men.   Considering the 'fecundity of "dirt"' (Stallings 2020, 4)
alongside Yusoff's work on 'political geology' (12) helps us to see
Ward's Bois Sauvage as a space of geological accumulation and re-
birth. The dirt which produces new life is found in abundance in
Ward's text. She writes of the communities of Bois Sauvage embedding themselves in the red clay, the dust of the red chalky clay of the
Mississippi Delta clinging to their bodies, and the red clay birthing
the Wolf River. These are a few examples of the details of Ward's
origin story, reading the South through the lens of history and the
physical landscape. The author reveals a hidden world in the shadow
of an existing one, demonstrating how revisiting and refocusing on
familiar territory opens the landscape to new interpretations and
considerations.

In Ward's South, Black subjects have engaged and continue to engage in placemaking out of necessity, often in response to societal
challenges. Herman Beavers writes, 'While places have a material
reality, their meanings evolve over time and not in wholly predictable or controllable ways. Places are constantly reinterpreted and
reconstituted, and entail ongoing power struggles and negotiations'
(Beavers 2018, 4). Ward centres her stories around the people of
a newer South whose concerns and struggles are not focused on

journeying elsewhere but rather anchoring themselves to the land on which they were born. While the South is historically identified as an 'immediate, identifiable, and oppressive power' (Griffin 1995, 4), and for some of the characters the reason for their disconnection, for other characters, the small town of Bois Sauvage is a safe space, an instance of what Griffin calls 'spaces of retreat, healing, and resistance' (9). Ironically, during the Great Migration, the South for many represented anything but, which lead to the mass exodus to the North. The DeLisles stay and find love for their land. Staying and evolving allows a new-found freedom.

Waterways and Interior Worlds

The geography at the opening of the text is a waterway. Ward takes her readers on a journey down an offshoot of the Mississippi River. Akin to an aerial shot in film, Ward then zooms in on the scene of the twins mentally preparing for their next steps in life. Water is an essential element of life and of Black cultural history, and, in the first paragraph of the novel, Ward brings us to the birth of the river and presents the waterway as a living entity. The water is a kind of womb for the brothers throughout the novel, nurturing them through their growth. Ward writes:

> The river was young and small. At its start it seeped from the red clay earth in the piney woods of southern Mississippi, and then wound its way, brown and slow, over a bed of tiny gray and ochre pebbles through the pines, shallow as a hand, deep as three men standing, to the sandy, green lowlands of the gulf of Mexico. (1)

From the first sentence, Ward alludes to the twins who are 'young and small' (1), like the river. Here, the brown river water is shallow and seems to ooze from the red clay earth, moving slowly over stones, through trees, to the sandy beach. Along with the natural terrain, there is a blending of natural colours – red, brown, grey and green – as well as natural materials with man-made elements – wood and concrete bridges and steel rails. The Wolf River seeps, winds, expands and shrinks accordingly with the land. Slithering like a snake, the river flows smoothly, undeterred by the multiple forms of the terrain. Further along, the river darkens and deepens reaching its apex, where the twins prepare themselves, both literally and figuratively, to jump. They are preparing to leap into adulthood, and Ward situates their leaping over the divergence of the river. The scene marks a beginning and an end, an important opposition. Ward taps into the strong elemental symbol of water which African American authors have often used as a symbol of cultural history.[1] As she maps the splitting of the Wolf River with the experiences of the twins, she also taps into the literary trope of the river, reminiscent of Langston Hughes's poem 'The Negro Speaks of Rivers' (1921) in which Hughes connects the African diaspora. The repetition of the simile from the line, 'My soul has grown deep like the rivers' punctuates the growth that the speaker experiences as a result of this rich history, just as Ward's river is enriched by the minerals its collects. With the water's journey comes a deepening of knowledge and understanding. The poet's use of synecdoche in the poem – 'I' and 'The Negro' in place of the African American community – helps us to understand how a people have travelled from the birthplace of humanity, the Euphrates, to various countries of the African continent to America and along the Mississippi River, learning and deepening their knowledge and understanding as they went. The poem emphasises the African presence across time and place and alludes to the passing of ancient African culture to the contemporary African American. Hughes tells us that the soul of a people has been enriched by the flow of the river waters.

Storytelling – through oral history, music or the written word – is an important element of placemaking for African Americans. Toni Morrison once said that 'fiction as an ancestor serves as a space for enlightenment, sustenance, and renewal' (Griffin 1995, 6). In her 1984 essay 'Rootedness: The Ancestor as Foundation', Morrison writes of characteristics of or elements in African American fiction including the presence of the ancestor, people who she explains are 'not just parents, they are sort of timeless people whose relationships to the characters are benevolent, instructive, and protective, and they provide a certain kind of wisdom' (Morrison 1984, 343). Keeping in touch with the ancestors keeps contemporary characters grounded. The ancestor is the community's North Star. The ancestor is also an essential figure in the construction of the South in *"Who Set You Flowin'?": The African American Migration Narrative*. Here, Farah Jasmine Griffin expands on Morrison's avocation of the ancestor, writing, 'the ancestor might be a literal ancestor; he or she also has earthly representatives, whom we might call elders . . . Ancestors are a specific presence in the text. They are found in both its content and its form' (5–6). Griffin notes that some narratives represent the South as the site of terror and exploitation as well as the site of the ancestor.

The elder-ancestor connection is a metaphorical avenue for passing on ancestral knowledge down through the generations and yet another example of the 'ungeographical'. The ancestors connected to these 'spaces of retreat, healing, and resistance' (Griffin 1995, 9). Characters such as Ma-mee, the twins' grandmother, and her parents migrated to and settled the land in Bois Sauvage, developing 'their own small, self-contained communities' (Ward 2008, 6). The next generation, the twin's parents, Cille and Sandman, lose their connection to the land. Cille's move from Bois Sauvage to Atlanta represents a minor migration which severs her connection to her home town and the lives of her sons. One can sense the distance between mother and sons in phone calls. During her visit, in the hospital after Christophe is stabbed, Cille tries to comfort him by placing a hand on his leg, but 'it was Ma-mee he leaned into, Ma-mee's neck he buried his face into' (228). Cille does not know or understand the twins in the way that Ma-mee does.

Similarly, familial and land ties have been broken for Sandman, who drifts from his sons and the town of Bois Sauvage. Even after rehab and a return to the town, Sandman quickly falls back into a pattern of drug use. Sandman, whose name reflects the natural motif of Ward's text as well as the mythological figure who lulls people to sleep and invites them to dream, may be an ironic figure. Sandman's life seems more a nightmare than a pleasant dream. The name Sandman also marries the man to the physical land which highlights the character's appearances and disappearances throughout the text. Sandman embodies the 'Black absented presence' (McKittrick 2006, 33). Cille and Sandman struggle with 'tight space', what Beavers calls 'a character's spiritual and emotional estrangement from community' which prevents a sustained connection to place (Beavers 2018, 6). Conversely, the twins are grounded in Bois Sauvage as their grandparents and great-grandparents were, and in a manner that the generation before is not.

What both Morrison and Griffin bring to this discussion of Black geography is the history of the Black experience in shaping space and the Ancestor as a figure both emblematic of and stuck in the South. Fiction is a vehicle for understanding what may have been passed down through oral storytelling or songs at one time. Ward builds upon the significance of the waterways connecting the African American history and literary history to her contemporary narrative. The river creates a strong presence in the novel. Water is a living being with a memory, an idea that intensifies the ominous tone in

Where the Line Bleeds. Ward's spaces are haunted by the stories of the enslaved. Waterways become harbingers of ghosts and memories, recognising:

> a molecular interconnectedness between humans and the sea; read through an African American historical prism, humans, who lost their lives in the current, have by their very materiality, changed the composition of the waters. Altering the bones that have lain on the ocean floor for centuries, the Atlantic is part of the ancestral past and thus inherent in the collective memory. (Wardi 2011, 7)

As scholar Anissa Wardi explains, water may haunt, but at the same time it may offer 'a clearer vision' (Wardi 2011, 10). Ward exploits this dual nature of water through her discussion of the twins who are haunted by a personal and collective past on the water but who also survive because of the nurturing aspects of the water. Throughout the novel, the brothers will call for the comforting and healing properties of water.

Alongside the importance of the waterways rests the power of the land and the private readings of the land by Ward's characters. One explanation for Ward's close attention to the physical earth of the Dirty South appears in her memoir. In *Men We Reaped*, Ward describes a natural underground cellar which holds symbolic importance for her – 'a physical representation of all the hatred and loathing and sorrow I carried inside, the dark embodiment of all the times . . . when I had been terrorized or sexually threatened' (Ward 2013, 161). She continues, 'Its specter would follow me my entire life' (161). Being haunted by spaces is an important aspect of *Where the Line Bleeds*; the remnants of personal and collective ancestral history haunt these characters as well as the author who writes to light the hidden stories of the land, both sustaining and inhospitable, and to bring them to our collective consciousness in order to confront, reflect on and learn from our collective past.

Private readings of the landscape also shed light on the interior worlds of the characters. Just as Joshua reads the aggressive seagulls as simply trying to survive, he reframes the brokenness of the landscape as comforting as it reflects the realities of life. Upon graduating, the boys are expected to find jobs and contribute to maintaining the household. The opportunities for work are scarce, and soon the twins must follow different paths to employment with Joshua working the shipyard doing manual labour and Christophe selling drugs. Insecurity, jealousy, family drama, as well as societal challenges shape the twins' experiences. However, they actively contemplate their lives and weigh what options they do have carefully. Carrying the frustrations and disappointments of the job search along with the growing conflict between brothers, the twins take to the basketball court and talk out their problems with 'wordless speech' (114). For days, tensions between the brothers have grown after Joshua realises that Christophe plans to sell drugs to make money. On the court, the twins team up against their friends and work through their own conflict at the same time. They 'grunt . . . bare their teeth . . . emit forceful breaths like expletives . . . This was their conversation' (114). The brothers breathe, lob, step, shake and score, communicating in a wordless language, their bodies expressing what they have been hesitant to say before. Once the game is done, they are ready to talk out loud about the return of their father and Christophe selling drugs, the source of tension between them. The neutral space of the basketball court becomes a stage for the feeling and acting out of emotions. When they return home from the court, their mother Cille calls, reminding the reader of the third issue hanging over the twins' heads. The reader recognises the wordless exchange as the brothers' way of entering their interior world and finding their way to possible solutions.

Just as Ward illuminates her characters' interior worlds, she highlights their presence on the land or in the water. At times, Ward does so metaphorically, making Joshua and Christophe part of the foundational dust of the land or transforming their bodies into living, growing creatures of the sea. They are part of the earth and waterways of Bois Sauvage. The brothers demonstrate how they use intuition and perception to understand their lives and work to survive on the land to which they are attached. This emotional intelligence is gained from the interior world that they inhabit. On the basketball court, the twins' bodies are used as tools of communication while in the kitchen scene with Ma-mee and elsewhere, we find metaphors linking the brothers to creatures of the sea. In fact, the fish is the essential metaphor in the final scene of the novel. Christophe watches long, striped fish sucking up the dirt from the bottom of the riverbed, imagining 'them running their large tongues over the insides of their mouths and feeling the scars where the hooks had bit them . . . They would survive, battered and cunning' (238–9). This scene provides hope for the brothers' survival among other mullets, bottom feeders who conjure Ward's dirty imagery. Earlier in the novel, both brothers suffer cuts: Joshua slices his hand at work, and Christophe cuts his tongue with a razor testing drugs. Their wounds – their scars – are likened to gills or a tear from a fishhook. Christophe's question harbours greater meaning for the twins, who now speak out loud. Tiffany Lethabo King argues for

Black fungibility as 'a spatial analytic' (King 2016, 1022). King, like Griffin, urges a break from reading Black fungibility in terms of labour (the enslaved manipulated for specific types of use), instead describing it as 'an always-unfolding space' which can be 'transformed into new geographies of Black freedom' (1037). King looks to Hortense Spillers and Sayida Hartman to employ a more 'open-ended' (1024) reading, recognising the Black fungibility as an ever-changing space which amounts to unlimited forms of freedom.

Ward also reimagines bodily fungibility. In Ward's South, bodies become 'liquid, dust, and more' (King 2016, 1025). While 'confederate emblems' (126) symbolise Black fungibility that benefits the oppressor, connecting fungibility to the production of space through the morphing of bodies into tools of communication, rather than tools of production or extraction, advances and benefits the lives of these characters, the formerly oppressed. Similarly, the metaphorical reading of the twins' bodies as fish and shrimp, living beings of the sea, broadens their physical space to include the waterways. Ward positions Ma-mee as the novel's elder, a bridge between the present moment and the past. In Chapter 4 of the novel, Ward turns our focus to the interior life of Ma-mee, who has partially lost her sight due to diabetes. Ma-mee's blindness heightens her ability to feel what the brothers feel. She senses their needs. In the aforementioned kitchen scene, Ma-mee asks her grandson to help her peel shrimp and recognises in his reply a tone which she has not heard since Christophe was a boy. Ma-mee helps Christophe to see that he must stop allowing his fear to stifle him, using the ancestors – his grandfather and uncle – as examples. Ma-mee addresses the economic issue weighing on Christophe's mind. Christophe's reaction is to fixate on the task at hand as he allows his mind to ruminate over the real problem weighing him down, his decision to sell drugs, just like the 'rock' God hands to the Black man in Pastor Troy's 'Vice Versa'.

Christophe's methodical pulling of the shrimp's flesh from the protective shell, mirrors the transformation happening in his own life and to his own body. He is pulling away the protection of his brother and Ma-mee and, sensing this, his grandmother works to lure him back. He wonders if the shrimp 'struggled against the thick fingers of the current created by the encroaching net in hope of escaping, of moving forward' (71). This image echoes the 'interconnectedness between humans and the sea' (Wardi 2011, 7). Christophe also transforms darkness into a soothing presence like the quiet underneath the water in the opening scene of the novel. Later, after seeing his father Sandman, he will again think about being in the water (140).

His ability to move through his fear by transforming his surroundings into a comfortable, safe space signals his maturation and proves vital to his survival.

Conclusion

By mapping the 'ungeographic' in *Where the Line Bleeds*, Jesmyn Ward opens often overlooked spaces of the Dirty South to her reader and guides her reader in observing the ways in which her characters – representatives of generations of African Americans – interact with the landscapes of the novel and challenge our own readings of this variation on the old South. By recognising the ways in which the places and people of Bois Sauvage have been influenced by the political and the sociological, by the past and the present, by familial and cultural history, one begins to see interconnectedness of people and spaces. The twins view what is familiar through the lens of their psychic world and Ward is asking her reader to do so in the real world. In order to finish the 'project of emancipation' (Sharpe 2016, 5), one must recognise the ways in which freedom has not been attained, to shed the '"always-already" death bound inflections' (King 2016, 1024) of Black fungibility, and to see new possibilities for expansion and growth. Ward offers a way to the light. She makes the imaginary possible. After all, Joshua and Christophe, like the fish in the Mississippi waters 'would survive battered and cunning' (239). By (re)framing this geography – the water and safe spaces along the physical and psychic landscape – Ward offers these men a chance.

Note

1. Representations of the Middle Passage and survival by escape on waterways such as the Mississippi River echo in African American works from the vernacular tradition to the contemporary written word. In songs such as 'Wade in the Water' to the plays of August Wilson, water serves as a significant element in the lives and literature of African Americans.

Works Cited

Beavers, Herman. 2018. *Geography and the Political Imaginary in the Novels of Toni Morrison*. London: Palgrave MacMillan.

De Nooy, Juliana. 2005. *Twins in Contemporary Literature and Culture: Look Twice*. London: Palgrave MacMillan.

Griffin, Farah Jasmine. 1995. *"Who Set You Flowing?": The African American Migration Narrative*. Oxford: Oxford University Press.

Gross, Kenneth. 2003. 'Ordinary Twinship'. *Raritan: A Quarterly Review* 22, no. 4 (Spring): 1–39. https://raritanquarterly.rutgers.edu/issue-index/all-volumes- issues/volume-22/volume-22-number-4.

Hughes, Langston. 1921. 'The Negro Speaks of Rivers'. *The Crisis* (NAACP).

King, Tiffany Lethabo. 2016. 'The Labor of Re(reading) Plantation Landscapes Fungible(ly)'. *Antipode* 48 (4): 1022–39.

Laymon, Kiese, and Jesmyn Ward. 2021. An Interview between Kiese Laymon and Jesmyn Ward for The New Mississippi Project and The African American Read-In at Augusta University. Zoom, 17 February. http://tinyurl.com/y3z9gtl4.

McKittrick, Katherine. 2006. *Demonic Grounds: Black Women and The Cartographies of Struggle*. Minneapolis: University of Minnesota Press.

Miller, Matt. 2008. 'Dirty Decade: Rap Music and The US South, 1997–2007'. 10 June. https://southernspaces.org/2008/dirty-decade-rap-music-and-us-south-1997-2007/.

Morrison, Toni. 1984. 'Rootedness: The Ancestor as Foundation'. *Black Women Writers 1950–1980: A Critical Evaluation*, edited by Mari Evans. New York: Anchor Books.

Moynihan, Patrick. 1965. 'The Negro Family: The Case for National Action'. Office of Policy Planning and Research. United States Department of Labor.

Sharpe, Christina. 2016. *In the Wake: On Blackness and Being*. Durham, NC: Duke University Press.

Spillers, Hortense J. 1987. 'Mama's Baby, Papa's Maybe: An American Grammar Book'. *Diacritics* 17 (2): 64–81.

Stallings, L. H. 2020. *A Dirty South Manifesto*: Sexual Resistance and Imagination in the New South. Berkeley: University of California Press.

Taylor, Danielle K. 2016. 'Literary Voice of the Dirty South: An Interview with Jesmyn Ward'. *CLA Journal* 60 (2): 266–8. https://www.jstor.org/stable/26355922?seq=1#metadata_info_tab_contents.

Ward, Jesmyn. 2008. *Where the Line Bleeds*. New York: Scribner.

—. 2013. *Men We Reaped*. New Jersey: Bloomsbury.

Wardi, Anissa Janine. 2011. *Water and African American Memory: An Ecological Perspective*. Gainesville: University Press of Florida.

Yusoff, Kathryn. 2018. *A Billion Black Anthropocenes or None*. Minneapolis: University of Minnesota Press.

Chapter 6

Salvaging Vulnerabilities: Climate Crisis and Marginalised Bodies in Jesmyn Ward's *Salvage the Bones*

Leah Van Dyk

In Jesmyn Ward's 2011 novel *Salvage the Bones*, an impending storm threatens to hit the Gulf Coast of Louisiana, where we meet Esch Batiste and her family navigating life as marginalised Black bodies in contemporary America. This novel – part coming-of-age narrative, part climate crisis narrative – resides in the space between waiting and knowing, as Esch's (forced) growth into adulthood is interwoven with the dangers and realities of the coming hurricane. In conversation with environmental theories of embodiment and marginalisation, I consider how Ward's focus on the dynamics of family and kinship relations, gendered labour and violence, and class barriers and racialised economic inequality also examines the disproportionate effect of climate crisis and environmental degradation on marginalised bodies. Through Esch's experiences of impending crisis – motherhood, natural disaster – I seek to explore the interconnections and importance of the natural and the personal in *Salvage the Bones*. As Kathryn Yusoff notes in their considerations of natural space, geology and Blackness, 'noticing the meshwork of anti-Blackness and colonial structures of the Anthropocene, which constitute the distinct underbelly to its origin stories, gives visibility to the material and bodily work that coercively carries the Anthropocene into being and challenges the narrative accounts of agency there within' (Yusoff 2019, 107). In embracing the narrative accounts of marginalised bodies and climate crisis, Ward's text confronts the histories of erasure and apathy towards particular bodies in discussions of climate crisis and environmental impact.

In the novel, Esch's experience is deeply tied to the land, with her understanding of selfhood growing out of the place and space which she inhabits. The connections of Esch's personal experience to natural space are, further, played out within the domestic sphere: as Esch grapples with the legacy of her mother (and mothering), other maternal figures and influences, and the unconventional family dynamics within the Pit. Esch inhabits a space of 'extreme domesticity', a term coined by Susan Fraiman which theorises a re-formation of domesticity in the face of dislocation, economic insecurity, queered notions of family and other non-traditional (heterogeneous, anti-capitalist, anti-colonial) family structures. In these formations of the domestic space, homes and families are 'vulnerable, hybrid, heterogeneous, and dynamic' attributes that 'serve to debunk received, naturalized notions of home as inert and one-dimensional' (Fraiman 2017, 123). Fraiman argues instead that the domestic is 'a site of change and complexity' (123). For Esch, the domestic is a site of vulnerability and building tension, and the 'change and complexity' of her situation – and its paralleling with the storm – is the central focus and intention of Ward's narrative. As each chapter brings us one day closer to Katrina's landing, the literal *sturm und drang* ('storm and stress') within the novel asks us to consider the multilayering of vulnerabilities experienced by those in the Gulf Coast, particularly nuancing the experiences of Esch as a young, disenfranchised, pregnant Black woman – as she poignantly asks '*Who will deliver me?* And the hurricane says *sssssssshhhhhhhh*' (235). Esch's experiences and identity are wrapped up not only in the domestic but also in the realities of (and the attitudes towards) the Gulf Coast, and its historical and contemporary social impact as a site of Black community formation. As Gigi Adair writes, an analysis of Black diasporic kinship can illuminate 'what it means to be a recognizable human subject, to have a place in a personal and shared history, to be a member of a political society, and a subject in relations with the world and other others,' ultimately suggesting 'ways of rethinking such relations and categories in less exclusive ways' (Adair 2019, 3). Though often absent in the discussion of environmental literature, *Salvage the Bones* is a critical text for our understanding of contemporary Black experience in and alongside the environment, recognising the specific and urgent interconnections of identity and place for Black bodies.

In *Salvage the Bones*, Ward considers the exploitative 'use-value' ascribed to Black bodies, particularly following the female protagonist through her pregnancy and exploring the multiple vulnerabilities that accompany her experiences as a marginalised, gendered and pregnant body: as we see in the novel, the well-being of Ward's protagonist Esch is only further complicated by her impending pregnancy, as she simultaneously hides and desires the reveal of her pregnancy to those she knows. Living in an impoverished area of the

Mississippi Gulf Coast in the days before Hurricane Katrina, Esch and her family live in the conditions of, what theorist Rob Nixon terms, 'displacement without moving' or the racialised, economic and environmental violence that sees communities of colour experiencing a 'loss of the land and resources beneath them, a loss that leaves communities stranded in a place stripped of the very characteristics that [make] it inhabitable' (Ward 2011, 19). The house is in 'a gap in the woods [Esch's grandfather] cleared and built on that we now call the Pit' (1) – Esch's grandparents cultivated this land, but it was ultimately deemed valuable as a site of extraction, for 'it was Papa Joseph nicknamed it all the Pit, Papa Joseph who let the white men he work with dig for clay that they used to lay the foundations for houses' (14). The extraction of clay for better-built and more expensive houses in the surrounding county's white neighbourhoods came to an end only when the land had no more to give, as:

> Papa Joseph let them take all the dirt they wanted until their digging had created a cliff over a dry lake in the backyard, and the small stream that had run around and down the hill had diverted and pooled into the dry lake, making it into a pond, and then Papa Joseph thought the earth would give under the water, that the pond would spread and gobble up the property and make it a swamp, so he stopped selling earth for money. (14)

The Pit came into being through the loss of land and resources to white buyers, who – upon using up anything of 'value' on the land – promptly forgot about its existence. The land gradually reclaimed itself, and in many ways claimed the Batiste family, who continue to reside on the land – recognising the differences of 'value' that can be placed on a space and acknowledging their connection with or responsibility to the Pit.

The Pit is a complicated haven for the Batiste family, a meeting place for the local teens – Big Henry, Manny, Marquise – to exist outside of white scrutiny, a multigenerational home space for the Batistes from Papa Joseph and Mother Lizbeth to Esch, and the site of birth and death within the family. The Pit is a multigenerational, kin-centric space that is, in many ways, defined by non-genetic relationality: a way of living and relating that has deep history in the (often ruptured) relationship-building of the American South para- and post-enslavement. As Adair notes in her analysis of Black diaspora and kinship:

> If kinship is reduced to questions of conjugality, blood and paternity, this risks, first, the inaccurate, limited description of relationality [. . .];

secondly, an accession to the colonial imposition of certain kinship norms upon colonized, enslaved and oppressed populations as a method of control, [. . .] and finally the elision or marginalization of the history of resistance, cultural creation and forms of alternative, sometimes subversive relationality that those enslaved and oppressed peoples developed and practiced – and still do today. (Adair 2019, 20)

The Pit and its inhabitants – whether permanent or transitory – demonstrate broad kinship dynamics, bringing into focus the centrality of community to the narrative and to understandings of Black diasporic experience in the Gulf Coast more generally. Everything within the Pit is hidden away, forgotten or discounted by the larger community of Bois Sauvage. Even their house attempts to become part of the natural environment surrounding it, as Esch remarks how 'our house is the colour of rust, nearly invisible under the oaks and behind the rubbish, lopsided. The cement bricks it sits on are the color of the sand' (16). Christopher Lloyd emphasises the connections between the land and those who dwell there as a critical part of understanding life in the American South/Mississippi Delta, remarking that 'there are clear overlaps and connections between the disparate materials, objects, and subjects in the Pit. The entangling of the novel's animals and environment [. . .] makes clear how embroiled its southeners are in the "natural" world' (Lloyd 2018, 143). The Pit is seen as a place of salvaged goods, cobbled together buildings and undesirable land – a perspective that is transferred onto the inhabitants of the Pit as a measure of their 'value' within the larger community.

Comparatively, when outside the space of the Pit, Esch, her brothers and their friends are subject to surveillance and scrutiny – their displacement and lack of belonging made apparent in their encounters with other teenagers at school or locals in Bois Sauvage and the nearby town of St Catherine. On one such trip into town to the grocery store, Ward describes how Esch, Skeetah and Big Henry are affected by this (white, unnatural, manufactured) space, as Esch tells us how 'inside, I follow Big Henry, who follows Skeetah, who bumps past carts pushed by ladies with feathery-light hair and freckled forearms pulling tall men wearing wraparound sunglasses. The rich ones wear khakis and yacht club shirts, the others wear camouflage and deer prints' (28). Each child navigates this space differently to avoid confrontation, suspicion and harm: 'Skeetah ignores everyone like they're pits of inferior breeding. Big Henry dances past, mumbles "Sorry" and "'Scuse me." I am small, dark: invisible. I could be Eurydice walking through the underworld to dissolve, unseen' (28). Unlike the Pit, where Esch and her family reside fully embodied and able to express themselves, there is an unease around navigating these other spaces. In this way, the Batiste children and their friends are entangled with the histories of and assumptions about the Pit, even when distant from it: as Ingrid Waldron notes, 'land value is deeply inscribed with ideologies about race in ways that illuminate how we value or don't value certain bodies' (Waldron 2018, 37), and Ward explicitly considers this valuation of bodies as commentary on and a critique of settler colonialism and white heteropatriarchy.

Existing within, and relying on, spaces transformed by colonialism and the transatlantic slave trade, Ward's protagonist Esch and her relations reside within spaces deemed undesirable or unsafe by the colonial state, emphasising the adaptation Nixon considers a central concern for marginalised peoples, as environmentally embedded violence 'is often difficult to source, oppose, and once set in motion, to reverse' (7). While Esch may reside outside the social structures and attention of society – hidden in the lands inhabited by her family for generations – her actions are continually informed by the fear and violence of the society which her family peripherally inhabits. In the consideration of embodied experience in the face of violent disembodiment, Esch understands her embodiment – and the violence threatened against her body – through the marginalised spaces she resides within. Esch's plight supports theories of disproportionate vulnerability in the climate crisis proposed by theorists such as Waldron, Laura Pulido and Andrew Ross, who seek to make visible the effect of racism and marginalisation within climate discourse, considering the old truism 'that we will *all* be impacted by the Anthropocene, but we will experience it differently [. . .] there are those who will be merely inconvenienced and there will be those who will die . . . with numerous positions between these two extremes' (Pulido 2018, 118, emphasis original). In many ways, Ward poses the safety of their protagonist's Black body as reliant on the land, connecting past understandings of land and kinship to present structures of disembodiment and displacement.

The consideration of vulnerable spaces in Ward's novel naturally connects to considerations of the contemporary climate crisis and environmental racism – for, as many environmental theorists argue 'the Anthropocene must be seen as a racial process' (Pulido 2018, 117). There is, as environmentalist Laura Pulido notes, 'abundant research [that] indicates that not only do many environmental hazards follow along racial lines, but also many of the meta-processes that have contributed to the Anthropocene, such as industrialization, urbanization, and capitalism, are racialized' (Pulido 2018, 117). The effects of climate crisis are neither neutral nor equitable, as we see in the disproportionate effect of flooding, wildfires, droughts and other acts of environmental destruction on marginalised communities, particularly communities of colour – and in the United States, specifically, communities of historically disenfranchised Black and Indigenous peoples. This effect is well documented in studies such as Ingrid Waldron's *There's Something in the Water*, where toxic land-bases and unhealthy living spaces are inhabited by those historically and continuously forced to the economic and social margins of colonial society. Waldron notes that 'environmental racism is violence – one of several forms of state-sanctioned racial violence perpetuated upon the lands, bodies, and minds of Indigenous and Black communities through decision-making processes and policies that have their roots in a legacy of colonial violence' (2018, 37). Similar to Waldron's study of toxic landscapes in Nova Scotia, Ward's locating of the narrative within the Mississippi Gulf Coast compels readers to consider the lives and experiences of those who reside in spaces deemed unfit by settler communities. Ward goes further in asking us to not only consider these undesirable spaces as spaces of marginalisation, but also to consider how these spaces support life and its flourishings outside of and in spite of the colonial state.

In the Pit, Esch and her family find meaning and safety in the routines and obligations of residing on land that is deeply familiar and yet simultaneously unknowable. Their impact on the landscape of the Pit is not altruistic – they burn their garbage and maintain only the areas which are of use to them (15) – yet it is a relationship formed out of mutual understanding, if not equal power. Kinship in the Pit extends its considerations of kin to the more-than-human world and to the land itself, offering a kin-centric ecology of this hidden community that 'far from presupposing that humans are a degrading force, sullying whatever we might touch, [. . .] expresses the view that humans can actually play keystone roles in our landscapes, creating mutual flourishing' (Van Horn 2021, 7). Or, as Gavin Van Horn writes, 'human beings are not merely kin by biological relation, but it is entirely possible that human communities and cultures can be good kin, salutary ecological collaborators alongside and with our nonhuman family members' (2021, 7). Ward's novel is filled with descriptions of the natural environment and its (human and more-than-human) inhabitants, building kinship between the inhabitants of the Pit and the land itself through the paralleling and minutae of their experience. In one such moment, Esch describes walking through the trees:

> the air has been clear these past couple of days. Bright, every day almost unbearably bright and hot and close [. . .]. Insects root under our feet, squirrels leap from tree to tree, crows glide between the tops of the pines, cawing. The beat of their wings sounds soft as the swish of Mudda Ma'am's broom when she sweeps pine needles from her sandy front yard. (45–6)

Despite being offered 'little to no protection from a sustaining social structure beyond their immediate kinship relations', the inhabitants of the Pit embrace – and find moments of joy in – their environment as an alternative sustaining structure (Morgenstern 2020, 107). We see the trust held between the Batistes and their land, 'good kinship' made tangible through the constant navigation of the woods, the games played in the Pit, the animals hunted and eggs collected, and the nights spent camping out in the woods where 'the cicadas in the trees are like fitful rain, sounding in waves in the black brush of the trees' (51). These kinship ties, I would argue, influence and reinvent the protagonist and her family, producing an alternative history in defiance of the world that surrounds them, and contextualising the acts of embodiment and vulnerability which eventually lead to the destruction of that same space. This interweaving of defiance and devastation epitomises the complexity of kinship formation for marginalised bodies, recognising that 'kinship is deep and wide – and dwells within the human body' (Van Horn 2021, 6).

While the Batiste family impose their daily happenings onto the land, the environment imposes its own power by the end of the narrative – wreaking havoc through a storm that, despite continual preparation, could not be defended against. Esch notes how most hurricanes 'don't even hit us head-on anymore; most turn right to Florida or take a left for Texas, brush past and glance off us like a shirtsleeve. We ain't had one come straight for us in years' (4). This absence of severe storms, however, comes at a cost: for in between major storms there is 'time enough to forget how many jugs of water we need to fill, how many cans of sardines and potted meat we should stock, how many tubs of water we need' (4). Hurricane Katrina is an awakening for Ward's protagonists, a recognition that their place-world is not exempt from the happenings of the world, but rather connected to the world and made simultaneously vulnerable and powerful through this connection.[1] In the face of disconnect and mistrust of the natural spaces around us, theorist Stephanie J. Fitzgerald calls instead for the recognition of the 'narrated place-world' which we inhabit, positioning ourselves in relation to the layered history of lands and places which are 'imprinted with physical, cultural, and spiritual narratives that have retained their resonance throughout the centuries' (Fitzgerald 2015, 4). The Batiste family's relationship to the Pit is imprinted on their bodies and in their lived experiences – an embodied rhetoric that, rather than separating experience from practice or bodies from land, embraces these interconnections as additions to, rather than diminishings of, understanding. The Pit is Esch's narrated place-world, and the driving force of Hurricane Katrina is (in the frame of this novel) their story: for, it is through the storm that Esch and the Pit's vulnerabilities are made tangible.

Through her environment, Esch's multiple vulnerabilities as a Black, pregnant, economically disenfranchised woman are defined – the storm similarly affects these definitions, but, in its rupturing of the known, also ruptures the expectations of these vulnerabilities. Storms are common imagery for narratives of growth (literal or metaphorical) within literature – particularly that literature which uses temporary natural spaces for the protagonist's growth, a 'return to nature' trope which sees the protagonist recognise their need for growth and change through their experiences in a natural setting before returning to 'civilisation', nature having served its function as an appropriated space of learning.[2] In *Salvage the Bones*, Esch's connection with nature is not temporary or metaphorical, but rather an unavoidable connection between her embodiment and the natural space which she inhabits: yet, the storm within Ward's narrative does act as a defining moment of Esch's growth (into self, into womanhood, into motherhood). Despite this metaphorical impulse, the analysis of storms in literature is complex, and provides valuable spaces and opportunities within a text for understanding climate impact and social commentaries on vulnerability, as Sharae Deckard notes:

> To interpret the literary uses of storm aesthetics is not to romanticize the human suffering that tropical storms can cause. However, it is crucial to acknowledge that tropical storms are not 'disasters-to-nature', but rather serve ecological functions, lowering seawater temperatures, maintaining the global heat balance by recirculating humid tropical air to mid-latitudes and polar regions, and periodically stripping away excess vegetation in order to restore open, sandy ecosystems and redeposit sediments. Hurricanes such as Katrina, Hugo, or Ivan are ecological disasters only when social conditions cause them to be experienced as such, exposing the hidden geographies that attend environmental crisis. (Deckard 2016, 26)

Storms are not, as Deckard indicates, in and of themselves destructive; rather, it is in their collision with or impact on human spaces that they become agents of devastation. Deckard goes on to state that 'the most vulnerable, disadvantaged populations often live on reclaimed or coastal land exposed to elemental forces, situated within landscapes of socio-economic inequity', as 'the social construction of "natural" disaster is largely hidden from view by a way of thinking that simultaneously imposes false expectations on the environment and then explains the inevitable disappointments as proof of a malign and hostile nature' (26–7). In Ward's text, Hurricane Katrina exposes the vulnerabilities of Gulf Coast communities, of those living at the Pit, because that's what storms do – yet, the storm also provides an opportunity for growth and the making of space within the narrative, recognising not only the destructive potential of hurricanes, but also their function as a force that strips away in order to restore (Deckard 2016, 6).

Esch's growth from adolescence to motherhood is mirrored by the arrival of Hurricane Katrina – the literal *sturm und drang* ('storm and stress') of living in the Gulf Coast.[3] Similar to other hurricane narratives, particularly those of traditionally marginalised coastal communities such as Caribbean and Creole narratives, Ward's storm performs the role of 'crystallizing the individual subjectivities of adolescents', depicts the 'drive to 'development' and 'resolution' within the *Bildungsroman*', and imagines 'future conditions of revolution or socio-ecological transformation' (Deckard 2016, 33, 35). The storm is a moment of simultaneous crisis and growth, a (literal) unstoppable force for Esch's development that also cannot be defined by its influence on the protagonist. The storm does not intend to facilitate this growth, but it doesn't intend not to – its impact and influence tied intrinsically to the environments it affects and those who live there.

Immediately prior to the storm's arrival Esch confronts Manny, the father of her child, with the knowledge of her pregnancy – a moment long anticipated by Esch, who saw Manny as a potential partner despite her continual referral to Medea and the vengeance which defines Medea's story.[4] Manny's rejection of Esch and their child leads us into the storm, the turmoil within Esch made physical in the storm's awakening: 'the storm screams, *I have been waiting for you*' (230). Esch watches the storm with a combination of horror and fascination, remarking that 'it is terrible', that it is the 'flailing wind that lashes like an extension cord used as a beating belt. It is the rain, which stings like stones, which drives into our eyes and bids them shut. It is the water, swirling and gathering and spreading on all sides' (230). This description of the storm just as easily applies to Esch's anger, heartbreak and vengeance at Manny's (pre-destined) betrayal. Esch, filled with wrath and resolution, embraces the storm's violence as her own, speaking back to the refrain she has carried throughout the novel: 'make them know' (171). Yet, the storm is also a manifestation of Esch's vulnerabilities, the realisation that she is powerless to stop the storm – just as she is powerless to stop her pregnancy. Despite their preparations, the Batiste family are unprepared for the strength and relentlessness of the storm. Water seeps in through the floors while the winds outside sound like freight trains, the Pit becomes a lake of swirling water, and the Batistes must leave the safety of their storm-proofed home in order to avoid being swept away (230). Seeking better shelter from the storm requires them to enter into the very heart of it; and in this moment of peril, Esch's pregnancy is revealed.

Ward's narrative is continually shaped by motherhood and the exposure or vulnerability that motherhood brings, a reality made tangible in the midst of the storm – where Esch's pregnancy, hidden so carefully throughout the novel, is revealed to her family: 'Daddy saw it, that second before he pushed me [. . .] My wet clothes show the difference. Daddy saw the curve of a waist, the telltale push of a stomach outwards. Daddy saw fruit' (234). In that moment of turmoil, in the battering winds and raging waters of the hurricane, Esch is finally seen as she is – this revelation a claiming of space for Esch as a woman and as a mother. It is the claiming of space despite, and in many ways because of, the 'complexity and underlying fragility' of inhabiting female bodies and domestic spaces as a marginalised or vulnerable person (Fraiman 2017, 23). Following the storm, Esch's making of space is grounded in imagining a future comprised of 'alternative communities all across the world, informed by alternative information, and keenly aware of the environmental, human rights, and libertarian impulses that bind us together in this tiny planet' (Nixon 2011, x). For Esch, these alternative communities are based in survival, a salvaging of strengths and vulnerabilities to see her through the next storm:

> Regardless of the political weather that conditions the terminology around environmental rupture, there is no getting away from the radical presencing of geology in our lives, as energy, sensibility, storm, rift, and a growing awareness of what that energy costs across corporeal and planetary bodies (an awareness that has had its 'quieted' witnesses since 1492).

When the storm is over, there will be another. The storms are always coming, with faster and greater intensity. From a very literal point of view, these storms might very well be the loudest and most insistent political message and material instantiation of the Anthropocene today. If today's storm is a prelude to another, what, in Baldwin's words, would help us get through the storm next time? (Yusoff 2019, 108)

Esch and her family's survival of Katrina has transformed them, ruptured them, reminding them of the power of nature and their connection to the violence and vulnerability that storms bring about – until the next storm comes. This knowledge is made all the more urgent for Esch, who knows she must teach these lessons to her future child (255), while making space for that child to build their own connections with the land and community they are being born into.[5]

Alongside Esch's own experiences of impending motherhood, we see her mother, Skeetah's dog China and the storm Katrina shaping Esch's understandings of and community within motherhood. Esch's mother – though dead before the outset of this narrative – acts as a cautionary tale, warning Esch that the effects of motherhood on the body are exploitative and deadly. China's motherhood is relatively contemporary with Esch's, her puppies arriving just before the storm hits, and her birthing experience causing Esch to realise her own impending motherhood. While Katrina's form of motherhood sees Esch transformed (like Medea) into a strong and formidable force: 'she left us a dark Gulf and salt-burned lands. She left us to crawl. She left us to salvage. Katrina is the mother we will remember until the next mother with large, merciless hands, committed to blood comes' (255). Each of these mothers are linked with violence in their own ways, informing Esch's understanding of motherhood as rooted in violence and vulnerability. Yet, these mothers are also connected with the land – they are a part of the narrated place-world of the Pit – and they offer comfort, guidance and community alongside their pain. When asked who the father of her baby is, Esch insists there is no father – rejecting Manny as Medea did Jason – but Big Henry corrects her: saying that 'this baby got a daddy, Esch. [. . .] This baby got plenty daddies' (255). In Ward's text, kinship and community responsibility reside outside of expected heteronormative bounds, encouraging rather relations built on mutual recognition and care. Returning in many ways to a kin-centric ecology – a recognition that 'all of our lives depend on the quality of relations between us [. . .] within an exuberant, life-generating planetary tangle capable of nurturing intelligences that can spin webs and words' (Van Horn 2021, 2) –

Esch's relationships and community ties are grounded in the sharing and making of collective space.

Hope is found in the unlikeliest of places after the storm: for Esch and her family, this space for rebuilding and renewal is found in their return to the Pit, a space that – by all rights – should not continue to exist after the devastation of Katrina. The Batiste children, along with Big Henry, return to the Pit after the storm to salvage what they can: finding shoes, cans of food and broken pieces of their home and yard (256). The storm has transformed their space into a 'a tangle of tree branches and wood and car and wire and garbage' (255), yet they do not rush to leave the storm-wrecked space, instead ending this narrative sitting around a campfire waiting for what comes next. As Esch sits by the fire, she considers her own future, facing her pregnancy – and all of the vulnerabilities that come with it – with an acceptance of the upheaval of boundaries and norms brought by the storm. While Nixon considers how 'attritional catastrophes that overspill clear boundaries in time and space are marked above all by displacements – temporal, geographical, rhetorical, and technological displacements' that underestimate the human and environmental costs (7), Esch's impending motherhood is validated and made tangible through the transformation of the catastrophic storm. The storm, while violent and catastrophic, paradoxically brings a sense of surety and calm to Esch, linking her survival of the storms (both literal and metaphorical) to her ability to successfully navigate her future.

As the children of the Pit sit together at the end of the novel, Esch reflects on her place in the narrative of the Pit, anticipating the return of Skeetah's dog (and fellow mother) China, who 'will return, standing tall and straight, the milk burned out of her. She will look down on the circle of light we have made in the Pit, and she will know that I have kept watch, that I have fought' (258). China represents an affirmation that Esch cannot receive from elsewhere, for she knows what it is to be a mother, and so Esch imagines how China 'will bark and call me sister. In the star-suffocated sky, there is a great waiting silence. She will know that I am a mother' (258). Motherhood forms a kinship bond between the various female bodies within the text, celebrating kinship created outside of a heteropatriarchal structure – a kinship that extends beyond even an Anthropocentric structure to recognise the complexity of embodiment, motherhood and marginalisation. In embracing her place and relationships in the Pit after the storm, Esch mimics the hurricane's act, stripping away the excess in order to restore (Deckard 2016, 6).

In the history and knowledge of the Pit, a space that Esch cannot escape as an economically disenfranchised, pregnant, Black woman, she is provided with a sense of agency and embodiment that resists linear understandings of marginalisation and displacement. As Christopher Lloyd argues, 'intimately connected to the natural world around them [. . .], Ward's [characters] are deeply linked to other forms of life in the South, even while their own is rendered throwaway' (Lloyd 2018, 143–4). This returns us to a recognition of the 'narrated place-world': finding places to enact one's own narrative that connect and resonate in spite of – and in many ways because of – the complex histories of those spaces and embodiments (Fitzgerald 2015, 4). As Ward reminds us, 'bodies tell stories' (83) and kinship resides in the body (Van Horn 2021, 6); Esch's story and her kinship ties are deeply connected to the land, her experiences and identity tied to the Gulf Coast and its impact as a site of Black community formation. When Ward's characters return home despite Hurricane Katrina's devastation of their house and land, they acknowledge a history of safety and reliance on a place that, unlike their abandonment by other spaces or social structures, and though still fraught with trauma and destruction, has always been connected to them and has witnessed with them many storms.

Notes

1. In keeping with the teachings of Keith Basso, Stephanie J. Fitzgerald writes of the 'narrated place-world' as a recognition of the interconnections of spaces/environments with history/stories. Basso and Fitzgerald ask us to consider how history is grounded in place and in experience, bringing into focus the multiplicity of histories that exist and the connections between these histories: these land-based histories are 'extremely personal, consistently subjective, and therefore highly variable among those who work to produce it. For these and other reasons, it is history without authorities – all narrated place-worlds, provided they seem plausible, are considered equally valid – and the idea of compiling "definitive accounts" is rejected out of hand as unfeasible and undesirable' (Basso 1996, 32).

2. This is particularly prevalent in narratives which centre a young adult protagonist. As Megan McDonough and Katherine A. Wagner note, the natural world is often a place of awakening or agency for the young adult protagonist, treating nature as a place to be appropriated for the duration of the character's needs (McDonough and Wagner 2014, 159). In this way, nature is seen as 'dangerous but purifying, innocent yet

wise, the only real touchstone of what is good and right and beautiful'
(157).

3. First coined by G. Stanley Hall, 'storm and stress' (adapted from the
German Romantic notion *sturm und drang*) describes the 'emotional
tempestuousness of adolescence' (Mason 2021, 10). While the term has
seen a significant amount of criticism and adaptation since Hall's coinage, it generally is used to describe how the moments of stress (physically, emotionally, etc.) that accompany an adolescent's growth into
adulthood are keystone moments in that adolescent's maturation.

4. Esch is assigned a book of Greek myths for summer reading from her
high school English teacher (7). This book, and its story of Jason and
Medea, in many ways grounds Esch's understanding of love and betrayal; while Ward's allusion to the fate of Medea foreshadows the outcome of Esch's own narrative.

5. 'I will tie the glass and stone with string, hang the shards above my
bed, so that they will flash in the dark and tell the story of Katrina, the
mother that swept into the Gulf and slaughtered' (255).

Works Cited

Adair, Gigi. 2019. *Kinship Across the Black Atlantic: Writing Diasporic Relations*. Liverpool: Liverpool University Press.

Basso, Keith. 1996. *Wisdom Sits in Places*. Albuquerque: University of New Mexico Press.

Deckard, Sharae. 2016. 'The Political Ecology of Storms in Caribbean Literature'. In *The Caribbean: Aesthetics, World-Ecology, Politics*, edited by Chris Campbell and Michael Niblett, 25–45. Liverpool: Liverpool University Press.

Fitzgerald, Stephanie J. 2015. *Native Women and Land: Narratives of Dispossession and Resurgence*. Albuquerque: University of New Mexico Press.

Fraiman, Susan. 2017. *Extreme Domesticity: A View from the Margins*. New York: Columbia University Press.

Lloyd, Christopher. 2018. *Corporeal Legacies in the US South: Memory and Embodiment in Contemporary Culture*. Cham: Palgrave Macmillan.

McDonough, Megan, and Katherine A. Wagner. 2014. 'Rebellious Natures: The Role of Nature in Young Adult Dystopian Female Protagonists' Awakenings and Agency'. In *Female Rebellion in Young Adult Dystopian Fiction*, edited by Sara K. Day, Miranda A. Green-Barteet and Amy L. Montz, 157–69. London: Routledge.

Mason, Derritt. 2021. *Queer Anxieties of Young Adult Literature and Culture*. Jackson: University Press of Mississippi.

Morgenstern, Naomi. 2020. 'Maternal Sovereignty: Destruction and Survival in Jesmyn Ward's *Salvage the Bones*'. In *Reading Contemporary Black

British and African American Women Writers, edited by Jean Wyatt and Sheldon George, 104–21. New York: Routledge.

Nixon, Rob. 2011. *Slow Violence and the Environmentalism of the Poor*. Cambridge, MA: Harvard University Press.

Pulido, Laura. 2018. 'Racism and the Anthropocene'. In *Future Remains: A Cabinet of Curiosities for the Anthropocene*, edited by Gregg Mitman, Marco Armiero and Robert S. Emmett, 116–28. Chicago: University of Chicago Press.

Ross, Andrew. 2011. *Bird on Fire: Lessons from the World's Least Sustainable City*. New York: Oxford University Press.

Van Horn, Gavin. 2021. 'Kinning: Introducing the Kinship Series'. In *Kinship: Belonging in A World of Relations*, edited by Gavin Van Horn, Robin Wall Kimmerer and John Hausdoerffer, vol. 1: Planet, 1–11. Libertyville, IL: Center for Humans and Nature Press.

Waldron, Ingrid. 2018. *There's Something in the Water: Environmental Racism in Indigenous and Black Communities*. Winnipeg, MB: Fernwood Publishing.

Ward, Jesmyn. 2011. *Salvage the Bones*. New York: Bloomsbury.

Yusoff, Kathryn. 2019. *A Billion Black Anthropocenes or None*. Minneapolis: University of Minnesota Press.

Chapter 7

'We are left to seed another year': Nature and Neglect in Jesmyn Ward's *Salvage the Bones*

Devon Anderson

Jesmyn Ward's *Salvage the Bones* tells a story of devastation. The novel takes place over twelve days leading up to and immediately following Hurricane Katrina's landfall in southern Mississippi: readers experience the storm's slow and menacing approach, face its overwhelming violence, and glimpse the aftermath of its brutality. The storm is a constant presence in the novel, yet it is not the sole source of ruin. Katrina may be the force that 'swept into the Gulf and slaughtered', as narrator Esch describes it (Ward 2011, 255), but other, slower, more systemic violences have already afflicted the communities most vulnerable to the storm's destruction. As Katrina's threat grows, so too do markers of poverty, race-based inequality, and systemic neglect accrue within the narrative, and these systemic violences cause harms that interweave with and intensify the danger of the storm.

Because Hurricane Katrina magnified racist and systemic inequities already in place in the Gulf Coast region, it has been labelled an 'unnatural disaster', a term that describes a catastrophic event whose harmful impact derives from a mix of natural forces and human (in)action.[1] 'Unnatural disasters' highlight the relationship between one's social position and one's vulnerability to environmental harms, since the social, cultural, economic and environmental injustices that afflict minoritised and disadvantaged populations also make these populations more susceptible than others to worse outcomes after natural events. Katrina's violence intensified and was intensified by a long history of social and systemic violences that left Black, rural and poor people particularly vulnerable to environmental destruction. In this respect, Hurricane Katrina exposed a complex interplay between cultural and so-called 'natural' forces of harm. By setting her novel amid Katrina's destruction, Ward highlights 'the

need to resist an easy separation between "nature" and "culture"'
given that, as Naomi Morgenstern argues, 'this supposedly "natural" disaster proved to be profoundly enmeshed with socioeconomic
forces, with years of failed and inadequate policy and its material
legacy' (Morgenstern 2020, 106). In *Salvage the Bones*, Ward's poor
rural Black characters experience, both before and after the storm,
what Morgenstern describes as a level of 'social abandonment that
undoes the very opposition between culture and nature' (Morgenstern
2020, 111).[2] It is this blurring of categories that I explore in this
chapter, as I examine how Ward makes social abandonment visible
through her descriptions of a natural world marked by poverty and
neglect. I argue that Ward's (un)natural setting prompts a cautious
ambivalence towards the non-human environment by calling readerly
attention to the slower violences that undergird unnatural disasters.

Ward structures her chapters around Katrina's slow build: the
hurricane first unfolds gradually, a looming threat that hovers on
the periphery of Esch's narrative concerns before erupting in sudden, overwhelming, destructive violence. But the depiction of poverty grinds steadily throughout the novel, consistent and constant.
Against the quick and instantaneous violence of the hurricane, Ward
depicts a natural environment suffused with 'slow violence', Rob
Nixon's term for the accumulation of negative impacts that industrial
development and socio-economic disparities under global capitalism
have wrought upon the natural world. Nixon defines 'slow violence'
as 'violence that occurs gradually and out of sight, a violence of delayed destruction that is dispersed across time and space, an attritional violence that is typically not viewed as violence at all' since
it is 'neither spectacular nor instantaneous, but rather incremental
and accretive' (Nixon 2013, 2).[3] Poor communities, communities of
colour and other groups seen as expendable through a lens of global
capitalism suffer a disproportionate share of these negative impacts,
so that 'slow violence' specifically names the effects of climate ero-
sion and other structural and environmental crises upon the most
socially disempowered. Because slow violence is far less visible than
sudden and destructive events, this subtle, accretive, attritional violence is difficult to represent or to narrativise, which means that it
can be difficult for us to identify and to empathise with its victims.
In *Salvage the Bones*, Ward offers an example of how to represent
and narrativise long-term harm by first highlighting the extensive
and accumulated effects of slow violence that are present within the
existing environment, and then describing the devastating hurricane
that is slow violence's 'spectacular' counterpart.[4]

Ward's presentation of nature embeds signs of human oppression within the non-human landscape. She mixes descriptions of nature (flora, fauna, dirt, water, weather) with descriptions of discarded and decaying materials that suggest poverty, neglect and social disenfranchisement.[5] In this way, Ward infuses the natural environment with the systemic violences that shape and condition her characters' lives. As Brian Railsback puts it, in Ward's work 'the toxicity of the environment is intertwined with the social poisons that the people of rural Mississippi must endure' (Railsback 2018, 27).[6] Far from naturalising these systemic and racialised inequities, Ward's descriptions make visible the ways that social and cultural forces have shaped the environmental context of the Batiste family. There is nothing natural about the neighbourhood's racialised segregation, or the Batiste family's poverty, or their father's unemployment, or their poorly served public spaces, or their decimated and unproductive land, or their lack of access to fresh food and adequate medical care, yet all of these circumstances dictate how the characters experience natural events such as illness, hunger, pregnancy and the storm. By contextualising Katrina among these systemic inequities, Ward challenges the straightforward narrative of a natural disaster's sudden and total environmental destruction. As Jessica Doble argues, Ward 'revis[es] racist and classist narratives of Katrina' by representing 'not only the event, but the impact of class and racial oppression, which deems [the Batiste] family as disposable to the social structures' (Doble 2018, 58). Ward complicates and expands our understanding of the human experience of Hurricane Katrina by highlighting long-term social and systemic disparities that rendered the nature-filled rural South 'unnatural' long before the storm.

The narrator of *Salvage the Bones*, teenaged Esch Batiste, spends her summer days at once immersed in the untamed beauty of rural Mississippi and surrounded by signs of crushing poverty. Her family live on a plot of land nicknamed 'the Pit' for the lake that formed two generations ago, after white men extracted its soil and rendered the land unstable and unfarmable. Today, this artificial lake, a lasting sign of exploitation, now serves as a swimming hole for the Batiste children and their friends, who find ways to carve joy out of the red mud. The fields surrounding the Pit are 'overgrown with shrubs, with saw palmetto, with pine trees', the plants flourishing in the absence of anyone who cares to maintain them (Ward 2011, 14). The 'trash-strewn, hardscrabble Pit' (Ward 2011, 94) is likewise overfull, littered with broken machines and discarded items, scrap metal and scrap wood, empty bottles, abandoned wire, and other detritus that indicate a life of salvaging, recycling and making-do. But although the Pit is marked with these signs of degradation and disuse, it is also a scene of generation. The Pit teems with animal life, with squirrels, gnats, fleas, and 'mosquitoes so big they look like bats' (Ward 2011, 95). The abandoned henhouse sags and rots, but the hens, now half wild, return to tuck their eggs into old car engines. Ward's description of this environment captures apparent contradictions, with abundance and poverty, new life and old trash, coexisting in one space. Plants and animals do not undo, overcome or triumph over the obstacles created by neglect and poverty, but they do find ways to navigate those obstacles and adapt to them. Ward sketches a landscape that has grown over and around extracted holes and discarded garbage, and her descriptions of the Pit invite us to see that these signs of social marginalisation actually precipitate nature's flourishing. Whatever nature survives in the Pit has had to struggle against human forces of harm.

Indeed, nature's deep connection with the experience of struggle in the novel blurs the line between nature and culture. Ward shifts fluidly between natural imagery and references to poverty when she describes her characters' encounters with both human and non-human adversaries. When Katrina finally strikes the fictional town of Bois Sauvage, the hurricane's power is visible in 'the water, swirling and gathering on all sides' (Ward 2011, 230), but also in 'the remains of the yard, the refrigerators and lawn mowers and the RV and mattresses, floating like a fleet' of abandoned materials (Ward 2011, 231). The hurricane shows itself by rearranging the family's salvaged garbage into a new order.[7] The storm's intensity, too, is coded in a metaphor of salvage, 'the flailing wind that lashes like an extension cord used as a beating belt' (Ward 2011, 230), one source of violence substituting readily for another. The language of refuse intensifies and highlights Katrina's violence, and it links the natural violence to the life of salvage necessitated by the family's poverty. At other moments, natural imagery softens communal violence. When a fight over money erupts at Randall's basketball game, the brawling boys are pushed out of the gymnasium, 'the crowd carrying them out of the dorm in the kind of frothing waves we only get before hurricanes' (Ward 2011, 150). The water imagery here lends a steadiness and an evenness to the surging crowd, which pushes the boys as an urgent but unified force rather than a cluster of individual, hateful human fists. Similarly, when Esch and Skeetah creep through fields, preparing to steal from their white neighbours, Esch imagines them 'like ants under the floorboard, marching in line toward sugar left open in the cabinet' (Ward 2011, 71). Esch and her brother do not target their white neighbours aggressively or even intentionally. Their crime is a matter of course, as they follow the pull towards something that has been 'left open' for them. Ward's natural metaphors do not present nature as univocally bad or good: nature can be brutal in its discipline, gentle in its support, desperate and flailing or rational and organised, but in all of these guises it articulates a pervasive sense of broader social struggles.

Ward's work thus engages with an African American ecoliterary tradition in which the natural landscape serves a complicated and paradoxical role. Kimberly Ruffin argues that African Americans, whom she labels 'environmental others' (Ruffin 2010, 2), have a 'collective experience of being placed among those at the bottom of human hierarchies' (Ruffin 2010, 16), and this colours their relationship with both natural and built environments (Ruffin 2010, 13), which serve as sites of trauma as well as sources of beauty and connection.[8] Similarly, Camille T. Dungy identifies an ambivalence in Black poets' relationship to nature, since legacies of enslavement and violence have generated a sense of 'connection to, but also alienation from, the land' (Dungy 2009, xxii). Violence is woven into the southern landscape such that, for Black poets and Black readers alike, scenes of nature can evoke a sense of exposure and vulnerability to violence even as nature offers the 'potential to be a source of refuge, sustenance, and uncompromised beauty' (Dungy 2009, xxv). To portray only nature's beauty and ability to sustain life, then, risks occluding the darker threats posed to minoritised people within 'natural' spaces. Indeed, Dungy points to Elizabeth Dodd's concern that 'the literary attempt to deflect attention away from human beings' and focus instead on the non-human world 'might not be appealing for writers who already feel politically, economically, and socially marginalized' (Dungy 2009, xxv). Ward is able to address this concern by linking the human and non-human worlds together. By incorporating markers of marginalisation into her descriptions of the environment, Ward preserves legacies of social inequality and injustice even as she opens new pathways to connection and community within the (un)natural landscape.

Early in the novel, Ward centres the connection between nature and social trauma by placing the Batiste family home on land damaged by soil extraction. The Pit is an environment that testifies to a long history of racist exploitative land practices. When Esch first describes the Pit, she represents it as a site of overt exploitation and injustice:

> It was Papa Joseph nicknamed it all the Pit, Papa Joseph who let the white men he work with dig for clay that they used to lay the foundation for houses, let them excavate the side of a hill in a clearing near the back of the property where he used to plant corn for feed. Papa Joseph let them take all the dirt they wanted until their digging had created a cliff over a dry lake in the backyard, and the small stream that had run around and down the hill had diverted and pooled into the dry lake, making it into a pond, and then Papa Joseph thought the earth would give under the water, that the pond would spread and gobble up the property and make it a swamp, so he stopped selling earth for money. (Ward 2011, 14)

The white men's exploitation has shaped the Pit into a newly mobile, newly threatening and unstable landscape. The Pit, once productive of food and money, now threatens to consume itself. The water is active: it runs, diverts and pools; it is eager to spread, to change and gobble up the land. Though this action seems to derive from the land itself – the *earth* would give, the *pond* would spread – Ward ensures that we are able to trace the threat back to its true source: the white men who took what they wanted. White people have used, destroyed and then abandoned the land to its now-inevitable self-destruction.[9] Later, during the hurricane, the Pit will pour out water uncontrollably like 'a cut that won't stop leaking' (Ward 2011, 230–1), a long-term bleed from a brief but destructive act of social violence. To continue to occupy the Pit is to build a life upon the shaky foundation of exploitation and to risk encountering the future effects of this lasting environmental trauma, as the family will do when Katrina strikes.

The barren, trash-strewn, modern-day Pit exemplifies economic injustice, but it also represents more than a long legacy of trauma and social violence. Ward captures the ambivalence that Ruffin and Dungy describe when she identifies the Pit as a site of connection and community for Esch and her brothers. After their mother's death, the Batiste children form a kind of extended family with other boys from their town, and together they find ways to inhabit the Pit's unnatural landscape. When the neighbourhood boys are there, the broken cars and old machines in the yard take on new roles: they serve as beds for sex (Ward 2011, 23), as safe spaces for sleep, and as playmates, such as when Junior ties his jump rope to an old lawn mower (Ward 2011, 193). The boys make homes out of the Pit's detritus when they tuck themselves in among its scraps and decaying spaces, and they seem to belong so fully to the Pit that Esch is caught off guard when they emerge from anywhere other than among the Pit's junk.

> I was surprised that they all came from other places, that one or two of them hadn't emerged from the shed with Skeetah, or out of the patchy remains of Mother Lizbeth's rotting house, which is the only other house in the clearing and which was originally my mama's mother's property. The boys always found places to sleep when they were too drunk or high or lazy to go home. The backseats of junk cars, the old RV Daddy bought for cheap from some man at a gas station in Germaine that only ran until he got it into the driveway, the front porch that Mama had made Daddy screen in when we were little. Daddy didn't care, and after a while the Pit felt strange when they weren't there, as empty as the fish tank, dry of water and fish, but filled with rocks and fake coral like I saw in Big Henry's living room once. (Ward 2011, 10)

With its scattered machines, the Pit is not a natural space, but it is made into a habitable environment by the boys, just as the fake coral in Big Henry's fish tank mimics a natural setting when the fish are there. Without the boys, the Pit is as 'strange' as the tank without its fish, 'dry' and 'empty' and 'fake'. The presence of family and friends makes this unnatural space into a version of a livable environment, but without them it is visible as what it is: 'rotting' wood and junk. This is one way in which Ward humanises the Batistes' experience of slow violence. Family connection, community and play are all possible in the Pit, but these positive experiences neither negate nor fully obscure the systemic harms that inform the family's unnatural environment.

Likewise, in Esch's memories, her mother's presence links her to a non-human environment that shows the unnatural signs of economic disenfranchisement. Rose Batiste – Mama – understands the animals of Bois Sauvage: she can coax a baby shark into submission, and she can interpret the movements of her chickens to discover eggs hidden in secret places. Yet even as Mama commands elusive knowledge of the natural realm, she complicates what counts as the natural world, for she navigates an environment littered with junk. As Esch recounts:

> Mama taught me how to find eggs; I followed her around the yard. It was never clean. Even when she was alive, it was full of empty cars with their hoods open, the engines stripped, and the bodies sitting there like picked-over animal bones. (Ward 2011, 22)

The machines in the yard have outlived their usefulness, and in their decay they resemble the leftover remains of animal carcasses more than the metal that makes up their remaining parts. The cars are 'stripped' and 'empty', but Mama's presence gives life to the scraps and renders the machines into bodies. When Esch describes the neglected cars as 'picked-over animal bones', she evokes her conception of her mother as a provider of food for the family. Rose knew how to break down wild animals and make them into food, how to efficiently break a chicken's neck (Ward 2011, 51), how to soak the wild out of her catch (Ward 2011, 85). Rose stripped her parents' house, too, taking from it any time she needed to replace a blanket or a pot until the house became 'a drying animal skeleton' (Ward 2011, 58). Comparing abandoned cars and homes to carcasses reminds us, here, that Rose's ability to hunt, catch and break down animals emerges out of necessity: she must feed her family and keep them warm, and she has little money with which to do so. While Esch remembers Mama as preternaturally linked to the natural world, we see Rose as a woman living in poverty and using all available resources to make her unnatural environment as inhabitable as possible.[10]

For Esch, Mama nearly disappears into the non-human landscape. Her colouring mirrors her surroundings so that she seems innately predisposed to blend in with the wooded environment that borders the engine graveyard, and her muted clothing choices make it difficult to track her through the shady growth.

> I can't remember exactly how I followed Mama because her skin was dark as the reaching oak trees, and she never wore bright colors: no fingernail pink, no forsythia blue, no banana yellow. Maybe she bought her shirts and pants bright and they faded with wear so that it seemed she always wore olive and black and nut brown, so that when she bent to pry an egg from a hidden nest, I could hardly see her, and she moved and it looked like the woods moved, like a wind was running past the trees. (Ward 2011, 22)

Mama's skin is an echo of the woods around her, and when she bends to fetch an egg, in her faded camouflage hues, she all but disappears into the scenery. Esch notes that the colours of her clothing may derive not from her choices but from the effects of time and decay on cheap materials. It may be Rose's poverty – the low quality of her old, worn clothing – that makes her seem one with the natural world. When Mama is present, her connection to the land seems natural, her movements linked to the movements of the wind, and Esch can barely discern her among the trees. After Mama's death, Esch comes to see that the connection is neither innate nor natural, but in fact a by-product of her low position within a social hierarchy: Mama likely fades into the trees and shadows because she cannot afford new clothing. Rather than romanticise Mama's connection to her environment, Ward uses the language of nature to highlight and make visible Rose's social and economic disadvantage.

Thus far, I have argued that Ward incorporates signs of social marginalisation into her descriptions of the 'natural' world in order to make visible the lasting effects of extractive capitalism, segregation, poverty and neglect on the non-human environment. By intermixing natural beauty with cultural harms, Ward creates an unnatural environment that reflects long-term social inequities, and she thereby captures an ambivalence towards the natural world: for the Batiste family, the non-human environment is as much a site of violence and struggle as it is a site of connection, community, family, joy and survival. For my final reading, I move away from the rural Pit and towards the city centre, where Ward presents us with a publicly owned space wherein neglect allows wild life to flourish and to challenge social order. In this way, Ward ensures that the complicated, ambivalent, paradoxical relationship between African Americans and the unnatural world extends into more urban representations of non-human life.

Esch and her brothers visit a public park which lies between the Pit and the nearby town of Bois Sauvage. As the group make their way into 'the center of Bois Sauvage, away from our Pit', the wildness of the woods recedes and the environment begins to resemble a settled, structured neighbourhood. Privately owned houses 'appear gradually, hidden behind trees, closer to one another until there are only ragged lots of woods separating them' (Ward 2011, 116). Nature here is tamed, forced into order as the individual houses shape the landscape into a built environment. The still-wild spaces diminish into 'ragged' lots, becoming scruffy and uneven next to the more ordered spatial organisation. The park, however, fails in its attempt to separate wild growth from the built environment. The state is responsible for maintaining this public park, but it neglects this responsibility. The park is poorly maintained, insufficiently cared for, and tended to just enough to keep it from total ruination.

> [T]he county park with the dirt parking lot [. . .] strives to impose some order, some civility to Bois. It fails. The woods muddle the park's edges. Mimosa trees arch over it with a basketball player's long, graceful arms and drop pink flowers like balls. Pines sprout up in the ditches along the edge of the park, aside the netless basketball goals, under the piecemeal

shade of the gap-toothed wooden play structure sinking into the earth, beside the stone picnic tables with their corners worn smooth by rain, even in the middle of the baseball field overgrown with grass. Maintenance workers, usually county convicts in green-and-white striped jumpsuits, come out once a year and halfheartedly try to trim back the encroaching wood, mow the grass set to bloom, the pine seedlings. The wild things of Bois Sauvage ignore them; we are left to seed another year. (Ward 2011, 117)

The park, all but abandoned by the county responsible for maintaining it, exists as a tribute to government neglect. Plants and flowers grow up around it, so that the park is a scene of both decay and renewal, a site of both government abandonment and natural reclamation. Again, we see a blurring of culture and nature, as state neglect precipitates and facilitates wild overgrowth. Life is passively permitted to flourish, but only through and in response to government neglect.

Against the encroaching forces of non-human life, the park cannot keep its shape; it is as though the land is swallowing the park, trying to return the steel and wooden structures to a more organic state. The woods creep towards the park and blur its edges, as the pine trees crowd the basketball court and invade the baseball field. Nature as depicted here is alluringly active, reaching out gently to assert itself in the cracks of the park's empty spaces. Nature muddles the effect of the built environment as it sprouts, blooms, expands, and with 'long, graceful arms' stretches across the park to play its own game on the empty court. Importantly, though, nature's active presence here does not undo the city's structure, but only works around it. Moreover, nature becomes this active force only when contrasted against the immobility of the park's static remains, and more broadly against the county's failure to act.

Government neglect has left the park's structures to 'sink', to grow gaps, and to be 'worn smooth', unshielded from the weather. Nature takes over in the wake of the state's abandonment, reclaiming neglected spaces and reshaping them into scenes of flourishing abundance. Lest this graceful, colourful, blooming scene lead us to hope that nature can overcome the violences of the past, lest we read too much redemption into nature's powerful and cleansing reach, Ward reminds us of the incarcerated workers who are sent, sporadically, to care for the grounds. As the convicts trim and mow and shape the space, they are separate from the scene and yet a part of it, their green and white uniforms mirroring the plant life around them. The ineffective maintenance workers serve as reminders of the state's more menacing forms of neglect, and the county park becomes another scene of paradox, with nature's beauty and humanity's violence coexisting. Indeed, in their contrast, each makes the other more prominently visible, so that violence and neglect both predicate and emphasise nature's beauty and unfettered growth. Social violence and state neglect become, in Ward's handling, the very conditions of nature's power.

By setting the incarcerated workers against the 'wild things' that ignore and negate their presence, Ward works against hopeful fantasies that position nature as a source of growth, progress, restoration and reclamation – fantasies that imagine escape from, or triumph over, environmental crises. If *Salvage the Bones* points to nature's generative possibilities, it does so only against the forces of abandonment that have left the neglected marginal spaces 'to seed'. In Ward's novel, neglect is the prerequisite for natural forces to become productive. At the end of her description of the county park, the narrator identifies herself as one of the 'wild things of Bois Sauvage'. In naming herself as wild, Esch aligns herself with the creatures that flourish in the Pit. Wild things continue to live and grow after the state has abandoned them; they ignore the state, they grow beyond their borders, they flourish, they tuck themselves away into safe spaces, they endure and they survive. Ward does not offer a redemptive or triumphant portrait of her characters overcoming their challenges. Rather, her depiction of the rural South is one that does justice to her characters by showcasing all that they live among. Ward depicts her characters existing, enduring and surviving amidst and alongside systemic oppression. The beauty of the natural world is not an alternative to that oppression, but an extension of it. Ward highlights the neglect that underlies both environmental degradation and nature's flourishing, and she refuses to let us see nature without the neglect that corresponds with it.

Ward's rendering of the unnatural landscapes of the rural South makes slow violence undeniably present and visible. In revealing the slow violence that undergirds apparently natural forces, Ward forestalls a redemptive reading of nature's power. Ward refuses to offer nature as an idyll, an escape from a culture suffused with racialised inequalities. Nor does she suggest that nature might reclaim degraded spaces and fully overcome the slow violences wrought upon marginalised populations. Instead of entertaining fantasies of escape and redemption, Ward illuminates the extent to which inequality and social neglect are preconditions for growth, survival and flourishing in the natural world. Neither nature's destructive nor its generative powers are altogether natural. Rather, they depend upon the neglect of structures, spaces and individuals no longer seen as useful to the financial and political systems responsible for maintaining them. Whenever nature seems to offer redemption and new life, Ward invites us to see that its redemptive qualities, its promises of sustenance and connection and beauty, are predicated upon violence, upon the history of abandonment and neglect that is the condition of the rural South after the continued and persistent dispossession of its poor and Black residents. Ward thus makes narrative space for the slow violences that made Katrina so destructive. In her complications of the 'natural', Ward becomes a version of what Nixon calls a 'writer-activist': she makes the 'insidious, yet unseen or imperceptible violence' wrought upon the environmental landscape visible, 'accessible and tangible' and human (Nixon 2013, 15). Annie Bares argues that 'the novel eschews narrative humanity's impulse to prove that the Batistes should be extricated from debility' (31) and instead offers an example of how literature can 'stridently object to the invisibility and inevitability of insidious modes of injustice' (Bares 2019, 36). Indeed, the reader does not have the option of imagining the Batiste family outside of the conditions of their existence. Instead, Ward invites us to look closely at those conditions, to see both the beauty and the violence visible in the non-human environment. Ward highlights the debility of the rural South, not to undo it, not to redeem it, but to ensure that it is seen.

Notes

1. For more on Hurricane Katrina as an 'unnatural disaster', see: Levitt and Whittaker; Dyson. Bullard offers a more general introduction to the term.
2. As Annie Bares succinctly writes, Katrina was 'an event that exacerbated and exposed – rather than created – scenes of injustice' (Bares 2019, 22). Similarly, Cameron W. Crawford, quoting Levitt and Whitaker, points out that 'in the days following the storm, Katrina's "floodwater exposed as much as it covered," revealing the ugly racism and systemic inequalities that persisted – and continue to persist over ten years after the storm – not only in the South, but throughout the country' (Crawford 2018, 73). More broadly, Christopher Clarke observes that the novel's rural Southern setting 'evokes a deeply embedded history of racism' and racialised poverty (Clarke 2015, 32), and Keith Mitchell notes that African American characters in Ward's novel are 'left largely to fend for themselves' as a result of a long history of economic deprivation, structural racism and de facto segregation (Mitchell 2018, 63).

3. In her chapter in this collection, Zsuzsanna Lénárt-Muszka describes this phenomenon using different terminology: where I use Nixon's term 'slow violence' to describe all lasting effects of social inequity, Lénárt-Muszka uses Christina Sharpe's terms *the weather* and *the wake* to distinguish between the ongoing, persistent, accretive harms done to bodies which experience marginalisation due to anti-Black racism and socio-economic inequalities (*the weather*) and the more expansive, persistent trauma of the afterlife of slavery (*the wake*).

4. A note: Nixon refers here to large-scale, specifically ecological destruction: 'Climate change, the thawing cryosphere, toxic drift, biomagnification, deforestation, the radioactive aftermaths of wars, acidifying oceans, and a host of other slowly unfolding environmental catastrophes' (Nixon 2013, 2). In contrast, the violences that Ward showcases mix racist environmental practices together with the effects of poverty and systemic oppression. I am not the first to utilise Nixon's term to refer to a broader range of social violences; see Bares (2019). Bares cites Nixon alongside Jasbir K. Puar's writing on debility and Saidiya Hartman's writing on quotidian violence, to argue that Katrina's destruction is an extension of the normalised daily social violences already done to Ward's narrator.

5. I use 'neglect' as an umbrella term for governmental policies that withhold care, that permit racist capitalist practices, that enable political and social disenfranchisement of minoritised communities (whether actively or passively), and that generally allow poor people, people in rural settings, and people of colour to live in states of poverty and disadvantage.

6. Railsback views Ward's novels as a coherent series of portraits of a 'dangerous, frightening environment' which 'reflect the 21st century, an Age of Anxiety in the USA rife with social division and scientific predictions of environmental collapse' (Railsback 2018, 31). Viewed together, Railsback argues, Ward's novels and essays sketch a damaged and dangerous environment in order to 'illuminate the *not right* world of today' (Railsback 2018, 31). But while Railsback concludes his reading of Ward's work by insisting upon a distinct separation between the human and non-human world – 'Nature turns away from us' (Railsback 2018, 31) – I see the human and non-human realms in Ward's work as more permanently intertwined.

7. Here, I refer to the salvaged and reused items in the Batistes' yard as signs of debility and economic disadvantage. However, Sinéad Moynihan suggests that 'the Batistes salvage and reuse as much as possible, thus calling into question the status of that which Esch herself calls "rubbish," "refuse," and "detritus"' (565). Moynihan argues that, 'whereas some post-Katrina discourses would frame the Batistes themselves as "so much garbage," Ward's emphasis on both recycling and salvaging constitutes a powerful counter-discursive gesture' by positioning Black

rural southern life as meaningful, valuable and viable (565). I don't think Moynihan's perspective is incompatible with mine, but I do want to articulate how our two views diverge: whereas Moynihan sees value and viability in the active gesture of salvage, I see value and viability in any relationship to refuse, whether or not the refuse is explicitly salvaged, recycled or reused. In my reading, nature's ability to work within and around garbage is a testament to life's viability – but that viability is without positive or negative moral value.

8. Christopher Lloyd makes a similar argument – though smaller in scope – when he emphasises the Batistes' close connection to animal life as that which reveals their social and environmental vulnerability: 'Surrounded by nature and connected to the animal world, Ward's southerners are companion species in the face of ecological and sociological collapse' (255).

9. The repeated verb 'let' in this passage implies permission and suggests that Papa Joseph had full power to decide what would happen to his property. But, of course, Papa Joseph is not in a position to choose. As Morgenstern observes: 'Contracts between black and white men – even those who work together – are not equal (the contract is not enforced by a sovereign state in whose eyes all persons would ostensibly enjoy the same standing)' (Morgenstern 2020, 114). See also Crawford: 'Esch's account implicates white people and their exploitation of black farmers' land as factors that further contribute to food access disparities, particularly in the rural, black community' (Crawford 2018, 82).

10. Crawford notes that the mother figures in *Salvage the Bones* evade simple categorisation: quoting Alice Deck, he writes that both Mama and Mother Lizbeth 'confound the role of "dark earth mother who represents fecundity, self-sufficiency, and endless succor" (Deck 69)' (Crawford 2018, 81). In my argument, Rose Batiste is indeed a fecund, self-sufficient and comforting presence, but these features are complicated by her social marginalisation.

Works Cited

Bares, Annie. 2019. '"Each Unbearable Day": Narrative Ruthlessness and Environmental and Reproductive Injustice in Jesmyn Ward's *Salvage the Bones*'. *MELUS: The Society For the Study of the Multi-Ethnic Literature of the United States* 44, no. 3 (Fall): 21–40. Project MUSE. DOI: 10.1093/melus/mlz022.

Bullard, Robert D. 2007. 'Equity, Unnatural Man-Made Disasters, and Race: Why Environmental Justice Matters'. In *Equity and the Environment (Research in Social Problems and Public Policy, Vol. 15)*, edited by W. R. Freudenburg, 51–8. Bingley: Emerald Group Publishing Limited. DOI: 10.1016/S0196-1152(07)15002-X.

Clarke, Christopher W. 2015. 'What Comes to the Surface: Storms, Bodies, and Community in Jesmyn Ward's *Salvage the Bones*'. *The Mississippi Quarterly* 68, nos. 3–4 (Summer–Fall): 341–58. *Project MUSE.* DOI: 10.1353/mss.2015.0002.

Crawford, Cameron Williams. 2018. '"Where Everything Else Is Starving, Fighting, Struggling": Food and the Politics of Hurricane Katrina in Jesmyn Ward's *Salvage the Bones*'. *The Southern Quarterly* 56 (1): 73–84. Project MUSE.

Doble, Jessica. 2018. 'Hope in the Apocalypse: Narrative Perspective as Negotiation of Structural Crises in *Salvage the Bones*'. *Xavier Review* 38 (2): 51–62.

Dungy, Camille T. 2009. 'Introduction: The Nature of African American Poetry'. In *Black Nature: Four Centuries of African American Nature Poetry*, edited by Camille T. Dungy, xix–xxxv. Athens: University of Georgia Press.

Dyson, Michael Eric. 2006. *Come Hell or High Water: Hurricane Katrina and the Color of Disaster*. New York: Basic Civitas Books.

Levitt, Jeremy I. and Matthew C. Whitaker, eds. 2009. *Hurricane Katrina: America's Unnatural Disaster*. Lincoln: University of Nebraska Press.

Lloyd, Christopher. 2016. 'Creaturely, Throwaway Life after Katrina: *Salvage the Bones* and *Beasts of the Southern Wild*'. *South: A Scholarly Journal* 48, no. 2 (Spring): 246–64. Project MUSE. DOI: 10.1353/slj.2016.0022.

Mitchell, Keith. 2018. '"Bodies Tell Stories": Between the Human and the Animal in *Salvage the Bones*'. *Xavier Review* 38 (2): 62–84.

Morgenstern, Naomi. 2020. 'Maternal Sovereignty: Destruction and Survival in Jesmyn Ward's *Salvage the Bones*'. In *Reading Contemporary Black British and African American Women Writers: Race, Ethics, Narrative Form*, edited by Jean Wyatt and Sheldon George, 104–21. New York: Routledge.

Moynihan, Sinéad. 2015. 'From Disposability to Recycling: William Faulkner and the New Politics of Rewriting in Jesmyn Ward's *Salvage the Bones*'. *Studies in the Novel* 47, no. 4 (Winter): 550–67. Project MUSE. DOI:10.1353/sdn.2015.0048.

Nixon, Rob. 2013. *Slow Violence and the Environmentalism of the Poor*. Cambridge, MA: Harvard University Press.

Railsback, Brian. 2018. 'Somewhere Over Emerson's Rainbow: Jesmyn Ward's Terrifying Environmental Vision'. *Xavier Review* 38 (2): 62–85.

Ruffin, Kimberly N. 2010. *Black on Earth: African American Ecoliterary Traditions*. Athens: University of Georgia Press.

Ward, Jesmyn. 2011. *Salvage the Bones*. London: Bloomsbury.

Chapter 8

The Weather and the Wake: Maternal Embodiment and Peril in Jesmyn Ward's *Salvage the Bones*

Zsuzsanna Lénárt-Muszka

Our eyes were scattered among T.V. images of So many poor, who without cars clung to interstate ramps like buoys young mothers starving stole diapers and bottles of baby food

Our families spread as ashes to the wind after cremation Our brothers our sisters our aunts our uncles our mothers our fathers lost

Stranded like slaves in the Middle Passages Pressed like sardines, in the Super Dome, cargo like on slave ships.

(Salloy quoted in Barajas)[1]

Jesmyn Ward's (1977–) second novel, *Salvage the Bones* (2011), recipient of the 2011 National Book Award for Fiction and the 2012 Alex Award, has been hailed as an exceptional fictional account of the 2005 Hurricane Katrina (Hartnell 2016, 206) and has helped solidify Ward's position as an eminent author of the American South. The reason the novel has sparked diverse responses is a testament to the potency of its subject matter: depictions of a Black family living in deep poverty during a national tragedy has captured the interest of the general readership and academia alike. *Salvage the Bones* traces the Batiste family's experiences with Hurricane Katrina in the fictional coastal town of Bois Sauvage, Mississippi. Four children – Esch and her brothers, Junior, Skeetah and Randall – live with their alcoholic father on an isolated plot of land called the Pit. As they anticipate Katrina, Esch realises she is pregnant by Manny, a local boy who only shows sexual interest in her; after the hurricane makes landfall and the family survives, Esch affirms her pregnancy. Since the Batistes already live in poverty and isolation, the novel allows for the potent illustration of how Katrina exposed racism, but the focus is not on the oft-criticised state and federal response to the natural disaster and its aftermath; rather, *Salvage* zooms in on the newly pregnant narrator. Following Katrina, the literal meaning of the wake (of the hurricane) intersects with its metaphorical meaning as understood by Afropessimist and Black feminist theoretician Christina Sharpe. The wake, as understood by Sharpe, is a multifaceted post-traumatic state in which the Black individual cannot be free of slavery's afterlife (Sharpe 2016, 8), that is, in *Salvage*, the acute, tangible danger of the hurricane is imposed on the chronic, quotidian state of being a Black (pregnant) girl in an already poverty-stricken region. The weather, as used metaphorically by Sharpe, refers to the unceasing, normalised and pervasive climate of anti-Back racism (2016, 90), which Katrina, a literal weather event, both exposes and exacerbates. Weathering is also present in the sense that is used by Arline Geronimus: the gradual harm to the protagonist's body, caused by years of inadequate nutrition, healthcare and stress – a harm that predominantly affects young Black mothers (Geronimus 1992, 207). The novel thus juxtaposes the literal and metaphorical meanings of (the) weather(ing) and examines the interlocking effects of both short- and long-term, psychic and corporeal, natural and social, catastrophes.

The following chapter demonstrates that while Esch's pregnancy is a significant plot line, it is decentred through the novel's narrative design; instead, several other mother figures are foregrounded and utilised as catalysts that foster Esch's understanding of her motherhood on the one hand, and throw into sharp relief her position as a single, poor, Black teenager in a masculinised environment on the other. Through the examination of the kaleidoscope of maternal figures that Esch merely sees the fragments of, I argue that she copes with the weather – in both its meanings – through fixating on several mothers but cannot escape the degendering and dehumanising aspects of being in that weather.

Literal and Figurative Mothers

Esch's mother dies shortly after giving birth to Junior seven years before the main events of the plot; however, her absence is felt continuously and her memory lingers. Not only do smells, situations, objects and physical touch trigger Esch to remember her, but since Mama was a centripetal figure in the family, Esch is also reminded of her care by the dilapidation of the house. Mama facilitated changes around the home by either fixing what was broken or initiating small projects that increased the comfort of the house. After her death,

Randall – the oldest brother – and Esch care for the newborn and do most of the housework. The mother's death not only upends the existing family structure and thrusts two young teenagers into parenting roles, but it results in the yard and house getting less and less comfortable and even habitable, while the fact that the dirty sheets make their skin itch evokes the lack of bodily comfort of the children as well. The sudden trauma of her death leaves a wake that is destructive not only in its immediate effects but accelerates the weathering of the family members and their surroundings.

Even though she is mostly remembered for her acts of care, the circumstances of her death also inform not only Esch's life as a daughter but her sense of self as an expectant mother. Esch witnesses her giving birth to Junior at home, and her agony lives on vividly in Esch's imagination. The way she visualises the process of giving birth and being born suggests that she conceptualises it as an inherently violent, traumatising event: she believes that the baby '[grabbed] hold of what he caught on to try to stay inside [the mother], but instead he pulled it out with him when he was born' (Ward 2011, 4). Experiencing the mother's absence and witnessing her suffering are compounded by the knowledge that Esch's grandmother, Mother Lizbeth, gave birth to eight children, all of whom died before their time, Esch's mother being the last one to pass away in her early thirties. The ambiguous structure, 'Mama, the only baby still living out of the eight that Mother Lizbeth had borne, died when having Junior' (Ward 2011, 14), does not clarify when her aunts or uncles died, but her use of the word 'baby' implies that the children died young. Losing her grandmother, then her own mother, and having hazy memories of them thus tie loss and suffering to motherhood in Esch's imagination.

Despite Mama's constant presence through the memories of Esch, there is a slippage of stable meaning associated with her as well. Mama often told the children to 'stop being orner' [*sic*] (Ward 2011, 25), and Esch upholds this practice and thus steps into the role of her mother by often repeating this to Junior without understanding that her mother meant 'ornery'. There is a discrepancy in how Esch remembers the details of Junior's birth: either Mama 'never screamed' (2011, 221) or she 'screamed toward the end' (2011, 1). She watches as her father drags her mother out to the truck to take her to the hospital and sees the trail of blood she leaves behind. Before they drive away, the mother maintains eye contact with her children and shakes her head, which Esch, at the intersection of being a daughter and a mother herself, struggles to interpret: 'Maybe that meant *no*. Or *Don't worry – I'm coming back*. Or *I'm sorry*. Or *Don't do it. Don't become the woman in this bed, Esch*, she could have been saying. But I have' (2011, 222, emphasis original). Skeetah recalls these events differently and believes the mother said goodbye to them (2011, 222). On the one hand, the siblings' differing versions attest to them being heavily traumatised by the sight of their dying mother. On the other hand, misunderstandings and misremembering stand in stark contrast with Esch's imperative to salvage her mother's legacy, underlining the impact of her mother's memory – and especially the fragmented nature of that memory – on Esch's motherhood.

While Randall and Esch emerge as Junior's primary caretakers, Skeetah finds another preoccupation and becomes a quasi-parent to his pitbull, China. Esch often perceives Skeetah and China's relationship as almost romantic when China only has eyes for Skeetah (2011, 2) and is like his woman (2011, 3). They even seem like equals to Esch: he sleeps curled up next to the dog on the shed floor in anticipation of the puppies' birth (2011, 3), and the intimacy between them leads Esch to conclude that when Skeetah and China look into each other's eyes, he looks like a dog (2011, 193). Esch maps a loving father-daughter dynamic onto Skeetah and China (2011, 98), but since Skeetah goes to great lengths to secure China's food, medicine and a safe living environment, he fulfils a traditional maternal role as well. His gentleness also reminds Esch of their mother: 'He wakes China like Mama used to wake us' (2011, 115). He endangers his health and even his life in order to steal medicine for the dog from a white family, and spends all his money to buy her quality dog food while the family starves. Again, these acts of care and sacrifice align him with the gendered selflessness traditionally imputed (or rather, prescribed) to mothers, so much so that he has been identified as a quasi-maternal figure (Keith 2012).

However, Skeetah's affection towards China is rooted in valuing her not as an equal partner or a beloved child – as Esch's descriptions would suggest – but as a tool that serves Skeetah's interests. While claiming to cherish her, he facilitates dogfights that endanger China's health and life, yanks her chain repeatedly, and forces her to walk and exercise when she can barely stand up (Ward 2011, 87), all supposedly for China's benefit. Skeetah forcing China to exercise can be interpreted as a desperate and loving attempt to help her recover: he accidentally gives her too much medicine, and he insists that China walk because he wants to make sure she recuperates. Nonetheless, dragging her, yanking her chain and forcing her to jog for miles in the heat seems excessive and less than compassionate to the onlookers (2011, 118). The pattern typical of his controlling behaviour is reminiscent of an abusive partnership, in which affection is deployed strategically: when coaxing her to fight viciously, Skeetah rubs her lovingly and whispers to her gently (2011, 171). Their dyad also mirrors an abusive parent-child dynamic in which the parent enjoys vicariously the praise given to the child. The qualities of China that Esch often refers to (her whiteness, cleanliness and strength) contrast with the decay in and around the house, which suggests that what Skeetah values about her is her being out of the ordinary: he finds it appealing that she stands out from her environment, making him feel special in turn. Her oft-referenced whiteness also alludes to the colour of cocaine – an expensive and rare commodity (Mitchell 2018, 72) – and to white skin colour (Clark 2015, 356). Esch also likens it to the whiteness of magnolias, a symbol of white Southern culture (Ward 2011, 94). These allusions attest to China's status as a rare and valuable possession, and reinforce that she is prized because she stands out from her bleak natural and social surroundings. Having a well-fed, healthy dog is rare and thus a status symbol in the community; having China fight and win confers an even greater value upon Skeetah too, giving him a chance at possessing something almost luxurious that makes him feel like he can transcend their condition.

While critics tend to sidestep the problematisation of Skeetah's relationship to China,[2] Esch sees and narrates the way he relates to the dog, which ultimately informs Esch's understanding of her own impending motherhood. While she is reassured by Skeetah saying that motherhood gives dogs (and thus women) strength to fight (Ward 2011, 96) instead of making them weaker, she witnesses him cruelly fighting the dog a week after she whelps. Although Esch does not reflect on China being analogous to an enslaved woman, a subtle parallel is certainly hinted at it in the text. Not only is China deemed more valuable as a mother, Skeetah even calls himself a breeder (2011, 21). This phrase evokes the practice of breeding, the enforced impregnation of Black women with the goal of increasing capital prevalent in the South during slavery; Skeetah certainly stands to gain money not only from China but from the sale of the puppies as well. While some of his behaviours (such as sleeping curled up next to China) align him with animality, by decrying that he is a breeder he distances himself from the animal and asserts his dominance over her. The moment China deviates from what is expected from her by refusing to feed one of her puppies, Skeetah lashes out at her by hissing 'you bitch!' (2011, 40). His sudden burst of anger might stem from seeing a mother reject her child, which evokes the painful absence of their deceased mother, but it certainly reveals that his relationship to China is far from the idealised symbiosis critics suggest. Esch sees China being respected on the surface but being bred, used for profit and insulted with a female-specific word at the same time, which unwittingly perpetuates her lack of self-worth.

Independently of Skeetah, China also influences Esch's maternal identification process. In a crucial scene, Esch witnesses the birth of the puppies, which is described in mythical terms: Esch watches the seemingly supernatural forces that move China's body during this intense, physical event. Evident in her using the register of natural disasters or a violent confrontation, she conceptualises the birth as an awe-inspiring yet threatening, primal experience: 'Her sides ripple. She snarls, her mouth a black line. Her eyes are red; the mucus runs pink. Everything about China tenses and there are a million marbles under her skin, and then she appears to be turning herself inside out. At her opening, I see a purplish red bulb. China is blooming' (2011, 4), mirroring the image of the hydrangea that the newborn Junior re-sembles (2011, 2). The integrity of China's body is undone and her agency taken away when her skin ripples and her body moves as if due to a divine intervention (2011, 8) or 'like she has caught the ghost, like the holiest voice moves through her' (2011, 6). Through the death of Esch's mother and China's suffering, labour thus takes on a destructive quality. China is also likened to Medea owing to her strength and because she kills one of her puppies, further reinforcing the link between wrath and motherhood.

Another maternal figure that has an impact on Esch's nascent ma-ternal identification is the mythical figure of Medea. While she has personal experience with and memories of her mother, and observes the most powerful, embodied event of China as a mother, she only reads about Medea as a school assignment, resulting in a heavily mediated knowledge that nevertheless has a profound impact on her. The assigned reading, Edith Hamilton's *Mythology* (1942) makes it clear that there are different versions of the myth, and Medea is more cruel and ruthless in one version (Ward 2011, 154), confronting Esch with a multiplicity of meanings and truths. The instability of Medea's and her own mother's stories mirror Esch's insecurity about becom-ing a mother, thus leaving her in a liminal space, without any stable point of reference. By identifying Medea as Greek and thus effacing her being a barbarian – that is, a member of a minority group – Esch marginalises Medea's ethnicity (Stevens 2018, 163). Medea's outsider status could provide Esch with another point of identifica-tion, but the facet that captures her imagination the most is Medea's passion for Jason: as she grapples with her desire for Manny, she understands the mythical figure's anger. However, as Stevens points out, by not turning against her own foetus, she does not emulate Medea's violence when it comes to motherhood (Stevens 2018, 159). The only incident in which she does follow Medea's example is when she lashes out at Manny, but their short physical confrontation is but a desperate attempt to take charge of her situation: it ends with Manny walking away. The main function of the multiple references to the mythical story is thus to illustrate Esch's repressed intensity and lack of choices: while she marvels at Medea's resourcefulness and fury, she herself is trapped in an environment that restricts her agency.

As the family prepares for, lives through and ultimately survives Katrina, Esch wonders about the hurricane's maternal qualities. As she experienced an earlier hurricane with her mother and heard stories of one that happened decades earlier, she connects hurricanes and motherhood, but Katrina takes on highly metaphorical meanings as well. After Esch sees her mother and China in labour and reads about Medea, notions of force and devastation are enmeshed in her perception of mothers. The hurricane figures not only as a mother – 'Katrina is the mother we will remember until the next mother . . . comes' (Ward 2011, 255) – but as birth itself, or as a force that facilitates birth. It is a transformative event not only because it is a life-threatening experience that almost destroys – or, at the very least, reorganizes – the family's and the community's living environment, but because it rearranges the family dynamic as well: as they are fighting for survival in the raging storm, Skeetah tells their father that Esch is pregnant. Katrina is thus a liminal, coming-of-age experience that uproots Esch's circumstances and thrusts her into motherhood, that is, it gives birth to Esch as a mother.

Katrina's power is conceptualised as bordering on the divine, elucidated by the metaphors of hands and grip. The first epigraph of the novel – 'See now that I, even I am he, and there is no god with me; I kill and I make alive, I wound and I heal, neither is there any can deliver out of my hand' (King James Bible, Deuteronomy 32: 39) – evokes the Old Testament image of a God capable of vengeance and healing. The image of God's hand is mobilised to provide a contrast with Esch's powerlessness. Human hands, when not used for an instrumental purpose in preparation for the hurricane, are either tender or steady in the novel: Big Henry's big hands and touch epitomise his reassuring presence (Ward 2011, 255), Skeetah's hands pet China, Mama's touch the children lovingly, and Randall's hold Junior firmly and dribble the basketball masterfully. In contrast, the father's hands are unsteady and vulnerable to injury, as the ironically named chapter 'A Steady Hand' evinces. Similarly, Esch's grip is posited as weak: her hands are injured, then unable to hold onto a tree branch and the bucket sheltering the puppies during the hurricane. She refers to Katrina's hand multiple times,[3] aligning it with that of God, both being mighty and destructive. Using another biblical reference, she asks in the eye of the hurricane, 'Who will deliver me?', quoting apostle Paul's rhetorical question ('Who will deliver me from this body of death?') in Romans 7: 24 that references God's mercy. Paul's question is answered definitively in the following verse, not quoted in the novel: he believes that Jesus will save him. Esch does not have the luxury of such hope but still emerges from Katrina's destruction with a renewed sense of vitality, saying that the hurricane leaves the survivors as 'newborn babies', 'puppies' and 'baby snakes' (Ward 2011, 255). She is endangered and salvaged by Katrina and by motherhood as well as by the members of her family. First, Claude pushes her into the water upon finding out about the pregnancy, that is, it is an angry *father* who puts her life at risk, recalling the 'I wound' of the epigraph. Then, instead of a divine intervention, Skeetah lends her a hand, prioritising his family over his dog (2011, 235). The twin images of life and death in both the Bible and the Katrina-related passages of *Salvage* thus conflate a divine power and a natural force in order to highlight Esch's initial powerlessness and nascent sense of agency.

Juxtaposed to the maternal figures of Mama, Skeetah, China, Medea and Katrina, Esch is the primary mother character in the novel. Her pregnancy progresses alongside the changes in the weather: as the wind gets stronger, her belly grows and she considers her options. The family's attempts to prepare for a hurricane mirror Esch's struggle to cope with the changes in her body. Their father, Claude, who is otherwise depicted as a less-than-pragmatic, less-than-capable parent, makes rational decisions in anticipation of Katrina, but their financial situation does not allow for proper preparations. Esch's plight is even more critical. While the slats are misaligned, the window is at least boarded up, and while their food stack lacks variety and nutritional value, at least they have enough food for a few days. Esch, however, finds that her 'options narrow to none' (2011, 103) as a Black, teenage mother in a poverty- and disaster-stricken, rural, Southern environment, without a supportive partner or financial means. While the novel depicts various mother figures' caring or fierce behaviour, it does not evade another facet of womanhood in rural Mississippi: the lack of access to reproductive healthcare. After his accident, Claude is taken to the hospital where he is given antibiotics, that is, emergency healthcare is not altogether unavailable to those in Bois Sauvage, but quality reproductive care seems to be elusive.[4]

Esch does not clarify the reason why 'Mama didn't want to go to the hospital' when Junior was born (Ward 2011, 2), nor does she elaborate on the price of healthcare and Black women's history of medical mistreatment, but she experiences the lack of resources available to her as a poor, young, Southern Black girl. While she risks her own life to steal medicine for China and knows that Skeetah spends a disproportionate amount of money on the dog's well-being, her reproductive health suffers because of the inadequate quantity and quality of food the Batistes have access to even before she gets pregnant: her menses are often irregular because she chooses to starve, overeating ramen and potatoes all the time (30). This effect of weathering is the very reason she is slow to realise she is pregnant; when she does, she has to steal a pregnancy test, in an act reminiscent of the siblings' scavenging for food or medicine (2011, 30). Considering dangerous ways to induce a miscarriage and being aware of her lack of options and limited agency, she muses:

> The girls [at school] say that if you're pregnant and you take a month's worth of birth control pills, it will make your period come on. . . . Only thing I wouldn't be able to find is the birth control pills; I've never had a prescription, wouldn't have money to get them if I did, don't have any girlfriends to ask for some, and have never been to the Health Department. Who would bring me? . . . These are my options, and they narrow to none. (Ward 2011, 102–3)

This passage also reveals the gaps in Esch's knowledge: she is withheld crucial information regarding birth control. Sexual education was not mandated in Mississippi in 2005, and if a school chose to incorporate it, state legislation required that emphasis be put on abstinence as the primary form of birth control (Moore 2014, 7). The institutionalised reproductive racism directed at Black women is thus represented in an oblique way, its presence seen through its absence: the reader never sees how Esch directly interacts with these systems simply because she receives no relevant education and has no means of even going to a clinic.

Without access to legal and affordable abortion or even healthcare, the process of pregnancy cannot be stopped, that is, there is a parallel between the weather's ruthlessness and her body's changes. As the storm approaches, her body's signals become more unambiguous as well: her frequent need to urinate and vomit reminds her of the pregnancy even when she tries to forget about it (Ward 2011, 78). In anticipation of Katrina, she says, '*Tomorrow*, I think, *everything will be washed clean*. What I carry in my stomach is relentless; like each unbearable day, it will dawn' (2011, 205, emphasis original), likening her pregnancy not only to the cycles of nature, but to the force of the impending storm as well. Water functions 'as a multivalent, organizing symbolic principle' (Mitchell 2018, 75): Esch also draws a parallel between amniotic fluid and rainwater when she listens to 'the watery swish of Junior inside' their mother's stomach during a hurricane (Ward 2011, 217). The association between water and birth is further reinforced when Esch says that Junior is the mother's last flower: a hydrangea (2011, 2). Nature, along with the Batistes' human-made environment, is depicted as unforgiving and less than habitable even before Katrina makes landfall. Even though being outside is favourable to being in the unbearably hot and dark, boarded-up house, there are frequent references to the unrelenting heat that exacerbates Esch's nausea. References to noises over which Esch has no control function similarly: rhythmic, unceasing hammering, hiccupping or barking contribute to this atmosphere of imminent danger. They make Esch's discomfort emphatic and highlight the parallel between the immutable nature of both her pregnancy and her environment.

Destabilising and Decentring Esch as a Woman

Through associating Mama with gentleness and remembering her dancing sensually with Claude, Esch posits her as a woman – a status not afforded to herself. While not only the mother, but even the hurricane and the dogs are gendered female, Esch is not. She wears the clothes handed down by her brothers (Ward 2011, 88), she thinks that her father often forgets that she is a girl (103), and instead of interacting with her peers – Black girls who live a few miles from the Pit – she watches them from afar. It is especially Manny's girlfriend, Shaliyah, who behaves and looks in accordance with feminine gender codes: she wears jewellery, a miniskirt, sits with her legs crossed, while Esch 'sit[s] ungracefully in the grass' (Ward 2011, 118). To Esch, Shaliyah's self-presentation looks sophisticated, just like Medea's grace: she yearns to be 'tall as Medea, wearing purple and green robes, bones and gold for jewelry' (2011, 170), but all she is left with is trying to rub Vaseline on her lips to make them glossy while being unsatisfied with her looks (2011, 137). In her chapter in this volume, Melanie Petch argues that her mother's early death impacted Esch's sense of self and self-presentation as 'Had her mother been alive, clothing might have been presented to her . . . from a female wardrobe rather than her brothers' hand-me-downs', which could have influenced how she relates to her looks (p. 157). Indeed, Shaliyah being a Black teenage girl living quite close to the Batistes implies that it is not only Esch's race, gender, age or isolation that foreclose the possibility of being feminine for her; rather, it is her poverty, masculinised community and the lack of female role models in her formative years.

The gender roles within the family are also problematised. The Batistes are presented as being outside of the traditional, heteronormative, nuclear family norm, but they diverge from those female-centred, often rhizomatically organised structures that are prevalent in African American literature. Instead of relying on the trope of the absentee father and a single mother, *Salvage the Bones* centres a diffuse family. The father is often present but absent at the same time, exhibiting a 'hands-off', neglectful approach to parenting (Moynihan 2015, 558). Randall and Skeetah are somewhat outside of the bounds of normative gender codes owing to their function as caretakers of Junior and China, respectively. Critics usually conclude that an alternative community forms around Esch, but specifically, it is a community made up of boys and men: even Big Henry, the only person outside the family who offers help to Esch and reassures her that 'this baby got plenty daddies' (Ward 2011, 255), is a man. This figuration is already non-normative, and caring for and raising a child without a partner will eventually force Esch to accept and seek alternative, queered[5] forms of relationality. These forms could provide her with much more affection and material help than the frequent failure and dysfunction of the traditional family unit as well as her own disrupted family. Nevertheless, her present and possible future community is predominantly a masculine one.

The way Esch relates to sexuality is illustrative of her feelings of insignificance in this specific social environment. She has had multiple sexual partners since the age of twelve, but she is often a reluctant participant (Ward 2011, 22–3). Regarding the advances made towards her by various local boys, she says that it is less complicated to 'take it' than having to explain why she does not want it (2011, 23). Her wish to avoid potential nagging questions anticipates the verbal or even physical violence the rejected male partner would resort to. The comparison she draws between sex and swimming – an activity she otherwise finds effortless and calming – might suggest that she finds enjoyment in the brief encounters, but her pleasure is certainly fleeting. Claude teaches the children to swim by throwing them into the water – another episode in their childhood that elucidates his parenting philosophy partly borne out of the need to force the children to adapt to their harsh circumstances – and Esch thrives in the water: 'I'd taken to it fast, hadn't coughed up the muddy pit water, hadn't cried or flailed . . . I'd pulled the water with my hands, kicked it with my feet, let it push me forward. That was sex' (Ward 2011, 23–4). Thus, the primary factor that sexuality and swimming have in common is not unqualified joy but a sense of effortlessness that results in feelings of temporary competence. Esch looks for the same ease but, without a partner who respects her desires and boundaries, fails to find it. She seeks out these experiences to feel like a girl at least temporarily (Green 2018, 133) – that is, to feel gendered at least to some extent. Her sexual behaviour, then, is a cry for help and attests to her lack of self-confidence, self-respect and agency, which in turn stem from her young age and, above all, the male-centred sexual culture prevalent in the community.

Not only is Esch de- or misgendered, but she is decentred as well: the above delineated images of animals as well as her sexual behaviour speak to her view of herself as an insignificant, marginal character in her own life. The narration confirms this as well: even though she is observant and sensitive, she barely speaks a few lines. The second epigraph of the novel ('For though I'm small, I know many things/ And my body is an endless eye/ Through which, unfortunately, I see everything'), taken from the English translation of a Gloria Fuertes poem, is an apt and compact illustration of this theme. The lyrical I informs the reader that she has observed how worms transform into butterflies 'because insects possess a bit of magic' (Fuertes 2005), then she reveals that 'Eloisa Muro/fourth mistress of Cervantes,/ was the author of Don Quixote.' The epigraph sutures the images of insects, gender and the hurricane ('an endless eye') to allude to Esch's internalised insignificance and her being in a position of an almost detached observer of her surroundings ('I'm small', 'I see everything') who, like Eloisa Muro, both is and is not the author of a narrative. She narrates everyone else's story except her own: different animals, nature, the weather, their own and their grandparents' house, and the Pit are described in detail and even humanised. Her perspective might be central (Doble 2018, 58), but she herself is not. The tension between Esch being the eloquent, poetic narrator and her invisibility highlights that she marginalises herself even further because her own insignificance is ingrained in her. She is not only invisible to mainstream society, but is on the periphery of her own family and community; as she says, 'where my brothers go, I follow' (Ward 2011, 53). As 'she resides between her mother's death and her own life' (Green 2018, 132) and thus occupies an interstitial position between being a daughter and a mother, she hopes motherhood would bestow her with agency, and indeed, this happens to an extent: she undergoes a minor transformation. In demanding Manny to look her in the eye during sex, Esch finally expresses her need to be seen as a partner; tellingly, however, Manny panics and leaves her alone after realising she is pregnant (Ward 2011, 146). Slowly, her voice begins to sound more confident; as she asserts, bringing back the image of a hand: 'I'm surprised at how clear my voice is, how solid, how sure, like a hand that can be held in the dark' (2011, 229). This comparison, in accordance with all the previous mentions of touch, suggests that both the impending catastrophe and motherhood allow her to have a grip suitable for both gentle and steady touch. The last four words of the novel – 'I am a mother' (2011, 258) – suggest that she is beginning to transcend her marginalised condition by attempting to *hold on* to the heavily limited agency afforded to her.

The third epigraph and its extended context, however, thematise the limits of Esch's 'grip'. Following the biblical quote emphasising God's authority and the Fuertes quote centring someone 'small' in awe of the unavoidable, the third one connects these perspectives by specifically alluding to Esch's predicament as a Black teenage mother. The lines 'We on our backs staring at the stars above,/ Talking about what we going to be when we grow up,/ I said what you wanna be? She said, 'Alive'' are taken from the song 'Da Art of Storytellin' (Part I)' by the Black Southern – Georgian – hip-hop duo OutKast, thus, this epigraph puts forward the contemporary and somewhat regional, culturally specific literary realm. The full lyrics relate the stories of two young women, one of them being an abused, pregnant drug addict who dies of overdose. Years after she speaks the quoted line, 'she got found in the back of a school/ With a needle in her arm, baby two months due' (OutKast, 'Da Art (Part I)'). The extended lyrics thus reference not only the vulnerability of Black youth in general, but the defencelessness of Black girls and young mothers in particular. The next song on the album, 'Da Art of Storytellin' (Part II)', though not referenced in the epigraphs, chronicles an apocalyptic storm the victims of which scramble to salvage what they can while likening the abused Earth to the female body selfishly used for sex, which echoes Esch's sexual practices, and, of course, Katrina.

The focal images of the epigraphs thus illuminate the intertwining of the mythological, the intimately personal, and the cultural layers, as well as the interplay of the micro and macro lenses the novel employs, thus allowing not only for heightening the aesthetic effect achieved in *Salvage*, but illustrating the ambiguity of the seemingly triumphant and positive ending: even though the Batistes survive – which is a feat at a time when hundreds of people of colour died because of Katrina – they still remain in a precarious position.

Esch affirming the pregnancy offers some comfort to the reader and to Esch, but, as Annie Bares argues, Ward's ethos of narrative ruthlessness precludes the possibility of a truly satisfying narrative resolution insofar as the narrative leaves open the question of how the Bois Sauvage community will be able to deal with the fallout of the hurricane (Bares 2019, 36). Esch finds some reassurance at the end of the novel when she claims that China, who has been carried away by the water, will come back and know that Esch has indeed become a mother, a fighter (Ward 2011, 258), but her fantasy of impressing China again misplaces *her* and centres a figure of reference outside of herself. Without a maternal figure with whom Esch can fully identify and who can guide her through the process, she is desperate to align herself with a mythical character, a dog and a weather event. Nevertheless, the maternal narratives she turns to are comforting but carry a lot of pain at the same time (see Leah Van Dyk's chapter in this volume, p. 95). The mythical and the down-to-earth intersect in the novel: Esch scavenges for food and witnesses China give birth, which is set against the constant presence of memories and Medea's story. Tangible and intangible maternal models meet and are superimposed on each other, relegating Esch's own experiences to the margins. The ambivalence regarding the mother's last words, the tension between the various extant versions of Medea's story, and China's muteness throw into relief the unknowability of the past and the 'truth', while the unfoundedly optimistic belief in China's return highlights the similar instability of the future. These are rendered unavailable, impossible to reconstruct or access, further stressing the epistemological uncertainty that compounds the existential precarity that Esch as a young mother is forced to navigate. The volatility of the weather is also foregrounded: the literal sense of weather, through the impending hurricane, intersects with its metaphorical meanings through the debilitating, weathering effects of the racist social climate that consigns the Batistes to the Pit.

We briefly see Esch again in Ward's 2017 novel *Sing, Unburied, Sing* – set after the events of *Salvage the Bones* – as someone perceived by the narrator to be 'lucky' to have all her brothers

(Ward 2017, 135), and we know that Big Henry attempts to reassure her by promising that 'this baby got plenty daddies' (Ward 2011, 255). All this, together with Esch's ease of identification with motherhood – 'I am a mother' (2011, 258) – points to an undeniable note of optimism in *Salvage*. I would still argue, however, that the wake of the hurricane, the wake of slavery and the eventual wake of the pregnancy coalesce to produce a uniquely vulnerable position for Esch and her baby: the demands of living in the Pit will soon be compounded by having to cope with the short- and long-term aftermath of a destructive weather event and the challenges of caring for a new life, thereby calling into question the restorative potential of Esch's decision to affirm her pregnancy.

Notes

1. An excerpt from 'Remembering that Katrina time & New Orleans' by Black poet Mona Lisa Saloy.
2. With the exception of Keith Mitchell: instead of foregrounding Skeetah and China's relationship in terms of a familial parent-daughter one, he argues that they exhibit a typical male-female dynamic of mistreatment (Mitchell 2018, 69).
3. For example, 'the arriving storm has put a strangling hand over the house' (Ward 2011, 218), 'the hurricane enfolds me in its hand' (2011, 232), 'my head bobs above the water but the hand of the hurricane pushes it down, down again' (2011, 235) and 'Katrina is the mother we will remember until the next mother with large, merciless hands, committed to blood, comes' (2011, 255).
4. On the inadequate quality and quantity of prenatal care given to Black women in Mississippi, see Cox et al.
5. I use the term queered to refer to Alexis Gumbs's formulation of non-heteronormative, non-patriarchal family structures (Gumbs 2010, 191).

Works Cited

Barajas, Joshua. 2020. 'How Poetry Helped These Hurricane Survivors Weather the Aftermath'. *PBS*, 1 September. https://www.pbs.org/newshour/arts/after-katrina-poets-wrote-our-trauma-until-it-was-numb.

Bares, Annie. 2019. '"Each Unbearable Day": Narrative Ruthlessness and Environmental and Reproductive Injustice in Jesmyn Ward's *Salvage the Bones*'. *MELUS* 44 (3): 21–40. Project MUSE.

Clark, Christopher. 2015. 'What Comes to the Surface: Storms, Bodies and Community in Jesmyn Ward's *Salvage the Bones*'. *The Mississippi Quarterly* 68 (3–4): 341–58. https://www.jstor.org/stable/10.2307/26468035.

Cox, Reagan G., et al. 2009. 'Prenatal Care Utilization in Mississippi: Racial Disparities and Implications for Unfavorable Birth Outcomes'. *Maternal and Child Health Journal* 15 (7): 931–42. doi.org/10.1007/s10995-009-0542-6.

Doble, Jessica. 2018. 'Hope in the Apocalypse: Narrative Perspective as Negotiation of Structural Crises in *Salvage the Bones*'. *Xavier Review* 38 (2): 51–62. https://issuu.com/xavierreviewpress/docs/xr382-final02-text.

Fuertes, Gloria. 2005. 'Now', translated by Brian Barker. *Words without Borders*. https://www.wordswithoutborders.org/article/now.

Geronimus, Arline. T. 1992. 'The Weathering Hypothesis and the Health of African-American Women and Infants: Evidence and Speculations'. *Ethnicity and Disease* 2 (3): 207–21.

Green, Tara T. 2018. *Reimagining the Middle Passage: Black Resistance in Literature, Television, and Song*. Columbus: Ohio State University Press.

Gumbs, Alexis Pauline. 2010. *We Can Learn to Mother Ourselves: The Queer Survival of Black Feminism 1968–1996*. PhD diss. Durham, NC: Duke University Press.

Hartnell, Anna. 2016. 'When Cars Become Churches: Jesmyn Ward's Disenchanted America. An Interview'. *Journal of American Studies* 50 (1): 205–18. https://doi.org/10.1017/S0021875815001966.

Keith, Rebecca. 2012. 'Jesmyn Ward by Rebecca Keith'. *Bomb Magazine*, 21 March. https://bombmagazine.org/articles/jesmyn-ward/.

Mitchell, Keith. 2018. '"Bodies Tell Stories": Between the Human and the Animal in *Salvage the Bones*'. *Xavier Review* 38 (1): 62–85. https://issuu.com/xavierreviewpress/docs/xr382-final02-text.

Moore, Elizabeth. 2014. *Sexuality Education in Mississippi: Progress in the Magnolia State*. Sexuality Information and Education Council of the US.

Moynihan, Sinéad. 2015. 'From Disposability to Recycling: William Faulkner and the New Politics of Rewriting in Jesmyn Ward's *Salvage the Bones*'. *Studies in the Novel* 47 (4): 550–67. Project MUSE.

OutKast. n.d. 'Da Art of Storytellin' (Part I)'. Lyrics. *Genius*. https://genius.com/Outkast-da-art-of-storytellin-pt-1-lyrics.

—. n.d. 'Da Art of Storytellin' (Part II)'. Lyrics. *Genius*. https://genius.com/Outkast-da-art-of-storytellin-pt-2-lyrics.

Sharpe, Christina. 2016. *In the Wake: On Blackness and Being*. Durham, NC: Duke University Press.

Stevens, Benjamin Eldon. 2018. 'Medea in Jesmyn Ward's *Salvage the Bones*'. *International Journal of the Classical Tradition* 25 (2): 158–77. https://doi.org/10.1007/s12138-016-0394-6.

Ward, Jesmyn. 2011. *Salvage the Bones*. London: Bloomsbury.

—. 2017. *Sing, Unburied, Sing*. New York: Scribner.

Chapter 9

'Something to save': Rewriting Black Teenage Motherhood in Jesmyn Ward's *Salvage the Bones*

Chiara Margiotta

Writing on Jesmyn Ward's *Salvage the Bones*, Sinéad Moynihan identifies the novel as an example of 'literary recycling', suggesting that Ward engages in a 'politically engaged model of rewriting' as a mode of resistance (Moynihan 2015, 551). While Moynihan focuses on Ward's relationship to the white canon, specifically William Faulkner's *As I Lay Dying*, this chapter adopts her model of recycling in order to consider the ways in which Ward's writing addresses a lineage of Black literary foremothers. The protagonist of *Salvage the Bones*, Esch, recalls a long line of pregnant Black girls, from Toni Morrison's Pecola in *The Bluest Eye* (1971) to Ursa in Gayl Jones's *Corregidora* (1975), Celie in Alice Walker's *The Color Purple* (1982) and Precious in Sapphire's *Push* (1996), and in each of these texts, recurring themes of troubled pregnancy and motherhood provide a fertile vein for the exploration of bodily and racial abjection. This chapter argues that Ward 'recycles' this motif: where, in these earlier texts, pregnancy has been traditionally marred by tragedy, Ward's work continually resists this narrative of Black teenage motherhood as necessarily destructive.[1] By refusing to dismiss Black teenage mothers as 'waste', she offers the potential of 'a redemptive horizon', while simultaneously remaining critically engaged with state neglect and abandonment (Moynihan 2015, 551; Hartnell 2016, 205–18). Expanding on the arguments set forth in Moynihan's article by applying them specifically to a tradition of Black women writers, this chapter looks to explore the ways in which Ward both draws upon this heritage and subverts it. Additionally, I will argue that the most notable aspect of Ward's rewriting is in her depiction of men: while the girls of these previous texts are isolated in their attempts to resist abjectification, Ward surrounds Esch with multiple Black men who support her demands for agency. By considering her work through the lens of abject theory, alongside contemporary criticism on race and class, this chapter investigates Ward's intertextual evolution of canonical Black women's writing, and positions her as a vital addition to this lineage.

Literary Recycling

Moynihan's theory of literary recycling is key to the framework of this argument, which focuses on literary tropes and ideas as forms of inheritance, handed down by literary forebears and then repurposed, or 'recycled', by later writers, such as Ward. In an essay which posits *Salvage the Bones* as a retelling of *As I Lay Dying*, Moynihan describes this process as 'a more politically engaged model of rewriting . . . a term with connotations of resolute social engagement and looking outward and forward, as opposed to the potentially solipsistic and retrospective textual worlds with which rewriting tends to be concerned' (Moynihan 2015, 551). Moynihan suggests that recycling is particularly relevant to works focused on those who are 'consign[ed] to the category of waste' by neoliberal discourses (Moynihan 2015, 551). Rooted in Henry Giroux's theory of 'the biopolitics of disposability', this sentiment asserts that Hurricane Katrina unveiled a 'systematic assault on the welfare state' by neoliberal policies, which sought to 'remove or make invisible those individuals and groups who are either seen as a drain' or who disrupt 'the neoconservative dream of an American empire' (Giroux 2006, 174–5). In this model, the neoliberal other – non-white, non-wealthy, non-'productive' – is positioned as disruptive to the neoconservative status quo, and so exiled to the borders of society. This framework recalls Imogen Tyler's conception of social abjection, a form of state-sanctioned social exclusion in which certain members of a society are figured as 'the border subjects of the neoliberal body politic – those whose lives are deemed worthless or expendable' (Tyler 2013, 10). This idea of being deemed worthless is repeated throughout the lineage of pregnancy narratives that, I argue, *Salvage the Bones* is in conversation with. In *The Color Purple*, when Albert tells Celie, 'You black, you pore, you ugly, you a woman. Goddam, he say, you nothing at all', he relegates her to the position of socially abject, where she is 'nothing' (Walker 2014, 205). In *Push*, Precious says she '[doesn't] exist': 'Don't nobody want me. Don't nobody need me. I know who I am. I know who they say I am – vampire sucking the system's blood. Ugly black grease to be wipe away, punish, kilt, changed, finded a job for'

(Sapphire 2021, 31). In *Corregidora*, Ursa speaks of her Great Gram as being 'sacrificed', and reflects on the ways female slaves had '*two alternatives, you either took one or you didn't. And if you didn't, you had to suffer the consequences of not taking it*', the alternatives being rape or death (Jones 2019, 69).

In this context, the poor Batiste family and especially Esch, who, as a Black teenage mother to be, is 'according to neoliberal logic . . . exemplary of a "mismanaged life,"' are defined as waste; or, in Esch's own words, 'human debris in the middle of all of the rest of it' (Moynihan 2015, 555; Ward 2012, 237). Esch, who describes herself as 'small, dark: invisible', can be understood as a manifestation of social abjection: poor, Black, female, young, and soon to be a teenage single mother, she is emblematic of a non-life, living outside the borders of neoliberal acceptance and order (Ward 2012, 28). Firstly, it is important to note that Moynihan's model does not support this othering of Black teenage motherhood, or arguments in which they are implied to be 'to blame for their own poverty', but rather, uses this theory to draw attention to the ways in which Ward subverts this notion of Black teenage mothers as 'waste' (Moynihan 2015, 556). Secondly, neither is this to say that the earlier novels condone the social abjectification of their protagonists, or agree with defining these girls as 'waste'. Rather, the key argument at hand here is that, while they are undoubtedly critical of this social position and utilise their work to depict the cruelty of such abjectification, their texts do not offer the same 'redemptive horizon' as Ward's (Hartnell 2016, 210). It is Ward's portrayal of hope, figured through positive depictions of kinship and community, that differentiates *Salvage the Bones*. This also supports the argument towards recycling, highlighting the ways in which Ward takes one aspect of the earlier texts – an honest, unyielding portrayal of social abjection and its resulting trauma – and transforms it into something with a new purpose. To unpack Moynihan's theory further, the language used frequently recalls abjection studies, particularly Tyler's contemporary theory of social abjection as well as Julia Kristeva's original theory of abjection – as that which exists within the liminal border-space between the Self and the Other, disturbing in its transgression of 'identity, system, order' (Kristeva 1982, 4). Moynihan defines recycling as an act in which 'an object is reused for a purpose different from its original function', however, she is clear that this need not be seen as a downgrading of the original function (Moynihan 2015, 564). Instead, she suggests, it offers a route towards developing the next object it is transformed into, citing the way in which Ward, by intertextually linking *As I Lay Dying* both explicitly and implicitly to *Salvage the Bones*, utilises Faulkner's literary and cultural capital as a vehicle to transport the Batistes – traditionally 'non-literary' subjects within the white canon – onto an equal stage. This notion can be strengthened by viewing it alongside abjection theory. There is a definite sense of disorder, an abject quality, in altering the original function of something, and yet it is difficult to see the transformative nature of recycling as anything other than positive. Recycling, then, can be seen to belong to the realm of the abject, as intrinsically tied to abjection as it is to waste and disorder, and yet its potential for transformation allows it to become a subversive act, one which accepts the abjection of a discarded object and transforms it into something with purpose.

However, this chapter posits that, despite the clear links to the white literary canon that Moynihan outlines, it is important to consider the ways in which Ward's work is also in intertextual conversation with seminal texts by Black women writers. While Moynihan's interest in the novel's connections to Faulkner are not pertinent to this chapter, her theory can also be used to analyse Ward's 'recycling' of the themes present in the work of her literary foremothers; namely, disrupted girlhood, abjectification, and pregnancy and motherhood. Pregnancy, as a theme, can be clearly seen as recycled: where it had been traditionally marred by tragedy – an unwanted hysterectomy in *Corregidora*, and repeated incestual abuse in *The Color Purple*, *Push* and *The Bluest Eye* – Esch's pregnancy is allocated space for positivity as well as concern. Particularly notable is the fact that although later rebuffed by Manny, her baby's father, Esch's pregnancy and sexual experience is the only one which involves her consent; in the other novels, it is forcibly denied to Ursa, and forced upon Celie, Precious and Pecola. Nevertheless, consent is still a key issue here. While the sex Esch has is consensual, her pregnancy cannot necessarily be defined as such. Considering the possibility of an at-home abortion, she notes 'one thing I wouldn't be able to find is the birth control pills; I've never had a prescription, wouldn't have money to get them if I did, don't have any girlfriends to ask for some, and have never been to the Health Department' (Ward 2012, 102). Ultimately, she concludes that her options 'narrow to none' (Ward 2012, 103). The pregnancy then, while not enforced (or denied) physically, as in the previous texts, is still enforced figuratively by forms of state-sanctioned neglect which leave girls like Esch without state-provided healthcare or financial aid to seek treatment. This issue is further highlighted through Esch's recollections of her mother, who died after giving birth at home. While Ward does not make this explicit, we can assume the 'choice' to give birth at home is due to the same narrow pool of options which deny Esch any choice regarding her pregnancy. By repeatedly calling attention to the ways in which poverty connects with state neglect and lack of healthcare access, Ward positions *Salvage the Bones* within the realm of current real-world issues affecting the kinds of people which the novel portrays. While this awareness makes it clear that Ward is hardly depicting Esch's circumstances as desirable, the way that the novel progresses, with Esch finding agency both within and in spite of her pregnancy and social position, is another indictment against arguments which would dismiss her as waste. As Moynihan argues, 'motherhood is put forth as an ambivalent and compromised form of power that combats the relegation of the maternal body to that of [discursive waste]' (Moynihan 2015, 561). While Ward utilises the trope of Black teenage pregnancy to draw attention to state abandonment, she also highlights the ways in which Esch's pregnancy helps her to find empowerment and agency, as I will go on to argue. Ward takes the trope, so regularly used to show the destruction wrought upon Black girls in the previous texts at hand, and repurposes it, showing how it can evolve beyond harm and be utilised as a tool of agency rather than ultimate depersonalisation.

The Act of Witnessing

The most important instance of recycling is found in Ward's reclamation of the act of witnessing, an idea which relates back to each of the four earlier texts. In *The Bluest Eye*, Pecola, who becomes mentally ill after becoming pregnant, is denied a witness: 'Every time I look at somebody, they look off' (Morrison 2014, 195). Claudia notes that the town 'tried to see her without looking at her . . . we avoided Pecola Breedlove – forever' (Morrison 2014, 205). In refusing to see her, they invalidate her personhood, casting her out as an object of revulsion. In *Corregidora*, Ursa is urged by her mother, grandmother and great grandmother to 'make generations' who can vouch for the truth of slavery: 'they didn't want to leave no evidence of what they done – so it couldn't be held against them. And I'm leaving evidence. And you got to leave evidence too. And your children got to leave evidence' (Jones 2019, 12). They hand down horrifying tales of their experiences in slavery so that the next generation can 'bear witness' (Jones 2019, 75). Witnesses and the act of witnessing, in this example, are crucial to identity, operating as a method of resistance through which to prove one's own history. However, this purpose is lost to Ursa when she has to have a hysterectomy after being pushed down the stairs by her husband. Without this inherited purpose, she is able to bear witness to her foremothers, but is left without someone who can witness her. In contrast, we see how a child can be positioned as witness in *Push*: early in the narrative, Precious states that 'I wanna say I am somebody . . . Why can't I see myself, *feel* where I end and begin' (Sapphire 2021, 31). However, by the end of the novel, she looks at her son Abdul and 'in his beauty I see my own': by invoking him as a witness, she is able to witness her own qualities (Sapphire 2021, 140). Whether this helps to clarify her borders, where she 'end[s] and begin[s]', however, is less clear: the blurred boundary between mother and child is of key importance to abjection studies, and while I am unable to fully examine it in depth here, there is scope for much more detailed discussion of how much agency – for mother or child – is to be gained through such mirroring, as well as warranted critique on the misogynistic elements of Kristeva's figuration of the abject mother (Sapphire 2021, 31).

With regards to witnessing, the text which *Salvage the Bones* most resembles is *The Color Purple*, in which Celie first establishes her own sense of agency when she states: 'And I come to myself. I'm pore, I'm black, I may be ugly and can't cook, a voice say to everything listening. But I'm here' (Walker 2014, 206). In this moment, she both commits to the act of witnessing – when she 'come[s] to [her]self' – as well as demanding she be witnessed by 'everything listening': 'I'm here' (Walker 2014, 206). Celie asserts that not only is she 'here', but her voice – one which has been so long repressed that it initially seems to her to be 'a voice' different to her own – will be heard: in Ward's words, she has found the power to 'make them know' (Ward 2012, 171). Where Pecola is denied the validation of being known, Ursa's ability to 'make generations' who will bear witness is taken from her, and Precious's borders around her Self remain somewhat troubled, Celie and Esch are able to find empowerment in being witnessed as Subjects. This stands to suggest that demanding the right to be 'known' can be utilised as a weapon against the depersonification of being made abject; by insisting that your Self is witnessed, and so affirmed by being witnessed, it becomes impossible to be estranged as Other. To be clear, though, this is not meant as an attempt to concur with feminist criticism which posits abjection as empowering on its own merit – Tyler has established the flaws in this argument in her essay, 'Against Abjection' – but rather to outline a mode of resistance against being made abject. Tyler's argument that 'criticism on the subversive potential of "abject parody" fails to address either the troubling premises of Kristeva's theory or the social consequences of living as a body that is identified as maternal and abject' is key to understanding this: Celie and Esch, in demanding to be 'known', are not attempting to lean into their abjection, but to force others to witness their Subjecthood (Tyler 2009, 78). In doing so, it becomes impossible to discard them as fully abject Others. However, the key difference between the protagonists is not just in their personal desires – Pecola, Precious and Ursa want to 'be known' just as much as Esch or Celie does – but in the response from those around them; one cannot be known without another to know them. While she was previously dismissed and diminished, like Pecola, Celie, in developing a relationship with Shug, finds someone through whom she can be known and know herself. Crucially, this differentiates from Precious's relationship with her son; where Shug is a clearly defined person in her own right, Abdul is a baby, and so the borders that separate one from the Other are much more ambiguous. Esch, however, has had this mirror all along in the form of her brothers, an argument I will return to shortly. In this, Ward presents a fascinating response to Tyler's account of being made abject: she reminds us that if being witnessed in your Subjecthood is a weapon against abjectification, it is not a weapon which can be wielded alone. Esch's 'people' are a necessary part of her survival, and her agency is preserved not by being alone, like Pecola, but by being supported by a community (Ward 2012, 150).

It is important to note, however, that it is not until the end of the novel that Esch truly taps into this sense of agency; up until that point, Ward shows her grappling with forms of abjection that trouble her identity. One of the main ways that Esch's shaky sense of self is illustrated is through her frequent identification with animals. In her interview with Hartnell, Ward says that, during her writing process, she 'would think about what are the metaphors for what [Esch] would see . . . what is informing what she's seeing, giving her context for what she's seeing' (Hartnell 2016, 212). Isolated within the Pit, their home in the woods, Esch's world is dominated by animals and nature, and so her metaphors are rooted within these contexts: Big Henry is 'graceful as a heron', Junior is 'forever the puppy weaned too soon', Randall and Skeetah hunch 'like birds, feathers ruffled against the bad wind', while her pregnant stomach is 'solid as a squash', a 'melon . . . ripe: intent on bearing seed' (Ward 2012, 120, 89, 232, 57, 102). In his chapter in this volume, Christopher Lloyd refers to such metaphors of 'complicated embodiments' as 'corporeal legacies', linked particularly to the ways in which bodies post-Hurricane Katrina are relegated to non-human status (p. 240). Focusing more specifically on the connotations of these animal metaphors, Christopher W. Clark notes that 'the characters' identities are merged with those of animals, much like derogatory cultural stereotypes that paint African Americans as non-human, or animalistic, in character', however, this chapter argues that we can view Ward's utilisation of this trope as another form of recycling, subverting racist stereotypes by 'overturning and investigating these figurations of animality and savagery' (Clark 2015, 349). On a similar note, Holly Cade Brown points out that when Skeetah refers to man and dog as 'equal', Ward resists 'the social allegory in which comparing a human to a dog inherently reduces the former's status' (Ward 2012, 29; Brown 2017, 8). This reflects my earlier arguments on recycling as something which can simultaneously boost the next interaction without reducing the capital of the last, suggesting that Ward is constantly thinking about relationships – between one work and another, between people, between people and animals – in a way that refuses to ascribe to binaries. This itself has abject themes, as an outlook situated within the liminal zone which exists in the push and pull of relationship dynamics. The kind of racial subversion Clark references is seen again in Ward's depiction of the Pit. Described as a 'refuse-laden yard' full of 'detritus' – 'pieces of engines' a rusted refrigerator, an old washing machine' – it is painted as a kind of graveyard of things which they have tried to salvage, but have been unable to (Ward 2012, 18, 89). The lack of purpose and order of things left to rust and rot has clear abject qualities, as does its isolated state, distanced from not only neighbours, but markers of neoliberal 'civilisation' like supermarkets. However, later in the novel, Ward flips its position when Esch says 'we live in the black heart of Bois Sauvage, and [the white farmer] lives out away in the pale arteries' (Ward 2012, 97). Where her previous descriptions allow us to assume that the Pit, isolated and marred by disuse, is a border-space, exiled from the civilised centre, this assertion subverts that. Instead, the Pit is 'the black heart' while the clear, fertile ground of the white farmer is the border-space (Ward 2012, 97). Brown notes that the novel represents those 'that have been positioned outside the boundaries of state protection', an idea reflected in multiple critical works on the portrayal of Hurricane Katrina in *Salvage the Bones*.

While the Batistes clearly represent the Black population neglected by the state in the aftermath of Katrina, Ward's positioning of the Pit as the 'black heart' brings assumptions about Black spaces as 'other' into question, and can be viewed as a defiant reproach to the kind of social abjection such state abandonment enacts (Brown 2017, 2). As the only 'other girl on the Pit', Skeetah's dog, China, becomes Esch's main point of comparison, and so, the most obvious example of her animal identification is seen in her persistent reflections on the connections between herself, her mother – who died in childbirth – and China. The opening sees China birthing her first litter as Esch watches: 'China's turned on herself. If I didn't know, I would think she was trying to eat her paws' (Ward 2012, 1). Posed like the ouroboros, China is immediately positioned as a symbol of both creation and destruction, a trained fighting dog who is now 'giving like she once took away' (Ward 2012, 1). This, in turn, links her to Esch's mother, with Esch's narration intersplicing memories of her mother dying after giving birth to her younger brother with her observations of China's labour. Motherhood, then, is intrinsically linked to death for Esch, setting the tone for her struggles to accept her own pregnancy. However, it is not just physical death that motherhood represents, but a death of the self; when Esch imagines her baby, 'who gives me that name as if it is mine: *Mama*', she imagines a loss of identity (Ward 2012, 219). In this idea of pregnancy as disruptive to identity, *Salvage the Bones* charts a noticeably Kristevan argument, suggesting that in the 'dual relationship' between mother and child, only one Subject can survive (Kristeva 1982, 64). However, while Kristeva's argument is focused on the child as the subject who fears their 'identity sinking irretrievably into the mother', here, it is the mother who fears losing her identity to the child, an issue which Kristeva's theory does not account for (Kristeva 1982, 64). As Tyler argues, in Kristeva's work the mother 'cannot exist as a subject in her own right, but only as the subject's perpetual other' (Tyler 2009, 85–6). Esch's insistence that she be witnessed, and her state as a subject be known, directly points to this hole in Kristeva's theory while also showing a potential route for resisting her assumption that to be a mother is necessarily to be abject. Indeed, if we accept the argument that, in Ward's work, resistance to abjection requires a supporting relationship with others, then motherhood can provide a way to regain agency *despite* abjection, rather than necessitate a loss of subjectivity.

Positive Black Male Influences

In multiple moments, *Salvage the Bones* seems to speak back to the texts of Ward's literary foremothers; consider the line 'a girl child ain't safe in a family of men', from *The Color Purple* (Walker 2014, 40). While this is proven many times over in Walker's text, in Ward's, often the opposite is true. The only girl in a house of four men, Esch is protected and loved by the men of her family, and devoted to her brothers: 'where my brothers go, I follow' (Ward 2012, 53). In this, Esch receives community: where Pecola is 'always alone', Esch is so used to being surrounded by her brothers and their male friends that her home 'felt strange when they weren't there, as empty as a fish tank, dry of water and fish, but filled with rocks and fake coral' (Ward 2012, 10). The crowds of boys are the Pit's natural inhabitants, the 'water and fish', comforting in their familiarity and sense of belonging, while a lack of them has the same sense of uncanniness that 'fake' replicas do (Ward 2012, 10). It must also be noted, however, that this results in a somewhat hyper-masculine environment, particularly prevalent when we consider the earlier example of China the pitbull standing in as Esch's only female mirror. Equally, she exclusively wears male clothing, handed down from her brothers, and admits herself to having no 'girlfriends' with whom she could seek advice from regarding her pregnancy, which raises questions about, firstly, whether her choices would have been different had she had other women to discuss the pregnancy with, and secondly, why she feels unable to broach the subject with her brothers or father (Ward 2012, 102). Her inability to tell them about her pregnancy – it is ultimately revealed to her father by Skeetah, who has worked it out of his own accord – suggests a shamefulness that could be rooted not just in the issue of the pregnancy itself, but in the *femaleness* of the issue. The pregnancy, and the inherent female quality of it, differentiates her from the men of her family in an unignorable fashion, and so she tries to hide it, to remain one of them, where she can 'follow' where they go (Ward 2012, 53). Her final demand to be witnessed, decreeing 'she will know that I am a mother', shows her growth: Esch is demanding to be seen, as a mother, in her femininity, as herself. This statement is also directed to China, the 'she' in question, reflecting a new-found respect for the feminine and a breaking free of her male-centric environment.

Although the Pit is an inarguably masculine environment, the passive effects of which I have outlined above, it is not a male space which is actively harmful or dangerous towards her. While the male family members characters of the preceding novels are consistently portrayed as abusive or dangerous – Pecola, Celie and Precious are all sexually abused by their fathers, Ursa's maternal relatives are incestually abused by their slave owner father/grandfather and Ursa herself is permanently injured by her husband – Esch is frequently protected by her elder brothers; and her father, while not particularly present or supportive, is nevertheless not a source of direct harm or abuse. Moynihan suggests that Ward's characterisation of the Batiste family, in which 'cooperation and empathy rather than atomization and selfishness are the distinguishing features' can 'be read as a strategy of resistance to the pathologizing of the Black family – albeit without romanticising their struggles' (Moynihan 2015, 557). In this case, we can consider this as an active rewriting of Morrison's Breedlove family. At the start of *The Bluest Eye*, Cholly Breedlove sets fire to their home, and the family is physically 'atomized': 'Mrs Breedlove was staying with the woman she worked for; the boy, Sammy, was with some other family; and Pecola was to stay with us. Cholly was in jail' (Morrison 2014, 18). The Pit, on the other hand, is not just a central base for the Batistes, but for extended family too, in the form of the boys who congregate there. The Breedloves also exemplify the kind of selfishness Moynihan refers to: Sammy, Pecola's brother, 'never took her' on his multiple escape runs from the home; her mother, Pauline, is too engrossed in her own self-hatred to care for Pecola, preferring the white child of her employers, and refuses to believe her when she confesses her father's rapes; Cholly, her father, spends all of the family's money on alcohol for himself, and rapes Pecola twice in a subconscious bid to assure himself of his own power (Morrison 2014, 45). By describing the various traumas of Pauline's and Cholly's childhoods, Morrison outlines the ways in which their self-hatred and pervading sense of their own abject ugliness has left them unable to love or empathise with Pecola, culminating in their various abuses towards her.

In contrast, empathy is a constant hum in *Salvage the Bones*. When Esch confronts Manny, the father of her unborn baby, and is rebuked, she silently returns to her brothers, isolated in the knowledge of her pain. However, they refuse to leave her in isolation: Big Henry, an adopted brother figure, notices and sends Junior to check on her, and Skeetah, with whom she has a particularly deep relationship, reaches out: 'it is as if he is touching the sadness in me with his hand' (Ward 2012, 147). Esch's relationship with Skeetah is frequently characterised by this kind of knowing touch. In an earlier moment, running through the woods together, hand in hand to keep pace, she remarks 'my body does what it was made to do: it moves. Skeetah cannot leave me. I am his equal' (Ward 2012, 66). With Skeetah, her body – or, her natural self – does 'what it was made to do': with him, her behaviour is organic, operating on an intrinsic bodily level, free from doubt (Ward 2012, 66). This is cemented further when she describes the sensation of running together as feeling like 'the running leap a bird takes before flight' (Ward 2012, 66). Returning, once again, to animal metaphor, this image is rooted in a sense of correctness, a moment in which nature is operating as it was 'made to' (Ward 2012, 66). In the safety of this experience with Skeetah, Esch is granted freedom to be her natural self. Crucially, they are 'equal' in the kind of moment of genuine togetherness that is so sorely lacking in the male/female relationships of the other texts (Ward 2012, 66). Ward makes it clear throughout the novel that Esch, even in the moments where she may feel as though she is alone, is always cared for and supported by an unspoken love and connection. Later, she tells Big Henry that her baby 'doesn't have a daddy', to which he replies: 'This baby got plenty daddies' (Ward 2012, 254). Breaking away from a traditional heternormative conception of family, this idea of 'plenty daddies' – daddy figured as someone who consistently cares, protects and supports – promises a future that, although different to the preconceived norm, is hopeful (Ward 2012, 254). In many ways, this is the environment in which Esch herself has grown up in, surrounded by protective men; however, the fact of her presence in the child's life allows for a more developed future for her baby. Where Esch had only men, the baby will have not only 'plenty daddies', but a mother, too, one who has found a sense of power and agency in that identity (Ward 2012, 254). In these moments, Ward emphasises the scope of Esch's support system – which includes her biological family as well as adopted family, like Big Henry – and their refusal to discard her to the realm of waste and the isolation of abjection. This support is critically absent from lives of the protagonists of the earlier novels, and provides a key example of Ward's recycling: Black teenage pregnancy is not rewritten as painless, but the unmitigated tragedy is cast aside in favour of hope and the potential for an alternative narrative.

By considering *Salvage the Bones* alongside works by Toni Morrison, Alice Walker, Gayl Jones and Sapphire, all seminal Black women writers, this chapter places Jesmyn Ward within a lineage of Black literary foremothers. Focusing specifically on Black teenage motherhood as a recurring motif – one which is loaded with meaning connected to abjection, race and class – this work looks to analyse the ways in which Ward's text is not only in conversation with these earlier novels, but actively revising and responding to them. Although constantly engaged with the effects of state neglect and abandonment, Ward goes beyond just depicting the experience of such social abjection, as is seen in the earlier texts, and homes in on modes of resistance. Esch, despite her social, financial and personal circumstances, is not relegated to 'waste': instead, Ward explores the ways in which she can find agency and power. Ultimately, where pregnancy becomes synonymous with tragedy and trauma in these earlier novels, Ward's work actively recycles the subject, refusing to conform to the narrative of Black teenage motherhood as a source of necessary destruction and, instead, finding within it a potential for hope and a 'redemptive horizon' (Hartnell 2016, 210).

Note

1. This comparison is most notable in *Salvage the Bones*, but, while outwith the scope of this chapter, is also a recurring theme throughout Ward's work, apparent in both her novel, *Sing, Unburied, Sing*, and her memoir, *Men We Reaped*.

Works Cited

Brown, Holly Cade. 2017. 'Figuring Giorgio Agamben's "Bare Life" in the Post-Katrina Works of Jesmyn Ward and Kara Walker'. *Journal of American Studies* 15 (1): 1–19.

Clark, Christopher W. 2015. 'What Comes to the Surface: Storms, Bodies and Community in Jesmyn Ward's Salvage the Bones'. *Mississippi Quarterly* 68 (3–4): 341–58.

Giroux, Henry A. 2006. 'Reading Hurricane Katrina: Race, Class, and the Biopolitics of Disposability'. *College Literature* 33 (3): 171–96.

Hartnell, Anna. 2016. 'When Cars Become Churches: Jesmyn Ward's Disenchanted America'. *Journal of American Studies* 50 (1): 205–18.

Jones, Gayl. 2019. *Corregidora*. London: Virago Press.

Kristeva, Julia. 1982. *Powers of Horror*. New York: Columbia University Press.

Morrison, Toni. 2014. *The Bluest Eye*. New York: Vintage International.

Moynihan, Sinéad. 2015. 'From Disposability to Recycling: William Faulkner and the New Politics of Rewriting in Jesmyn Ward's *Salvage the Bones*'. *Studies in the Novel* 47 (4): 550–67.

Sapphire. 1998. *Push*. London: Vintage.

Tyler, Imogen. 2009. 'Against Abjection'. *Feminist Theory* 10 (1): 77–98.

—. 2013. *Revolting Subjects: Social Abjection and Resistance in Neoliberal Britain*. London: Zed Books.

Walker, Alice. 2014. *The Color Purple*. London: Phoenix.

Ward, Jesmyn. 2012. *Salvage the Bones*. London: Bloomsbury.

Chapter 10

Being Touched by Cloth: Imprints on Community, Body and Self

Melanie Petch

Introduction

This chapter makes cross-disciplinary connections between the fields of material culture and contemporary literary studies of Black literature of the American South. In doing so, it positions Jesmyn Ward's work within the context of cloth and clothing. The interaction between these two disciplines takes material deprivation as its focus, and considers how the presentation of community, body and self bear the imprints of cloth and the material world. These themes are most evident, although not exclusively so, in Ward's text *Salvage the Bones* (2011) and her memoir, *Men We Reaped* (2013). Within American literary studies, Christopher Lloyd and Zsuzsanna Lénárt-Muszka's chapters in this collection, and Sinéad Moynihan's (2015) work offer rich readings of Ward's texts that make explicit reference to the body and memory. While attentive to American studies scholarship, the theoretical narrative in this chapter centres on cloth and draws upon Yeseung Lee's (2016) perspective of a concept she calls the 'garment ego'. Lee presents this as the idea that cloth acts as a second skin by becoming the layer between the body and the outer world. Lee urges us to recognise the weight that cloth holds in the creation of identity. Similarly, Stella North (2013, 64) tightly aligns cloth with the lived experience of human life. Cloth, she writes 'is at once the layer of the world closest to the body, and the layer of the lived body closest to the world'. North and Lee both talk of the terrific power of cloth to 'intervene' between body and world. Another thread in this chapter is inspired by Catherine Harper's (2014) views that cloth is inherently readable and allows for the expression of a tangible language that has the potential to reveal past experiences. While the theoretical link between body and cloth is clear, this chapter pivots this discussion to consider how Black literature of the US South can be viewed through the lens of material culture. Writing as a white, British scholar, I am forever mindful of the fact that I am 'looking in' from outside America's Black literary imagination. As such, contextualisation of Ward's work in this way offers a parallel account of material deprivation that gives special attention to Ward's characters' intimate experiences of skin against cloth. While this is not, by any means, an experience that can be viewed separately from race and place, the *sensation* of body and cloth might at least be recognised as a universal experience, if only as a point of departure.

Ward often reveals her personal relationship with cloth as something conflicted that can be traced back to her childhood. In *Men We Reaped*, she presents cloth as something that evokes nostalgia and maternal love as she recalls her mother's roles as laundress and housekeeper. Her mother's relentless acts of scrubbing, kneading, hanging and folding fabric are likely to have etched a sense of curiosity in Ward for the tactile relationship with the material world. She recollects how her mother would show her how to hang a 'fresh basket of clothes from the washing machine' (Ward 2013, 133). Likewise, in *Salvage the Bones,* the young narrator, Esch, fondly recalls the hanging of washing with her mother before she died. Yet, cloth is also seen to be a contentious concept for Ward, and it is the more subversive angle of cloth, rather than nostalgia, that is the primary focus for this chapter. At times the absence of 'reliable' cloth – cloth that is durable, intact, opaque – is hard to find in Ward's narrative. Indeed, this chapter reveals how the lives of the youths in *Salvage the Bones* are blighted by the imperfect surfaces and impressions of cloth. Bodies tussle with cloth, they pull and pick at it as it lodges in crevices, sticks to skin, stretches and gapes.

To outline a framework for exploring these ideas, the first section of this chapter considers how ownership of the body, or the 'community body', can be understood through the act of borrowing clothing. While sharing clothing is sometimes seen as a necessity for Ward's characters, it is far from the innocent act of 'handing down' or 'handing across' to which many of us are accustomed in our everyday lives. Sharing clothing places the young character, Esch, in a position where she must relinquish her body to the male owners of the borrowed items. Exploring this tension further, this chapter will then consider the eerily unseductive concept of gaping cloth and how this leaves the body open to exposure, desensitisation and loss of anonymity. Making connections to Lloyd's notion of 'corporeal legacies' where he argues that bodies frequently unravel in Ward's work, I will similarly argue that the threat of bodies spilling out of cloth and, paradoxically, being constricted by it, shows how clothing brushes uncomfortably with the surface of the skin and challenges our understanding of both modesty and nudity. Bodily excretions, soils and stains provide the focus for the final section of the chapter where considerations are given to expressions of class and power. Ward's characters seem to bear the social burden of these soils and stains as they wear them as badges of shame. This chapter concludes by acknowledging Ward's representation of a community that is blighted by poverty and frustrated by the absence of functional objects and dependable clothing items.

Cloth and the Community Body

Ward recognises the value that clothing plays in terms of belonging to a community. In *Men We Reaped*, there is a poignant reflection where she retells her experience of 'sifting through' cast offs and making decisions based on what would fit and what might be considered 'reasonably fashionable' (Ward 2013, 185). In affluent Western communities, the concept of wearing second-hand clothing is encouraged on sustainable grounds as an opportunity to display 'conspicuous non-consumption as the new signifier of self-worth' (Mair 2018, 85). Carolyn Mair notes that the sole purpose of wearing certain clothing need not be to look prosperous. Ward is well aware, however, that clothing – whether new or second-hand – is very much a symbol of self-entitlement from which she was often exempt. The kids in her class wear their entitlement, she says, in their 'collared shirts and khaki shorts' (Ward 2013, 5). Later, she recalls how her 'ragtag wardrobe gleaned from her schoolmates' would 'function as a camouflage' and allow her to 'fit in' (Ward 2013, 185). Similarly, for the Bois Sauvage community in *Salvage the Bones*, the sole aim is to wear clothing that fits and provides a layer of modesty for areas of the body most in need. The privilege associated with conspicuous non-consumption is simply not an option for Esch and her siblings. For Esch, the act of dressing every day is identity-erasing as we witness her slim pickings when making clothing choices. She says: 'We all share clothes, so it's mostly men's T-shirts for me, loose jeans and cotton shorts.' Esch reveals that the clothed-community is seen solely in male form, and Esch as the only female, has little autonomy. Later in the text, Esch acknowledges that it is masculine clothing that conceals her pregnant body from Skeetah and the community. 'I will not let him see until none of us have any choices about what can be seen . . .' (Ward 2011, 88). Esch has totally relinquished the right to make decisions about her pregnant body as it is clothed, and indeed, over-seen, by the male community, as Ward's use of the protective pro-noun 'us' suggests. This raises interesting issues around the idea of a young, single girl, and the prospect of motherhood in a masculinised community. We might ask whether this sense of shared identity, ex-pressed through clothing, protects or disempowers Esch.

Further in the text, we see how Esch's body, both clothed and un-clothed, becomes something to be viewed as a community event and becomes as Harper (2014) would say 'inherently readable'. This un-settling concept is also raised in an important discussion on violence against women by Paris Connolly (2019) who claims that ownership of the body does not always belong to the individual but sometimes the entire community. Similarly, Chimaraoke O. Izugbara and Chi-Chi Undie (2008, 162) refer to 'the communal body' as an entity which is 'privileged over the body and personhood' of the individual. In *Salvage the Bones*, there are examples of how personhood is very much diminished in the way Esch's body is viewed by males in the community of Bois Sauvage. The way the male community is repre-sented in Ward's work is discussed in Lénárt-Muszka's chapter in this collection where she notes that Esch's family diverges 'from those female-centred, often rhizomatically organised structures that are prevalent in African American literature. Instead of relying on the trope of the absentee father and a single mother, *Salvage the Bones* centres a diffuse family' (135). Sociologist, Joanne Entwistle conveys the relevance of the body within society and how it interacts with dress. She always sees the dressed body as inseparable from its context. She claims that dress is always 'the outcome of social pressures' (2015, 7). As Entwistle would have it, clothing and community are intertwined and we see similar patterns in Ward's work where the dressed, and undressed, body is viewed as subversive when it does not obey the rules of the social group. An illustration of community ownership can be seen when Esch, her brothers, Randall and Skeetah, and their friend Manny, wash in the black water of the Pit near to their home.

Ironically, the youths go to the dirty water in the Pit to scrub away the 'contamination' after Skeetah buries one of China's dead puppies. Esch's role is not wholly communal as she sets herself apart. While the boys strip off their clothes and throw them at the water's edge, for Esch, the knowledge of her secret pregnancy means that her entry into the water is self-conscious and different from theirs. As such, she stays fully clothed and, as a ruse, performs the washing of these garments while they still envelop her body. This act seems to reveal the social inappropriateness of her physical being, particularly as the boys lounge naked in the water. Again, Entwistle (2015) discusses the cultural significance that clothing plays in terms of creating meaning and recognises that both the dressed and undressed body must be appropriately located for it to be socially valued. Entwistle recognises that there are certain spaces where bodies are accepted in their naked form, and other spaces where they are not. We see that by keeping her body clothed and discarding her garments only when she is fully submerged, Esch subverts the cultural conventions expected of someone bathing. Clothing here, is a means of protection from the prying eyes of the community, yet falls inadequately short in terms of social acceptance. Lee's concept of the 'garment ego' (2016, 51) defines the textile surface as a tool that mediates the body in order to produce 'smooth narratives of the self to others'. While Esch's shape is veiled from prying eyes, the narrative she conveys is far from 'smooth' as her clothed body sits self-consciously apart.

Once in the water, Esch presents what might be perceived as a subversive and anti- erotic striptease. She says:

> I walk into the water with all my clothes on. When I am all wet, I grab the soap from Skeetah and rub the suds into my clothes, too. I make them white before I pull them away, one by one, until I am naked in the water, my clothes a dirty, slimy pile on the mud bank. (Ward 2011)

Ward might have chosen a more seductive lexicon for Esch's stripping down, and yet she uses the antagonistic 'pull' rather than the more alluring 'peel'. Anne Hollander claims that 'the erotic aspect of . . . nudity is always present' (2005, 84), and yet as Esch refers to the 'dirty, slimy pile' of clothes on the bank, eroticism has been reduced to the filth and grime of the Pit's innards. It is the boys' response to her performance that is more unsettling as they convey their vested interest in her body as a community object. After her public performance of undressing, Manny taunts 'Scared to let everyone see what you look like?' (Ward 2011, 55). Even more unsettlingly, under her brother's scrutinising gaze, she observes: 'Skeetah watches me swim to him and the dirt, watches me dress in my soapy clothes, and says nothing before turning to lead the way through the dark, naked' (Ward 2011, 57). Moynihan (2015) recognises Ward's conscious use of themes around sexuality and reproduction as they 'provide touchstones for social anxieties and fears that had been circulating since at least the 1980s' in Black literature of the US South (552). Ward is well aware of the literary legacy of 'pathologizing . . . the African

American family' (552). Having broken the social conventions of the community by remaining clothed, Esch must suffer the social anxiety and humiliation of dressing her pregnant body under the watchful eye of her brother.

Gaping Cloth and Exposure

The suspicious nature of cloth is evident throughout the text, and the female body, once again, is open to scrutiny and the threat of exposure. Interestingly, in the context of fashion and textiles, exposure of the body is rarely seen as an unsettling concept. Rather, the gaping garment often signals seduction. Fashion historian, James Laver (1969) recognises the way clothing is consciously designed to reveal some parts of the body and conceal others. He argues that: 'when a particular body part becomes overexposed it is no longer sexually enticing' (cited in Reilly 2014, 40). Laver also recognises that this is why we are so hungry for new fashion; the prospect of seeing fresh areas of the body provides welcome relief lest we become bored with the parts we know too well. Likewise, in *The Pleasure of the Text*, Roland Barthes (1990) expresses the idea that the gaping sleeve alluding to bare skin is far more erotic than the fully exposed body. Despite the widespread and multidisciplinary recognition of Barthes's ideas and the frequency with which they have been cited, it is still worth recalling how he alludes to the idea that clothing acts as a kind of social cue, or enticement; an open invitation, perhaps, to view a tantalising glimpse of skin beneath. Lee (2016, 51) considers another social aspect of cloth through her discussion of the garment ego. She sees the garment ego involving the intimate interaction between the body and clothing. Lee urges us to consider how they 'tame each other' in many ways. She imagines this relationship as reciprocal – both body and cloth impressing their significance in an equally balanced exchange. There is also the assumption, here, that there is choice in how, when and where the cloth might gape.

However, Ward does not view cloth in such an even-handed way as Lee, nor does she see it as a particularly seductive concept in the way that Barthes or Laver might. For her, cloth always takes on a far more problematic guise, particularly through the portrayal of Esch wearing her conspicuous 'short shorts'. While there is an argument that she wears these not through choice, but necessity, it is the case that Esch is deeply infatuated with local boy, Manny, and perhaps selects these shorts as an attempt to arouse his interest in her.

Either way, her choice is curtailed and as we saw in the previous section, the luxury of being able to make a choice about clothing was also limited for Ward when she was growing up. We see this tension echoing in her work and particularly in the garments Esch 'chooses' too. The precariousness of Esch's situation is felt keenly when she is in the presence of her brothers Skeetah and Randall, and the other boys. While they fixate on her body that is barely contained within the pair of shorts, we sense Esch's frustration as the garment seems discordant with her body. This can be observed on a particularly oppressive day in the yard where a sweaty Esch accidentally slides down a strip of metal to land on Marquise's back. Fear that her body might spill out, Esch slides behind a car 'to pull her shorts so they are not bunching' in her groin, and therefore 'showing' her (Ward 2011, 139–40). In his chapter in this volume, Lloyd argues that writers such as Ward, draw 'attention to bodies that are, in one way or another, registering internal and external forces at once: these are bodies whose interiors and exteriors are caught in an in interrelated cycle of coming apart'. Again, Lloyd's notion of 'corporeal legacies' bears witness to the overriding power of the body to collude and enmesh with the material world. We see this in *Salvage* as Esch's body both absorbs and expels the cloth, revealing her competing sense of desire and shame.

Despite the ever-present threat of bodily exposure, Ward chooses to portray Esch as a young woman who transcends the racialised hyper-sexual depictions of Black women to which we often bear witness (hooks 2014). While Esch's male peers are intent on closely watching her, she does not indulge them by parading her inadequately clothed body. Yet, Ward depicts a no less disempowered young woman. In her, we see a young teen, her sub-naked body blighted by material deprivation, and open to the eyes of the male community. While cloth, here, does expose Esch uncomfortably, it cannot be denied that she simultaneously covets Manny's attention. However, cloth does betray a secret. We notice how it clings to the 'ripe melon' that betrays her pregnancy (Ward 2011, 99, 111–12). The pressure of a growing baby on Esch's abdomen and her desire to urinate creates a sense of agonising suspense. Not only is Esch's body always on the edge of failing her, but the tiny shorts she wears, we fear, will be unable to contain the flood of urine when it comes. Cloth as a means to expose Esch is an ever-present threat throughout the novel, from the sheets that 'were so thin we could almost see through them' (Ward 2011, 179) to the precarious positioning of towels that are tacked to the bathroom window as Esch sits on the toilet. Cloth is depicted as substandard in its function, even when taking on a multipurpose role. Towels are not simply used to absorb water, but also act as threadbare privacy screens or curtains. In their cycle of poverty, we see signs that Esch and her family, but particularly Esch, are often subdued by the material world that surrounds them.

For the young men in Esch's peer group, cloth has the opposite effect of exposure. Their garments are often seen to be suffocating. During a searing bout of summer heat, clothing acts as a means of incarceration for Randall who 'picks' at his shirt 'so his skin can breathe (Ward 2011, 143). Skeetah has a similar reaction to the neck on his shirt 'stretched as a bib' which he proceeds to 'grab . . . with both hands, and pulls. The shirt rips' (136). Whether exposing or constricting, again, we witness how cloth continues to behave badly; as something that must be tamed and managed as Lee's argument alluded to earlier. In his chapter in this volume, Lloyd argues that it is often through depictions of the body, that 'contemporary texts set in the US South seem to gesture towards an ongoing and as yet unfinished project of making sense of the past' (241). We might argue that this impoverished Black community, and others before theirs, are haunted by the inadequateness of their material surroundings and we see this played out through the niggly micro-aggressions with the clothing they wear. Similarly, Esch notices how Daddy's T-shirt 'has a gaping hole at the neck, and is uneven at the hem, as is someone has been pulling at it' (Ward 2011, 127). Ward shows how the disfigured and torn garments reveal an aggressive tussle with the body. Cloth becomes a canvas for expressing frustration, anger and desperation. We notice the mark that bodies leave on clothing and the 'physical traces of everyday life' (Lee 2016, 51). We might liken this to Didier Anzieu's (1974) coinage of the 'transitional object' that is something that is both 'self and not self' (cited in Lee 2016, 47). Daddy's T-Shirt is clearly not Daddy – it is a material object that sits on, yet outside, his body – but it does reveal his past torments, his frustrations, aggressions even, at being contained in woeful material surroundings. Sadly, clothing renders many of Ward's characters impotent. Chiming with Daddy's tired and stretched old T-Shirts, and providing stark contrast to the poor clothing in Ward's work, luxury fashion designer, Martin Margiela, creates clothing that gives the impression of 'being worn hundreds of times' (Wilson 2008). Numerous collections are peppered with exposed stitching in a deconstructivist style and overstretched arms as if they have been tugged over hands to keep them warm. Away from the reality of poverty, we might argue that there is something delightfully nostalgic about this battered and time-worn approach to producing new, luxury garments. Yet unlike Margiela, nostalgia is not Ward's intention at all. When reflecting on her own childhood, Ward remembers how her 'shirts were constantly stretched out at the hem and [would hang] on our bony frames like A-line skirts' (2013, 134). Ward would have been all too familiar with the actions that her characters display as they pull and pick at their disfigured clothing. She documents a tense relationship between body and cloth that is made more hopeless by the lack of useable possessions, and the poverty she has endowed on the Bois Sauvage community.

Bodily Excretions, Soils and Stains

We have seen how cloth acts as a second skin by becoming the layer between the body and the outer world – traditionally, it protects, but with Ward's characters, as we recognise, cloth is also punishing in its betrayal of the body. However, there is more to cloth than superficially brushing or, indeed, battling with the skin's surface. Fashion historians, Ingrid Mida and Alexandra Kim (2015, 16), argue that 'dress is subjected to the demands and whims of its owner, bearing the marks and strains of wear, as well as decomposition from the effects of light, moisture, pests and soiling'. Mida and Kim take a forensic approach to observing historical garments and adopt a premise of 'slow seeing' in order 'to patiently observe the subtle clues that are embedded in a dress artefact'. They delight in the peculiarly positioned tear of cloth, or a surreptitious stain on a cuff. As Mida and Kim reveal, cloth has a rich, inner life that is imbued with the particles of the people and environments it comes into contact with. These remnants can reveal unspoken stories about identity and the associated feelings of shame that are hidden from the outer, social world. As such, the role of textiles, particularly in Ward's work, are not just antagonistic, or a concept that seeks to work against the body. We might also argue that cloth sometimes becomes a passive carrier for bodily remnants and, as such, human experience (Barnett 1999).

In Bois Sauvage, material is frequently seen as a receptacle that holds the detritus of both environment and its inhabitants. As Daddy prepares for the arrival of Hurricane Katrina, Esch reflects on how their old domestic items have been adapted and repurposed since her mother died. Exposing the family's garments to the unrelenting dust of the Pit, she notices a clothes line that has been repositioned by

Daddy. She notes, 'when Randall and I wash clothes and hang them out with wooden clothespins, the line sags, and our pants dangle in the dirt' (Ward 2011, 108). This is a reminder that cloth is always under threat of succumbing to the corrosive elements of the landscape. Not that this has always been seen in negative ways. Reflecting on happier times when her mother was alive, Esch recalls: 'We spent the summer dusted an orange colour, and when we woke up . . . the sheets would feel powdery like red clay' (Ward 2011, 23). These examples demonstrate the triadic connection between body, environment and cloth. This is not always harmonious. Ingun Grimstad Klepp, for example, advises us how 'clothes can protect the surroundings from the body's impurities, or conversely protect the body from the surroundings' (2007, 259). We note how the Pit's residue transfers from their bodies to become ingrained between the threads of the sheets. The 'protection' that Klepp speaks of is perhaps true in a more sterile environment, but the pervasiveness of the Pit rules out protection for Esch and the Bois Sauvage boys. And later, in a detached tone, Esch recalls how their sheets and clothes are indistinguishable from rags. Watching Skeetah root through a box of material that might comfort his pitbull, she wonders, 'I can't tell whether the material is old clothes, old sheets or old towels . . .' (Ward 2011, 98). To explain the social significance of dirt, Jenni Sorkin (2000) also draws attention to the idea that soils and stains on cloth often evokes deep-rooted feelings of shame. It could be argued that we do not see shame played out in Ward's narrative so much as apathy, but this might be because the youths are surrounded by their own kin. Nevertheless, we know from earlier examples, that Ward as a child, was keenly aware of the social impact of wearing inappropriate clothing, and in a different context with visiting friends, say, the dirty sheets would be perceived as damningly shameful. Instead, the speaker's detached observation seems more disarming, as if the dirt has become so much part of Esch's lived experience that it is no longer noteworthy.

Conversely, there are occasions in the text where the stigma of soils and stains on cloth becomes socially apparent. We might even argue that 'fashion' is a more desirable term to use here than the more abstruse term, 'clothing', especially when contemplating Ward's numerous comparisons between white and dirty sneakers. For example, we see how Manny's 'once white Jordans were the colour of orange sherbet' (Ward 2011, 15). Jordans are sometimes thought to be a class status symbol, especially for Black youths emulating the prowess of Michael Jordan. Robin Chandler and Nuri Chandler-Smith (2008) discuss how young, Black youths, emulating a hip-hop subculture, are often defined by the clothing they wear. Ironically, in Bois Sauvage, we see that even though items like the Jordans might be perceived as 'good gear', they are blighted by the dust of the Pit. Klepp's (2007) views are worth recalling here as she perceives dirt as a cultural construct that is, crucially, an indicator of power. Even older sneakers belonging to less poverty-stricken boys from the nicer end of town wield more social value than the stained Jordans belonging to Manny: the speaker describes 'some other older dark boy who has worn white shoes that look new to a dog-fight in the woods' (Ward 2011, 161). Manny and the other boys in the Pit community are denied the very few signifiers of social status afforded to Black individuals from more hospitable surroundings. Clearly, the staining on their sneakers overshadows their fancy branding and logos. As we see, in *Salvage the Bones*, Ward offers the grime in the Pit as a stark contrast to clean clothing which affords its wearers many of life's rich pleasures: 'boys wear white tees, sleeveless shirts, caps, basketball shorts. There is laughter, shrill calls. Everyone is flirting . . .' (Ward 2011, 143). In keeping with Ward's unflinching message that identity formation cannot simply be built by tugging on a luxury item, Susan Kaiser (2013) reminds us that dirt is often tied to manual labour and social class. Therefore, for those involved in physical work, it was impossible to keep clothing clean and therefore cleanliness becomes one of the signifiers of social status. Likewise, Klepp (2007) recognises the need to protect a clear boundary between respectable and not-respectable, and that this often comes about through the act of washing our clothing too. For Ward's characters, then, the everyday struggle to do ordinary jobs in unforgiving surroundings has resonance and we are reminded of Esch as she prays 'tomorrow . . . everything will be washed clean' (Ward 2011, 205). We accept, therefore, that Ward's soils and stains are worn as badges of shame for Esch and her kin.

Ward also places great emphasis on the way her textiles hold and absorb the debris of living beings. This fascination with remnants of the human body is seen as artistic and aesthetic fodder for textile artists as well as writers. There is a long tradition of creating a sense of community and selfhood through folk textiles. In Black culture of the American South this can be seen in the form of the Gee's Bend quilters from Alabama, who use scraps of domestic fabric from their lives, such as corduroy and cotton sheets that have a close alignment with the body. They use these scraps to create stories about community and self (Fox 2002). Undeniably, there is a degree of sensuality in handling both colour and texture which is often seen as soothing and pleasurable (Hunter 2019). For the Gee's Bend quilters, their approach to cloth selection is very much based on necessary pieces they have to hand, but they are often bold and visually uplifting. The imperfection of cloth and its relationship with the body can also be seen in Anne Wilson's textile piece entitled 'Mendings No. 7', where she creates holes in her cloth and weaves human hair around their openings. In another piece, 'Mourning Cloth', holes and hair feature again, yet this time the hair is swirled haphazardly on reconstructed cloth replicating the patterns of the imperfect human body (Barnett 1999, 20–1). Wilson's bodily scraps are not beautifully designed within the textiles, as the Gee's Bend constructions are, but rather, much like Ward's themes, these remnants impose themselves within and on the fibres of the cloth. We see this profoundly towards the end of *Salvage the Bones* where Ward gives a primal description of body particles and their imprint on the material world. Esch's family are seemingly suspended in time, doing mindless tasks, waiting for the hurricane to hit. Skeetah, cleaning his pitbull's meagre possessions, pegs her blanket to the clothes line. We notice how he beats the blanket with a large stick and then:

> Dirt showers down, fitful as cold rain. Some of it floats a little longer than it should, a slow cloud, and I realise that some of China is in the blanket, that her hair is coming away. It makes me think of cereal in milk, of Rice Krispies in sugar. (Ward 2011, 196)

In this poignant moment, and through the vehicle of the textile object, Esch seems to contemplate both life and death at once. China has been plagued by illness and the death of her puppies, her body is physically purging, and yet this urges Esch to nourish her own body with sugary sustenance. We see Ward echoing another, even more appalling, paradox of death and gluttony touched upon in Shakespeare's *Titus Andronicus*, where characters are punished cruelly by being either force-fed familial body parts or famished and left to die.

In his chapter in this volume, Lloyd also draws attention to 'the physicality of vomit (and the body's methods of evacuation)' in Ward's later text, *Sing, Unburied Sing*, and suggests that it is 'clearly part of Ward's point that the body is the site in, and on, which the world etches itself' (244). Likewise, in *Salvage*, Ward offers a reminder that the body both omits and consumes – it takes and it gives – and this is captured through the symbolic action of beating China's old dirty blanket.

Throughout the novel, bodies continue to secrete. This can be seen in the imprint of Skeetah's blood on the fence of a local white man: 'when I look at the boards in front of me, I see one dark splash like paint, one maroon tear from where Skeetah fell out of the window; it's his blood' (Ward 2011, 207). There is pain soaked in Esch's memory of this poignant tear, and yet, as if desensitised, she notes simply: 'it's his blood'. Interestingly, Christopher Clark's discussion sees Ward's representation of the Bois Sauvage residents as 'tired, hungry children who appear more like a scab rather than the flowing waters of a flourishing landscape' (2015). Equally, having witnessed Ward's examples, we might also argue that the detritus of these fractious, leaking bodies, both human and canine, are represented as crust-like scabs that coat the fibres of cloth and clothing, or as Lloyd would say, 'etching' upon them. Similarly, we see the aching inadequacy of the material world to protect, to comfort and to hold.

Conclusion

This chapter has discussed the readability of cloth which is arguably distinctive when positioned in the context of Black Southern American literature and the representation of poverty. Unlike other narratives in material culture that seek to understand the role of cloth and clothing in modern society, this chapter has shown how representations of cloth evoke contradictory issues in Ward's text, especially in the way the self is created, and how the body is perceived, in a materially deprived community. In Ward's texts, clothing is often laden with the burden of social expectation and choice is rarely an option. As we now know, items of clothing frequently subscribe to a community ideal which is made problematic for Esch as the only female. For her, clothing provides a way to camouflage herself within the group even as it simultaneously diminishes her autonomy. As we have seen, there is also a juxtaposition in the way cloth both exposes the body and incarcerates it. In other words, cloth is a trickster – a friend one moment, a foe the next. Cloth betrays. On an aesthetic level, it holds very little value – and when it does, fleetingly, it is soon ruined by the inhospitable landscape and the permeating red dust from the Pit. Items are tainted and their owners wear them as tokens of shame that highlights the labours of a Black community aware of the connotations of wearing dirty clothes. We have, however, observed Ward's representations of cloth forensically, to understand that it also harbours body detritus that gives us valuable insight on her characters. This insight allows us to grasp the unheard stories of her characters in the way they inhabit and interact with the material world that imprints upon them.

As mentioned at the start of this chapter, there is also a counternarrative that runs through *Salvage the Bones*, that sees cloth as evocative and maternal. It was not the intention of this chapter to diminish this interpretation of nostalgia, but more to show that cloth complicates Esch's sense of selfhood after her mother dies, as the only woman in a community of men. Had her mother been alive, clothing might have been presented to her in the form of handmade garments of brightly patterned and coloured fabrics from a female wardrobe rather than her brothers' hand-me-downs. While this might not have raised her entirely out of the deprivation that has been part of her family's heritage, these small acts of maternal kindness might have afforded her a sense of joy and delight in the material world and a bond that led her away from the dust.

Works Cited

Anzieu, Didier. 2016. *The Skin Ego*, translated by Naomi Segal. Oxford: Routledge.

Barnett, Pennina. 1999. 'Folds, Fragments, Surfaces: Towards a Poetics of Cloth'. In *Textures of Memory: The Poetics of Cloth*, 25–34. Nottingham: Angel Row Gallery.

Barthes, Roland. 1990. *The Pleasure of the Text*. Oxford: Blackwell.

Cavanagh, Sheila L., Angela Failler and Rachel Alpha Johnston Hurst, eds. 2013. *Skin, Culture and Psychoanalysis*. London: Palgrave Macmillan.

Chandler, Robin, and Nuri Chandler-Smith. 2008. 'Flava in Ya Gear: Transgressive Politics and the Influence of Hip-Hop on Contemporary Fashion'. In *Twentieth-Century American Fashion*, edited by Linda Welters and Patricia Cunningham, 229–54. London: Berg.

Clark, Christopher. W. 2015. 'What Comes to the Surface: Storms, Bodies and Community in Jesmyn Ward's Salvage the Bones'. *Mississippi Quarterly* 68 (3–4): 341–58.

Connolly, Paris. 2019. *Female Genital Cutting in the United Kingdom: a feminist phenomenological study of perceptions and lived experiences*. PhD thesis. De Montfort University, Leicester. https://ethos.bl.uk/OrderDetails.do?uin=uk.bl.ethos.783316.

Entwistle, Joan. 2015. *The Fashioned Body: Fashion, Dress & Modern Social Theory*. Cambridge: Polity Press.

Fox, C. 2002. 'Pieces of the Past from Gee's Bend'. *The Atlanta Journal – Constitution*, 7 February.

Harper, Catherine. 2014. 'Sex, Birth and Nature Unto Death'. In *Love Objects: Emotion, Design and Material Culture*, edited by Anna Moran and Sorcha O'Brien. London: Bloomsbury.

Hollander, Anne. 2005. *Seeing through Clothes*. New York: Penguin Books.

hooks, bell. 2014. *Black Looks: Race and Representation*. Abingdon: Taylor & Francis.

Hunter, Clare. 2019. *Threads of Life: A History of the World Through the Eye of a Needle*. London: Hodder & Stoughton.

Izugbara, Chimaraoke O., and Chi-Chi Undie. 2008. 'Who Owns the Body? Indigenous African Discourses of the Body and Contemporary Sexual Rights Rhetoric'. *An International Journal on Sexual and Reproductive Health and Rights* 16 (31): 159–67.

Kaiser, Susan B. 2013. *Fashion and Cultural Studies*. London: Bloomsbury.

Klepp, Ingun Grimstad. 2007. 'Patched, Louse-Ridden, Tattered: Clean and Dirty Clothes'. *Textile: The Journal of Cloth and Culture* 5 (3): 254–75.

Lee, Yeseung. 2016. *Seamlessness: Making and (Un)Knowing in Fashion Practice*. Bristol: Intellect.

Mair, Carolyn. 2018. *The Psychology of Fashion*. Abingdon: Routledge.

Mida, Ingrid, and Alexandra Kim. 2015. *The Dress Detective: A Practical Guide to Object-Based Research in Fashion*. London: Bloomsbury.

Moynihan, Sinéad. 2015. 'From Disposability to Recycling: William Faulkner and the NewPolitics of Rewriting in Jesmyn Ward's *Salvage the Bones*'. *Studies in the Novel* 47 (4): 550–67.

North, Stella. 2013. 'The Surfacing of the Self: The Clothing Ego'. In *Skin, Culture and Psychoanalysis*, edited by Sheila L. Cavanagh, Angela Failler and Rachel Alpha Johnston Hurst, 64–89. London: Palgrave Macmillan.

Reilly, Andrew. 2014. *Key Concepts for the Fashion Industry*. London: Bloomsbury.

Shakespeare, William. [1594] 1998. 'The Most Lamentable Roman Tragedy of Titus Andronicus'. In *William Shakespeare: The Complete Works*, edited by Stanley Wells and Gary Taylor. Oxford: Clarendon.

Sorkin, Jenni. 2000. 'Stain: On Cloth, Stigma and Shame'. *Third Text* 14 (53): 77–80.

Ward, Jesmyn. 2011. *Salvage the Bones*. London: Bloomsbury.

——. 2013. *Men We Reaped*. London: Bloomsbury.

Wilson, Eric. 2008. 'Fashion's Invisible Man'. *The New York Times*, 1 October.

Chapter 11

'Life had promised me something when I was younger': Biopolitics and the Rags to Riches Narrative in Jesmyn Ward's *Men We Reaped*

Maria Elena Torres-Quevedo

Jesmyn Ward's *Men We Reaped* tells two concomitant stories: that of her own ascension from bright young student to author, and that of the violence, physical, environmental and biopolitical, suffered by the Black community of DeLisle, Mississippi at the hands of white supremacist power structures. The narrative pans between the intimate, personal details of the character Jesmyn's life to the broader issues that are connected to and influence that life. It weaves together the story of Jesmyn's coming of age, narrated chronologically, with that of the death of five men close to her, narrated in reverse chronology: Rog dies of undiagnosed heart disease, Demond is shot dead before acting as a witness during a drug trial, C.J. is hit by a train at a crossing with perpetually broken lights, and Ronald commits suicide. The two chronologies meet with the death of Jesmyn's younger brother, Josh. Across these converging narratives, Ward relates her developing consciousness of other women's coming-of-age stories and later the writing of civil rights activists, connecting her local and family history to the practice of oral storytelling and probing the communicative and emancipatory limits of storytelling. In this essay, I argue that Ward's memoir subverts the generic convention within American autobiography of a sovereign subject, replacing this with a posthumanist biopolitical subject. I show how Ward's memoir subverts the prevalent ideological underpinnings of mainstream American life-writing, in particular the narrative of upward mobility, and questions the ways this genre conceptualises and reifies 'the good life' and neoliberal subjects within the American imagination. Through a sustained analysis of state-sanctioned biopolitical violence, a reconceptualisation of the sovereign subject and agency, and a rejection of the racist and classist teleology of the upward mobility narrative, Ward posits a radical understanding of what it means to be an American subject. In particular, Ward's work centres on groups who are marginalised from the sovereign subject of the Enlightenment that the autobiographical genre has been central in constructing. Ward's undoing of this sovereignty is performed through intertextual references, generic innovations and metatextual commentary that serve to assert the relationship between the story and the subject, and to establish the lacunae and failures of that relationship for marginalised writers. Moreover, through her navigation of the relationship between biopolitics, narrative technologies, and lived experience, Ward's memoir exemplifies posthumanist subjectivity within the context of the experience of African American subjects in the rural South.

One of the central tropes of American autobiography is the 'sovereign subject', the 'I' constructed through narration. Leigh Gilmore affirms that 'autobiography helps to install a sovereign subject' (Gilmore 2001, 21), while Rachael McLennan (2012) comments on the indebtedness of this figure to European Enlightenment philosophy. The idea of the sovereign subject, however, is oxymoronic. The Western subject is, as Foucault argues, constructed through discourse, including that of autobiographical writing, and always already subjected by that constitution and the normative discourses that inform it (Foucault 1986, 60). The fantasy of sovereignty is persistent in American autobiographical writing and the mythology of the American subject, individual and nationally representative, that such writing constructs.

This conceptualisation of the ideal American subject as a sovereign individual undergirds one of the quintessential American narrative trajectories: the upward mobility story. The upward mobility story has close ties with American autobiography and *The Autobiography of Benjamin Franklin* is a predecessor of both genres. Franklin's autobiography establishes the prototype of American self-reliance in a way that is bound to both class mobility and morality. Franklin offers himself, his life and his story as models of moral behaviour, industriousness and rationality, which are rewarded by prosperity and communal respect. The underlying ideology put forth by the legacy of Franklin's autobiography holds that the good American citizen will work hard and be rewarded by wealth and freedom. Ironically, far from contributing to a meritocratic system across gender, race and class lines, this generic and ideological trope reinscribes the forms of oppression on which America was built by denying their existence and placing the blame for economic disenfranchisement on individuals.

Berlant's concept of cruel optimism is a useful lens through which to read this narrative tendency in American literature and autobiography in particular, as well as Ward's intervention into it. For Berlant, cruel optimism refers to 'a relation of attachment to compromised conditions of possibility whose realization is discovered either to be *impossible, sheer fantasy, or too* possible, and toxic' (Berlant 2011, 24). Berlant relates this concept to life-writing specifically, stating that 'the genre of the "life" is a most destructive conventionalised form of normativity: when norms feel like laws, they constitute a social pedagogy of rules for belonging and ineligibility whose narrowness threatens people's capacity to invent new ways to attach to the world' (Berlant and Prosser 2011, 182). Rags-to-riches narratives, the trope of the self-made sovereign subject, and the upward mobility trajectory in American literature and culture are forms of cruel optimism because they offer an object that is almost impossible to attain for working class subjects. Ward's text shows that communities like hers are not just excluded from but are a by-product of the American dream. *Men We Reaped* exposes the idea of meritocracy as a form of cruel optimism, which entraps marginalised subjects through notions of hard work or political reform and obscures the oppressive foundations of contemporary American society.

Joyce Sparrow suggests Ward's narrative is actually an example of the upward mobility narrative:

> Through Ward's narrative, readers come to know her own struggles as the only black female in a private high school and as a budding writer finding her place in the world. Ward's candid account [. . .] proves that education and hard work are the way up for the young and downtrodden. (Sparrow 2013, 111)

Sparrow's emphasis on 'lapsed personal responsibility' reinforces the conservative bootstrap-pulling rhetoric of American autobiography, and in doing so undermines the structural oppression Ward evidences. Sparrow's suggestion that 'education and hard work are the way up for the young and downtrodden' is a serious misreading of the text, wherein Ward notes the inescapability of class and racial oppression for most of her community. Ward presents her own upward mobility as being as much down to luck and coincidence as to her own efforts, and often presents those who do not have the opportunities she had as having to work considerably harder than she did. Ward does not position herself as exemplary, in the Franklinian tradition, but as an outlier. Where the individual narrative of development in the classic *Bildungsroman* mode sees its prototypical protagonist leaving a community behind to make it on their own, Ward advocates for her community and uses her success as a platform for exposing state violence.

Berlant's concept of slow death, which is connected to cruel optimism, usefully contextualises Ward's framing of the oppression facing the inhabitants of DeLisle. Slow death 'refers to the physical wearing out of a population in a way that points to its deterioration as a defining condition of its experience and historical existence' (Berlant 2011, 95) and aligns with Ward's description of life in DeLisle, where 'we felt like death was stalking us, driving us from one another, the community falling apart' (Ward 2014, 31). Moreover, it is through the concept of slow death that the importance of biopolitics emerges. Berlant situates their theory as a descendent of Foucault's concept of biopower, the power of the state to 'make something live or to let it die' (97) and describes biopower as the system that 'allow[s] political crises to be cast as conditions of specific bodies' (105) and thus 'gets to judge the problematic body's subjects, whose agency is deemed to be fundamentally destructive' (105–6). Biopolitics, in these terms, aptly describe America's relationship to poor Black communities, where the violence of 'letting die' has become apparent through the (lack of) response to Hurricane Katrina in 2005, the Flint water crisis, Hurricane Maria in 2017, and the general weaponisation of the environment and effects of the climate crisis as a form of institutionalised racism, to name a few examples. In this context, the poverty and violence often endemic to these communities are routinely read as the inherent failings of community members, rather than the result of state violence and neglect. Berlant's discussion of slow death focuses on notions of individual agency under biopolitical capitalist regimes and the ways in which the individual is held responsible for maintaining life-extending behaviour and pursuing 'the good life'.

Alexander Weheliye also deploys a biopolitical approach to reconceptualising the individual, but offers necessary expansions on the approaches of Foucault and Berlant in ways that are relevant to *Men We Reaped*. Weheliye argues that, despite the 'unacknowledged influence of the Black Panther Party . . . on Foucault's work' (Weheliye 2014, 62), race is rarely considered in theories of the human and posthuman. Conversely, he argues that Black studies 'illuminates the essential role that racializing assemblages play in the construction of modern selfhood, works toward the abolition of Man, and advocates the radical reconstruction and decolonization of what it means to be human' (Weheliye 2014, 4). For Weheliye, the experiences of subjects of racialised political violence are essential to understanding the human as a biopolitical construction. While Weheliye's work overlaps with a posthumanist critical framework, he situates himself within the tradition of Black humanism and references Hortense Spillers and Sylvia Wynter as critical race theorists working towards the abolition of 'Man'.

Wynter contests the concept of Man and the attending naturalisation of a particular construction of the human born of racist historical circumstances. She relates the construction of the human to a naturalisation of the properties of Enlightenment Western Man and the associated racial and gendered exclusions. From this, she argues for 'genres of the human', wherein humans are constructed narratively and teleologically, with a cosmogenic origin, and on a hierarchy of humanness, value, and power. Wynter traces the transition from dominant conceptions of the human as divinely created to evolutionarily selected and notes the relationship of this history to capitalism and a 'bioeconomic conception of the human' (quoted in Scott 2000, 160), within which Black people have been positioned as resources in the form of free or cheap labour, rather than consumers. She renders the implications of this clear, posing the rhetorical question:

> How did [people] come to conceive of what it means to be both *human* and *North American* in the *kinds of terms* (i.e. to be White, of Euroamerican culture and descent, middle-class, college-educated and suburban) and within whose logic, the jobless and usually school dropout/ push-out category of young Black males can be *perceived*, and *therefore behaved towards*, only as the *Lack* of the human, the Conceptual Other to being North American? ('No Humans' 43)

Wynter therefore provides a salient framework for unpacking the racial implications of the Enlightenment Humanist subject in America. Her arguments highlight the conditions under which many of the men Ward discusses fall victim to racialised marginalisation because of precisely these concepts of the human and their attendant care and protection on behalf of the state and the broader community. Both Ward and Wynter therefore evidence the ongoing historical and material conditions that have contributed to the construction of a hierarchical humanness.

Men We Reaped can be usefully read as a *Künstlerroman*, in which the narrative follows the development of an artist: in this case, Jesmyn's development as a writer. In the context of biopolitical violence and cruel optimism, Ward eschews the narrative trajectory that would render her story an aide to perpetuating such phenomena, instead testifying to its violence. Jesmyn's subjectivity, far from being sovereign and individualistic, is constructed via and constituted by narrative.

Jesmyn as a writer and creator of narrative is also self-consciously the product of narratives, textual, cultural and national. These come in different forms: the stories and family histories passed down through generations, the changing bodies of literature that she reads at different life stages, and the customary knowledge she develops through lived experience. This initiation into narrative fundamentally determines Jesmyn and the other members of her community and culminates in Jesmyn's understanding of herself and her life as a particular story intersecting and informed by a broader web of stories. Her own textual production navigates the broader narrative landscape to signal the ways in which generic conventions and the knowledge they produce are inherently political. Far from a straightforward *Künstlerroman*, *Men We Reaped* takes advantage of this narrative form, and the distance it makes possible from the sovereignty traditionally associated with autobiography, to construct a posthuman iteration. Even as the *Künstlerroman* genre proves useful in interpreting the text, Ward navigates the attachment to 'being generic' with ambiguity, allowing her text to express its own forms of double consciousness.

The grammars of *Men We Reaped* underscore the ways in which these posthumanist subjectivities function within this reimagined *Künstlerroman*. Across the narrative, Jesmyn's burgeoning consciousness is informed by the stories she reads at different points of her life and development as a writer. She reflects on her motivation to read, stating:

> my love for books sprang from my need to escape the world I was born into, to slide into another where words were straightforward and honest, where there was clearly delineated good and evil, where I found girls who were strong and smart and creative and foolish enough to fight dragons, to run away from home to live in museums, to become child spies, to make new friends and build secret gardens. (85)

The texts Jesmyn references in her adolescence are coming-of-age stories about white girls, and immediately she signals her divergence from these models. For Jesmyn, words are not straightforward and honest, and morality is compromised by the exigencies and limitations on agency imposed by the racial and class oppression amongst her community. While she notes wanting to explore the woods 'like the characters in *Bridge to Terabithia* did in their forest' (86), instead, she 'wandered around the shed in the backyard, leapfrogging over the sceptic tank, sliding along the slippery slope where what had been an artesian well slowed to a slick trickle to create a bog in the middle of the yard' (86). These scenes mark the difference between Jesmyn's childhood heroines and her own life. The innocence of the white canon and the coming-of-age genre is unavailable to Jesmyn, even as that same canon is provided as a model for the construction of her subjectivity. She is a constructed subject, but one that is constructed through an awareness of her alienation from the dominant models of subjectivity in her society.

As she gets older, Jesmyn begins to resist the narratives she encounters. She is horrified by *Gone with the Wind* and moves to texts related to African American resistance: 'By the time I was in my junior and senior years of high school, I was reading *Roots* and *Invisible Man* and *Native Son* and *The Color Purple* and, at my father's insistence, *The Autobiography of Malcolm X*' (207). These texts give her tools with which to understand America; she notes, in particular, an essay by Toni Morrison that allows her to contextualise her Asian friend's lack of support when she received racial abuse at school. Perhaps the most explicative of her own experience, though, is W. E. B. Du Bois, whose work supplies her with the term *double consciousness*: 'When I read it, I thought about sitting in my mother's employer's family room, watching my mother clean' (202); she is referring here to the same employers who are paying for her to attend an elite private school, which in turn will provide the educational foundation for her writing. Jesmyn makes sense of herself, her family and her social world through a combination of texts that rise and fall in importance throughout her development.

Alongside her reading, Jesmyn also begins to situate herself within her own family's history, which functions on two levels. First, there is the material history of violence, wherein she can trace her lineage back to slavery, after which her mother's great-grandfather was murdered by a group of white men (12), her own great grandfather was shot dead (13) and her father lost an eye from a BB gun at the age of six (15). She locates herself and her siblings as the inheritors of 'a line of men and women who have fought hard to live' (44), noting 'Men's bodies litter my family history' (14). Second, Jesmyn understands herself as the product and inheritor of narrative history that delivers these histories through words and stories. History and narrative, fact and fiction, bodies and texts therefore exceed their generic boundaries in Jesmyn's life.

In episodes where she learns about her family's history, she emphasises the storytelling qualities of that knowledge acquisition: 'My grandmother Dorothy tells me stories about them, says some of them were Haitian, that others were Choctaw, and they spoke French that they came from New Orleans or a nebulous elsewhere, searching for land and space, and they stopped there' (9). On other occasions, she notes the stories that are made significant through their omission: 'Mama often told us stories about him, her dead husband, but never spoke of Aldon, the son who died in Vietnam after stepping on a land mine' (14). For Jesmyn, history is a story that sets the narrative conventions and generic determinism for future generations; she describes her parents as 'children of history and place' and notes their 'history bearing fruit in each other' (15). Rather than reading the failure of their marriage as personal failings of individuals neglecting their life-building duties, Jesmyn reads her parents as a generic inevitability, the subjects of particular stories. Ward therefore allows the overdetermination of narrative to undermine the concept of sovereignty throughout the text.

Jesmyn's understanding of history as a narrative trajectory expands from her family to DeLisle and beyond. She connects her community's suffering to a broader national story, literalising the relationship between material reality and personal narrative through the technology of the text. Her parents' relationship is contextualised in a:

> tradition of men leaving their families here [that] seems systemic, fostered by endemic poverty. Sometimes color seems an accidental factor, but then it doesn't, especially when one thinks of the forced fracturing of families that the earliest African Americans endured under the yoke of slavery. (131)

Jesmyn therefore emphasises the structures in which individuals in her community are embedded, those of the town, the nation, and the oppressive historical trajectory of African Americans in America. She continues to make these connections, stating, 'In my research for words to tell this story, I found more statistics about what it means to be Black and poor in the South' (236); she affirms that 'These are the numbers that bear fruit in reality' (237). These statistics are linked to 'Reagan's policies in the eighties' (84), the absence of public housing in DeLisle (6), alongside the Vietnam war, widespread riots, and the constant violence of white supremacy.

The violence that Jesmyn's community endures at the hands of a racist, classist and white supremacist state finds its present-day continuity under a different form, the biopolitical violence of the neoliberal state. As Luz Horne and Daniel Noemi Voionmaa point out:

> Now that the state is (supposedly) almost invisible, or has been transformed into a system that, like god, is everywhere but nowhere to be seen; now, under these circumstances, state violence is not only reproduced through its presence but also, and perhaps more so, through its absence and abandonment towards its subjects. (Horne and Voionmaa 2009, 3)

This form of neglect, or 'letting die' rather than 'making die', is what Jesmyn highlights as the contemporary condition of her community, such as when C.J. gets hit by a train because of a missing reflexive gate and warning lights that 'didn't consistently work, and because it was located at a crossing out in the country in a mainly Black area, no one really cared about fixing them or installing a reflective gate arm' (125).

The relationship between her community's history and her story also becomes a point at which the text is generically destabilised by Gothic tropes and forms of dramatic tension. For example, after Jesmyn's friend Demond is shot dead before he can testify to a crime he witnessed, an event that she could interpret as tragic but entirely disconnected from her own fate, she instead wonders:

> If Demond's family history wasn't so different from my own, did that mean we were living the same story over and over again, down through the generations? That the young and Black had always been dying, until all that was left were children and the few old, as in war? (68)

This framing invokes ideas of haunting and iterative, inescapable loss that exceed the narrative traditions of a *Künstlerroman* and resonate most within the Gothic. Similarly, Jesmyn's assertion that 'Men's bodies litter my family history. The pain of the women they left behind pulls them from the beyond, makes them appear as ghosts' (14) is replete with Gothic imagery, as is her description of feeling 'like death was stalking us' (31) and finding a cellar 'off in the darkness in the future, gaping as a grave' (152) which 'had become an omen for me' (161). In Ward's use of the Gothic in her non-fictional text, it is not the master that is satanic, but the system. Likewise, the haunting in Ward's memoir is not just the haunting of the horrific past of slavery, but the haunting of the invisible and malignant forces at play in the white supremacist structures of an allegedly post-racial America. *Men We Reaped* constructs DeLisle not as a static place but as almost a character itself, with its own history and occasionally an appearance of its own violent agency, a 'wolf town' (9) that is hunting its Black inhabitants.

DeLisle's inhabitants instinctively feel the oppressive overdetermination that this history has on them. When Jesmyn, as a child, gets sent to an elite and majority white school through funding from the rich white family her mother cleans for, she affirms that she wanted 'to leave Mississippi, to escape the narrative I encountered in my family, my community, and my school that I was worthless, a sense that was as ever present as the wet, closing heat' (195). Indeed, much of her childhood and youth is marked by an anxiety about the future. In one episode, she and her siblings and cousins are playing a game where they identify passing cars as omens for their fates, an experience she describes as heavy with anticipation. When it becomes her younger brother Josh's turn, Jesmyn ends the chapter, stating only 'We listened intently for a whoosh, for a loud bang, for a flash of color, for anything that would signal our future' (103). The car that would signal Josh's future never arrives, and this functions as an unsettling foreshadowing of his premature death. As her brother ages, the attempt to grasp at the possibility of a future is exacerbated by the accelerating force of neoliberalism, one which disproportionately affects racially marginalised communities; she notes the collapse of living-wage jobs across the country, stating 'only dead-end service jobs remained, and my brother was burning through those in search of something with a future' (219). Indeed, the history outlined by Jesmyn is one that not only conditions the present, but likewise serves as a generic precedent that shapes future life stories.

Christina Sharpe describes this relation to temporality as part of the experience of existing in the wake of racial violence: 'In the wake, the past that is not past reappears, always, to rupture the present' (Sharpe 2016, 9). The non-linear relationship to temporality likewise appears in Lillvis's *Posthuman Blackness*; she describes Black identity as 'temporally flexible based in the history of what has occurred as well as the potential of what is to come' which corresponds with 'the views of being and time found in the wider field of posthumanism [. . .] In posthuman theory, the subject – the individual, both body and mind – exists in networks of knowledge, discourse, and power that influence and are influenced by the subject' (Lillvis 2017, 3). Jesmyn's use of the past is an example of this; the relationship she establishes with history is one that roots the subject in precisely such networks. In a later episode, Jesmyn describes repeatedly driving aimlessly with her brother, stating, 'We rode like we could drive far and long enough to outrun out story [. . .] But in the end, we could not' (248–9 emphasis added). This emphasis on 'we' is significant; while it is only Josh that dies, and Jesmyn escapes DeLisle, its dead-end jobs and its youth mortality rates, she understands her story as one that is inextricable from her community. The deaths of the men around her are part of her story to the point that they are the centre of her memoir. Jesmyn undermines the individualism of the upward mobility story to affirm her solidarity with the marginalised people of DeLisle.

The focus on the absence of futurity emphasises the ways in which certain communities have no inherited narrative future and no teleological happy ending, a fact that is in stark contrast with the promises of the American dream. Jesmyn describes one episode, after several of the deaths detailed in the text, in which, 'I played one song over and over in my car parked on the street, felt the acute sense that life had promised me something when I was younger, that it wouldn't be this hard, perhaps, that my people wouldn't keep dying without end' (79). C.J., she affirms, 'saw no American dream, no fairy-tale ending, no hope' (121). These episodes highlight the stark contrast between the relationship to free will and determinism that exists in her community and that of the broader American imagination. While she understands herself and the people around her as being set in a particular story with a particular fate, she also evokes the American promise of agency and meritocratic reward. This too is a generically determined story, though one she can resist. The relationship between the events of Jesmyn's life and the story of *Men We Reaped* is manifested as one of construction; a memoir based on Ward's life could well have taken the form of an American dream narrative with certain emphases and omissions. The choice to present it in its current form dramatises the relationship between genre and the construction of truth and knowledge. The genre of the upward mobility narrative is complicit in constructing and maintaining the idea of the American dream and obscuring the axes of oppression and exploitation on which the American economy has relied. *Men We Reaped* does not just dramatise the ways in which different narratives are applied to different bodies, it undermines the individualism that permeates the genre and the neoliberal ideology underpinning American national identity, an ideology that discourages solidarity. Jesmyn, in lieu of this, highlights the relationship between the discourse of the American enlightenment individual in the form of memoir and systemic disenfranchisement.

In *Men We Reaped*, systemic disenfranchisement has not just external, material effects but constitutive effects on individuals and communities, wherein marginalisation becomes a central and internalised narrative and hence becomes self-perpetuating. In reference to her earlier cited statistics, Jesmyn states:

> These are the numbers that bear fruit in reality. By the numbers, by all the official records, here at the confluence of history, of racism, of poverty, and economic power, this is what our lives are worth: nothing. We inherit these things that breed desire and self-hatred, and tragedy multiplies. (237)

Ward dramatises this internalisation through her representation of the lives of the men who die throughout the book. Rog's dropping out of school is contextualised through an educational system that targets

Black boys: 'Sometimes they are passively forced out by school authorities, branded as misfits or accused of serious offences like selling drugs
or harassing other students: sometimes they are pushed to the back of
the classroom and ignored' (26); C.J.'s pessimism is depicted as wisdom, 'In the end, our lives are our deaths. Instinctually, C.J. knew this'
(128); Ronald's suicide is imagined as the response to a knowledge
of his situation in history: 'Ronald looked at his Nothing and saw its
long history, saw it in all our families and our communities, all the
institutions of the South and the nation driving it. He knew it walked
with all of us, and he was tired of walking' (176). The internalisation
of their inherent lack of value within the national structure is a central
factor in these men's subsequent deaths insofar as it bars them from
the steps that are supposed to lead to social mobility, creates mental
health problems, and contributes to addiction and substance abuse.

Jesmyn pays special attention to the way that internalised racial
narratives are gendered. She describes the burgeoning differences
between the roles she and her brother are taught, stating:

> Both of us on the cusp of adulthood, and this is how my brother and I
> understood what it meant to be a woman: working, dour, full of worry.
> What it meant to be a man: resentful, angry, wanting life to be everything
> but what it was. (162)

For Jesmyn, the pressures of womanhood are exacerbated by race in a
country where, as Kimberlé Crenshaw notes, 'many women of color,
for example, are burdened by poverty, childcare responsibilities, and the
lack of job skills' (Crenshaw 1991, 1245). Joshua, on the other hand,
receives less care, is expected to make his own money at a younger age,
and expected to be tougher, a quality he develops through violence at
the hands of his father. The latter is described as an act of protection
as much as violence: 'Perhaps my father dreamed of the men in his
family who died young in all the wrong ways, and this forced his hand
when he woke to my brother standing next to my parents' bed: pink-
mouthed and grinning, green to the world, innocent' (52).

Innocence, a quality so intimately bound with American identity,
is, as Jesmyn demonstrates, not a quality that Black children, especially boys, are afforded. After Joshua moves in with their father as a
young adult, Jesmyn notes a change in him:

> [I] thought for the first time: *He knows something I don't.* [. . .] Perhaps
> my father taught my brother what it meant to be a Black man in the South
> too well: unsteady work, one dead-end job after another, institutions that
> systematically undervalue him as a worker, a citizen, a human being. (211)

Within this context, Jesmyn affirms 'We are never free from the feeling that something is wrong with us, not with the world that made this mess' (240). While the gaining of knowledge is typically represented as empowering in the upward mobility narrative, the knowledge gained by Joshua and the other men here is the internalised knowledge of white supremacy and is hence inherently and explicitly productive of subjugated and subjected subjects.

Jesmyn builds on this foundational understanding of internalised oppression to evidence the ways in which acts that are typically thought of as individual failings or 'lapses in personal responsibility' are systemic and predictable effects of the multifaceted violence faced by racially marginalised communities. As Berlant notes, 'In this habit of representing the intentional subject, a manifest lack of self-cultivating attention can easily become recast as irresponsibility, shallowness, resistance, refusal, or incapacity' (Berlant 2011, 99). Indeed, the belief in the generically determined autonomous individual of Enlightenment humanism obscures the oppressive conditioning of subjects and environments that render 'self-cultivating attention' impossible, undesirable or fruitless. Ward's narrative not only undermines the notion that such an autonomous individual could exist, but makes it clear that the continued belief in this trope reinscribes oppression, disguising it as personal failure.

Jesmyn confesses to her own complicity in this mindset with regards to C.J.'s selling of drugs, stating: 'I, like many others in the neighbourhood, judged him for it. What I did not know at the time was that he hated sitting on that tree, that he wanted more for himself, but he didn't know how to do it' (110). She contextualises the drug epidemic in similar terms: 'I knew that I lived in a place where hope and a sense of possibility were as ephemeral as morning fog, but I did not see the despair at the heart of our drug use' (34). Later, she explains the errors in her understanding:

> What I did not understand then was that the same pressures were weighing on us all. My entire community suffered from a lack of trust: we didn't trust society to provide the basics of a good education, safety, access to good jobs, fairness in the justice system. (169)

This lack of trust and belief in the American dream, is one that she proves to be rooted in material reality.

These representations of what would normatively be understood as 'lack of self-cultivating attention' stand in contrast to Demond's behaviour. Demond is one of the few people in Jesmyn's community who managed to avoid legal problems and the drug scene, and to hold down a steady job: 'Not only did [Demond] have responsibilities, but he also had spent the last couple of years dodging the kind of bad luck that afflicts the innocent in drug-plagued neighbourhoods' (75). Nevertheless, Demond is shot dead outside of his house. His murder is an example of the inescapability of the tragic narrative within which Jesmyn feels her community is trapped and undermines once again the notion that individuals will be rewarded for 'acting in a life-building way – the way that liberal subjects and happy people are supposed to' (Berlant 2011, 100). João Costa Vargas and Joy James state that 'to be sinless or angelic in order to be recognized as citizenry has been the charge for postbellum blackness' (Vargas and James 2012, 2), yet for Demond even that does not suffice. Indeed, this promise is exposed as the form of cruel optimism it is, coercing citizens into accepting exploitative jobs and obeying the laws of a state that is oppressive in the hope of the fulfilment of the American dream. While Jesmyn climbs the social mobility ladder, she makes explicit that she has been a fortunate exception.

Berlant's reference to the liberal subject resonates with the concept of liberal subjectivity that Weheliye describes in analysing the relationship between the oppression of certain modes of 'enfleshment' and the concept of the human. Weheliye draws on Sylvia Wynter's work to argue that the white liberal subject has come to constitute the Western genre of the human, and that:

> In the context of the secular human, black subjects, along with indigenous populations, the colonized, the insane, the poor, the disabled, and so on serve as limit cases by which Man can demarcate himself as the universal human. Thus, race, rather than representing accessory, comes to define the very essence of the modern human. (Weheliye 2014, 24)

In other words, the exclusion of Black and other marginalised subjects from the construction of the white liberal subject is an essential aspect of that construction. The genre of the human in this context is inherently racist, and hence behaving according to the rules of the white liberal subject does not entail the same telos for Black subjects. Wynter's understanding of the 'genre of the human' is particularly relevant to *Men We Reaped* in that the text simultaneously exposes and resists the genre of the human in the literary form that most prominently reinforces it: the memoir. Ward shows that the American dream is intimately bound with this genre, and both are bound to Wynter's concept of the genre of the human. Weheliye describes Wynter's view of Black studies as 'liminal spaces, simultaneously ensconced in and outside the world of Man, from which to construct new objects of knowledge and launch the reinvention of the human' (Weheliye 2014, 25). Ward's memoir is itself a liminal case, simultaneously ensconced in and outside the genre most central to constructing the human and reinventing it aesthetically and politically.

Jesmyn's frequent use of the terms 'story' and 'narrative' to understand the events occurring in DeLisle is notable. It is particularly important that she thinks of this story as one written by someone else, the same 'they' that is hunting her community in the many Gothic-inflected passages and episodes of *Men We Reaped* (38). For Jesmyn, narratives are a vital lens through which to render systems visible. Notably, Jesmyn has not merely inherited the Gothic; she has conscientiously deployed its generic features to make her own intervention into the broader narrative of the Black rural South. The events of her life are presented within the conventions of the Gothic, rather than the upward-mobility story and this is important to note in a *Künstlerroman*. While the Gothic has historically been used to represent the experience of America in general and the South in particular for Black subjects, Ward's intervention into this history is significant. Teresa A. Goddu notes that, traditionally, 'the slave remains stuck playing the terrified victim in the antislavery movement's Gothic story line' (Goddu 2013, 79); in other words, the Gothic genre is useful for depicting racial oppression, but has not proven to be a liberatory tool.

Part of this inherent pessimism is no doubt due to the social constraints of the material world; as Rachel DuPlessis notes in *Writing Beyond the Ending* (1985), 'To compose a work is to negotiate with these questions: what stories can be told? How can plots be resolved? What is felt to be narratable by both literary and social conventions?' (DuPlessis 1985, 3). *Men We Reaped* takes an innovative approach to this dilemma by writing beyond the ending and resisting social and literary conventions in doing so. In one episode, Jesmyn comments:

> I knew the boys in my first novel, which I was writing at that time, weren't as raw as they could be, weren't *real*. I knew they were failing as characters because I wasn't pushing them to assume the reality that my real-life boys, Demond among them, experience every day. I loved them too much: as an author, I was a benevolent God. (70)

This comment metatextually explains Ward's own approach to writing: she deploys the trappings of the Gothic to escape the trappings of the upward-mobility narrative and to contribute to the discursive production of knowledge of structural oppression, yet she writes her characters outside of the Gothic genre in her descriptions of the episodes that solidify her affective relationships with them and in her imaginings of the last hours before their deaths. The latter are written through use of the subjunctive and conditional modes and are in many ways not 'real', in the sense that they create ameliorative alternative realities. When imagining the hours before her brother is hit by a drunk driver while not on his usual ride home, she states, 'I'd like to think it was a beautiful night, which is why he would have taken Highway 90 home. That the moon was full out over the Gulf, that it shone cool and silver in the clear sky, that the water glittered with its reflection' (230). This scene goes on for half a page, constructing a peaceful image of her brother enjoying his detour. For Demond, she imagines 'another night' where he 'would have driven to DeLisle, turned into Rob's mother's driveway [. . .] and stopped to the side of Rob's mother's house' (76).

Lillvis notes that 'Posthuman theorizing, when executed with an awareness of black humanist histories, acknowledges the significance of the past to present and future ideas of black identity and simultaneously considers alternative temporal reference points for the origin of black autonomy and authority' (6). In *Men We Reaped*, Ward deploys temporalities beyond the past, present and future to reassert the value of Black lives. The subjunctive and conditional are primary examples of this. Despite the texts' focus on state violence and necropolitics, Jesmyn avoids settling on representations of suffering, choosing instead to offer versions of events that emphasise her loved ones' potentiality for freedom, reinstating their inherent value. She notes that, 'Most of the men in my life thought their stories, whether they were drug dealers or strait-laced, were worthy of being written about' (69), and her own writing reaffirms that belief. Nevertheless, the text is anxious about the unknowable and inexpressible. Representations of the men who died are not adequate substitutes. Jesmyn notes the failures of her memory, failures that are significant in the holes that they leave in her memoir. She is unable to recall the last time she saw Joshua, and notes that 'As the years pass, I find my memory shrinking and adhering to photos' (241). She remembers:

> Sometimes at night, on one of his rides, Josh would stop and sit with [an elderly man], talk to him, ask him questions: *What do you know about God? Why are we here?* [. . .] This older gentleman would have smiled and said – I do not know what answers this Black man gave my brother, nor if they made sense to Joshua. (244–5)

This sense of epistemic and narrative loss is reiterated when she states: 'When Joshua died, he took so many of our stories with him' (249). This frustration with her failing memory is not mitigated by photos; instead, they signify the shortcomings of representation, even in the genres that most convincingly retain the aura and authority of reality. She describes the picture of Rog on his memorial shirt as an 'insult to the living man, too blurry, too static for the smiling, open-armed twenty-three-year-old he'd been' (41). When trying to photograph C.J. playing basketball, she recalls:

> he was too fast and my camera was too old. I could hear the shutter snap open, lick against metal, and then snap shut again. Too slow. Later, when I developed that film back at college, C.J. would look all wrong in the air: awkwardly bent, blurry, all his terrific grace lost in the frozen moment captured by the camera. (108)

The frustration of being incapable of capturing and immortalising moments with these loved ones is a testament to the limits of textuality and language, and yet marks an awareness that the act of taking photographs itself is a form of rendering moments and people meaningful. Indeed, many of Jesmyn's childhood and affective memories are mediated through photographs. This mediation takes on particular significance after death, marking its own kind of haunting in its reminder of absence: photographs are not people. These anxieties about representation also emerge as anxieties about language. Throughout the text, Jesmyn describes episodes where words fail her. Many of the moments where Jesmyn insists 'I have no words' (127), relate to her brother. Towards the end of the narrative, her mother asks her to write a poem for her brother's funeral and she states:

> 'I can't do it,' I told her, 'I can't write a poem.' [. . .] My mother asked me what I wanted my brother's funeral shirt to say, and I replied: 'Nothing.' [. . .] My voice broke when I read it to my family, to our friends, to the boys who would later lie in caskets, but who stood alive on that day in the back of the church. (232)

This anxiety is resonant for two reasons. One is that her ability to craft words is what enabled her ascent into a literary career and her escape from the trajectory in which the rest of her community are trapped. Thus her failure to find words at times when she is reminded of the violence they continue to endure represents a mourning of the gap between her experience and theirs, and a refusal of the assumed gap in value between them. Another is the sense that language, far from being a neutral tool with which to communicate reality, is in some way determined by and complicit in the very structures her writing is trying to combat. She notes 'We dream of speaking when we lack the gift of oratory, when we lack the vision to see the stage, the lights, the audience, the endless rigging and ropes and set pieces behind us, manipulated by many hands' (180). She does, of course, eventually find the words to write this story, despite a full awareness of the stage, the ropes, the set and the manipulation, but she is clear about the limitations of words: 'This story is only a hint of what my brother's life was worth, more than the nineteen years he lived, more than the thirteen years he's been dead. It is worth more than I can say. And there's my dilemma, because all I can do in the end is say' (243). Jesmyn tells her story, she acknowledges the power of stories, but she never settles on the belief that the story is enough. To refer back to Berlant's critique of women's memoirs appealing to the sentimental as if it were enough to create material change, Ward's memoir emphasises the need for action outside her text.

Nevertheless, stories do matter. Stories are key to subject construction and to developing a relationship to the past and future. They are central to imagining alternatives, and necessary for informing and inspiring action. While Jesmyn acknowledges the limitation of 'just saying', she tells this story at great personal cost. She notes that to 'say this is difficult is understatement; telling this story is the hardest thing I've ever done' (7). Her stated aim in writing it is to 'understand why my brother died while I live, and why I've been saddled with this rotten fucking story' (8). This said, the public nature of memoir suggests she wants to do more than understand; she wants others to understand the injustice to which she is testifying; she wants a different future.

Lillvis argues that 'Posthuman Blackness asserts that the boundary crossings that exist within posthuman cultures enable black subjects to make connections to diasporic history in the present and also imagine the future as a site of power' (Lillvis 2017, 8). Ward attempts to cross such boundaries in her rejection of the generically inscribed class separation of her upward mobility and in her temporal experimentation. She states that

> because this is my story just as it is the story of those young men, and because this is my family's story just as it is my community's story, it is not straightforward. To tell it, I must tell the story of my town, and the history of my community. (8)

It is not straightforward both in that it is not just her story, not just her teleology, but also in that it seeks to fight the teleological fate of her community through both form and content. In the final chapter, the alternating temporalities (from the beginning and from the end) come together. Jesmyn states 'This is where the past and the future meet [. . .] This is where my two stories come together. This is the summer of the year 2000. This is the last summer that I will spend with my brother. This is the heart. This is. Every day, this is' (213). With this use of temporality, not only does Ward construct a subject that connects history to the present, but she makes her brother both centre and climax. Her form mirrors her words in its assertion of the value of his life, in spite of all generic determination to the contrary.

The stories that Jesmyn finds empowering are not directed at white America; they do not seek affirmation and recognition from the system that has grown from the oppression of Black people. They are tools for survival and expressions of love and care for the community out of which they come. This is the blueprint for her own memoir. Autobiographical passages appear frequently in scholarship contesting the construction of the human and the violence against Black people woven into the development of the United States. Both Christina Sharpe and Sylvia Wynter deploy the autobiographical 'I' and root their theorising in personal experience. This is not coincidental. Ward's story gives concrete examples of abstracted statistics; it shows the lived experience of Black biopolitical subjects in a country founded on concomitant white supremacy and an insistence on the freedom and agency of humans. It exposes the relationship between material reality and social and rhetorical construction. Ward uses the genre most closely tied to the promise of the American Dream to delegitimate its subject.

Works Cited

Berlant, Lauren Gail. 2011. *Cruel Optimism*. Durham, NC: Duke University Press.

Berlant, Lauren, and Jay Prosser. 2011. 'Life Writing and Intimate Publics: A Conversation with Lauren Berlant'. *Biography* (Honolulu) 34 (1): 180–7.

Crenshaw, Kimberlé. 1991. 'Mapping the Margins: Intersectionality, Identity Politics, and Violence against Women of Color'. *Stanford Law Review* 42 (6): 1241–99.

DuPlessis, Rachel. 1985. *Writing Beyond the Ending*. Bloomington: Indiana University Press.

Foucault, Michel. 1986. *The Will to Knowledge: The History of Sexuality*. Volume 1. London: Penguin.

Gilmore, Leigh. 2001. *The Limits of Autobiography: Trauma and Testimony*. Ithaca, NY: Cornell University Press.

Goddu, Teresa A. 2013. 'The African American Slave Narrative and the Gothic'. *A Companion to American Gothic*. Oxford: John Wiley.

Horne, Luz, and Daniel Noemi Voionmaa. 2009. 'Notes Toward an Aesthetics of Marginality in Contemporary Latin American Literature'. *Latin American Studies Association Forum* 40 (1): 36–41.

Lillvis, Kristen. 2017. *PostHuman Blackness and the Black Female Imagination*. Athens: University of Georgia Press.

McLennan, Rachael. 2012. *American Autobiography*. Edinburgh: Edinburgh University Press.

Scott, David. 2000. 'The Re-Enchantment of Humanism: An Interview with Sylvia Wynter'. *Small Axe* 8 (September): 119–207.

Sharpe, Christina Elizabeth. 2016. *In the Wake: on Blackness and Being*. Durham, NC: Duke University Press.

Sparrow, Joyce. 2013. 'Ward, Jesmyn. Men We Reaped: A Memoir'. *Library Journal* 138 (14): 111.

Vargas, João Costa, and Joy A. James. 2012. 'Refusing Blackness-as-Victimization: Trayvon Martin and the Black Cyborgs'. *Pursuing Trayvon Martin: Historical Contexts and Contemporary Manifestations of Racial Dynamics*, edited by George Yancy and Janine Jones. Lanham, MD: Lexington Books. ProQuest Ebook Central. https://ebookcentral.proquest.com/lib/ed/detail.action?docID=1076201.

Ward, Jesmyn. 2014. *Men We Reaped*. London: Bloomsbury.

Weheliye, Alexander G. 2014. *Habeas Viscus: Racializing Assemblages, Biopolitics, and Black Feminist Theories of the Human*. Durham, NC: Duke University Press.

Wynter, Sylvia. 1994. 'Human Being as Noun? Or Being Human as Praxis? Towards the Autopoetic Turn / Overturn: A Manifesto'. Unpublished essay. 'No Humans Involved: An Open Letter to My Colleagues'. *Forum H.H.I. Knowledge for the 21st Century* 1, no. 1 (Fall 1994): 42–73.

Chapter 12

Releasing the Heavy Repercussions of Black Death in Jesmyn Ward's *Men We Reaped*

Candice N. Hale

Sick and Tired

Mississippian and Civil Rights activist, Fannie Lou Hamer, knows the heavy burdens Black people face in America and her long-used idiom to describe the injustices of the Jim Crow South, in which, she remarks that she's 'sick and tired of being sick and tired' is enduringly relevant in the US today.[1] Not only are Black people 'sick and tired of being sick and tired' but we are also tired of dying in record numbers to endemic poverty, overlooked health disparities, police brutality and drug-related deaths. While Jim Crow may seem like it absolved itself from any further reckoning in the South after the civil rights era, it simply dons a new set of masks in present-day America to punish, penalise and criminalise Black men and women.[2] And though chattel slavery no longer remains, due to the 13th Amendment, and frees Black people from such physical harm, it does not mean that systemic and institutional racism and white supremacy in the US have continued to uphold practices, policies and procedures that exert power, create fear and choke the life out of its Black citizens. Let's not forget that this fear is most realised in the US South, and even more so in rural and poorer neighbourhoods.

The fear is something Black people have carried for generations and passed on reluctantly to their children like thick cough syrup, hoping their throats would regurgitate it, but it goes down a bit too smoothly instead, settling to find a snug place to hinder their children's futures. When the fear rises and bubbles though, it turns into a palpable kind of anger that consumes most Black people when they feel that first moment of nothingness – that sting and betrayal of their own skin. In *The Fire Next Time*, James Baldwin cautioned us with his raw depiction of race relations in 1960s America. Penning a letter to his 14-year-old nephew, Baldwin writes, 'You were born into a society which spelled out with brutal clarity, and in as many ways as possible, that you were a worthless human being. You were not expected to aspire to excellence: you were expected to make peace with mediocrity' (Baldwin 1993, 7). Confronting the reality of white supremacy as a Black man is as traumatic in 1963 when Baldwin pens these words as it is today in 2022. Why? Then is now. Times have not changed much since Rev. Dr Martin Luther King, Jr had a dream: 'It is paradoxical that with all the attention over the last 50 years on social justice and diversity and inclusion, we have made little progress in actualizing the vision of an equitable society' (Winters 2020, xiv). Progress is slow and dreams are halted by the scourge of white supremacy that continues to seep into every part of society. In that regard, white supremacy casts a wide net in devaluing, traumatising and killing the Black body. Since the first arrival of Africans in Jamestown, Virginia in 1619, the lived experience of what it means to be Black in America and how that carries its own set of traumas and experiences – undeniably keeping us 'sick and tired'. In this chapter, I focus on the ways Jesmyn Ward's memoir *Men We Reaped* addresses the situation wherein Black men are being dispossessed of their lives, and the related situation wherein Black women are being reduced to a rising, unsurmountable grief that is nearly impossible to hold down. In *Men We Reaped*, Ward opens the floodgates for the Black death, trauma and grief of those that must bear witness to the injustices exacted by decades of white supremacy for Black Southerners. In what follows I show how Ward's memoir can be informed by fellow Mississippi writer Kiese Laymon's work *Heavy* and Mary-Frances Winters's *Black Fatigue*. Using these specific texts in conversation with *Men We Reaped* later in the chapter, I can offer a sliver of hope to the wounded Ward references because transformation and healing are both capable and near for the communities and families surviving from the sour of white rage.

Black Women – A Voice Like Rage

Black women are sick and tired, but they don't get a day off, especially when their roles in motherhood, marriage, relationships and the workforce present the overflowing burdens of fear, poverty, sexism, racism and death at every turn. Malcolm X made this painfully clear in the 1960s: 'The most disrespected person in America is the black woman. The most unprotected person in America is the black woman. The most neglected person in America is the black woman.'[3] In *Men We Reaped*, Ward recognises early on the disrespect Black women will face, and her own personal experience begins as the 'only Black girl in a school' full of white peers that stare and ridicule the lives of Black people during her tenure at middle and high school (2013, 2). Not only do the white peers attempt to place Ward in an inferior status because of her Black race, but they also use her class status as a 'scholarship' recipient to further demean her and the communities from which she comes from – both DeLisle and New Orleans – as impoverished and a 'murder capital'. Ward refuses to let other people (e.g. outside of her community) discredit the beauty of the Black men she loves and honours because outsiders fail to know them, fail to understand them, and fail to provide for the basic needs of a community. That love is extended especially to her brother and close family friends who function as 'play cousins' in the South. Although a young 'Mimi' comes to understand what Black women like her own mother and grandmother had to endure with lousy husbands and absent fathers, she builds strong and loving relationships with her brother and male friends.[4] Ward's mother and grandmother struggled to hold down these Black men for little to no reward because that's what Black women have always done to keep their families intact for generations. *Men We Reaped* is comprised of alternating chapters where Ward discusses the story of her family and her community and then the deaths of five Black men. Ward informs us that one story cannot exist without the other story – the five men are a part of Wolf Town – they are born to this community, watched by this community, wounded by this community, this community learns to ignore their concerns, and Ward is now mourning their deaths because the outrage wasn't loud enough in this community. Ward's memoir isn't linear but neither is time, memory, nor grief, when we consider death or the past. Furthermore, Ward's intention here is to better understand the purpose of her brother's death – why is he able to die while she lives? Ward's findings lead her to assess how the unfathomable losses she suffered were at the hands of the endemic poverty and racism in Mississippi – the wolf that preys on Black life. Black women like Ward, and those agonising over the deaths of Black boys and men, have every right to have a voice of rage. To battle the ghosts of the past is no easy task – it's a double-headed dragon – if one is living in the deep South. Black people are fighting the ghosts of slavery and the ghosts of their own people, as Ward reiterates, 'But my ghosts were once people, and I cannot forget that' (2013, 7). The South will never let one forget the damage it's done.

Ward's memoir is a testament to its menacing effects. Trying to get through to the other side of pain is a journey that most people find to be a hard terrain to cross – so for Ward to find a straight path to normalcy after five unexpected deaths is beyond unfathomable – her courage and spirit to move forward through grief is extraordinary. From the testimony in her memoir, it is understood that grief is certainly not a linear process, but one that moves with ebbs and flows. In *Notes on Grief*, Chimamanda Ngozi Adichie explains, 'We don't know how we grieve until we grieve' (2021, 65). Understanding grief is unpredictable and is a different process for everybody.

There may not be any comfort in grief; sadness may be the only comforter. Navigating grief may sound like rage and look like sadness, but Ward demands that we must not forget our grief and let it silence us. Ward speaks for all the men she lost: 'I wonder why silence is the sound of our submerged rage, our accumulated grief. I decide this is not right, that I must give voice to this story' (2013, 8). *Men We Reaped* is a hard story for Ward to tell, to write, and to remember for others, but it helps to clear out the rage and spread the beauty of life and value of Black men. Ward writes:

> Grief doesn't fade. Grief scabs over like my scars and pulls into new, painful configurations as it knits. It hurts in new ways. We are never free from grief. We are never free from the feeling that we have failed. We are never free from self-loathing. We are never free from the feeling that something is wrong with us, not with the world that made this mess. (Ward 2013, 239)

Grief stays in place, lulls and pulls, never making a bargain with convenience. In *Men We Reaped*, the weight of grief is not simply heavy, but it is complex, imposing, haunting, lonely, insidious and silencing. Ward states that 'this grief, for all its awful weight, insists that [Joshua] matters. What we carry of Roger and Demond and C.J. and Ronald says that they matter' (2013, 243). To be a Black man in the South is a daily grief for Black women and mothers. Black women hold up the strength and soul of their homes and their communities. According to Mary-Frances Winters in *Black Fatigue*, 'Black women are taught that they should protect Black men and boys at all costs' (2020, 115). More often than not, Black women not only thrive but survive in hostile communities like DeLisle, Mississippi – able to still create an environment where Black boys and men can feel love, respect and value in the community. In *Men We Reaped*, we see it not only from Jesmyn, but from her mother and her grandmother as well – those traits of Black motherhood and womanhood are passed down – giving her the ability to quell the grief and pain that ransacks her life in the early 2000s. Ward's strength and resilience are undeniable, but not limitless:

> Without my mother's legacy, I would never have been able to look at this history of loss, this future where I will surely lose more, and write the narrative that remembers, write the narrative that says: *Hello. We are here. Listen.* It is not easy. I continue. Sometimes I am tireless. And sometimes I am weary. (2013, 251)

Although weary and tired, and repeatedly pointing to the difficulty of composing her memoir, Ward is ultimately able to confront her own grief and gives voice to the pain in our lives and our communities. However, here I direct us to writer-historian Imani Perry, another Black Southern woman, who cautions readers in *Breathe: A Letter to My Sons*, 'Be careful to what you are bound. Otherwise, you might author your own bitterness and bile' (2019, 107). Ward's grief from the deaths of the five Black men whose stories partly structure *Men We Reaped*, represents a deep wound, which creates an understandably intense rage, and one might worry about how this could function as a breeding ground for rancor and hostility. For this reason, I argue for the value in placing Ward's work in conversation with other healing texts like Laymon's *Heavy*, which focuses on Black men and vulnerability, and Winters's *Black Fatigue*, which centres on social justice, self-care and transformation, allowing us the space not to fall prey to incapacitation and antagonism.

Black Men – DeLisle's Invisible Prey

In Ward's emotionally charged memoir she chronicles the deaths of five young Black men, including her younger brother, who died from the years 2000 to 2004 in the small town of DeLisle, Mississippi. These young men die from terrible accidents, murder and suicide. Even though these deaths are clearly unrelated in nature and time, they are intrinsically linked by a glaring truth where racism and economic struggle kills them: 'Only this loss, this pain. I could not understand why there was always this' (Ward 2013, 41). Ward strongly believes their identity as young Black men and their place and circumstance in rural Southern Mississippi affords them little to no advantages. Ward, aware of Dr King's dream in 1963, realises it does not hold true decades later for the beloved Black men in DeLisle that she loses.[5] Because Roger Eric Daniels, Demond Cook, Charles Joseph Martin, Ronald Wayne Lizana and Joshua Adam Dedeaux end up being judged by the colour of their skin and not by the content of their character. It is interesting here that Ward offers us five different versions, personalities and attitudes of Black men in her memoir, but, too often, white America fails to rightfully see Black men as they are. Ward's testimony of these men's experiences here are so reminiscent of Ralph Ellison's narrator in *Invisible Man*. The unnamed narrator explains:

> I am a man of substance, of flesh and bone, fiber and liquids – and I might even be said to possess a mind. I am invisible, understand, simply because people refuse to see me . . . They see only my surroundings, themselves, or figments of their imagination – indeed, everything and anything except me. (Ellison 1995, 3)

Within their imaginations is where the danger lies because white people refuse to acknowledge Black men as real people with families, futures, and hopes – they are instead controlled by their fears, hate and psyches. In *Black Fatigue: How Racism Erodes the Mind, Body, and Spirit*, Mary-Frances Winters notes what happens when Black men hide behind that invisibility themselves: they carry the weight of invisibleness with many different and sometimes destructive responses. Black men have a number of different personas, including nurturing father figure; supportive partner; strong, don't-show-emotion macho man; laid back (nothing bothers me); a hard, mean outward vibe (I'll kick your ass if you mess with me). Behind these different personas hide deep wounds from intergenerational denigration. (Winters 2020, 155) These Black men share the trauma of generational pain and sorrow that keeps their vulnerability at bay, allowing white America to use their imagination to paint their own narratives of Black men that dement and destroy.

In *Men We Reaped* we learn that these Black men only reap a harvest of endemic poverty and systemic racism in the South unable to manifest their freedom or an oasis. Before Ward can even make sense of the Black death present in her memoir and convey the grief of so much loss, she must recognise the place she calls home as a place that mangles the life out of its people, even if it is also a place of kinship and solidarity. Ward shares with us both the personal testimonies of death and the lovely condemnations about DeLisle, Mississippi: 'I knew there was much to hate about home, the racism and inequality and poverty, which is why I'd left, yet I loved it'

(2013, 22).[6] Merging together the connections and feelings of family and memories, flickering hope and love to a home space that doesn't always love you back is the sentiment Ward proposes here. Her love-hate relationship to DeLisle is one very common to Black residents often stifled in the tightened grip of indifference and incapacity in small, rural, poor and racist Southern towns. Ward's family line of (white) Dedeauxes that live in Wolf Town (DeLisle) endure the first cases of brutal racism at the hands of white men that set the tone for how the future generations are thus treated in the family – especially the men – both grandfathers on Ward's mother and father's sides are killed.[7] Ward reiterates here, 'Men's bodies litter my family history. The pain of the women they left behind pulls them from the beyond, makes them appear as ghosts . . . Sometimes, when I think of all the men who've died early in my family over the generations, I think DeLisle is the wolf' (Ward 2013, 14). The metaphor of the wolf becomes a recurring image of death and destruction that preys on the Black men in DeLisle like a prized hunt of the season. Like the wave of white supremacy that attacks the South, the wolf in DeLisle is a savage beast uncontrolled by its desires to feed on the bodies of Black men.

Yet, Ward issues a fierce call to action to save her community from the hunt. In *Between the World and Me,* Ta-Nehisi Coates riffs on the importance of Black bodies in America and how valuable they are to white consumption then and now. Coates even exclaims, 'In America, it is traditional to destroy the black body – *it is heritage*' (2015, 103). However, our Black boys and men are no longer for sale and the oppression and destruction and devaluing of our Black bodies must cease. Ward makes them real people because they are. More specifically, Ward mentions her own late-night rendezvous during her breaks from college where she often did things like drinking too many shots, smoking Black-n-Milds, listening to Outkast too loud, and taking club pics with her cousins and friends. Ward remembers, 'I knew that I lived in a place where hope and a sense of possibility were as ephemeral as morning fog, but I did not see the despair at the heart of our drug use' (Ward 2013, 34).[8] However, the only difference is that Ward was able to escape Wolf Town by going back to college and getting away while her siblings and her friends remained back home in the midst of the poverty, racism and drug use that plagued her small town. Clearly, Ward made sense of the situation between her circle of family and friends, 'We crawled through time like roaches through the linings of walls, the neglected spaces and hours, foolishly happy that we were still alive even as we did everything to die' (2013, 76). It's just that young people sometimes think they are invincible – but in DeLisle these young Black men were invisible to a system that failed to give them a chance to be successful Black men that could actually prosper and take care of themselves socially and economically. Ward states:

> My entire community suffered from a lack of trust: we didn't trust so-
> ciety to provide the basics of a good education, safety, access to good
> jobs, fairness in the justice system. And even as we distrusted the society
> around us, the culture that cornered us and told us were perpetually
> less, we distrusted each other. We did not trust our fathers to raise us,
> to provide for us. Because we trusted nothing, we endeavored to protect
> ourselves, boys becoming misogynistic and violent, girls turning duplic-
> itous, all of us hopeless. Some of us turned sour from the pressure, let it
> erode our sense of self until we hated what we saw, without and within.
> And to blunt it all, some of us turned to drugs. (2013, 169)

Inequality and racism don't meet Black people on equal ground and make amends – those people wanting to be heard and feel seen usu-ally must fight for what they need and deserve. More importantly, this memoir testifies that Black men possess a strong sense of value and worth and not just this capacity to suffer and to get choked out in the South.

Within the span of four years, Ward aches over the death of five beloved Black men that she could not save. In the memoir, she ded-icates a section to each young man, so readers get a full glimpse of their life as human – not a statistic or an invisible Black man in the media – with a sense of dignity, integrity, love, hope, future and family. By using this type of narrative choice to eulogise them, Ward gives these men a memorial space forever etched in her memoir, even if DeLisle chooses to forget they ever existed. From the alternating chapters, Ward's witnessing in *Men We Reaped* is impactful and effective. 'We' affects not only Ward but also other relatives, friends and the community.[9] She tells us how 'Death spreads, eating away at the root of our community like a fungus' (Ward, 2013, 239).[10] Even after the death of these five men, the community still suffers even more loss that Ward is devastated by and wonders how DeLisle can breathe moving forward. In spite of everything Ward experiences in these moments, she finds a lesson to pass on: 'My mother had the resilience to cobble together a family from the broken bits of another. And my mother's example teaches me other things: This is how a transplanted people survived a holocaust and slavery' (2013, 251). The living are still here to make their way past the wolf.

Trauma: Bending and Healing to Survive White America

While *Men We Reaped* examines America's impact on the destruction of Black families, Kiese Laymon's *Heavy: An American Memoir* unpacks the traumas, oppressions, truths, expectations and bodies weighing down the lives of Black men in America.[11] Laymon's and Ward's texts are both poignantly heavy in their approaches to the plight of Black men, and they speak to one another in vital ways. Ward's text highlights some of the male struggles that are present in Laymon's text, but I am also attempting to connect moments of healing and transformations that arise through comparison. Laymon and Ward are fellow Mississippians with a clear understanding of the Black man's struggle in the post-civil rights South.[12] The deaths experienced in *Men We Reaped* are products of the cultural silence around generational trauma, institutional racism and abuse we find revealed in Laymon's *Heavy*. These Black men's untimely deaths result in a faulty society and a failed community where they could not voice their concerns, fears or shame to keep them alive. However, unless we learn to bring the truth to the surface as Laymon decides to do in his painfully honest memoir, then the impacts of generational trauma and violence will continue to destroy families and communities. Just as *Men We Reaped* deploys its innovative narrative structure, Laymon is also formally innovative as *Heavy* is presented in the form of a letter to his mother in which he is finally able to discuss the lies that have harmed him during his childhood and shaped him as an adult. Loving yet abusive, Laymon's mother's only goals are to protect her Black son and deter him from being mediocre in a white world, but she did so often at his own detriment with her strict upbringing, verbal jabs and frequent beatings. Laymon remembers, 'Every time you said my particular kind of hardheadedness and white Mississippians' brutal desire for black suffering were recipes for an early death, institutionalization, or incarceration, I knew you were right. I just didn't care' (Laymon 2018, 5). Like any young Black boy, Laymon attempts to wiggle into his own existence the hard way, which no Black mother wants her son to do, so she beats him into a shape she can form instead. But his mother stresses vehemently to him, 'At some point, you are going to have to understand that people outside of Mississippi never know what to do with us when we're excellent. So they do what they can to punish us' (Laymon 2018, 80). His mother does what she thinks is best to keep him safe even when it may not be enough. While it is evident that Laymon does not always understand the reasons behind his mother's logic, he comes to understand the suffering Black men endured simply for existing and breathing in Jackson: 'It seemed like just driving, or walking into a house, or doing your job, or cutting a grapefruit was all it took to get shot out of the sky' (Laymon 2018, 83). By the same token, in *Men We Reaped*, Ward's brother Joshua is incessantly punished and disciplined for even the slightest infractions in ways Jesmyn is not. Ward learns quickly:

> My brother would have to be stronger than that. My brother would have to grow up and be a Black man in the South. My brother would have to fight in ways that I would not. Perhaps my father dreamed about the men in his family who died young in all the wrong ways. (2013, 52)

In both texts we see unspoken rules about how a Black boy conducts himself around white folks.

Coming of age as a Black boy in Mississippi is particularly complex for Laymon because not only does he divulge his struggles in his family but he also exposes those struggles of America – the constant damage white society continues to do that injure Black people.[13] Laymon aptly reminds us, '*America seems filled with violent people who like causing people pain but hate when those people tell them that pain hurts*' (2018, 88, emphasis original). Unresolved trauma festers like a sore that will never heal, if families do not speak the truth to one another. The pain never leaves if it is not brought to the surface. In *Heavy*, Laymon experiences sexual assault at the age of twelve with his babysitter on several occasions and also witnesses sexual acts at a neighbour's house, but fails to effectively communicate about his trauma.[14] Instead, food becomes his outlet and he gorges on peach preserves and box wine to cope with his trauma, starting his initial problems with his weight.[15] From high school to college, Laymon struggles with his weight, sexuality and racism and these struggles structure the memoir. The truths he reveals to his mother are thus transformative and healing for him as a Black man:

> Every time I lied, I wanted to control you, control your memory of us, control your vision of me. I was afraid to talk about being emotionally abusive, about gorging, about starving, about gambling all my money away, about wanting to disappear. I didn't talk with you about those days at Beulah Beauford's house, about what my body felt in the bedrooms of our house in Jackson. I didn't think there was any way you could love me if I really showed you more of who, and what, and where I'd been. (Laymon 2018, 224)

At once, Laymon is open, vulnerable and free to finally be himself without shame and judgement to be the Black man he chooses – even if it is a heavy existence – it's his – his Black body – his Black life. Learning from a parent's mistakes is not always a failure because Laymon gained an important lesson from his mother: 'I learned indirectly from you that we cannot responsibly love anyone, and especially not black children in America, if we insist on making a practice of hiding and running from ourselves' (2018, 230). As Laymon shares the various trauma inflicted throughout *Heavy*, readers are quick to acknowledge that surviving trauma is chaotic, confusing and non-linear. Throughout *Men We Reaped*, Ward and her family experience intergenerational traumas well before they experience the death of Joshua and the other four family friends. For example, Ward's maternal family is wounded by men's infidelity, Reaganomics and scathing survival:

> This is a common refrain in my community, and more specifically in my family. I have always thought of my family as something of a matriarchy, since the women of my mother's side have held my nuclear family and my immediate family and my extended family together through so much. (2013, 83)

Ward's immediate family becomes unravelled when her father leaves – it is traumatic and consequential for all involved. Ward reminds us, 'My mother knew the family was her burden to bear. She could not leave' (2013, 131). Fractured families, endemic poverty and systemic oppression, and the business of raising children alone are definitely traumas experienced in Ward's household that deserve room for proper healing. (2013, 131). Both Ward's and Laymon's memoirs suggest that we must be willing to unburden the secrets of our traumas in order to fully heal and endure the struggles that are harming us in this life.

Laymon offers a brutal and honest account of his trauma and not once does he expect our sympathy. The risks and the regrets that Laymon sacrifices in putting his memoir out into the world are indeed heavy, but so perhaps are the rewards of giving voice to the traumas of the past. In an effort to evoke solidarity and empathy with readers and communities at large, Laymon believes there is 'a more meaningful process of healing. If we fall, give us a chance to fall honestly, compassionately together. The nation as it is currently constituted has never dealt with a yesterday or tomorrow where we were radically honest, generous, and tender with each other' (Layman 2018, 239). There can be interweaving of trauma, pain, abuse and violence with joy, laughter, friendship and love done within a community of friends and family that can jump-start a moment of transformative healing. While Laymon may not keep all the promises he made his mama in his life, he can show us all the ways of 'getting through the other side of suffering' (2018, 170) and just 'where we bend' (2018, 240). Trauma lingers and remains with us so that it becomes ingrained and indistinguishable from the reality of what it means to be human – to experience dignity in the everyday – which is what Ward's five beloved Black men were denied in death. Laymon's *Heavy* bends and holds a space for every Black body denied freedom and possibility to get to the other side in Ward's *Men We Reaped*. We observe in *Men We Reaped* how the traumas often begin in the home and then manifest into the communities, impacted by socio-economic factors like racism, violence and drug use, that it turns 'all of us hopeless', making its Black men and women feel like they are *nothing* (Ward 2013, 169). Ward acknowledges her stories are hard to tell, but the traumas do not get to have the final say: 'We raise children and tell them other things about who they can be and what they are worth: to us, everything. We love each other fiercely, while we live and after we die. We survive; we are savages' (Ward 2013, 250).

Black Fatigue and Wilful Ignorance

In her work, *Black Fatigue: How Racism Erodes the Mind, Body, and Spirit*, Mary-Frances Winters identifies and describes the forms of systemic racism that lead to the symptoms of 'black fatigue'.[16] Black fatigue is defined as:

> the fatigue that comes from the pain and anguish of living with racism every single day of your life. It is about being fatigued by those who are surprised and express outrage (with no action) that such inequities still exist. It is about the constant fatigue of not knowing whether you or a loved will come home alive. It is about enduring the ravages of intergenerational racism. (Winters 2020, 2)

Black Fatigue is usefully read alongside *Men We Reaped* because it not only uncovers the negative impacts of systematic racism on Black men, but it also provides practical strategies to resist Black fatigue in one's everyday life. Black fatigue is very real and shares the exact sentiment Fannie Lou Hamer shared during the 1960s:

> Then is now. Black people are fatigued because of the lack of progress in dismantling centuries-old racist systems. The forces that maintain the status quo are deeply entrenched. The widespread denial that racism is at the root of these interconnected issues is fatiguing and literally killing those who are the victims of this system. (Winters 2020, 67)[17]

For example, this system keeps many of the men in DeLisle, Mississippi in dead-end jobs (such as a store clerk, casino worker or janitor) with no room for advancement, forcing many to sell drugs as a side hustle to provide for their families. Ronald, Ward tells us, 'Maybe in his low moments, when he was coming down off the coke, he saw no American dream, no fairytale ending, no hope' (2013, 121) because he couldn't tell the difference between the living and the dead in DeLisle. This cycle of futility that Ward mentions just recycles new Black men each season like crop. First, it kills their spirit, then their mind and their body. Unfortunately, the targets are misplaced. Both Ward and Winters advocate for racial policies and legislation to address generational trauma and systemic racism so that it may experience its own timely death.

This wilful ignorance of the racial injustices, discrimination and violence Black people sustain at the hands of white America shows how the continual stress affects the body, mind and spirit of Black people. Winters's text is resourceful, informative and educational for individuals that need knowledge of anti-racist advocacy. It does the double duty of showing white people the dire consequences of 'living while Black' and how white people as allies can help mitigate Black fatigue.[18] Although Winters finally dons 'black fatigue' a proper moniker, it will serve a futile purpose if white America grows tired of anti-racist advocacy and Black people continue being sick and tired of racism in America. Because what we realise from Ward's *Men We Reaped* and Laymon's *Heavy* is that 'Racism exhausts Black people [and] has dehumanized, ostracized, murdered, and otherwise violated [their] human rights' (Winters 2020, 69). We cannot keep living in a society that is complicit with the fact that racism is killing Black people, but refusing to do much about changing it in their everyday lives. *Black Fatigue* argues for collective action and transformative healing to dismantle the racist systems that place a physical and emotional toll on the lives of Black people.[19]

Breathe, We Are Still Here

We are still here. What does that mean in a world so exhausting and fatiguing for Black people? Does it mean they give up or does the fight continue? In 2020, the world surely slowed us all down with the deadliest of viruses: Covid-19. Winters reminds us, 'Hundreds of thousands of people all over the world died from the highly contagious virus, for which there was no vaccine at the time. Black and Brown people were disproportionately affected, dying at rates two to four times the rate of white people' (Winters 2020, ix-x).[20] Seeing death parade around and collect bodies for sport is a triggering and alarming response the world couldn't quite fathom. Covid-19 shocks, and grief runs out of available rooms to hold all of its victims. Covid-19 doesn't discriminate in its cases, because in January 2020 Ward lost her beloved husband Brandon Mitchell to the disease.[21]

In a *Vanity Fair* article, titled 'On Witness and Respair: A Personal Tragedy Followed by Pandemic', published seven years after her memoir during the Covid-19 pandemic, Ward reflects on another personal tragedy that is deeply connected to *Men We Reaped*.[22] Through grief, Ward comes to understand that she was not simply mourning the loss of her partner – 'her beloved' or 'tender second skin' (2022, 203), but that she was getting to know herself as a different person. While Ward's life has been stacked with pain forcing her to move forward with grace, others may sometimes gloss over the suffering and injuries Black people endure, but the death of George Floyd in May 2020 changed race relations across the world. Ward recalls, 'I sat in my stuffy pandemic bedroom and thought I might never stop crying. The revelation that Black Americans were not alone in this, that others around the world believed that Black Lives Matter broke something in me, some immutable belief I'd carried with me my whole life' (2022, 205). Finally, the world gives a collective voice to the pain and struggles of Black people. Ward sees a 'witnessing' of her own people in action with every protest and march because they have now manifested Hamer's notion of being 'sick and tired of being sick and tired'.[23] In *Breathe*, Imani Perry provides a moving meditation on race in a letter to her sons, but also extends to Black people a lesson on pride and becoming the best version of themselves. Perry demands:

> Breathing life back into the past, pulling from the ranks of your history, is how you build yourself. You are born to something and someplace; you become of a living accord in road. This is how we move forward. Letting the constraints of the moment die a little bit, to breathe life into the process of becoming. (2019, 141)

We can breathe. We can become. We can live. We can never tire of doing good for Black people and the culture. Black men deserve to live a life full of hope and vitality instead of one that reaps of destruction and death.

Notes

1. Throughout this project, I will capitalise the 'b' in Black to honour the years of abuse, humiliation and degradation Black people faced at the hands of white slave owners during chattel slavery and thereafter during Reconstruction and Jim Crow. The lower-case 'b' represents inferiority and denotes disrespect and a lack of dignity. The capital 'B' is bold and demands respect for Black culture, history and people. The capital 'B' is an act of agency and defiance that holds the spirit of our people moving forward.

2. In *The New Jim Crow* (2010), Michelle Alexander states, 'We have not ended racial caste in America; we have merely redesigned it' (2). In the span of thirty years, the American US penal system expanded from 300,000 to 2 million, with drug conviction accounting for much of the increases. However, the most disparaging feature of mass incarceration is the racial dynamic. There is no other country imprisoning so many of its racial or ethnic minorities than the US (6–7). Alexander further contends that 'In some states black men have been admitted to prison on drug charges at rates 20 to 50 times greater than those of white men. And in major cities wracked by the drug war, as many as 80% of young African American men now have criminal records and are thus subject to legalized discrimination for the rest of their lives' (7).

3. The excerpt is from a speech Malcolm X gave on 22 May 1962 in Los Angeles to a crowd of Black women. The focus centred around the oppression of Black women in America.

4. Mimi is Jesmyn's family nickname that is used throughout the memoir.

5. Dr King attests in his 'I Have a Dream' speech: 'I have a dream that one day even the state of Mississippi, a state sweltering with the heat of injustice, sweltering with the heat of oppression will be transformed into an oasis of freedom and justice. I have a dream that my four little children will one day live in a nation where they will not be judged by the color of their skin but by the content of their character.' <https://www.npr.org>.

6. Ward always returned home to DeLisle during breaks and holidays – she had a literal homesickness when she was away at school. When she graduated, she even returned home to live at her mother's house until she found a job in New York.

7. In the section titled 'We are Wolf Town', from *Men We Reaped*, Jesmyn Ward describes the history behind the name of DeLisle, Mississippi and its French history: 'Before DeLisle was named DeLisle, after a French settler, the early settlers called it Wolf Town. Pine and oak and sweetgum grow in tangles from the north down to the south of the town, to the DeLisle Bayou. The Wolf River, brown and lazy, snakes its way through DeLisle, fingers the country in creeks, before emptying into the bayou. When people ask me about my hometown, I tell them it was called after a wolf before it was partially tamed and settled. I want to

impart something of its wild roots, its early savagery. Calling it Wolf Town hints at the wildness at the heart of it' (2013, 9).

8. Ward never did hard drugs – she mentions how Roger and Ronald always forbade her to do them. She did drink heavily though during this time and smoke Black-n-Milds.

9. Here I include the ways each young man died: Roger Eric Daniels III dies of a heart attack from a cocaine overdose (20). Demond Cook is murdered in a shooting that is rumoured to be drug related (62). Charles Joseph (C.J.) Martin is burned alive in a train accident (104). Ronald Wayne Lizana suffers from a cocaine addiction but succumbs to suicide by shooting himself in the head (163). Joshua Adam Dedeaux is killed by a drunk driver (213).

10. Using the Scribd e-book version of *Men We Reaped*, I was able to register Ward's use of the words 'dying', 'dead' or 'death' around seventy-five times throughout the length of the memoir here. It goes to show just how important the act of dying or death is to the memoir's overall subject matter here and how it shapes the narrative.

11. Specifically, *Heavy* tackles the issues of sexual assault, racism (structural and institutional), fat phobia and body image issues, anorexia, gambling addiction, drug addiction, police brutality, parental and child abuse, and domestic violence.

12. Laymon is from Jackson, Mississippi while Ward is from DeLisle, Mississippi. The two writers are less than three hours apart from each other when at their home residences. Currently, Laymon teaches at Ole Miss in Oxford, Mississippi and Ward teaches at Tulane in New Orleans, Louisiana. Both still remain situated in the Deep South. Laymon and Ward are well-known friends in the literary world and have dubbed themselves as 'country cousins'. Their relationship is personable, endearing and warm. (I'm privy to this information from several Zoom interactions during the 2020–1 web seminars they've both had.)

13. In a heart-to-heart conversation with his grandmama, Laymon discusses his reasons for not attending graduation. He vividly remembers the lack of resources and concern to fully educate and fund Black students in Mississippi schools. His white teachers failed to make their 'best better' (Laymon 2018, 114). In fact, Laymon attests, 'They never once said the words: "economic inequality," "housing discrimination," "sexual violence," "mass incarceration," "homophobia," "empire," "mass eviction," "post traumatic stress disorder," "white supremacy," "patriarchy," "neo-confederacy," "mental health," or "parental abuse," yet every student and teacher at that school lived in a world shaped by those words' (Laymon 2018, 114).

14. Laymon is asked if he wants to 'run a train' on his friend Layla after several other boys leave the bedroom after having sex with her, but he refuses (Laymon 2018, 17–18). On another occasion, he accidentally sees his friend Dougie licking the older boy Delaney's penis when he goes looking for him in Beulah Beauford's house that afternoon (Laymon 2018, 40–1).

15. Laymon explains, 'You made me read more books and write more words in response to those books than any of my friends' parents, but nothing I'd ever read prepared me to write or talk about my memory of sex, sound, space, violence, and fear' (2018, 24)
16. Mary-Frances Winters is the founder and president of The Winters Group, Inc., a global diversity, equity and inclusion consulting firm.
17. Those systems yet to change include areas in the workforce, unemployment, voter suppression, gentrification, mass incarceration, etc. (Winters 2020, 67).
18. Winters defines 'Living while Black' as 'a term coined to embrace the myriad unjust and inequitable experiences that are relentless and too often lead to violence against Black people' (2020, ix). Winter further explains, 'There are many aspects of living while Black that can induce negative health consequences. The most serious source of this is fear for our lives. It is stress inducing to worry about your safety and that of your loved ones' (2020, 76).
19. The latter chapters in *Black Fatigue* provide strategic outlines, steps and resources for allies, readers and DEI groups to follow in their collective efforts to help protect the lives of Black people.
20. Covid-19 is still doing numbers to affect Americans two years later. According to the Centers for Disease Control website, 977,402 Americans died between 4 January 2020 and 19 March 2022 from the Covid-19 virus in the United States <www.cdc.gov>.
21. Losing her husband is now the sixth Black man in Ward's life, which is simply devastating for any Black woman to have to experience in a lifetime. In addition, Ward also follows the legacy of her mother and grandmother by being left alone to raise her children as a single mother. As Faulkner, another Mississippian would say, 'The past is never past.'
22. The essay was originally published in *Vanity Fair* on 1 September 2022, but I include the printed version copy that is forthcoming in an edited collection forthcoming in April 2023.
23. Ward mentions candidly the way the horrible conditions of Covid-19 have riddled Black and brown communities: 'Witness Black people, Indigenous people, so many poor brown people, lying on beds in frigid hospitals, gasping our last breaths with COVID-riddled lungs, rendered flat by undiagnosed underlying conditions, triggered by years of food deserts, stress, and poverty, lives spent snatching sweets so we could eat one delicious morsel, savor some sugar on the tongue, oh Lord, because the flavor of our lives is so often bitter' (2022, 206).

Works Cited

Adichie, Chimamanda Ngozi. 2021. *Notes on Grief*. New York: Knopf.
Alexander, Michelle. 2010. *The New Jim Crow: Mass Incarceration in the Age of Colorblindness*. New York: New Press.

Baldwin, James. 1993. *The Fire Next Time*. New York: Vintage International.

Coates, Ta-Nehisi. 2015. *Between the World and Me*. New York: Spiegel & Grau.

Ellison, Ralph. 1995. *Invisible Man*. New York: Vintage International.

Laymon, Kiese. 2018. *Heavy: An American Memoir*. New York: Scribner.

'Martin Luther King Jr.'s "I have a dream" speech in its entirety'. 2022. NPR. https://www.npr.org.

Perry, Imani. 2019. *Breathe: A Letter to My Sons*. Boston: Beacon Press.

'Provisional Death Counts for Coronavirus Disease 2019 (Covid-19)'. 2022. Centers for Disease Control and Prevention, www.cdc.gov.

Ward, Jesmyn. 2013. *Men We Reaped*. New York: Bloomsbury.

—. 2022. 'On Witness and Respair'. Reprinted in *The Lonely Stories: 22 Celebrated Stories on the Joys & Struggles of Being Alone*, edited by Natalie Eve Garrett. New York: Catapult.

Winters, Mary-Frances. 2020. *Black Fatigue: How Racism Erodes the Mind, Body, and Spirit*. Oakland, CA: Berrett-Koehler Publishers, Inc.

Chapter 13

A Prophetic Tension: Bearing Witness Against Black Nihilism in Jesmyn Ward's *Men We Reaped*

Mary McCampbell

Towards the end of Jesmyn Ward's grief-soaked memoir *Men We Reaped*, the author accompanies her beloved brother, Joshua, on a final car ride. Joshua's car, like the many featured in Ward's book, is a sacred space of intimacy and freedom, operating as 'a church can function, or has functioned in the past, in the community' (quoted in Hartnell 214). As Mimi (the young Ward) and Joshua cruise both from and towards the nothingness of their fragile internal/external worlds, they repeatedly listen to the track 'All That I Got is You' by Ghostface Killah. It is the soundtrack of their last moments together, the soundtrack of their family, the soundtrack of their community and the soundtrack of their collective longing. When listening to the lyrics, 'To all the families that went through the struggle', Mimi's face is covered in tears of grief, lament and confusion: 'We rode like we could drive far and long enough to outrun our story . . . But in the end, we could not' (249). Although the car is the siblings' 'church', it is also a moving target. There is no safe space for the poor, Black, Southern men of this memoir, nor for the women that love them; they are pursued by the police, by death, by the haunting of both the past and their own impending stories. Just hours after Mimi's sacred ride with her brother, he is in a collision with a drunk driver that ends his life.

As Ward reflects on the life and death of her brother, the painful emotional 'heart' of the story, one of her most compelling and tragic descriptions of Joshua is that he 'wanted meaning' (213, 244). She remembers her brother confronting a street evangelist/ street vendor selling 'crucifixes' fashioned from 'plastic and string' with questions erupting from his core: '*What do you know about God? Why are we here?*' (244–5). These sorts of questions are also echoed in his favourite Ghostface Killah song, a narrative of devastating poverty that sidesteps nihilism because of its thirst for sense-making:

'Sometimes I look up at the stars and analyze the sky/ And ask myself was I meant to be here . . . why?' The final short narrative of Joshua's life, coupled with the questions he raises, are perhaps the existential underpinning of the book itself. Although both Mimi and Joshua search for meaning, they struggle to reconcile their brutal lived reality, the experience of what Cornel West deems 'Black Nihilism', with the idea of a benevolent God who directs their lives and provides purpose and meaning.

As Ward explains in the book's prologue, 'From 2000 to 2004, five Black young men I grew up with died, all violently, in seemingly unrelated deaths' (7). The tragic loss of Joshua, Ronald, C.J., Demond and Roger create a 'brutal list, in its immediacy and relentlessness' (Ward 2013, 7). In this chapter, I will explore Ward's raw depiction of both the causes and lived reality of 'Black nihilism' in her Southern, Black, rural community. The author's devasting account of the deaths of five men close to both her life and soul is also an analysis of the desire to make meaning out of emptiness, despair and trauma. In looking at the nihilistic aspects of the story, I will also explore its prophetic qualities, the subversive tools that work as a buffer against all-consuming nihilism. Although the list of deaths that punctuate Mimi's young life 'silences people' and silenced the author herself 'for a long time', she regains her voice in retelling her part of their stories, both the memories and the presumably meaningless grief and pain (7). While Ward is questioning the cruel circumstances that lead to the 'seemingly unrelated' violent deaths of these men that she knows and loves, she is also questioning the absence or presence of a God behind the scenes, possibly orchestrating or ignoring these tragedies. In this sense, *Men We Reaped* functions as a prophetic work, bearing witness to and critiquing the amoral, systemic racism that leads to tragedy upon tragedy. It is also a work of theodicy, questioning both the presence/absence and goodness/badness of the God of the author's beleaguered, forgotten community. It is both a testimony, bearing witness to grief, and a set of theological questions that seeks, rather than abandons meaning. Alongside its tender despair, *Men We Reaped* is also a testament to survival, dignity, and the search for both hope and elucidation. As Ward explains in an interview with Anna Hartnell, 'Hope equals meaning, and to me there has to be some sense of meaning to any story, to whatever I write' (216).

As a child, Ward sought this hope through a belief in God while attending an Episcopal day school and, in her teenage years, while volunteering for a Christian camp. But as she grew into the reality of Black life in the South, her youthful faith transformed into an acute sense of abandonment. Ward's recollections of the micro-aggressions she experienced in school signal her awakening to the paralysing injustices that result in inequity, exhaustion and despair. She recalls that 'My school peers would often glance at me when they spoke about Black people' (2). She was a 'scholarship kid' and, in their eyes, her Blackness was associated with gangs, violence towards white people and a lack of 'common human decency' (2). Even as she was self-aware and discerning, 'studying the entitlement they wore like another piece of clothing' (5), their subtle but ever-present social cues inevitably contributed to her growing sense of worthlessness. When working for the Episcopal day camp 'All God's Creatures', a programme for 'underprivileged kids', she meets Ronald, a copper-skinned, freckled child that would soon begin to sense the 'Nothing over his shoulder, bearing down on him while spurring him into action' (177). This personification of despair is a vivid example of what Cornel West sees as the 'nihilistic threat' to the very existence of Black America. He deems this form of nihilism 'a disease of the soul' (12) rooted in a 'profound sense of psychological depression, personal worthlessness, and social despair so widespread in Black America' (19). When Ronald unexpectedly commits suicide, Mimi understands his motives. They share the same sense of hopelessness, a need to 'silence the self' and, in turn, 'silence the world' through an act of self-extinction (Ward 176). Ronald and Mimi are both pawns in a game beyond their control, reaping the death and cruelty that they had not themselves historically sewn. As Lorraine Hansberry's Walter Lee Younger explains, 'I didn't make this world! It was give to me this way!' (143). As Mimi and the important men in her life attempt to navigate a system that was created to oppress them, it feels almost impossible to move from dehumanisation to rehumanisation. Like Walter Lee, the young men Ward loves must play the game created by the system in order to define and retain their manhood. But the game is often pointless, the rules are unfair or invisible, and the winners are predetermined. The lure to abandon the search for meaning or hope is strong, especially when trapped in an unfair game created by the mechanisms of white supremacy. The unjust reaping of poverty, pain and death are often, and ironically, the only 'prizes'.

The memoir's title, *Men We Reaped*, speaks to the book's tension between the prophetic, a resistance against the creeping nihilism birthed by the hopeless game, and the theodical, a sense of divine injustice within both the system and the world. The title is taken from words spoken by Harriet Tubman in 1863 after the Union Army's 54th Massachusetts Volunteer Infantry (an all-Black military unit) failed in their attempts to defeat the Confederate army, losing many of their own men. Tubman's words are copied, in full, as one of the book's three epigraphs:

> We saw the lightning and that was the guns; We heard the thunder and that was the big guns; We heard the rain falling and that was the blood falling; and when we came to get in the crops, it was dead men that we reaped.

The brutal imagery within this quote bears witness to an unjust tragedy; recipients of unearned oppression and agents of desired justice are defeated by an enemy that embodies and enacts senseless evils. That which is seemingly natural, organic ('lightning', 'thunder') becomes inhuman, mechanical ('guns', 'big guns') and leads to the 'rain' of human blood.

Harriet Tubman was a deeply religious woman, an indefatigable believer who frequently saw what she deemed prophetic dreams and visions that provided her with both hope and direction in her fight for justice. It is interesting to note that these visions are also attributed to an earlier episode of abuse, thus the good and prophetic arising even out of an abusive circumstance.[1] Although Tubman had an unwavering belief that her Lord was on her side, she uses biblical language ironically to describe the tragic outcome of the last battle. The living young Black men, fighting for freedom and justice, soon become the 'dead men that we reaped'. Jewish and Christian scriptures include over a hundred descriptions of humans 'reaping', receiving the consequences of their own actions: 'Do not be deceived: God is not mocked, for whatever one sows, that will he also reap' (Galatians 6: 7). But in Tubman's account, those standing for justice and liberation are reaping unearned pain and, ultimately, the death of those they love. The sharp irony of Tubman's use of the word 'reap' is even more evident when looking at Proverbs 22: 8: 'Whoever sows injustice will reap calamity.' Tubman's life and freedom-fighting work was grounded in the Black prophetic rhetorical tradition, what Andre Johnson defines as 'discourse grounded in the sacred, rooted in a community experience that offers a critique of existing communities and traditions by charging and challenging society to live up to the ideals they espoused, while offering celebration, encouragement and hope for a brighter future' (270–1). Prophetic language and actions serve an apocalyptic function, both unveiling the truth of injustice and working towards a corrective. But in Tubman's quote here, the only logical biblical sense to the death that has been 'reaped' is a reflection of human degradation, a result of the Fall. Tubman's quote bears poignant witness to the cruelty of an unjust world where suffering is often not earned but thrust upon the victims of both systemic and individual depravity.

In *The Prophetic Imagination*, Walter Brueggemann's understanding of the twofold nature of the prophetic writings of the Old Testament would be very familiar to Harriet Tubman and others in the prophetic tradition. Brueggemann sees the 'prophetic', not so much about forecasting a vision of the future, but of both the subversive power of lament/ critique and the 'energizing' power of hope grounded in doxology (3). He explains that the prophetic voices of Israel boldly proclaimed an 'alternate reality' to the empire mentality that was bolstered by the 'politics of oppression and exploitation' (6). According to Brueggemann, one of the ways that the 'empire' gains and retains power is by attempting to convince its subjects that things are normal, that they are incorrect in perceiving that their realities are painful, the results of injustice.[2] It is a form of gaslighting used in both personal and systemic contexts. In this sense, the act of lament, 'the language of grief', is countercultural, revolutionary, subversive (46). It refuses to accept that the oppressive, whitewashed status quo is reality itself, it fights against the normalisation of oppression. We see this very clearly in Frederick Douglass's narrative when he relates the spiritual and political importance of the spirituals: 'Every tone was a testimony against slavery, and a prayer to God for deliverance from chains', revealing 'at once the highest joy and the deepest sadness' (36). The dual emotions of these spirituals reflect Brueggemann's twofold conception of the 'prophetic' – holding together both lament/critique and the hope of deliverance. In *Men We Reaped*, Ward mentions the spirituals only as opportunities for mockery in her friend Rog's childhood classroom: 'Rog sat in the back of one such class and beat-boxed while his cousins sang spirituals that substituted the teacher's name for Jesus' (27). Although this is silly child's play, it is also a subversive response to trauma. These songs that are a fabric of the African American prophetic tradition speak of liberation, joy, freedom from pain after authentic lament. But the young men singing them have only experienced the trauma of life as 'products' of the school-to-prison pipeline. Thus, the name of the great redeemer is traded out for their teacher – the man, the purveyor of the system. In retelling her story and the story of the men whose lives she loved and lost, Ward's prophetic voice is a testament against normalised injustice. At the same time, it is unable to conjure up the joy, the hope of any sort of deliverance or transformation. She does not, however, completely deny the possibility of any sort of meaning to be found alongside such despair.

Once again, her emphasis that 'Hope equals meaning' is key: 'In everything I write I like to at least leave the reader with something to hang onto – this was harder with *Men We Reaped*. I think there has to be hope in any story' (quoted in Hartnell 216). Ward's use of the Tubman quote reminds us that the world inherited by the author's community is not inherently different from the world that produced the blood-soaked fields of dead Black soldiers. Her sense of powerlessness in an environment that is unsafe for the Black men that she loves is intensified by her sense of divine abandonment. A gradual rejection of faith makes sense as a protective measure because, as James Cone notes, 'Suffering naturally gives rise to doubt. How can one believe in God in the face of such horrendous suffering as slavery, segregation, and the lynching tree?' (132). Once Mimi bears her own witness to the fragility of Black existence, losing five young men within a span of four short years, she struggles to believe in a loving God. Ward explains that, as a young teenager, 'I found irresistible the idea of a God who loved me unfailingly' but 'In the end, I realized sometimes, some people were forsaken.' Interestingly, she emphasises that not all people were 'forsaken,' only 'some people' (Ward 2013, 244). Mimi sees herself as one of these 'some people' both pursued by nothingness while existing as a 'nothing' (244). Perhaps the most acute sense of abandonment is the systemic abandonment of 'White politicians in Mississippi' speaking in 'coded language' (244). As Arin Keeble observes, 'In none of Ward's works is there any support or intervention from the American state. In fact, government agencies are almost entirely invisible except for when they pose a violent threat' (2020, 41). Ward's description of the short, tragic life of her sister's boyfriend, C.J., is a testament to the poverty, lack of opportunity and sense of defeat that result from the abandonment of the state.

C.J. did not grow up with dreams of being something or someone great. In talking about his future with girlfriend Charine, he merely said, '*We can hustle . . . make money . . . Live*' (121). A lack of both family and systemic support led to a lack of motivation, self-care and sense of future hope. C.J. worked minimum-wage service jobs between selling drugs, what Ward calls 'a cycle of futility' (121). She pondered that perhaps C.J. 'looked at those who still lived and those who'd died, and didn't see much difference between the two; pinioned beneath poverty and history and racism, we were all dying inside' (121). A spiritual, mental and emotional death simply preceded the physical, thus completing the 'cycle of futility' (121). C.J.'s life was governed by a fatalistic view that '*I ain't going to be here long*' (120). His macabre prediction becomes a prophecy. After a ride 'upcountry with his cousins' (125) C.J. was hit and killed by a train because the reflective gate arm at the railway crossing was missing, and the flashing lights did not always work. C.J.'s avoidable death was a symptom of systemic abandonment. Because the crossing where he was killed was 'out in the country in a mainly Black area, no one really cared about fixing them or installing a reflective gate arm' (125). A willful silence, a lack of attention, care and support from the systems formed by whiteness killed C.J. He was forsaken.

These same systems also taught Mimi to hate herself, teaching her a single, repeated internal mantra: '*You're nothing*' (244). In *Men We Reaped*, she documents the beginning of this cultural indoctrination while in her predominantly white Christian school. Interestingly, her first awareness of systemic oppression occurred alongside a period of youthful faith. Although she was very involved in school activities, she always felt '*other*', and the White boys that she was attracted to were forbidden to date her both by their (Christian) parents and (Christian) peers. As she became more aware of her 'otherness', the existential result was the lack of 'true' or unified 'self-consciousness', because she could only see herself 'through the revelation of the other world' (Du Bois 2). The 'other world's' mythology became visible to her one day when she came across the novel *Gone with the Wind* in the school library. While reading, she was 'horrified' by a novel that positioned the 'defeated Confederates' as heroes, enshrining their 'vilification of the freed slaves' (207). Her introduction to the Lost Cause ideology so beloved by white Southerners, including her Christian classmates, led her to a crucial question: 'Do they really think of Black people like this?' (207). Although this episode led to a greater awareness of the toxic mythology within which her peers were socialised, it was not possible to fully stop seeing herself through the eyes of a culture that still sees her as inferior, degraded, useful only as a commodity. At the end of the memoir, Ward writes that, when she was twelve years old, she looked at herself in the mirror and felt a sense of 'loathing' that 'came from others' hatred of me' and 'fostered a hatred of myself' (Ward 2013, 250): 'I thought being unwanted and abandoned and persecuted was the legacy of the poor southern Black woman' (250).

Mimi's development of a fractured double consciousness is not only her story; it is the story of an 'entire community' that 'suffered from a lack of trust' because of the ways in which it was denied access to education, safety, justice (Ward 2013, 169). Because of this, we 'trusted nothing' and suffered from a deep sense of hopelessness: 'Some of us turned sour from the pressure, let it erode our sense of self until we hated what we say, without and within' (169).

This fragmented self-hatred is, again, at the heart of the nihilism that West believes is threatening the mental and spiritual health of many Black communities in America:

> Nihilism is . . . the lived experience of coping with a life of horrifying meaninglessness, hopelessness, and (most important) lovelessness. The frightening result is a numbing detachment from others and a self-destructive disposition toward the world. (14)

West sees a lack of love as the most insidious and devastating cause of Black nihilism. By this, he is speaking mostly of the lovelessness that manifests itself in unjust systems and structures, and the ways this impacts Black familial and other interpersonal relationships.[3] In Ward's own life, this is intensified by the absence of her father, something that must also be understood in the historical context of the separation and oppression of Black families. She explains that 'the tradition of men leaving their families here seems systemic, fostered by endemic poverty' as well as the intergenerational trauma of 'the forced fracturing of families that the earliest African Americans endured under the yoke of slavery' (131). These collective abandonments lead to a sense of despair and worthlessness that is as endemic as poverty and the racism that led to it. Like most children, the young Mimi would have identified her parents as 'god' figures, and her father's departure made it impossible for him to help affirm her sense of dignity after it was relentlessly bruised by her indoctrinated peers. The repeated abandonment by her father, the perpetual systemic abandonment of her community, and a perceived abandonment of God all resonate in the core of Mimi's eroding being: '*You're nothing*' (244).

In understanding the result of these abusive forces on her own psyche, Ward also knew that she needed to be honest about the impact of them on the lives of her characters. She found it hard to 'abuse' her characters, and she addresses this difficulty in her role as creator by contrasting her understanding of the differences between the God(s) of the Old and New Testaments. In *Men We Reaped*, she notes that in writing her first novel, *Where the Line Bleeds* (2008), her characters were 'failing' to be real because she 'loved them too much' (Ward 2013, 70). She felt that 'as an author, I was a benevolent God', protecting them, lavishing grace and mercy on them rather than detailing the impact of the raw injustice that they reaped:

> I protected them from death, from drug addiction, from needlessly harsh sentences in jail for doing stupid, senseless things . . . All of the young Black men in my life, in my community, had been prey to these things

in real life, and yet in the lives I imagined for them, I avoided the truth. I could not figure out how to love my characters less. How to look squarely at what was happening to the young Black people in the South, and to write honestly about that. (Ward 2013, 70)

To be more truthful in depicting the suffering of these young Black men, she felt she needed to love her characters less, and in writing, to be more of an 'Old Testament God' (Ward 2013, 70). Ward is contrasting this to her posture of writing as a 'benevolent God', perhaps reflecting the mercy and grace embodied by Christ in the New Testament. The implication here is clear: that the God of the Old Testament is devoid of mercy, allowing famine, poverty and slavery to play out, leaving humans subject both to their own devices and the forces of injustice. Once again, this reinforces her perception that both she and her characters (both fictional and non-fictional) were among the 'some people' that 'were forsaken' (Ward 2013, 244).

But Ward's understanding of the 'Old Testament God' is, interestingly, very out of step with traditional, historical Black church theology. Her polarising comments about the Old and New Testament depictions of God's character have more in common with the theology of William Blake than that of Richard Allen, Martin Luther King, Jr, or C. L. Franklin. In *Reading While Black*, Esau McCaulley notes that, while many white evangelical churches in the United States orient their theology around the Pauline epistles, most Black churches begin with the Old Testament book of Exodus. This is the inheritance of enslaved Africans who found their own story of oppression contained in the story of the Israelites enslaved in Egypt. According to McCaulley, both the enslaved faithful and their Christian descendants 'viewed events like God's redemption of Israel from slavery as paradigmatic for their understanding of God's character' (17). Because of this, 'they viewed God fundamentally as a liberator' (17). This was (and is) the dominant contextualised understanding of the God of the Old Testament. And this, of course, relates directly to the understanding of Christ as one who was, as James Cone famously proclaims, innocent yet 'lynched' at the hands of the unjust empire: 'The cross and the lynching tree interpret each other' (187). This gospel of liberation, shared by both Harriet Tubman and many Black theologians and activists after her, seems foreign to Ward's forgotten community. As Cone explains, 'Without concrete signs of divine presence in the lives of the poor, the gospel becomes simply an opiate; rather than liberating the powerless from humiliation and suffering, the gospel becomes a drug that helps them adjust to this world by looking for "pie in the sky"' (181). It is a painful challenge to 'reconcile the gospel message of liberation with the reality of Black oppression', so painful that it becomes absurd, easier to abandon belief than enter into another dimension of pain caused by wrestling with spiritual questions (21).

This challenge in Ward's own writing practice is enough to deeply depress her and make her feel powerless. So much so that, 'To avoid all of this, I drank' (Ward 2013, 70). While she rejects the idea of embracing a gospel which might be only an 'opiate', she turns directly to using a drug that will temporarily kill her pain. Her drinking is a response, not just to her writing, but to the sense of existential meaninglessness, to acknowledging the reality that perhaps, if there is a God, this God does not care about the plight of young Black men. In a chapter detailing the untimely death of her friend, Demond, Ward elaborates on the perpetual need to extinguish both thought and feeling through the use of drugs and alcohol. 'All I wanted in the world was for it to go dark, to not exist' she writes. 'I wanted to black out again. Then I did' (Ward 2013, 74). During this period, she spends time with her friends at the 'Delusions' club, ironically inviting the delusion of momentary happiness, feeling 'drunk and sentimental', and loving all of her party companions 'for still being alive' (74). When reflecting on those moments of temporal despair-tinged joy, she recognises the desperation that she and her friends felt. And in describing this, she sees their powerlessness and perceived unworthiness as they try to escape the pain of death by scurrying towards it: 'We crawled through time like roaches through the linings of walls, the neglected spaces and hours, foolishly happy that we are alive even as we did everything to die' (Ward 2013, 76).

Ward's disturbing metaphor of roaches running both towards and from death is reminiscent of the famous, nihilistic scene of ants on a log in Hemingway's *A Farewell to Arms*:

> Once in camp I put a log on a fire and it was full of ants. As it commenced to burn, the ants swarmed out and went first toward the center where the fire was; then turned back and ran toward the end. When there were enough on the end they fell off into the fire. Some got out, their bodies burnt and flattened, and went off not knowing where they were going. But most of them went toward the fire and then back toward the end and swarmed on the cool end and finally fell off into the fire. (374)

Ward's existential despair is the result of a profoundly different lived context than Hemingway's, but both sets of scurrying insect images point to the cruel senselessness of abandonment. Like the ants in

Hemingway's novel, Ward, her friends, and her family feel power-lessness in the face of impending death no matter how much they run away from the growing flame. Ultimately, many resign themselves to run towards it, falling off the edge, tunnelling headfirst into the fire. Hemingway uses this metaphor to express the impact of the absence of an empty universe, devoid of a loving God. As previously mentioned, the despair depicted in Ward's memoir also grapples with this sense of spiritual abandonment – but the concrete, daily examples of social and political 'abandonment' are often more overt and more pressing, contributing to the ongoing malaise within her community.

The perverse, puzzling inequity highlighted in the Harriet Tubman epigraph is also the perverse, puzzling inequity at the centre of Ward's story that makes hope 'harder' to find. A relentless presence of both actual Black death and the fear of Black death in rural Mississippi parallels the unjust reality of Black death and Black fear of death in an urban context as described in Ta-Nehisi Coates's *Between the World and Me*. His depiction of what King calls the 'two Americas' is the unspoken backdrop to Ward's memoir: 'Fear ruled everything around me, and I knew, as all Black people do, that this fear was connected to the Dream out there, to the unworried boys, to pie and pot-roast, to the white fences and green lawns nightly beamed into our television sets' (King; Coates 2015, 29). The absurdity of this injustice is the absence of the fear of death in white communities, those who are yet to 'reap' the injustice of systems created by the ideology of whiteness. Both Coates and, before him, Baldwin, note the perceived 'innocence' of the 'those who think they are white' chasing after and benefiting from the heavily mythologised American dream (Baldwin 3; Coates 2015, 10). Yet the inhabitants of Black bodies are denied access to the dream that was built upon the labour and torture of their very bodies. Coates sees in this, 'a cosmic injustice, a profound cruelty, which infused an abiding, irrepressible desire to unshackle my body and achieve the velocity of escape' (21).

The 'cosmic injustice' that is seemingly at the heart of 'two Americas' is skilfully depicted near the beginning of *Men We Reaped* when Ward describes a reckless party at 'Delusions', one of the many spaces in the story where Mimi and her friends gather to self-medicate. Suffocated by grief while fearing the ghosts of the dead, they gravitate closer to the 'Nothing', an empty, hungry spirit of death that is always 'stalking' (31) them. While at the club, the drunken friends take a photo in front of a fantasy backdrop, 'a city-coast sky-line that was completely alien' (71) to life in the fields and bayous of their native Mississippi. Around the photograph is a border with the words 'God's Gift' (71) cradling the image of a shiny, momentarily happy, ever despairing group of young friends. The ironic notion that their lives are a gift from a seemingly absent God is perhaps, to Ward, the greatest delusion. Where is the 'gift' of God in the friends' current circumstances? The photo border phrase 'God's Gift' is also eerily reminiscent of the title of her childhood Christian camp, 'All God's Creatures'. Both describe gatherings of her friends looking for an alternate reality, either through Christianity or drug use. While Ward believes that all her stories need to end with a sort of 'hope' that produces 'meaning', she acknowledges that this is perhaps a 'foolish impulse' because 'hope can often make it easier for people to be deluded and to not deal with what is in front of them' (quoted in Hartnell 226). In this sense, hope connected to faith is especially 'foolish', an 'opiate', the drug that helps them adjust to this world and accept its perversions rather than confront them (Cone 181). And in the end, for Ward and her community, this perceived 'delusion' of faith is perhaps more painful than comforting when confronting the lived cruelty that is so relentless, so absurd, so omnipresent in the lives of these young, Black Southerners.

Although an absence of faith might make it seem as if the prophetic strand of the Black theological tradition is absent from Ward's Mississippi, her writing is not without any prophetic tincture. Anne Hartnell positions *Men We Reaped* within the tradition of the American literary 'jeremaid':

> American literary endeavors that have wanted to highlight a nation that has lost its way is not new: this literary landscape is full of prophetic voices – 'jeremiads,' as they have come to be known in American studies – that have wanted to illustrate the gap between the American dream and the American reality. African American voices have played a very particular role in this project, so often positioned as whistleblowers in relation to the national myth. (209)

Men We Reaped vividly depicts the underside of the 'American Dream', a dream experienced only by those for whom the country was built. Instead, her friends were often dreamless, including C.J. who 'saw no American dream, no fairy-tale ending, no hope' (121). And this dreamlessness began in childhood, when little Black boys began walking a tightrope to try and escape prison or death, even for doing things that little white boys could do freely. Ward's childhood friend, Rog, and Rog's cousins decided to prank some neighbours by putting some Fourth of July firecrackers in their mailboxes. The mailboxes eventually exploded, and when the police came, Rog's cousins were taken to juvenile detention for committing the 'federal offense' of tampering with the US mail. This extreme treatment, 'how silly pranks by Black kids are handled in the South' indicates that even childhood is not a time for carefree play, fanciful dreams or fairy tales. The reality of what Malcolm X deemed the 'American nightmare' (24–25) is lurking far too close to the surface of everyday experience. Like C.J. and Rog, Ward's brother, Joshua, did not have lofty dreams, did not have a vision of 'the American dream shining like some wishing star in the distance' (Ward 2013, 212). Ward's words are tinged with guilt and sadness when she writes that 'Joshua would hustle. He could do what he had to do to survive while I dreamed a future' (212). In telling the stories of the young Black men that she lost, she often highlights their lack of access to the dream, thus prophetically subverting both the underlying mechanism and the outcome of life in an 'empire' originally built upon the backs of her people.

Although creating a sort of meaning through her own acts of storytelling resistance, Ward ultimately seeks a larger meaning, perhaps even a transcendent one, to explain the reasons why 'my brother died while I live, and why I've been saddled with this rotten fucking story' (Ward 2013, 8). As with many a prophet, the weight of the news Ward has to bear is both painful and frightening. The more those close to her died, the more she realised that 'death was stalking us' (31). But was this death-bringing force personal or impersonal, an act of chance or predestination? Throughout the memoir, Ward continually explores the notion that the Black men in her life are being hunted: by a mythical 'wolf', by the 'nothing' that they feel inside, by the ghosts of the dead, by death itself. When Mimi's friend Rog dies of a cocaine-related heart attack, his sister, Tasha, cries, 'They killed my brother!' (37). Her cousin Brandon then utters, 'They picking us off, one by one' (38). Mimi is left trying to discern who the 'they that wrote our story might be' (38). Is the one creating and moulding their story, operating both outside and within their community, a cosmic or human-made force? Why is this force targeting them? The repeated use of 'us'[4] as opposed to 'they' solidifies the absurd opposition, with one side being embodied and abused, the other faceless, omnipresent, impossible to name, escape or catch. The central question at the core of the memoir concerns the author of these stories of recurring tragic death, a result of the larger story of poverty, despair, desperation, injustice. Who is behind all this? In the shadow of death and doubt, Mimi continues to self-medicate, nursing the 'illusions that our youth might save us, that there was someone somewhere who would have mercy on us' (64). But is this 'someone somewhere' a politician, a magician, a deity? After her friend, Demond, is hunted and executed by the spectre of death in the form of a drug lord's vigilante, Mimi sleeps snuggled up next to her sister, Charine, and 'thanked *something* that she still breathed, even as I was sick about it. Whatever it was, that killed us one after the other. *Senseless*, I thought. This is never going to end, I thought. Never' (79). As she thanks this nameless, possibly malevolent force, the author of her tragic loss, she is 'sick about it', trying to reconcile the central tensions of these 'senseless' cosmic injustices that plague the inhabitants of Black bodies.

But these tensions are never resolved. Ward bravely sits in them, asking the questions that gesture towards meaning and hope but never directly point to its source. In *The Future of the Race*, West explains how the 'guttural moan' testifying to Black grief is a 'fragile existential arsenal – rooted in silent tears and weary lament' that 'supports Black endurance against madness and suicide' (106). The prophetic tradition of bearing witness to injustice through lament, whether in song or writing, underpins the central existential tensions in Ward's memoir. She has inherited the long tradition, as Chiara Patrizi notes, of both 'survival and witness' to that survival (70). Although Ward's story is written in the shadow of a seemingly absent God, her storytelling serves a prophetic function, exposing injustice, bearing witness to pain, and pushing against the despair that leads to death. She has not inherited a privilege-based, Enlightenment-tinged secularism, but an honest, sad and struggling agnosticism built on questions that are seemingly never resolved. These very questions seeking meaning provide a sliver of hope in some sort of sense to be made of her community's unjust reaping. Most of all, *Men We Reaped* reiterates the undying 'power of the voice' in trauma literature, particularly the literature of the African diaspora (quoted in Taylor 268). This voice is a means to 'bringing to reality' the very truths that are so often hidden, ignored, lied about (Brueggemann 46). In *Men We Reaped*, Jesmyn Ward's sacred storytelling is an act of resistance against the silence that wants to consume the author into its nothingness.

Notes

1. When she was thirteen years old, Tubman was accidentally struck on the head with a weight. An overseer was attempting to whip a field hand, when the young Ariminta stood in the way to try and prevent this from happening. She was struck so hard that her skull was broken.

This is yet another example of righteousness and justice that was thwarted by cruelty. See Clinton, especially 22–3, for more information.

2 We see this, of course, in the oppressive uses of decontextualised Christian scripture used to control and oppress those enslaved in the United States. As Douglass notes, the cruellest slave masters were those who used religion to justify their practices. See Douglass 77, as well as the entirety of the Appendix.

3 It is important and interesting to note that West's *Race Matters* was published in 1993 when Jesmyn Ward was sixteen years old. In this sense, it very much reflects the sociopolitical and economic climate of Ward's teenage and young adult years as described in the memoir.

4 For a discussion of the repeated use of 'for us' in the text, see Travis 222.

Works Cited

Baldwin, James. 1991. *The Fire Next Time*. New York: Vintage International.

Brueggemann, Walter. 2018. *The Prophetic Imagination*. Minneapolis: Fortress Press.

Clinton, Catherine. 2004. *Harriet Tubman: The Road to Freedom*. Boston: Little, Brown.

Coates, Ta-Nehisi. 2015. *Between the World and Me*. New York: Spiegel & Grau.

Cone, James. 2011. *The Cross and the Lynching Tree*. Maryknoll, NY: Orbis Books.

Douglass, Frederick. 2016. *Narrative of the Life of Frederick Douglass*. New York: Dover Publications.

Du Bois, W. E. B. 2016. *The Souls of Black Folk*. New York: Dover Publications.

Ghostface Killah. 1995. 'All That I Got is You'. *Ironman*, Razor Sharp.

Hansberry, Lorraine. 1988. *A Raisin in the Sun*. New York: Vintage Books.

Hartnell, Anna. 2016. 'When Cars Become Churches: Jesmyn Ward's Disenchanted America. An Interview'. *Journal of American Studies* 50 (1): 205–18.

Hemingway, Ernest. 1929. *A Farewell to Arms*. New York: Scribner.

Johnson, Andre E. 2010. 'The Prophetic Persona of James Cone and the Rhetorical Theology of Black Theology'. *Black Theology: an International Journal* 8 (3): 266–85.

Keeble, Arin. 2020. 'Siblings, Kinship and Allegory in Jesmyn Ward's Fiction and Nonfiction'. *Critique: Studies in Contemporary Fiction* 61 (1): 40–51.

King, Martin Luther, Jr. 1967. 'The Other America'. Speech Transcript. https://www.crmvet.org/docs/otheram.htm.

McCaulley, Esau. 2020. *Reading While Black*. Downers Grove, IL: IVP Academic.

Patrizi, Chiara. 2021. '"We Ain't Going Nowhere. We Here": Survival and Witness in Jesmyn Ward's Fiction and Nonfiction'. *RSA Journal* 32: 69–86.

Taylor, Danielle K. 2016. 'Literary Voice of the Dirty South: An Interview with Jesmyn Ward'. *CLA Journal* 60 (2): 266–8.

Travis, Molly. 2016. 'We Are Here: Jesmyn Ward's Survival Narratives. Response to Anna Hartnell, "When Cars Become Churches"'. *Journal of American Studies* 50 (1): 219–24.

Ward, Jesmyn. 2013. *Men We Reaped: A Memoir*. New York: Bloomsbury.

West, Cornel, and Henry Louis Gates, Jr. 1997. *The Future of the Race*. New York: Vintage.

West, Cornel. 1993. *Race Matters*. Boston: Beacon Press.

Chapter 14

'Something like praying': Syncretic Spirituality and Racial Justice in Jesmyn Ward's *Sing, Unburied, Sing*

Lucy Arnold

On 5 November 2020, the University of Southern California hosted 'Spiritual Protest: The Role of Faith in the Fight for Racial Justice', an event exploring the role of spirituality within the Black Lives Matter movement. In her keynote speech, Hebah Farrag recalled her experiences of that summer's BLM protests and described seeing 'protestors clad all in white, burning sage across militarized police lines, chants and the pouring of vivations in front of court houses invoking the spirits of ancestors and those killed by police' (Farrag 2020). The actions Farrag describes have their roots in African religious traditions such as Ifá, which became syncretised as part of African American spiritual traditions including Hoodoo, and Haitian and Louisiana Vodou. It is these systems of belief and practice – including root work and root medicine, conjuration, and the invocation of loas and other deities – which structure the metaphysical landscape of Jesmyn Ward's *Sing, Unburied, Sing* (2017) and, for some characters, interact with the sensory disorganisation resulting from drug use, and with traumatic hallucinations. The novel tells the story of the African American Stone family, who live in the fictional town of Bois Sauvage, Mississippi. The family comprises patriarch Pop, who in his youth served a jail sentence in the notorious Parchman prison, Mam, who is dying of cancer and practises Hoodoo, the syncretic form of religion native to America's Gulf coast, their daughter Leonie, whose white partner Michael is serving a sentence in Parchman for drug dealing, and Michael and Leonie's children, Jojo, thirteen and Kayla, three. As the novel opens Leonie has received the news that Michael is being released and has decided to take their children with her on a road trip to collect him.

In this essay I map Ward's deployment in her fiction of the practices, language and iconography of Hoodoo, and Haitian and

Louisiana Vodou, a deployment that is neither a straightforward documentation, nor uninterested in historico-social specificity. An analysis of Ward's representation of syncretic African-based spiritualities is begun in James Mellis's 'Continuing Conjure: African-Based Spiritual Traditions in Colson Whitehead's *The Underground Railroad* and Jesmyn Ward's *Sing, Unburied, Sing*' (Mellis 2019). However, here I contextualise Ward's engagement with the intersection between African-based spiritual traditions and political protest, resistance and protection, by placing it in conversation with the manifestation of these practices within the Black Lives Matter movement specifically. Furthermore, I propose that this representation is more complex than has previously been suggested, offering a vision of a potentially politically protective set of spiritual practices which are, for young African American subjects in the South, unevenly available and unevenly efficacious. In so doing, I place Ward's literary strategy in dialogue both with wider contemporary trends in the intersections between political activism and African American spirituality, and with less well-recognised manifestations of such spirituality as protection and protest. I argue that *Sing, Unburied, Sing* demonstrates the complex evolution and presence of Hoodoo in Southern African American life and culture, and the ways in which the protection, subversion or resistance it might be understood to facilitate has become more complex or difficult to access for younger African Americans, whose ability or desire to engage with these belief systems and practices should not be understood as homogenous.

Ward's representation of the African-based spiritual traditions predominantly practised in the south of America, including Hoodoo and Mississippi, Louisiana and Haitian Vodou,[2] and their relationship with political protest and protection is complex. To appreciate their nuances various contexts must first be established. The first is the long-standing relationship between African American spirituality (both in terms of mainstream Christian traditions and in terms of traditions such as Hoodoo) and African American social justice movements from the slavery era to the present day. A significant body of research has emerged in recent decades on the relationship between African American Christian traditions and social justice activism in America. From analyses of the ways in which Black Christianity shaped politics in the antebellum South (Ford 2012) to studies of the significance of evangelism and religious experience in Black women's activism (Booker 2021), the interactions between African American Christianity and the civil rights movement and its forebears is well documented. A more recent development in scholarship in this area is the analysis of how practices taken from African-based spiritual traditions have historically formed a concealed praxis of political protest and resistance and have recently started to form a key element of the activism of the Black Lives Matter movement. Elise M. Edwards states, the Black Lives Matter agenda 'is holistic, and the movement embraces spiritual practices' (Edwards 2017). Despite these spiritual practices being invoked in often profoundly visible and explicit ways during Black Lives Matter rallies and protests,[3] this facet of the movement has been largely excised from its mainstream media representation. To quote Hebah Farrag:

> What is generally missing from these depictions are images like the white-clad black woman burning sage across a militarized police line; documentation of the chants in front of the Los Angeles courthouse declaring 'summon our ancestors,' and grassroots organizations' use of spiritually infused tools to heal those directly impacted by state violence. (Farrag 2018, 76)

It is within this sociopolitical context, where what Farrag terms 'traditional African faith practices' are being self-consciously and visibly mobilised as part of a 'very new toolbox' for political protest, resistance and healing (2018, 87), that Ward's representations of these practices in *Sing* must be analysed.

Defining Hoodoo

As Zora Neale Hurston noted in 1931, the American Gulf Coast, where Ward has set all her novels to date, is a location which has historically had the highest development of African spiritual practices in the United States (1931, 318). These spiritual practices, which are syncretic in nature, developed as a result of the forcible displacement of people by the transatlantic slave trade. As Yvonne Chireau puts it: 'While Africans were unable to replicate their religious institutions, they usually created new, sometimes clandestine traditions that served their collective needs' (2003, 31). While there are numerous such syncretic belief systems which developed under these circumstances, the belief system which became dominant in the American South, and in Mississippi in particular, was known as Hoodoo.[4] To quote Timothy Ruppel et al.:

> Hoodoo [...] combined African ethnic beliefs with elements of Christianity and Islam. In the late nineteenth century, Hoodoo spread across the United States wherever African Americans moved after emancipation.

> In this process, African based spiritual practices from across the South merged into a fairly cohesive practice. (Ruppel et al. 2003, 326–7)

Despite Ruppel's contention that Hoodoo as practised in the American South formed a 'fairly cohesive practice', it is vital to recognise, as Billy Middleton does, that 'in seeing "Southern black" or "slave" culture as a single uniform culture or Voodoo and Hoodoo as a uniform set of folk practices, we are being reductive' (Middleton 2016, 158) and to acknowledge that the practice of these spiritual systems was always, to quote Danielle Clausnitzer 'highly individualized and contextualized' (2017, 213). This is borne out in Ward's work, where her protagonists (particularly Mam), draw on Hoodoo alongside elements of Haitian Vodou, including the invocation of loa.[5] Nonetheless, two key features of Hoodoo and Haitian Vodou can be identified as central to *Sing*. The first of these is the presence of a specific understanding of the natural world. As Katrina Hazzard puts it '[s]ince the forces of nature were everywhere and highly accessible, the transference from lost African divinity back to nature could be accomplished. Evidence of this process is observed in later Hoodoo rituals which responded to and honored these forces' (Hazzard-Donald 2011, 199). This blending of the material and the spiritual also registers itself in another feature of Hoodoo and associated syncretic religious systems: the significance of family, community and spirit. To quote Elizabeth West:

> [f]or early African Americans, one's place in the community constituted a spiritual belonging – one's soul, one's humanity was confirmed through community. Early African American communities consisted of enslaved people who formed bonds that guided them in living through the commonplace violence and terror of slavery, maintaining their collective understanding of the world and themselves as sacred. [. . .] Moreover, when slavery was abolished, freed black people continued and passed on this tradition of community and spirit. (West 2020, 427)

The specific relationship with the animal and botanical world, an emphasis on the significance of community and 'spirit' in the specifically African American spiritual sense, the invocation of loa, the practice of herbal medicine: all of these features of Hoodoo and Haitian Vodou are present within *Sing*. The question then arises of what functions they serve and effects they create within Ward's novel, in the context of the recently visible and self-conscious presence of African-based spiritual traditions in Black Lives Matter and other African American social justice movements.

Hoodoo, the Human and the Non-Human

The intertwined relationship between the human and the non-human found in Hoodoo and Vodou belief is present thematically throughout *Sing*. This is illustrated in Pop's understanding of the mutually beneficial exchange which is possible between the human and the natural world. As Chireau outlines, within numerous African cultures there exists a concept of the

> force vitale, an omnipresent energy [. . .] [t]he power of this life force was believed to dwell within organic and inorganic objects, in the elements of nature, and in the bodies of all animate beings. Through ritual, it was thought that human beings would be able to tap supernatural power for manifold purposes. (Chireau 2006, 39)

While cutting wood Pop explains to Jojo how his great grandfather:

> 'Said there's spirit in everything. In the trees, in the moon, in the sun, in the animals. [. . .] You need a balance of spirit. A body, he told me, is the same way. [. . .] Like this. I'm strong. I can split this wood. But maybe if I had some of the boar's strength, a little bit of wild pig tusk at my side, something to give me a little bit of that animal's spirit, then maybe, just maybe,' he huffed, 'I'm better at this. Maybe it come a little easier to me. Maybe I'm stronger.' (73)

This intertwined quality of the human and the non-human is borne out in Jojo's ability to comprehend the communications of the animal world. However, it is also reproduced linguistically by Ward, where it structures the metaphorical ground of the novel. Pop is described as 'straight and slim and brown as a young pine tree' (1), his bones 'indomitable as cypress', while Mam, suffering from cancer, is 'dried [. . .] up and hollowed [. . .] out the way the sun and the air do water oaks' (3).[6] Ward's linguistic invocation of the interrelation between the human and animal world is at its most potent in Richie's description of Jojo as carrying the 'scent of leaves disintegrating to mud at the bottom of a river, the aroma of the bowl of the bayou, heavy with water and sediment and the skeletons of small, dead creatures, crab, fish, snakes and shrimp' (133). This description chimes with Mam's metaphorisation of her family's bloodline, and the spiritual skills and cognisance which come with it, as the flow of the Mississippi waterways: '"I think it runs in the blood, like silt in water. Builds up in bends and turns, over sunk trees. [. . .] Rises up in the water over generations"' (40).

'Because humans is animals': Dehumanisation and the Rhetoric of Racism

Ward's use of metaphor to underscore the inextricable relationship between the human and the animal within the novel is in the above instances indicative of a source of power and connection. However, in *Sing*, the instability of the boundary between the human and the animal is paralleled by a dehumanising equivalence drawn between Black communities and animals which underpinned the logic of slavery and its legacies. The division between these two categories of being is one which the biopolitical regime exploits 'to mark racialized bodies as non-human [. . .] By projecting animality onto socially subjugated groups, these individuals are framed as neither animal nor human' (Cade-Brown 2017, 3). Ward's novel acknowledges this in Pop's recollection of his enslaved great-grandmother: 'her mouth shaped to a muzzle. [. . .] made into an animal under the hot, bright sky' (69). Creaturely life is what Eric Santner refers to as 'the dimension of undeadness, the space between real and symbolic death' and it is to the creaturely that I wish to turn now (Santner 2006, xx). Santner defines the creaturely as 'signify[ing] less a dimension that traverses the boundaries of human and nonhuman forms of life than a specifically human way of finding oneself caught in the midst of antagonisms in and of the political field' (2006, xix). While the troubling of the animal/human boundary permeates *Sing*, it is Ward's child characters who are subjected to the most painful entanglements with creatureliness.[7]

Such entanglements can be found as stand-alone metaphors, as in the case of the image of Kayla as 'her most animal self, a worm-ridden cat in [Jojo's] arms' (110) or when Jojo, aware of the danger involved in being introduced to his racist white grandparents, is described as 'hear[ing] like an animal' (203). However, the comparison is at its most visceral in the novel's opening depiction of the slaughter of a goat by Pop, an event which underscores the disposability of animal bodies. Jojo experiences the odour of the animal's entrails and observes the tenuous quality of the border between life and death: 'It's the smell of death, the rot coming from something just alive, something hot with blood and life' (6) while in his mind Jojo is unable to separate the goat's body from the body of his sister:

> I grimace, wanting to make Kayla's stink face, the face she makes when she's angry or impatient; to everyone else it looks like she's smelled something nasty [. . .] I know it's stomach and intestines, but all I can see is Kayla's stink face and the soft eye of the goat. (6)

As Crownshaw puts it: 'the distinction between [Ward's characters'] humanity and the surrounding animal life is blurred; their bodies are caught in an interminable process of evisceration revealing the animal within' (2016, 228). This pairing of Black bodies with animal carcasses is repeated in the image of Given's corpse which is doubled with that of the buck he shoots, found 'lying long and still in the pine needles, his blood a black puddle beneath him [. . .] A hundred yards off, the buck lay on his side, one arrow in his neck, another in his stomach and all of him as cold and hard as my brother, their blood congealing' (49–50). The repetition of the comparative 'as' in this sentence combines with the use of the phrase '*their* blood congealing' to conflate Given and the buck, a conflation continued in the repeated lie that Given's death is a hunting accident, a situation in which a human is substituted for the intended prey.

The repeated comparison of the Black and dual heritage children in the novel to animals acknowledges an equation of Black bodies with animal bodies which bolstered white supremacist thought and which still underscores race relations in Ward's America, as illustrated in Jojo's recollection of his white father, Michael, telling him about his experience of the Deep Water Horizon oil spill which has killed whole pods of dolphins on the Gulf Coast:

> then Michael said something I'll never forget: *Some scientists from BP said this didn't have nothing to do with the oil. That sometimes this is what happens to animals. They die for unexpected reasons. Sometimes a lot of them. Sometimes all at once.* And then Michael looked at me and said: *And when the scientist said that, I thought about humans. Because humans is animals.* And the way he looked at me that night told me he wasn't just thinking about any humans; he was thinking about me. (226)

Jojo's recognition of his father's complex and disturbing attribution to him of a potentially 'animal' status is shocking precisely because it takes place in a stream of consciousness rather than in an overt discussion of race. The passage confirms the 'creaturely' existences which are conferred upon children such as Jojo and Kayla by a society still structured by the legacies of slavery, even by those who might be expected to most energetically acknowledge and defend their human status.

The insistence upon the instability of the human animal binary in *Sing* performs, then, two oppositional functions. This strategy offers a vision of an African-based spirituality which 'revolve[s] around exchange and connectivity between the spirit, the human, the animal and the plant realms in a way that maintains a cosmic balance'

(Nweke and Okpaleke 2019, 250). Such a vision is powerfully evoked in Jojo's ability to '[hear] *as* an animal', not merely in terms of the sharpness of that sense, but his capacity to comprehend the animal world. Early in the novel he recalls how, while in his grandparents' yard: 'it was impossible not to hear the animals, [. . .] and it was like I was looking at a sentence and understanding all the words, all of it coming to me at once. [. . .] I knew the animals understood me then too' (14–15). Conversely, Ward points not to a communication between the human and the non- human but a perverse substitution of one for the other which facilitates acts of racial violence, a substitution which is possible only through the Puritan Christian separation of the material and the spiritual. If in many African spiritual traditions, '[h]umans have the responsibility of keeping this equilibrium through the process of respect and relevance of all things', then it is in contrast to the white Christian traditions also present in the American South (Nweke and Okpaleke 2019, 250). This institutes a separation between spirituality and the material world which desacralises the animal and makes it available for literal and ideological exploitation.

The status of Hoodoo as not solely religious but also serving a political function is vital to acknowledge. Clausnitzer positions conjure, and other belief systems like it, as 'facilitating the overthrow of oppressive forces in the lives of countless Hoodoo practitioners who shared this experience of empowerment', enabling such practitioners to 'realiz[e] their own agency in such a dehumanizing system' (2017, 216). Crucially, however, Hoodoo as a force political resistance and subversion was also a *concealed* force. The necessity of such concealment was theorised by political anthropologist James C. Scott in his notion of the 'hidden transcript'. To quote Ruppel et al.:

> James C. Scott [. . .] argues that oppressed groups challenge the dominant order by constructing and utilising what he terms a 'hidden transcript,' an interlocking series of veiled cultural practices designed to dispute and disrupt the absolute power of the 'official' and 'public' transcript. Scott draws attention to prosaic, everyday forms of resistance that remain largely invisible to the dominant culture because their meanings are not understood by those in power. (Ruppel et al. 2003, 324)

Such 'disputes' and 'disruptions' are recorded in *Sing*, as Pop remembers his ancestors producing their own hidden transcripts in which the 'old ways' are set in contrast to the 'official stuff' of white bureaucracy:

> *his mama and daddy avoided them census takers, never answered their questions right* [. . .]. *Said them people came sniffing out that information*

[. . .] *to cage them like livestock. So they never did any of that official stuff, held to the old ways. Papa taught us some of that before he died: some hunting and tracking, some animal work, some things about balance, about life.* (17)

Gris-Gris Bags and Protection in Plain Sight

Another of the 'old ways' which Pop utilises in order to protect himself and his family from the threats posed by white society is the gris-gris bag (Calustnizer 2017, 213). A gris-gris bag is a pouch containing 'an amalgamation of objects, both natural and manufactured, that connect the individual directly with the sacred.' (Clausnitzer 2017, 213). Gris-gris bags embody the deeply syncretic nature of spiritual systems like Hoodoo, incorporating elements drawn from Algonquin traditions, in addition to those drawn from African contexts. They are also profoundly individualised, as 'various constructed and natural elements as well as a clear "intention" are utilized to create the ideal "bag" for each individual practitioner' (Clausnitzer 2017, 216). In *Sing* the gris-gris bag is almost exclusively invoked in the context of providing protection against racist violence, explicit, structural or otherwise. It is one of the key objects through which the novel posits traditions such as Hoodoo as possible tools for political resistance, particularly given that to survive is a political act in these circumstances. As Loretta J. Ross puts it: '[i]t is a radical act to nurture the lives of those who are not supposed to exist' (Booker 2021, 221). In Ward's novel, this individualisation is evident in Jojo's discovery of the gris-gris bag his grandfather has created to protect him on the journey to and from Parchman. Ward not only emphasises the relationship between the maker of the bag and its intended recipient – as Jojo acknowledges 'I know it's Pop who wrote the note, Pop who gathered the feather, the tooth, the rock, who sewed the leather pouch' – she also describes the contents of the bag in minute detail:

> a white feather smaller than my pinkie finger, tipped with blue and a slash of black. Something that at first looks like a chip of white candy, [. . .] some kind of animal tooth, lined with black in the chewing grooves, sharp like a canine. [. . .] a small grey river rock, a little perfect dome. [. . .] a piece of paper rolled thin as a fingernail. In slanted, shaky script, in blue ink: *Keep this close.* (70–1)

While Ward's description reproduces the traditional construction and contents of such objects within Hoodoo tradition, her use of language here incubates a feeling of fragility. Everything the bag contains is miniscule, the feather 'smaller' than Jojo's little finger, the tooth a 'chip', the rock both 'small' and 'little', the note 'rolled thin as a fingernail'. The image of the fingernail, pared away from the human body combines with the shakiness of Pop's handwriting to pair the cultural accuracy of Ward's depiction of the gris-gris bag with an inescapable precarity. This sense is present also in Ward's description of Jojo's discovery of the bag, as he finds: '[a] small bag, so small two could fit in the palm of my hand, secreted in the middle of my bundle of clothes. Like the dot of blood the size of a pin at the centre of the yolk in an egg: life that would have been life but not' (70–1). However, this emphasis on fragility (both in the curation of the bag's contents, and the invocation of the fragility of the human, specifically childhood, state) is paired in the text with an emphasis on secrecy. Jojo attempts to conceal the bag from his mother and her friend Misty in the cramped confines of the car, 'making a small room with [his] body, a screen', and holding his 'palms, a warm open bowl, over the things that Pop has given [him]'. However, for Jojo, there is a need to conceal this protective object not only from Leonie's white friend Misty, but also from his own mother. This concealment ruptures the kinds of communal and familial connections upon which spiritual traditions such as Hoodoo are based, pointing to the parallel representation of Hoodoo in *Sing*, wherein this potentially protective and resistant spiritual practice is insufficient, unavailable or otherwise fails for Ward's characters, in the face of persistent racial violence and its traumatising legacies. Such failure is writ large when we recognise the overdetermined parallels which exist between Jojo's gris-gris bag and the bag of crystal meth which Leonie swallows to conceal it from the white police officer who pulls the family over during a traffic stop. While Jojo has access to a bespoke spiritual object created with the intention of keeping him safe from precisely the kinds of racialised violence he is threatened with, Leonie has no such object to draw on. Instead, the bag of crystal meth – 'scored' and 'jagged' in contrast to the 'smooth' and 'soft' gris-gris bag – poses both an internal and external threat to Leonie's life. However, this incident also articulates the precarity of the kinds of protection Hoodoo practice appears to confer on its adherents. When Jojo is asked to leave the car and instinctively reaches for the gris-gris bag, the police officer interprets his action as a threat: 'then the cop has his gun out, pointing at me. Kicking me. Yelling at me to get down in the grass. Cuffing me. Asking me, "What you got in your pocket, boy?"' (170). At the end of this terrifying altercation the police officer says dismissively 'Boy had a damn rock in his pocket' (166).

This exchange, where the objects of bag, 'baggie', river rock and 'rock' of crystal meth become dangerously interchangeable and in which the white officer calcifies the 'soft' complexity of the gris-gris bag into a 'rock' which justifies the violent restraint and threat with a firearm of a thirteen-year-old boy, attests to the heterogenous nature of Ward's representation of Hoodoo as generative of politically protective tools and practices, and evidences its potential fragility in the face of white violence, even as its potency is also attested.

The Yard as Space of Resistance

While existing scholarly work on *Sing* and African-based spiritual practice has focused on the gris-gris bag, within Hoodoo and within Ward's novel a hitherto unacknowledged facet of Ward's evocation of Hoodoo and its related cultural practices is the status of the yard or garden as a spiritually significant site of resistance. This is perhaps unsurprising given that these spaces are only recently being recognised in the fields of archaeology and anthropology as playing a part in the practice of spiritual systems such as Hoodoo. To quote Ruppel et al., 'African spiritual spaces were created in [. . .] gardens in the form of coded landscapes that were often hidden – though in view' (Ruppel et al. 2003, 321). According to Ruppel's research the gardens of enslaved African and African American subjects 'contested the public transcript of social death and natal alienation with a diasporic transcript in the same manner as the spirituals, folklore, and quilts of enslaved Africans and African Americans' (Ruppel et al. 2003, 325). Moreover, these spaces also facilitated covert independent economic activity, characterised by secrecy and vigilance, as Ruppel et al. describe:

> these landscapes and gardens also served a more prosaic function: they produced cash crops or side money. Despite the vigilance of the masters, an unregulated internal economy developed, one which allowed those who were enslaved to make crucial decisions about the allocation of time and resources used for family and community. (Ruppel et al. 2003, 325)

Certainly, Pop's attitude to his yard is characterised by a desire to keep hidden from view his economic activities, and contrasts his organisation of this outside space with Jojo's overtly racist white grandfather:

> Pop [. . .] put his pigpen and his goat yard and the chicken coop in small clearings in the trees. [. . .]
> 'Why you ain't got more of this cleared out, Pop?'
> 'Ain't enough space,' Pop says. 'And don't nobody need to see what I got back here.' [. . .]
> 'Who you know got all they animals out in the open?' Pop says. [. . .]
> 'The big Joseph,' I say [. . .] Pop snorts [. . .]
> 'Well there you go,' Pop says. (2)

The Stone family yard isn't solely a site of the 'unregulated internal economy' which Ruppel speaks of. It is also the space in which the majority of Jojo's spiritual encounters take place, be that in terms of his ability to understand the communications of animals or in terms of where he most frequently comes into contact with Richie. Ward's situation of Richie in the yard, its trees 'hold[ing] him like a baby' (237), its earth 'making a cot' for him (240), acknowledges how for African and African American communities in the American South, gardens were 'places to find and manage spirits [. . .] Spirits lived there, came there, were discovered there and could be brought and fed there' (Gundakar cited in Ruppel et al. 2003, 332). In populating the yard in this way, with conventionally unheard non-human voices and the spirits of the unmourned dead, Ward acknowledges how: '[l]andscapes throughout the African diaspora were encoded with meaning, [. . .] with signs, or hidden transcripts, that recognised the mystical nature of the world, the immanence of the other world in this one' (Ruppel et al. 2003, 321).

The final aspect of the practices of Hoodoo and Louisiana Voodoo through which Ward explores the tension between its utility and its accessibility for her younger characters is that of root medicine. This branch of folk medicine emerged from and is underscored by a profoundly political rationale. To quote Middleton: 'mainstream medicine was for slaves yet another part of the systemic repression that devalued them as mere chattel. Slaves in the antebellum South approached the healing process, therefore, very similarly to Haitian Vodou communities, using self-treatment as the first strategy' (2016, 161). Such an understanding of the links between medicine, care broadly defined, and political resistance to racial violence and oppression is also present in the contemporary moment and underpins much of the work done by activists in the Black Lives Matter movement, as discussed by Hebah Farrag with reference to the embedding of practices of traditional and alternative medicine within the movement's activities.[8] By contrast, in Ward's novel this trifecta of medicine, care and resistance is embodied by the figure of Mam, a caregiver whose practice of medicine is both shaped and necessitated by the oppressive and active legacies of racial violence in the American South. Ward's novel represents root medicine as both an inherited way of understanding the world, which 'runs in the blood, like silt in the water' (40), and as a practice which requires study and instruction. Mam recalls how the local midwife, Marie Therese, 'trained [her], taught [her] everything she knew' (41) and, significantly, offers her daughter what Leonie dismissively refers to as 'plant lessons' (48). For Mam particularly, imparting this knowledge to her children is a bulwark against racist violence and oppression. Leonie recalls a conversation her mother has with her:

> *This is the kind of world*, Mama told me [. . .], *that makes fools of the living and saints of them once they are dead. And devils them throughout.* [. . .]. She thought that if she taught me as much herbal healing as she could, if she gave me a map to the world plotted orderly by divine order, spirit in everything, I could navigate it. (105)

For Leonie, though, the 'plant lessons' she is offered by Mam fail to connect with her, and she recalls how during these lessons she would 'roll [her] eyes to the pines, wishing [she] were in front of the tv' (103). The 'map to the world' Mam hoped her teaching would provide likewise proves insufficient. When Kayla becomes ill on the drive to collect Michael from Parchman, Leonie attempts to put some of her mother's root medicine teachings into action. However, far from Mam's promise that 'if [Leonie] look carefully enough, [she] can find what [she] need in the world' (102), Leonie concludes that '[s]ometimes the world don't give you what you need, no matter how hard you look. Sometimes it withholds.' (104). Ward connects Leonie's lack of fluency and confidence with root medicine to her position as a young Black woman in contemporary America. During her attempt to gather the wild strawberries which she hopes will cure Kayla, Leonie reflects that '[i]f the world were a right place, a place for the living, where men like Michael didn't end up in jail, I'd be able to find wild strawberries' (104). Leonie's attempts to practise root medicine in this passage are syntactically bound up with Michael's incarceration; Leonie conjectures how she could 'boil the leaves at Michael's lawyer's house, where we're staying before we go pick Michael up in the morning' (104). Relatedly, while the ability to see the dead can form an element of Hoodoo practice, Leonie gains this ability following Given's death, but is only able to see her brother. It is significant that it is an act of racist violence which triggers Leonie's ability to see beyond the human world but in a way which cannot take in the rest of 'what the world sings' (42) as Mam puts it. For Leonie racist violence both provokes and delineates her ability to engage with this vision and these practices, almost until the end of the novel. They don't protect her, or provide her with a subversive voice or tool, in the way they do for her children. As a character, Leonie depicts the collision between syncretic belief systems such as Hoodoo, which emerged specifically in the context of slavery-era America, and a contemporary American context, whose racial dynamics, and the violence and oppression they generate, pose challenges which these belief systems may not be able to accommodate.

Conclusion

To conclude, it is essential when undertaking an analysis of the significance of syncretic spiritual practice for *Sing*, to do so with an awareness of a political context in which these practices have, with increasing visibility, been folded into social justice movements. However, while such practices are present in these contexts, Ward's treatment of them calls on her readers to acknowledge not only the possible site of protection, resistance and subversion Hoodoo and belief systems like it might offer, but also the heterogeneity of that experience for young African Americans who may not be able or willing to connect with them, or for whom they are not capable of offering the kinds of reparative or protective resource which Jojo experiences, and which many of Farrag's interviewees attest to. As such, Ward's representation of these beliefs and practices attests to Clausnitzer's position that: '"conjure" culture continually rethinks and reshapes itself to both adapt and develop in opposition to this changing American culture' (Clausnitzer 2017, 218) and supports Hazzard-Donald's proposal that African American communities 'still tell of Hoodoo's efficacy [and] the[se] potential believers still seek help from a tradition now forced to the margins of black culture' (Hazzard-Donald 2013, 162). *Sing* is a text which refuses to homogenise the practice and representation of these syncretic belief systems, and demonstrates a commitment to articulating its history and potential limitations in the face of contemporary manifestations of racial violence and oppression. Through mapping Ward's dramatisation of the paradoxical pain and power of engaging with the cultural and spiritual practices formed in the crucible of slavery, her acknowledgement of the potential impossibility for some subjects of doing so in any meaningful way – the way in which the trauma of racial violence might preclude such engagement in the first place – it becomes clear that *Sing* both unflinchingly attests to 'unrightness' of the world, and asks what strategies one might use not only to survive in it, but to achieve 'something like relief, something like remembrance, something like ease' (284).

Notes

1. I use this term in Eric Santner's sense, where the creaturely is understood as 'signify[ing] less a dimension that traverses the boundaries of human and nonhuman forms of life than a specifically human way of finding oneself caught in the midst of antagonisms in and of the political field' (2006, xix).
2. Ina Fandrich helpfully differentiates between the connotations of the various spellings of this term (Vodun, Vodou, Voodoo and Voudoo). In this chapter the spelling 'Vodou' will be used, owing to the closer resemblance of the spiritual practices depicted in Ward's novel with the religious system which emerged in Haiti (2007, 778).
3. A key example of this phenomenon was the ceremony carried out in the Ifá tradition (a Yoruba religious system) in June 2015 in front of the house of Ezell Ford, a young, Black, disabled man shot in the back by Los Angeles police officers. Protests held in response to Ford's death also saw many participants attend 'dressed all in white, a custom often required in many traditional Ifá ceremonies' (Farrag 2018, 77).
4. Hoodoo, particularly as practised along the Gulf Coast, was also associated with practices such as conjure and root work, and in some sources these terms are used interchangeably. Likewise, locally specific forms of other syncretised religions, including Louisiana Vodou and Mississippi Voodoo, share some features with Hoodoo while being distinct in other respects. Yvonne Chireau's *Black Magic: Religion and the African American Conjuring Tradition* (2006) offers a detailed account of the development of these traditions, with a particular focus on conjure.
5. 'Loa' refers to 'the pantheon of gods and spirits [in Haitian Vodou], effective in healing both spiritual and physical illnesses; these spirits inhabit "rocks, trees, and other inanimate objects" (Tarter 91), and thus represent the holism of the spiritual and the physical' (Middleton 2016, 160).
6. The prevalence of tree imagery in Ward's descriptions of her characters resonates with the significance of the tree within Haitian Voodou

traditions, where they are understood to be favoured by the loa as places to reside, and with the metaphor frequently used in Afro-American religions of the universe as a cosmic tree, 'with its branches above and roots below' ([Rashford 2013,] 313). (Middleton 2016, 160).
7. For further analyses of the function of the creaturely in Ward's work see Christopher Lloyd's 'Creaturely, Throwaway Life after Katrina: *Salvage the Bones* and *Beasts of the Southern Wild* (2016).
8. In her article 'The Spirit in Black Lives Matter: new spiritual community in black radical organizing', Faragg recounts how 'many organizers involved in DPN and more broadly BLM, [. . .] have begun to reinterpret African spiritual practices and beliefs, [. . .] along with healing practices such as acupuncture, reiki, therapeutic massage, and plant medicine for a variety of personal and professional functions' (2018, 78).

Works Cited

Booker, Vaughn A. 2021. 'Mothers of the Movement: Evangelicalism and Religious Experience in Black Women's Activism'. *Religions* 12 (141): 221–45.

Cade-Brown, Holly. 2017. 'Figuring Giorgio Agamben's "Bare Life" in the Post-Katrina Works of Jesmyn Ward and Kara Walker'. *Journal of American Studies* 51 (1): 1–19.

Chireau, Yvonne. 2003. *Black Magic: Religion and the African American Conjuring Tradition*. Oakland: University of California Press.

Clausnitzer, Danielle. 2017. 'Adorned by Power: The Individualized Experience of the Mojo Bag'. *Religions* 8: 213–21.

Crownshaw, Richard. 2016. 'Agency and Environment in the Work of Jesmyn Ward. Response to Anna Hartnell's "When Cars Become Churches"'. *Journal of American Studies* 50 (1): 225–30.

Edwards, Elise M. 2017. '"Let's Imagine Something Different": Spiritual Principles in Contemporary African American Justice Movements and Their Implications for the Built Environment'. *Religions* 8: 256–78.

Fandrich, Ina J. 2007. 'Yorùbá Influences on Haitian Vodou and New Orleans Voodoo'. *Journal of Black Studies* 37 (5): 775–91.

Farrag, Hebah. 2018. 'The Spirit in Black Lives Matter: new spiritual community in black radical organizing'. *Religion* 125: 76–88.

—. 2020. 'Keynote Speech'. 'Spiritual Protest: The Role of Faith in the Fight for Racial Justice', 5 November. https://youtu.be/CZt5OjM25jk.

Ford, Bridget. 2012. 'Black Spiritual Defiance and the Politics of Slavery in Antebellum Louisville'. *The Journal of Southern History* 78 (1): 69–106.

Hazzard-Donald, Katrina. 2011. 'Hoodoo Religion and American Dance Traditions: Rethinking the Ring Shout'. *The Journal of Pan African Studies* 4 (6): 194–215.

—. 2013. *Mojo Workin': The Old African-American Hoodoo System*. Chicago: University of Illinois Press.

Hurston, Zora Neale. 1931. 'Hoodoo in America'. *The Journal of American Folklore* 44 (174): 317–417.

Lloyd, Christopher. 2016. 'Creaturely, Throwaway Life After Katrina: *Salvage the Bones* and *Beasts of the Southern Wild*'. *South* 48 (2): 246–64.

Mellis, James. 2019. 'Continuing Conjure: African-Based Spiritual Traditions in Colson Whitehead's *The Underground Railroad* and Jesmyn Ward's *Sing, Unburied, Sing*'. *Religions* 10: 403–17.

Middleton, Billy. 2016. 'Two-Headed Medicine: Hoodoo Workers, Conjure Doctors, and Zora Neale Hurston'. *The Southern Quarterly* 53 (3–4): 156–75.

Nweke, Kizito Chinedu and Ikenna Paschal Okpaleke. 2019. 'The Re-emergence of African Spiritualities: Prospects and Challenges'. *Transformation* 36 (4): 246–65.

Rashford, John. 2013. 'Candomblé's Cosmic Tree and Brazil's Ficus Species'. *African Ethnobotany in the Americas*, edited by Robert Voeks and John Rashford. New York: Springer.

Ruppel, Timothy, Jessica Neuwirth, Mark P. Leone and Gladys-Marie Fry. 2003. 'Hidden in view: African spiritual spaces in North American landscapes'. *Antiquity* 77 (296): 321–35.

Santner, Eric L. 2006. *On Creaturely Life: Rilke, Benjamin, Sebald*. Chicago: University of Chicago Press.

Tarter, Andrew. 2015. 'Trees in Vodou: An Arbouri-Cultural Exploration'. *Journal for the Study of Religion, Nature & Culture* 8 (1): 87–112.

Ward, Jesmyn. 2017. *Sing, Unburied, Sing*. London: Bloomsbury.

West, Elizabeth J. 2020. 'Community and Naming: Lived Narratives of Early African American Women's Spirituality'. *Religions* 11: 426–41.

Chapter 15

Ghosts in Mississippi: Jesmyn Ward's *Sing, Unburied, Sing*

Christopher Lloyd

Jesmyn Ward's third novel *Sing, Unburied, Sing* (2017), like her other writing, reaches into US (southern) history and memory to lay bare the deep legacies of racial violence that still striate the nation's landscape. Through multiple first-person narratives, we follow Jojo, his younger sister Kayla, and their mother Leonie, as they drive to Parchman prison to pick up Leonie's white boyfriend Michael who is being released. This journey through the delta landscape, I argue, is also a journey into the region and nation's past. The family drive across an unrelentingly hot landscape that is also marked by the criminal justice system and the legacies of slavery. As they drive, their bodies are pushed to the limit, and we witness different responses to that claustrophobic geography. The book also is, at the title suggests, about giving voice to the dead, and this novel is a ghost story deeply rooted in incarceration. *Sing*, like Ward's previous novel *Salvage the Bones*, can be framed through what I call 'corporeal legacies': representations of embodiment in contemporary culture that index or register the ongoing and historical subjugations of, and violences done to, Black lives in the US South and beyond.

In this chapter, I want to extend some of the arguments I have made previously (Lloyd 2018) and tie them to *Sing* because it exemplifies the analytic of corporeal legacies, but also gestures to other futures and uses of that framework. In short, by thinking through the novel's attention to memory-work, which is activated by attention to bodies and the landscape, I show how *Sing*'s corporeal legacies reveal much about Black life in the US South. By looking at bodies that are coming apart and then tying that corporeal instability to the novel's broader concerns with haunting (both personal and cultural), I show how Ward's novel traces a memorative line through the heart of Mississippi and thus of the nation. I begin by showing how corporeal legacies can be mapped onto *Sing*'s narrative; then analyse key scenes in which bodies are shown to be coming apart; then look at the ghostly figures haunting this family and the US South; before turning to the way that these corporeal representations instruct us about the ways that the novel thinks about regional and national memory. The novel can be read in many ways – as Southern Gothic, as a road novel, as a ghost story and so on – but threaded through these signifiers and tropes is an attention to the body in specific environments which calls up regional and national histories. As such, corporeal legacies offer a way in (but not a totalising framework) for reading the novel's layers.

Sing is narrated by thirteen-year-old Jojo, his mother Leonie and Richie (the ghost of a boy who was in prison with Jojo's grandfather), and the oscillating narrative perspectives flesh out a story of multiple generations of Black precarity in the US South. Each character offers a way of seeing and working through the past, especially as that past is registered through particular embodiments: vomit, blood, addiction, sweat, captivity and various kinds of violence. I have previously explored at length some of the ways that injuries done to Black Southerners are substantiated in contemporary cultural representations of corporeal vicissitudes. Through depictions of the body, contemporary texts set in the US South seem to gesture towards an ongoing and as yet unfinished project of making sense of the past. As historical corpora, these textual bodies and lives reveal material substantiations of the past – they show the continued memory-work of US race relations. As the protagonist of *Salvage the Bones* says, in an oft-quoted line, 'Bodies tell stories' (Ward 2011, 83). Corporeal legacies, as I have described them previously, point to a range of complicated embodiments: (1) as the plantation and prison are connected, those people living in and around its shadow are vomiting, fat, sexualised and breathless; or even undead and/or zombies (*Monster's Ball*; *The Walking Dead*); (2) as discourse around racial cleanliness attempted to segregate the races, bodies are shown to be defecating, urinating and bleeding (*The Help*); (3) and in the light of Hurricane Katrina and other forms of ecological collapse, bodies are non/human, creaturely, prehistoric and, indeed, dying (*Salvage the Bones*; *Beasts of the Southern Wild*). In numerous textual analyses, I show how the body – in all its variety – registers something both fleshy and historic, both material and abstract. This argument builds on the work of Southern studies scholars like Jay Watson (2012) and Patricia Yaeger (2000) who foreground the body as a site of continued exploration in Southern fiction, especially if we are to think about the ongoing histories located in the region and the larger nation.

In the conclusion to *Corporeal Legacies*, I suggest that *Sing* might be an encapsulation of its arguments due to the novel's interests in tying together Black, white, dead, alive, free, incarcerated, human and non-human subjects, all within a particular Southern (Mississippi) landscape. Shadowed by the prison (and its plantation histories), the novel's characters are shaped by, though not delimited to, its anti-Black logics and violence. Doing a 'corporealised Southern studies', one attuned to the variegations of the body as it is represented in literary and other cultural texts, enables us to see both the long and short-term narratives of the US South, as well as the region's imbrication in larger (trans)national networks. This is not to re-provincialise the US South, nor make it exceptional in any way, but to show how particular (i.e. material) histories live on through bodily representation. As I am arguing here, *Sing* shows us bodies primarily coming apart, being haunted, and as shadowed by incarceration.

The ghost, as we will see, is a main figure in the novel, principally because they manifest the ongoing workings of the past. As Megan Ashley Swartzfager argues, there are many ghosts in the novel – Richie and Given (Leonie's murdered brother) among them – who are 'unburied' because they 'never achieved manhood' (what I would qualify as a less gendered 'adulthood') and 'neither youth's untimely death receives adequate recognition' (2020, 314). In short, Swartzfager writes, 'A lack of closure, of burial, allows these ghosts to haunt the living' (2020, 314), which means that the novel has to do the work of exhuming their histories so that they can finally be put to rest. *Sing*, in other words, testifies to those Black deaths that have gone unmarked and unacknowledged in the US South, or what we might in Judith Butler's words call 'ungrievable' lives, because they 'never counted as a life at all' (2009, 38). In her other novels and non-fiction, Ward is similarly interested in the ways that death is either processed or ignored, how Black life is both forgotten and unacknowledged. In *Men We Reaped: A Memoir* (2013), for example, Ward tracks the deaths of five Black men, including her brother, who died within a four-year time span. This 'brutal list' of deaths is one that she felt she had to finally tell, moving from 'silence' and 'subsumed rage' to a mode of 'giv[ing] voice to the story' (Ward 2013, 8). Giving voice, in this memoir, is achieved primarily through telling the stories of both the men themselves and the Mississippi environments in which they lived and died. In the final section of the book, Ward frames the men's deaths through state statistics: 'Mississippi ranks dead last in the United States on the UN's Human Development Index' (2013, 236). In relation to *Sing*, and for our focus here, Ward notes that 'about one of every 12 Black Mississippi men in their 20s is an inmate in the [. . .] prison system' (2013, 236). However you frame Black life in Mississippi (and the US South, and the United States more broadly) Ward writes, 'here at the confluence of history, of racism, of poverty, and economic power, this is what our lives are worth: nothing' (2013, 237). Ward sees contemporary Mississippi as a geography of, among other things, Black dispossession and negation. Ward carries this idea through to *Sing* – in the way it foregrounds death and the prison's ubiquity – but the novel also gestures to the ways that bodies, and the memorative legacies that they testify to, might just exceed the violences of the past.

One of the central ways that cultural texts register corporeal legacies and testify to historical violence, is through attention to bodies that are, in one way or another, registering internal and external forces at once: these are bodies whose interiors and exteriors are caught in an interrelated cycle of coming apart. In psychoanalytic terms, we might say that the bodies are materialising hysterical symptoms: physical (external) representations of psychic (internal or internalised) phenomena. There are numerous scenes in *Sing* where bodily evacuation (of the body being turned inside out) testifies to violences and unarticulated traumas: such as when River (or Pop) kills, skins and dissects a goat with the help of Jojo; or then later, when on the car ride to Parchman and back, Kayla becomes sick and cannot stop vomiting. In her chapter in this volume, too, Cydney Phillip has suggested that 'thirst' is a dominant image in the novel that links the prison to a transatlantic hydrologic history, from slavery and the Middle Passage onwards.

In the opening lines of the book, Jojo says 'I like to think I know what death is. I like to think that it's something I could look at straight', a sentence that links the novel's interest in life and death, Jojo's sense of self, and the idea that men should look at suffering head-on. Though Jojo is ostensibly talking about River killing a goat, the lines gesture towards the ways that Jojo is socialised into being a Black adult before his time – having to partly raise himself and his sister while their mother is absent – and the way that death saturates this Southern locale. The suffering that opens this novel, and thus sets the scene for what follows, is the slaughter of a goat; but more than that, Ward focuses on the way that River takes the animal apart: he 'cuts the goat along the legs, giving the goat pant seams, shirt seams' (2017, 4). The flayed skin is a kind of human outfit to Jojo, a way for this child to make sense of what's happening, but then they have to skin the goat: Jojo pulls and 'The goat is inside out' (5). This 'inside out' image is a key example of corporeal violence, because it spotlights the relationship between interiors and exteriors, the way a body can be something other than it is. The skin 'peels off like a banana' (similes like this abound in Ward's fiction) and smells 'musty and sharp'; and once the goat is hanging up, they bleed it. River 'slices down the center of the stomach, and the innards slide out', an image of the literal messy interior of the body (5). Jojo is also attuned to the way that the goat is warm, and warmer 'near the heart', which he imagines might be because his 'panicked heart beat so fast it made his chest hotter' (5). Throughout the opening chapter, Jojo and River are tied, bodily, to the dead goat, a reminder of their own fragile mortality and the way a body can be rendered merely flesh, merely meat ('the tender liver for Mam', 'the haunches for [Jojo]') (8). As Alexander Weheliye (2014) has written, the flesh becomes a key site in and through which Blackness is constructed within and after slavery. Here, the flesh is attended to as a substance that links humans and non-humans, a common – if differentially precarious – material condition. In other words, the opening scene of River and Jojo taking the goat apart forebodes the way that other bodies (like Kayla's and Richie's) come apart in this novel and are subject to the mechanics of racism, or what Ruth Wilson Gilmore calls 'group-differentiated vulnerability to premature death' (2007, 28). Kayla's fleshiness is connected (though not equated) to the goat's; from the start of the car journey to Parchman, she is ill. Ward's attention to Kayla's sickness – her vomit, in particular – is, I suggest, a way of articulating the sociopolitical and geographical environment's effects on the body, or how the cultural is manifested in the personal. The journey to the prison, which is also a journey into cultural memory, has a physical effect on Kayla: she throws up her food in the car, producing a 'harsh and intense' smell, from the 'puffy Cheetos, digested soggy' and the ham sandwiches, a mixture of yellow and pink (97). The distinct viscerality of the images like this that Ward uses highlights how the novel wants to attend to the significance of the corporeal. We see this kind of fleshy depiction, too, in relation to Mam, who is dying from cancer. Throughout the novel her slowly failing body (tangled in sheets, sweating, struggling to eat) is called attention to. There are so many ways that the characters in this novel (and indeed Ward's other fiction) are so embodied in material and metaphorical ways.

For the next few chapters, Kayla's sweaty and vomit-soaked body is the centre of the car journey: it is as though the vomiting body is trying to register something to or for the other characters. Even Jojo's tenderness towards Kayla – soothing her, cuddling her – transforms into his need to get the sick out of her: at the house of Michael's lawyer Al, when they take a break from the journey, Jojo 'stick[s his] finger down her throat and make her throw up' (118), even as Kayla fights him, sobbing. He makes her 'do it three times, [. . .] over my hand, hot as her little body, three times, all of it red and smelling sweet, until I'm crying and she's shrieking' (118). Through this layered, comma-heavy prose, the siblings' bodies are deeply entwined in a way that foregrounds the interpenetration of self and other, inside and outside, body and psyche. Such relentless attention to the physicality of the vomit (and the body's methods of evacuation) is clearly part of Ward's point that the body is the site in and on which the world etches itself. We see this in *Salvage*, too, when the pregnant teenager Esch has morning sickness, and wants to 'throw it all up' even though 'Inside, at the bottom, something remains' (Ward 2011, 14). For Esch, vomiting is a chance to expel that which she does not want to face; for Kayla, I suggest that she is also trying to get rid of the knowledge that haunts the prison and the surrounding landscape. While I think more about haunting below, there is a sense that Kayla's vomiting, a physicalising of the trouble within the family and region, is also a kind of exorcism. She is tortured from within by something that cannot be pinpointed, but nonetheless needs to come out. For psychoanalytic thinkers like Freud, vomit can be seen as a kind of hysterical symptom: a materialisation of an internal conflict or unconscious process. Something psychic and perhaps unacknowledged is brought up, literally, as a manifestation. Kayla's sickness is clearly tied to the road trip the family are taking to Parchman prison. We could argue that the vomit is a bodily manifestation of fear, or indeed of resistance or rejection. Kayla's sickness halts the journey numerous times, as though warning them of what lies ahead at the prison: the histories of violence that will haunt them all until the end of the novel. Nicole Dib (2020) makes a related claim about the novel, seeing the road narrative as one of immobility (in the face of racism and incarceration) rather than mobility, as the genre has been so popularised in the white imagination. The journey to Parchman and back, then, is not a simple quest narrative, but a materialisation of the stark racist world in which these characters travel.

The vomit is also a way of registering the continual anti-Black violence, in the past and present, that suffuses the delta. Later in the novel, Leonie also mentions sickness, as, when they take Michael back to his parents' house and the parents are rude to Leonie and the kids, she thinks:

> I would throw up everything. All of it out: food and bile and stomach and intestines and esophagus, organs all, bones and muscle, until all that was left was skin. And then maybe that could turn inside out, and I wouldn't be nothing no more. Not this skin, not this body. Maybe Michael could step on my heart, stop its beating. (207)

Here, the earlier image of the goat's inversion is connected to Kayla's vomit, so that the expelling of the interior is also a reorienting of inside/outside to the point of obliteration. Leonie's image of being sick testifies to self-destruction, principally because of Michael's white racist parents, and also to the larger system of white supremacy that they epitomise. In a way, Michael's returning from Parchman to this racist household is a reminder to Leonie of the ways that whiteness dominates the carceral landscape of the US South, in turn linking to the anti-Black violence from slavery onwards that still marks this setting.

The second way in which corporeal legacies are visible in *Sing* is through Ward's attention to ghosts and the material violence they symbolise. As noted above, the scars of slavery that linger in the US South are registered in Ward's novel at the level of the body, but this materialisation also happens, paradoxically, through the *im*material ghost. While haunting has, perhaps, become one of those hoary concepts within Southern studies – gesturing, for some, to a backwards-looking vision of the US South, stuck in the past (which potentially feeds white exceptionalist narratives) – *Sing* is nonetheless a novel replete with ghosts and the matter of haunting. While the novel's narrative engine is the drive to Parchman to collect Michael, more significant is that the ghost of Richie travels back with the family because he cannot come to terms with his own death many years before. The spectre of haunting is introduced much earlier in the book when Leonie sees her murdered brother Given whenever she takes drugs: 'Last night, he smiled at me, this Given-not-Given, this Given that's been dead fifteen years now, this Given that came to me every time I snorted a line, every time I popped a pill' (34). That drugs enable Leonie to see this ghostly Given is perhaps an acknowledgement of the way in which such substances open Leonie up to things beyond one's usual perceptions. Drugs produce a state in which absence is present; that state is also one which the whole family, children included, can tap into, most of them seeing ghosts at one moment or another in the novel.

Avery Gordon's oft-cited definition of haunting, in which it is a structural condition of modernity, is useful here. For Gordon, we do not have adequate language to discuss haunting, but we must nevertheless reckon with its presence in our lives. Gordon writes: 'If haunting describes how that which appears to be not there is often a seething presence, acting on and often meddling with taken-for-granted realities, the ghost is just the sign, or the empirical evidence [. . .] that tells you a haunting is taking place' (2008, 8). The ghost then becomes not only a singular person (as with many of *Sing*'s ghosts) but also a 'social figure', a (non)materialisation of that which is lost or unseen. Ghosts, as social figures, index the presence of something we cannot often see, but is nonetheless shaping our world. In *Given*'s case, Leonie is haunted by her dead brother whose life was ended too soon, when he was shot (or, as the novel suggests, lynched) on a hunting trip by Michael's cousin. There are ways in which we might tie the brotherly haunting of Michael in this novel to the story that Ward tells about her own brother in *Men We Reaped*, noted above. In both cases, the ghost of the brother is also a social figure for the subjugation of Black men in the United States and the ongoing disappearing of them, whether literally through murder or symbolically through the mechanics of incarceration. Given's ghost gives 'body' to a broader absence of Black US men. The ghost of Richie is more instructive however about how *Sing* uses haunting, principally the way he registers the legacy of slavery as it is tied and connected to the prison.

Parchman prison (Mississippi State Penitentiary) is an institution that itself haunts the US South, as a structure with links to slavery and its aftermath. Like many other prisons in the region, Parchman is connected to slavery, as it was built on the grounds of an old plantation. David Oshinsky has detailed the history of this prison in *"Worse Than Slavery": Parchman Farm and the Ordeal of Jim Crow Justice* (1996), which, as the title suggests, shows the thread that runs between enslavement, Jim Crow and incarceration. Caleb Smith explains that in the US South slavery was replaced by convict leasing on the 'prison farm', which 'enforced a new version of the old labor discipline under the sign of criminal justice'; in essence revealing that 'slavery had endured' (2009, 19). He goes on to say that after opening in 1904, Black convicts – including children, like Richie in *Sing*, arrested for petty crimes like 'vagrancy' or 'loitering' – were leased, in a sense, to the state to make it money. 'In its discipline', Smith notes, 'as in its architecture and landscape, Parchman Farm reproduced the old regime of the plantation' (2009, 150–1). (We might say, too, that the spectre of law enforcement, as an emblem of 'discipline', also haunts the characters in *Sing* as they drive through the state and are stopped and accosted on the roadside.) In short, Parchman both replicates and extends slavery's form and logic; which is not to say that the prison *is* the plantation but that the latter is echoed in the former, or as Katherine McKittrick says, 'prisons mimic, but do not twin, the plantation' (2011, 955). When Pop describes Parchman to Jojo, the links between the two worlds are clear: 'I worked in the fields, planting and weeding and harvesting crops', he says; and 'I'd worked, but never like that. Never sunup to sundown in no cotton field' (22). In *Sing*, plantation geographies and practices linger in the ways that River and Richie toil in the Southern landscape, but there are also other corporeal legacies at play.

At the end of the novel, we find out why Richie has followed Jojo back to River: which is that River killed Richie to save him from even worse violence. One day, we are told, Richie stumbles upon a mentally ill inmate called Blue who rapes a Black woman on a baseball visit day. Blue knows that he will be killed for what he has done, and tries to escape, but Richie tags along. As they try to get away, they run into a white girl at a spring, and Blue knocks her down, ripping her dress. The spectre of the criminal Black rapist emerges instantly, and a gang of men gather that day, 'eager as hounds to the hunt' (253). River and his dogs run after the men, traversing a literal landscape of Black servitude: 'the earth turned to scrub and balded from them black hands. All them black hands' (253). The toil of Black Americans is literally underfoot as River hears gunshots, connecting slavery and Jim Crow to the prison: the men shoot Blue and, River finds out later, tear him apart: 'cutting pieces of him off. Fingers. Toes. Ears. Nose. And then they started skinning him' (254). Here, the body is literally disassembled, through a ritual lynching. As Amy Louise Wood notes (2011, 76), the white people who lynched Black men often took bodies 'apart piece by piece to obliterate [their] human and masculine identity', in order to render the dead both inhuman and desexed. Where this novel has put emphasis on the body coming apart, here that process is made literal through the memory of lynching that is both personal (for Pop) and collective/cultural within the nation more broadly. Knowing that this fate would await Richie, River kills him swiftly with a knife. For Greg Chase, this scene echoes the opening of the novel, 'with River's modeling for Jojo the art of humanely killing a goat, so he now tells his grandson of the hardest mercy killing he has ever had to perform' (2020, 212). River then tells the dogs to consume Richie's body: they 'Tore into him' (256). In life and death, the Black body is deconstructed in this novel; it is the flesh on/in which history and memory are materialised.

Delayed, then, until the end of the novel, Richie's death – and the violence done to other Black men that he also symbolises – has been haunting the story from the very beginning. The ghosts were there from the start (we meet them, as Nicole Dib says, 'before learning how the ghost came to be' (2020, 142)), as if the novel is suggesting that the US South is perpetually haunted. As in Gordon's definition above, haunting is the structural condition of the modern world, and it is the ghost that signals haunting is happening. The novel takes seriously the notion that haunting is, perhaps, a constituent element of the Black South, given the long-standing connections between violence done to Black people (often unacknowledged, forgotten and un-memorialised) tied to specific geographies and landscapes. Indeed, the 'unburied' at the heart of the book – Richie, Given and so many more – are given the chance to 'sing' or to articulate their histories, their memories. While we have seen how that memory is often embodied, quite literally through bodies that are coming apart, evacuating their insides, or indeed are dismembered, the final images of the novel are of ghostly bodies at something like peace.

After Richie hears the story of his own death, he is stricken and vengeful and tries to take Jojo's grandmother (Mam) – who is dying – with him. Richie intervenes, and Leonie performs a litany that summons up the healing powers of Maman Brigitte, the mystical woman who delivered Leonie and passed spiritual knowledge on to Mam. Richie relents, knowing that the family do not owe him anything – his story has been told, in essence, remembered collectively – and leaves the house. The haunting he has been enacting is not merely of his own death but, as I am suggesting, a larger memory of violence done to Black people in the US South. The particular remembrance of Richie's death is synecdochal of the novel's broader role in cultural memory of the region's history. The novel's end ties together, albeit provisionally, the political and cultural power of haunting.

At the end of the novel, we find Richie outside River's house, reclining on a tree branch, and surrounded by lots of other ghosts: 'the branches are full'. Though none of them speak to Jojo in the way that Richie does, they communicate 'with their eyes' the multitude of violences done to them: '*He raped me and suffocated me* [. . .] *they came in my cell in the middle of the night and they hung me*' (282). This litany of abuses goes on for several lines, highlighting the seemingly endless subjugation of Black people in the US South and beyond. The dead have gathered, as if manifesting and indexing

the condition of haunting in this Mississippi landscape. We are returned, in a sense, to Ward's statement in *Men We Reaped*, that, in
this Southern context, 'this is what our lives are worth: nothing'.
The novel attends to that nothingness by giving the ghosts a 'voice',
even if it is only on the page, or only to Jojo and Kayla. The ghosts
sit restless and traumatised, but Kayla sings to them, 'a song of mismatched, half-garbled words, nothing that [Jojo] can understand'.
She 'waves her hand in the air as she sings', mirroring the movement
of when Leonie would rub their backs as children. This reimagining of Leonie's attentive and physical mothering (something we do
not see much of in the novel) is Kayla's way of calming the ghosts,
who 'smile with something like relief, something like remembrance,
something like ease' (284). Kayla's performance enables the ghosts to
relinquish some of the trauma that they are carrying.

The final words of the novel, '*Home*, they say, *home*' (285) seems
to suggest that the ghosts can either return home (leave this world for
the afterlife), or that this moment of reprieve together is already some
kind of dwelling. How we read this final scene instructs us about the
role of haunting and memory in the novel. For Greg Chase, Kayla's
performance 'represents the final push these ghosts need to take their
leave from this world' (2020, 213), but for Nicole Dib, Kayla's communication is not a 'scene of closure for the ghosts' (2020, 149), but
rather a temporary moment of calm through memory. Dib suggests
that this unfinishedness mirrors Jojo and his family's 'coming home'
from the prison, which is far from 'cut-and-dried' and left ambigu-
ously open, particularly for Leonie (2020, 149). In both readings,
the work of memory is central: by attending to the ghosts, Kayla
and Jojo enable a process of remembrance and its attendant affects.
Within the frame of corporeal legacies, what is key is that Kayla's
communion with the ghosts, via singing and gesturing, is primarily
embodied. That is, where Kayla's singing is garbled and beyond language (either pre- or post-linguistic), it aligns with Jojo's understanding of the ghosts' stories through their eyes. For both children – and
there is much to say about the role of children in mediating this ghost
story, beyond the scope of this chapter – the link to ghosts and haunting is a material and corporeal one. Talking to the dead, and doing
the work of memory, happens primarily through the body.

In concluding this chapter, I argue that attending to *Sing*'s corporeal legacies not only shows us the ways in which cultural memory is
enacted through the body, but also how to read the novel's glimpse
of the future. In other words, attention to memory is as much about
the past in the present, as it is how that recollection of the past might

point towards other futures. Anna Deavere Smith (2018) suggests that the novel as a whole 'honors paying attention: seeing, listening, and finally, singing' and that happens principally through the memory-work registered at the level of corporeality. To think finally about the role of memory in understanding Ward's novel, and perhaps the broader field of a Southern studies/American studies attuned to the body and to the material traces of history, I want to turn back to an early scene from the book. Just after Jojo and River kill the goat, Jojo remembers his mother and father arguing on the porch; when River calls him in, Jojo tries 'to leave the memory [. . .] outside, floating like fog [. . .]. But it follows, even as I follow the trail of tender organ blood Pop has left in the dirt, a trail that signals love as clearly as the bread crumbs Hansel spread in the wood' (11). In this moment, memory is seen to be active, following Jojo (rather than something in his control), but it is also twinned with the trail of goat blood that Pop leaves behind, which is metaphorically linked to the fabled breadcrumbs in the wood. Ward is gesturing here to the embodiment of memory (fog, blood) and its attendant affects (love, hurt), which are central to the novel as a whole. *Sing* is concerned primarily with the way that homecoming is a kind of memory-work: not only stitching together memories that link the plantation to the prison, but also that braids personal and historical narratives together, rooted in the Southern landscape.

Discussing Toni Morrison's *Beloved*, Sharon P. Holland writes that, in the novel, we see how 'memory is jolted from its moorings in forgetfulness' (2000, 1); that is, memory is an active process, and that literature itself might have an important role to play in its remediation. In *Sing*, memory is 'jolted' from forgetting principally by the trip to Parchman and the confrontation with history that this geography and architecture evokes. The violence of the prison in both the past and present is materialised by River and Richie, in both life and death, and the violence of lynching is embodied in Richie and Given, but in different ways. The spectres of racial violence more broadly in the US South are indexed by the ghosts that attend Jojo's family and River's home. The end of the novel suggests that the ghosts in Mississippi will not just disappear and must be actively listened to; that, as in the Butler quote above, grievability is only possible when lives are apprehended as lives in the first place. *Sing* suggests that in death, the unburied can still be seen and heard and, in time, be let free.

To gloss the end of the novel – Kayla's communion with the dead – another way, we can argue that Ward points towards a moment of Black fugitivity, an escape from the anti-Black violence that has lingered in the US South, and the rest of the nation, for so long.

Returning home, the novel seems to say, is both a confrontation with the violence of history – and the ongoing memories that are still being worked through – and an escape, of sorts, from them. In Rinaldo Walcott's words (2021, 2, 3), 'glimpses of Black freedom' are those 'moments of the something more that exist inside of the dire conditions of [. . .] present Black unfreedom'; they are a 'set of eruptions that push against and within' what freedom has come to mean. Glimpses, eruptions of a 'something more': Ward has used corporeality in this novel to figure some of these moments. Bodies have literally erupted over and over again, as though making mani-fest – or making room for – an alternative embodied existence, one that breaks with the 'plantation logics and economies' of the 'long emancipation' (Walcott 2021, 2), even as they testify to those mem-ories. Though Walcott notes that 'One might plausibly argue that all forms of Black terror and death lead us back to the plantation and its afterlife as the institutionality of all life and death in the Americas' (2021, 19), and Ward's novel has shown just that, the novel has also revealed how corporeal legacies might be remembered and reworked.

If the bodies that come apart, evacuate themselves, and turn inside out show us the workings of historical violence, embedded in the flesh and the landscape, they also show how those memories might be exorcised, how 'glimpses of Black freedom' can be found by going home, following the trail of breadcrumbs, or goat blood, and finding there the past which can, in time, be set free. It is by leaving home, to go to the prison, and confronting Parchman's history, that Jojo and Kayla, at least, can begin to shake loose the hauntings and violences of their family's past which might otherwise confine them to repeti-tive futures.[1]

Note

1. While I haven't used the language of trauma in this chapter explicitly – for my interest in memory tries to shift away from the now fraught discourse of trauma studies and incomprehensibility towards the means and methods of representing the past – this final moment of freedom, however fleeting, could offer a way out of the trauma bind. In other words, corporeal legacies might enable us to see *beyond* being stuck 'in' or 'around' trauma, as though trauma is the only way of conceiving and unpacking one's relationship to personal or cultural pasts.

Works Cited

Butler, Judith. 2009. *Frames of War: When is Life Grievable?* London: Verso.

Chase, Greg. 2020. 'Of Trips Taken and Time Served: How Ward's *Sing, Unburied, Sing* Grapples with Faulkner's Ghosts'. *African American Review* 53 (3): 201–16.

Dib, Nicole. 2020. 'Haunted Roadscapes in Jesmyn Ward's *Sing, Unburied, Sing*'. *MELUS: Multi-Ethnic Literature of the United States* 45 (2): 134–53.

Gilmore, Ruth Wilson. 2007. *Golden Gulag: Prisons, Surplus, Crisis, and Opposition in Globalizing California*. Berkeley: University of California Press.

Gordon, Avery F. 2008. *Ghostly Matters: Haunting and the Sociological Imagination*. Minneapolis: University of Minnesota Press.

Holland, Sharon Patricia. 2000. *Raising the Dead: Readings of Death and (Black) Subjectivity*. Durham, NC: Duke University Press.

Lloyd, Christopher. 2018. *Corporeal Legacies in the US South: Memory and Embodiment in Contemporary Culture*. Cham: Palgrave Macmillan.

McKittrick, Katherine. 2011. 'On Plantations, Prisons, and a Black Sense of Place'. *Social & Cultural Geography* 12 (8): 947–63.

Smith, Anna Deavere. 2018. 'Ghost Whisperers: *Sing, Unburied, Sing* by Jesmyn Ward'. *The New York Review of Books*, 8 March. https://www.nybooks.com/articles/2018/03/08/jesmyn-ward-ghost-whisperers/.

Smith, Caleb. 2009. *The Prison and the American Imagination*. New Haven, CT: Yale University Press.

Swartzfager, Megan Ashley. 2020. '"Ain't no more stories for you here": Vengeful Hauntings and Traumatized Community in Jesmyn Ward's *Sing, Unburied, Sing*'. *Mississippi Quarterly* 73 (3): 313–34.

Walcott, Rinaldo. 2021. *The Long Emancipation: Moving Toward Black Freedom*. Durham, NC: Duke University Press.

Ward, Jesmyn. 2011. *Salvage the Bones*. London: Bloomsbury.

—. 2013. *Men We Reaped: A Memoir*. London: Bloomsbury.

—. 2017. *Sing, Unburied, Sing*. London: Bloomsbury.

Watson, Jay. 2012. *Reading for the Body: The Recalcitrant Materiality of Southern Fiction, 1893–1985*. Athens: University of Georgia Press.

Weheliye, Alexander G. 2014. *Habeas Viscus: Racializing Assemblages, Biopolitics, and Black Feminist Theories of the Human*. Durham, NC: Duke University Press.

Wood, Amy Louise. 2011. *Lynching and Spectacle: Witnessing Racial Violence in America, 1890–1940*. Chapel Hill: University of North Carolina Press.

Yaeger, Patricia. 2000. *Dirt and Desire: Reconstructing Southern Women's Writing 1930–1990*. Chicago: University of Chicago Press.

Chapter 16

Experiencing the Environment from the Car: Human and More-than-Human Road Trippers in Jesmyn Ward's *Sing, Unburied, Sing*

Michelle Stork

Introduction

The back cover of Jesmyn Ward's *Sing, Unburied, Sing* (2017) suggests that the author's third novel 'brings the archetypal road novel into rural twenty-first century America'. Arguably though, social, ecocritical and transcultural issues intersect in this narrative: instead of repeating myths of freedom and self-fulfilment found on the open road, it is sceptical about the road's liberating potential. In her reading of *Sing*, Nicole Dib rightly points out that 'contemporary critical approaches' to the road narrative 'counter the notion of the road as a free and open space for all, whether the notion is depicted in literature or film. However, [. . .] these studies prove the hold that the image of the open road has on the American imagination' (2020, 140). Scholarship on the road narrative has drawn attention to racialised im/mobilities (Lackey 1997, Laderman 2002, Seiler 2008, Brunnemer 2009), but critics have been slow to mobilise ecocritical perspectives for the study of this genre. Yet, some such perspectives have been emerging in recent years (LeMenager 2012, Seymour 2016, Obernesser 2018, Pesses 2021, Bowman 2022) as scholars begin to conceive of the road novel genre as fertile ground for ecocritical debates. Following the protagonists' road trip from Bois Sauvage to Parchman prison and back against the backdrop of the Deepwater Horizon oil spill, *Sing* links historical and ongoing racialised violence to environmental concerns. Though anxiety about the impact of resource extraction and consumption, such as driving fossil-fuelled cars, is growing, Nicole Seymour stresses that the road novel genre cannot be dismissed a priori as anti-environmental (2016, n.p.). Expressing unease with notions like 'moving west', 'individual mobility', 'progress' and 'freedom', Seymour draws attention to 'how visions of mobility might be enticing or at least meaningful to historically oppressed groups – and conversely, how experiences of oppression are often defined by immobility' (2016, n.p.). My reading of *Sing* seeks to think together racialised im/mobilities, ecological concerns and 'histories of oppression' which nevertheless allow for 'new and more caring relations to the land' (Dillender 2020, 131). All these issues are linked *via* the road trip, although they have been treated separately in previous scholarship. While Dib accounts for *Sing*'s portrayal of the legacies of slavery and racism on 'haunted roadscapes' (2020) and Dillender highlights the novel's potential to 'portray landscapes that perpetuate black vulnerabilities yet also accommodate affiliative relationships' (2020, 131) across species and into the more-than-human world, I show how the car itself functions as a literal and symbolic vehicle for connecting and 'transporting' these concerns.

In an interview with Anna Hartnell, Ward herself suggests that her portrayal of cars is multifaceted: 'they symbolize freedom' (Hartnell 2016, 214), they allow characters 'to be introspective and reflect and connect' (214) and they can fulfil the function of the church (214) allowing members of a community to experience 'connection' and 'intimacy' (214). These are 'new and more positive meanings', as Hartnell comments. They contrast with earlier perspectives such as Paul Gilroy's comment in 'Driving While Black' that car culture may be 'foreclosing the possibility of any substantive connections' (Gilroy 2001, 90), particularly for marginalised Black communities in the US. In *Sing*, the car's meaning is ambivalent and oscillates between connection and separation, introspection and extrospection. The characters also feel ambivalent about the car journey: claustrophobia, confinement and survcillance prevail, while the tantalising, yet elusive promise of freedom, escape and connection remains. In *Sing*, the car is haunted by ghosts and thereby opened up to the more-than-human world. *Sing* thus reconfigures the notion of disconnect – from other humans and the more-than-human world – which remains pervasive in research on automobility. Mobility studies scholars often understand the car as a 'cocoon' (Urry 2004), making the car 'a vessel of the "unnatural world"' (Hartnell 2016, 213). I argue that *Sing* deconstructs and reworks this notion of the car as a 'cocoon' by figuring it as an integral part of the environment and as a space for encounters with the more-than-human world. The novel blurs the distinctions between the car, nature and culture; the character's embeddedness in 'petroculture' (Szeman 2017) and the evocation of creolised African and Native American belief systems are both integral to this reconfiguration. I begin by briefly defining the road novel and outlining the notion of the car as cocoon, before moving on to analysing, firstly, how risk and dis/connection inform the characters' experience of driving, and secondly, how the porosity of the car and memories of the Deepwater Horizon oil spill offer a more nuanced understanding of the car's ambivalence from an ecocritical point of view. It becomes clear that the car plays a central role in experiencing the more-than-human world, but the encounters elicit diverging responses from the main protagonists. Lastly, the historical embeddedness and creolisation of the automobile as a carrier of traumatic stories speaks to lingering histories of slavery, racial segregation as well as environmental[1] and social injustices, which *Sing* explores through the road novel genre.

Beyond the Car as Cocoon

Before introducing the notion of the car as cocoon, I will provide a working definition of the road novel. Drawing on Špela Virant, I define the road novel as a narrative that is largely set on the road with protagonists using a motorised vehicle to move from one place to another. The journey structures the plot and is often related to an internal transformation of the travelling characters. Dib notes how the road trip and its preparations signal Jojo's 'rushed maturity' (2020, 139), an element *Sing* shares with other coming-of-age road trip narratives.[2] Moreover, the road narrative often combines quest and chase elements (Laderman 2002, 20). Drawing on this idea of moving *towards* or *from* something, Dib suggests Ward's characters 'understand the perils one drives away from and the ones encountered on the road' (2020, 145). John Ireland similarly foregrounds risks and more figurative obstacles when he notes:

> The journeys undertaken in these stories frequently are associated with the search for the elusive American Dream, and the obstacles (or road-blocks) hindering the search for the Dream – racism, class division, government or police oppression, gender discrimination, and cultural differences, for example – are obstacles America as a whole has yet to overcome. (Ireland 2003, 474)

In Ward's novel, the road trip becomes a means of negotiating positive and negative potentials inherent in driving. The journey is marked by experiences of policing, racial discrimination, and Jojo's unintentional discovery of his family's past with Richie's ghost as the catalyst. *Sing* grapples with the issues identified by Ireland, but does not suggest a simple overcoming through the journey. There is no easy end to centuries of racial violence, and so the ghosts, memories of violence and environmental destruction linger. While Leonie's impulse is to escape, to keep journeying, Jojo and Kayla find a way to live in recognition of and in company with these legacies of the long- and short-term past.

Large parts of *Sing* are set *within* the car, in which the reader feels to be journeying alongside the characters in their 'low maroon Chevy Malibu' (13). The notion of the car as cocoon has been explored by Deborah Lupton, John Urry and a number of scholars in the field of mobility studies as an integral part of modern discourses of progress and individuality supported by automobility. Lupton's 'Monsters in Metal Cocoons: "Road Rage" and Cyborg Bodies' (1999, 60) highlights the duality between a hard exterior and soft interior and points out the false sense of safety. While Lupton does not question the car's capacity for providing privacy, she does not buy into the narrative of safety and security, stressing the wishful thinking involved here. In his influential 'The "System" of Automobility', Urry argues that driving means 'being encapsulated in a domestic, cocooned, moving capsule' (2004, 28), echoing key ideas already put forward by Lupton. He goes on to describe the car as 'the literal "iron cage" of modernity' (28). He claims that '[p]eople have come to inhabit congested, gridlocked, and health-threatening city environments through being trapped in cocooned, moving iron bubbles' (Urry and Dennis 2009, 42). The imagery of the cocoon reappears, but its metaphorical implications are not entirely dissected. It is interesting that Urry implies certain features of the cocoon that have been perceived as positive – security and privacy among them – but already addresses many of its shortcomings in a disillusionment with this myth of the car.

The cocoon, in terms of its imagery, is an interesting choice, as it attributes animalistic qualities to the car that simultaneously imply a process of transformation. In Urry's description, the cocoon is marked by a hard, allegedly protective shell that encloses the passenger within itself, containing the individual worlds of each driver or passenger. The idea of the 'iron bubble', in its conflation of hard, almost militaristic and soft, highly fragile material conditions, seems to take up a similar duality in which the illusion of safety gives way to fragility in the face of danger. Of course, the sense of being trapped in the car runs contrary to the car's promise of freedom, as Gordon M. Sayre comments. He notes that

> Urry [. . .] emphasized the insulation of car-drivers and car-passengers, who enjoy sound systems and climate control while externalizing the

costs and risks of automobility onto 'a "nasty, brutish, and short" world of millions of moving and crashing iron cages' (23) that imperil pedestrians, children, the poor, the disabled, and others who cannot drive. (2020, 129)

Sayre rightly points out the potentially negative social and environmental impact of driving and the 'externaliz[ation] of risks' seen as a cumbersome part of driving.

This chapter builds on some of the complexities and contradictions already highlighted in Urry's and Sayre's accounts, but will more thoroughly engage with how *Sing* reworks and revises the notion of the car as a cocoon. While the idea of encapsulation and separation from the surrounding world is thoroughly questioned, the analysis brings to the fore a number of the cocoon's actual attributes – porosity, transformation and proximity to the environment. In *Sing*, the car becomes a risky environment, subject to policing, and its meaning oscillates between connection and disconnection. Not only does it become a window onto the environment, it runs on organic matter (oil) and carries the more-than-human world which allows for an ecocritical reading of *Sing*. Finally, the notion of the untethered cocoon is revised when analysing cultural and historical conditions that make a road narrative such as Ward's possible. In other words, Ward's novel deals with histories of creolisation in the American South and, as the road trip unfolds, traces the story of traumatic family events linked to the history of racial segregation under the Jim Crow laws, and by extension the transatlantic slave trade, on the one hand and the disastrous Deepwater Horizon oil spill on the other. The car thus becomes central to the novel's larger interest in capturing the creolisation of cultural and linguistic traditions. This both leads to and is captured by the opening of the cocoon to transnational histories and their afterlives.

The Car's Ambivalence: Risk and Dis/Connection

Following the family's road trip, *Sing* both reflects and reflects on the everyday reliance on cars as spaces to inhabit, perhaps particularly acutely felt in the rural American South.[3] However, rather than providing comfort and entertainment, Leonie's Chevy quickly becomes uncomfortable, as the small space begins to feel crowded with people, their bodies and bodily fluids. The automobile feels cramped and unwelcoming, especially since Jojo would have preferred to stay home with Mam and Pop in the first place. A sense of foreboding is experienced by the reader, innately aware of the potential for accidents and surveillance on the road and the mistreatment suffered by the siblings. The narrative neither omits the fact that accidents are an inevitable part of automobility, nor does it gloss over the racial discrimination and the drug tripping, which has lost all the rebellious connotations it used to enjoy in many 1960s and 70s road stories.[4] Jojo is not keen on setting out on the road trip (60). He does not want to share a ride with his mother, whom he has taken to calling by her first name rather than '*Mama*' (7, emphasis original) since she became addicted to drugs, showing his disapproval and distance from her. In fact, Jojo initially experiences the car as an oppressive space, 'listening to country which [he] hate[s]' (70). For Jojo, who is more exposed to his mother's neglect in the car than in his grandparents' house, the desire to get away from the car is most acutely felt. The road trip is rendered more and more difficult for Jojo and his sister, as his mother and Misty fail to feed them. Jojo scavenges food for himself and his sister wherever possible. Here, the novel clearly decouples the narrative of automobility from the idea of progress and well-being: the children suffer from hunger and neglect; the automobile, subject to the American South's socio-economic hardships and racialised regimes of power, is not a guarantor for prosperity, well-being or health.

One striking scene in particular illustrates the risks inherent in driving and shatters the illusion of safety. While Michael is behind the wheel on the way back from Parchman, Leonie asks Jojo to pass Kayla to the front of the car. Jojo relents, and just as he is passing his little sister, there is a wild hog on the road, causing Michael to swerve. Narrated from Leonie's perspective, she confesses: 'I clutch Michaela but I can't hold her and she flies forward, hitting her head on the dashboard' (201). Having let Kayla slip out of her hands, Leonie notices, without any particular alarm, that there is a 'purple knot weeping red on her forehead' (201). As a result, Kayla wants to be back in Jojo's arms. Leonie is overwhelmed and seems relieved when giving in to her daughter's request. With Leonie repeatedly 'watching [her] children comfort each other' (101), she starts to feel useless as a mother. This incident combines parental inadequacy with the dangers of driving. The car turns out not to be the safe space idealised narratives would have drivers and others believe. Not only does the car become dangerous, but it is also soon filled with the stench of numerous ingested and regurgitated bodily fluids. While Kayla falls sick during the trip to Parchman and is repeatedly throwing up all over the seats in the back of the car, with Leonie trying but failing to keep the mess at bay, on the way back Leonie drinks and throws up charcoal milk in an attempt at remediating the impact of the drugs she swallowed when stopped by the police. The car is clearly not a pleasant space anymore and the encounter with the police highlights how racism and racial profiling shape the family's experience of automobility. Here, the act of throwing up not only speaks to the underlying 'affective aesthetic of [. . .] surveillance and anxiety' Dib identifies (2020, 142), it also renders the mother's, daughter's and the car's bodies porous, since neither can contain these fluids.

Remarkably, it is Kayla's throwing up outside of the car, perhaps evoked by the appearance of Given-not-Given's ghost, and onto the police 'officer's uniformed chest' (166) that saves the family here, rendering sickness their saviour. While vomit contaminates the car and speaks to the underlying threat and unease Kayla feels during the trip, in this particular scene the act of throwing up just outside the car speaks to the porosity of the human body and the car.

In a later scene, *Sing* projects the racism Leonie and her children are exposed to onto the car itself. When Leonie stops at her racist parents-in-law's house on the drive back from Parchman, the car once again becomes suffocating while Leonie and the children wait for Michael to return. Leonie contemplates leaving with the children but is unable to. In this scene, the car comes alive; it is not simply an object: 'The car chokes and cranks to life. I drive slowly down the driveway, swerving around muddy potholes, the bugs scatting our way' (211). More than that, the car itself echoes Leonie's struggle for air, the feeling of drowning (see Cydney Phillip in this volume). This imagery also evokes the experience of Black Americans arrested, restrained and choked to death by police on the road which led supporters of the Black Lives Matter movement to protest against police violence, adopting the slogan 'I can't breathe' (see Lucy Arnold in this volume). Here, the anthropomorphism serves to dissolve the difference between the passengers and the car, highlighting that those who are 'Driving While Black' are not sheltered by the automobile's allegedly protective shell. Unlike Jojo, Leonie is initially keen to set out on the road trip. For her, the trip becomes coterminous with a reunion with Michael, whose connection she seeks despite his violent and, at times, racist behaviour. Driving offers a floating sense of liberation and she articulates a sense of belonging to the road that is at odds with Jojo's experience:

> The road winds through fields and wood, all the way south to the Gulf [. . .] I wish it ran straight over the water [. . .] wish it was an endless

concrete plank that ran out over the stormy blue water of the world to circle the globe, so I could lie like this forever, feeling the fine hair on his arm, my kids silenced, not even there [. . .] I'm already home. (152–3)

This scene encapsulates the tantalising promise of mobility for marginalised communities (Seymour 2016). Moreover, this passage suggests a deep connection between the 'roadscape' and the 'landscape', which of course includes the 'waterscape' here. Leonie's notion of driving over the Gulf evokes the history of the 'hydrological hauntings' of the transatlantic slave trade, as Phillip suggests. Rather than articulating a broken relation with the environment, the water as an 'affiliative landscape' (Dillender 2020, 140) promises healing. This scene also captures a connection with the environment enabled by the road and the car, which I will discuss in more detail later on. Here, Leonie may experience momentary relief on the road, but she knows this alleged freedom comes at the cost of eventually leaving her children behind and the guilt attached to this abandonment. The ending scene is worth discussing, because the car, now without the two children in the back seat, begins to function as a safe haven for Leonie: 'The car shrinks the world to this: me and him in this dome of glass' (274). Michael suggests that they 'just [take] a ride', but Leonie knows she can convince him to 'drive for hours into the black-soiled heart of the state', because 'something in him also wants to leave' (274). Consequently, they 'move forward, and the air from the open windows makes the glass shudder, alive as a bed of mollusks fluttering in the rush of the tide: a shimmer of froth and sand. The tires catch and spit gravel. We hold hands and pretend at forgetting' (275). They pretend, but they cannot forget: driving is not a means of escaping the past, but continues to bear the traces of memories, of unwanted ghosts that Leonie has not, and perhaps cannot, come to terms with.

Looking Out: An Ecocritical Reading of the Road Trip

The collapse of binaries – such as nature and culture – can be found throughout the novel. *Sing* deconstructs the myth of the car as a 'metal cocoon' altogether in one of the climactic scenes and reimagines it as an agent in itself. The car is 'alive' in a sense that goes beyond notions of the driver-automobile-complex as formulated by mobility studies scholar Richard Randell (2017, 664). Rather, Bruno Latour's term adopted by Stephanie LeMenager to describe the human body as 'a petroleum *natureculture*' – defined as an 'inevitable

intermixture of the self-generating (organic) and the made' (2012, 62) –
can also be applied to the automobile here, as it assumes organic,
animalistic and human traits.

Moreover, the rhetorics drawn on during the final departure obscure the car's clear identification as 'technology': it is likened to a
human or animal as the bodily expressions of shuddering and spit-
ting suggest. This, in fact, echoes an earlier scene in which Jojo describes the car as 'an old animal, limping to another clearing in the
woods' (110), effectively rejecting narratives of speed by means of
this comparison. Similarly, Big Joseph's tractor is theriomorphised[5]
when he threatens Leonie. Leonie hears 'a buzz, which loudens to a
humming, which loudens to a growl' (55). Here, the animal qualities
convey danger and indicate how Big Joseph's threats inhibit Leonie's
mobility and freedom. In both scenes, the vehicles assume animal
qualities but to different ends: while the 'old' 'limping' car-animal
has been harmed by the circumstances under which it moves (i.e. racialised mobility), Big Joseph's growling tractor together with his rifle
and gestures towards the trees resembles the dogs at Parchman used
to keep prisoners in check and evokes 'the haunting history of black
lynching' (Dib 2020, 145).

Ward's novel erodes the car's boundaries and emphasises its per-
meability, with Jojo's focus on what is outside the window. The road
trip allows Jojo to observe the landscape in Mississippi, and his descriptions suggest that he is highly attuned to life outside the car, reworking the myth of the cocoon and taking seriously its connotations
of connection to the more-than-human world. The car windows offer
at least some respite from the oppressing interior of the car, as he observes the landscape pass by. Having learned about animals and healing plants from Pop and perhaps also from Mam, Jojo is empathetic
to the world outside. While the scene in which Leonie flees from her
father-in-law's threat connects trees to lynchings in the American
South (see Dillender 2020, 135), entangling human history with the
more-than-human world – a reading further supported by the fact
that ghosts mostly inhabit trees in *Sing* – Jojo's view of trees suggests
a fascination for them. From the back seat, he observes:

> I like the way the highway cuts through the forests, curves over hills
> heading north, sure and rolling. I like the trees reaching out on both
> sides, the pines thicker and taller up here, spared the stormy beating
> the ones on the coast get that keeps them spindly and delicate. But that
> doesn't stop people from cutting them down to protect their houses
> during storms or to pad their wallets. So much could be happening in
> those trees. (63)

His curiosity and wonder propel his urge to preserve the trees, as he imagines the lives lived by animals and insects inside them; this scene perhaps also foreshadows his curiosity for the trees' ghostly inhabitants. Through Jojo's eyes, the trees attain almost fantastic qualities opposed to the monetary profits and the presumed safety humans 'gain' from cutting them down. The notion of the 'stormy beating' that 'keeps' the trees in a certain shape in the present is highly evocative of enduring racial violence inscribed into the environment. While it is tempting to read this trope as a reference to human violence only, it is equally possible to interpret the 'stormy beating' as the repeated force of hurricanes impacting trees and forests in the American South when 'hitting' the coastline, over and over again, their impact, of course, increased by more extreme climate. Building on Crownshaw's observation regarding Ward's portrayal of Hurricane Katrina in *Salvage the Bones* (2011), this passage is indicative of the 'environmental neglect [that] is part of a long and varied history of racial oppression in the South and in the nation more generally, which intersects with a long history of industrial fossil fuel emissions and anthropogenic climate change' (Crownshaw 2016, 229). Jojo's observations are extremely detailed, even though they are made from within the space of the car. When driving through a burnt forest, Jojo describes the scenery as follows: 'To the right of the car, the forest looks recently burned. The trunks are black halfway up, and the undergrowth is thick and bright green. I wonder at the stillness of it all. We are the only animals rooting through' (78). Jojo does not specify the causes of the fire, but it is likely that the trees have either burnt down in wildfires or have been burnt in 'prescribed burnings', a 'complex forest management tool that, when done correctly, leads to healthier and more productive forests', as the Mississippi Forestry Commission states (Mississippi Forestry Commission, n.d.). However, if it is the result of controlled burning, it does not seem to have led to a 'productive forest' at all. In fact, Jojo is confused by the absence of other animal life in the forest; he craves and mourns all that 'could be happening in those trees' (63) in its absence. Jojo undergoes all these feelings while inside the car, so his observational skill deconstructs the notion of the car as a cocoon that precludes a deeper engagement with the environment.

In the early days of her relationship with Michael, Leonie's observation of the environment from the car seems to resemble Jojo's during the road trip. Leonie thinks back to her first months with Michael when they went on dates in her car. She recounts how they spent 'a month of riding everywhere but near his house in the Kill' (193). The car becomes a refuge, a space of connection and intimacy, as Ward indicates in her interview with Hartnell (2016, 214). Beyond this personal connection which Leonie experiences within the car, she articulates her feelings through imagery that draws on the environment beyond the car window: 'The world outside the car is a green, shaky blur, the color of Michael's eyes, of the trees bursting to life in the spring' (194). This cliché image of spring and love sprouting simultaneously is used to interlace the world outside the car with Michael's and Leonie's small world within the car. However, Leonie's relationship with the environment remains largely anthropocentric – or rather, 'Michaelcentric'. It is less healing than Jojo's, because not only is Leonie uninterested in Mam's herbal remedies, she is also the only character who litters the environment when 'throw[ing] [. . .] napkins on the asphalt' (98). This gives expression to her indifference to and disconnect from the environment.

Since Jojo demonstrates a keen interest in the environment, he is introduced to a new world view by Richie. In the age of the Anthropocene, where oil spills, wildfires and thunderstorms increasingly often occur beyond the confines of Ward's storyworld, Richie's articulation of the earth as 'home' provides an urgent and necessary reframing of the environment that goes beyond the local scale the novel so strongly stresses. It is relevant that Richie's following observation is articulated from within the legroom of the car; as Dib emphasises, 'the journey narrative meets the story of Richie's incarceration *in the space of the car*' (2020, 141, emphasis added). While cowering in the car, he explains to Jojo:

> 'Home ain't always about a place. [. . .] Home is about the earth. Whether the earth open up to you. Whether it pull you so close the space between you and it melt and y'all one and it beats like your heart. Same time.' (182–3)

This is a striking example of how road novels *can* articulate alternative value systems that seem to be at odds with the basic premise of the genre. The porosity of the car, its ambivalent status as neither natural nor unnatural space, does not foreclose connection with the environment and sometimes, though not always, even fosters it.

Ward's novel does not promote driving and automobility as an entertaining pastime; rather, the road trip allows for Jojo to articulate his ideas about *natureculture* and for Richie and Jojo as well as the siblings to connect. Thus, while the previous generation represented by Leonie and Michael seems to remain more thoroughly embedded in and reliant on an understanding of automobile culture as disparate from the environment, Jojo and Kayla seem to seek alternative forms of being by paying attention to the environment and by being with and learning from the ghosts from within the car. In this way, the novel – *despite* or precisely *because* it is largely set on the road – is exemplary in its questioning of what freedom means, responding to Szeman's question of whether 'we [. . .] as a society [are able] to re-map some fundamental ideas of freedom' (Szeman 2014, as cited in Obernesser 2018, 33) with a careful, but nonetheless unwavering 'yes'.

Rethinking the Environment and the Car: Deepwater Horizon and Creolised Belief Systems

While Jojo's and, to some extent, Leonie's observations are one way in which the novel deconstructs the traditional notion of the cocoon, highlighting instead its proximity to the environment that also de-stabilises the boundary between technology and nature, the novel repeatedly conflates the categories of human and animal. This, I suggest, is rooted in the creolised belief systems on which the novel builds. Richie's and other ghosts are prime examples for this blurring, but even the characters are constantly likened and compared to ani-mals. This becomes apparent when Leonie remembers the Deepwater Horizon oil spill, also highlighting again how her understanding of the environment contrasts with Jojo's. *Sing* is one of the few road novels that includes references to the process of oil extraction in the narrative and explicitly describes the devastating environmental im-pact oil drilling can have.[6] Notably, this memory resurfaces when they stop at a gas station: it is here that the resource required for driving is sold. Jojo briefly hints at Michael's work and focuses on the glorious life surrounding the oil rig, but Leonie recalls in a later chapter how the oil rig 'accident' unfolded:

> I'd spent the days after the accident with Jojo in the house watching CNN, watching the oil gush into the ocean, and feeling guilty because that's not what I wanted to see, guilty because I didn't give a shit about those fucking pelicans, guilty because I just wanted to see Michael's face, his shoulders, his fingers, guilty because all I cared about was him. He'd called me not long after the story broke on the news, told me he was safe, but his voice was tiny, corroded by static, unreal. *I knew those men – all eleven of them. Lived with them*, he said. When he came home, I was happy. He wasn't. (92)

Here, Leonie's reaction to the event suggests a divide between hu-mans and animals that the novel constantly seeks to undermine –

arguably, precisely for this reason: distinguishing between humans and animals leads to the illusion that there is a disconnect from an othered 'nature', in which humans only care about fellow humans, or more precisely for humans they personally know and care about. Arguably, readers are not invited to empathise with Leonie here, as they have just heard from Jojo about the splendid, yet largely invisible wildlife, making her lack of interest in its devastation seem inappropriate and selfish.

The narrative does not suggest Leonie's reaction as the only possible or the right one either. Michael's memory of the events foregrounds how 'humans is animals', which is why he 'cried one day after the spill, when he heard about how all of them [animals] was dying off' (226). What he is criticising is how BP was trying not to take responsibility for the dying animals and the environmental damage, arguing against the '*scientists for BP*' who '*said this didn't have nothing to do with the oil, that sometimes this is what happens to animals: they die for unexpected reasons. Sometimes a lot of them. Sometimes all at once*' (226, emphasis original). However, Michael's position is equally problematic as Leonie's, since his seeming care for the environment is juxtaposed with his abuse of Kayla. While he announces that he is 'here to stay' after he is back from prison one minute (227), the next he threatens 'to whip' his daughter, and actually follows through with it, 'smacking Kayla hard on the thigh, once and twice, his face as pale and tight as a knot' (228). Michael's sadness for the loss of human and animal lives on the oil rig seems to stand in stark contrast with his lashing out at his children without any apparent remorse (228–9). While this well may be the only way Michael knows for expressing his feelings, it suggests that the cycle of violence – against humans and more-than-humans – cannot easily be broken. The cover-up of the Deepwater Horizon oil spill might therefore relate to a purity politics in which the cover-up of BP resembles a cover-up or suppression of traumatic memories. Purity and innocence have long been lost though. Neither the traumatic experiences which turn individuals into ghosts, nor the environmental pollution linked to oil consumption and the oil spill can be reversed: both are an inextricable part of the environment. Not only the 'ghosts linger in this landscape because the cruelty that extinguished their lives is inscribed on the land' (Dillender 2020, 136), but also the traces of the oil spill and of road kill (Ward 2017, 6, 44), consequences of fossil-fuel consumption. By representing Richie's ghost as oscillating between human shape and animal shape as a 'scaly bird' (141), *Sing* establishes an aesthetic connection between the oil spill, Parchman prison and, by extension, the transatlantic slave trade.

Richie's ghost, the oil spill and the traumatic memories of all these entangled events share multiple characteristics: they are ungraspable, uncontainable and linger for centuries. While Richie's ghost has a diffuse quality to it, as his 'blurring' upon entering through the car window indicates (131), the ghosts also have striking material, embodied qualities, as Christopher Lloyd (in this volume) rightly notes. Against the backdrop of Deepwater Horizon, Richie's embodiment as a 'black bird' (262) inevitably evokes the image of the hundreds of thousands of birds covered in oil slick in the aftermath of the 2010 disaster (Balmer 2014) as well as of scaly sea life, including fish and reptiles, who have to live among the oil traces. As Melody Jue notes, the use of Corexit and other chemicals aimed at 'sinking and dispersing oil into smaller droplets within seawater' rendering the spill and its aftermath 'out of sight and out of mind' (Jue 2019, 527). However, as *Sing*'s portrayal of the 'scaly bird's' haunting of the present suggests, efforts at a clear-up failed to contain both material traces and memories of Deepwater Horizon. While Richie's blackness as a bird can simply be read as a translation of his Black skin, it is perhaps more vital to understand his ghost not only as a reminder of racial violence, but as carrying the more recent but equally haunting history of destructive acts against the environment. These events and their timeless and restless im/material traces will continue to shape the American South for centuries to come. The road trip is haunted *and* fuelled by memories of the Deepwater Horizon oil spill on the one hand, and by the afterlives of slavery, racism and Parchman prison on the other. Not only does the car evoke the 'belly' of the slave ship and the killing of enslaved people by drowning (see Phillip), but the novel's reference to an offshore oil drilling disaster also offers a tentative link between these two, connecting the harm and injustices done to humans with those done to the environment in the Gulf. Bearing in mind that the consumption of oil is also the consumption of dead organic matter, it makes sense to understand the car as one part of the haunted environment and as a contributor to further destruction. The car carries ghosts and 'releases' dead matter: again, the road trip suggests violence and death are not obstacles to be overcome but legacies to be grappled with. If understood in these terms, the road trip highlights the characters' ongoing imbrication in these systems of violence.

It is worth considering why Given's and Richie's ghosts are the only ones linked to the car, while the anonymous ghosts at the end of the novel all reside in trees (though one of the ghosts reports having been drowned (283)). Given's ghost is sought by Leonie when she takes drugs and the car seems a safe space in which to connect;

the fact that Mam planted a tree for Given after his death (50) but Leonie never goes to encounter his ghost there is perhaps more telling of Leonie's relation to the environment than of Given-not-Given's whereabouts. Unlike Given, Richie's ghost imposes his presence on the road trippers. For Richie, the car ride promises freedom; he hopes to learn about his death which will release him from his restlessness – a promise that is not entirely fulfilled. Here, it is worth reconsidering the idea of cars as churches: not only does the car allow for some of the family members to connect, but it also becomes a place which establishes the connection with the dead, a connection later extended beyond the car. Ward arguably builds on the Gothic notion of the haunted house (see Michlin 2012 and Petrelli 2020), with Pop and Mam's house certainly displaying these characteristics after the road trip. Notably, she enlarges this notion to encompass the car as well, offering the first opportunity for the children to access the more-than-human world. While the car is not, as I have suggested, an 'unnatural' space, it becomes evident that ghosts are increasingly inhabiting all spaces, no longer just living in trees or haunting houses.

So far, I have shown the close connections between the car, the Deepwater Horizon oil spill and the ongoing hauntings which can be understood in terms of 'the end of nature' (McKibben 1990). This collapse of nature, culture and the more-than-human world can also, to a great extent, be attributed to Creole belief systems directly referenced in *Sing*. Shape-shifting ghosts and elemental forces do not allow for a clear distinction between nature and culture in the first place. I have already discussed the oscillation between human and animal shape in the human and in the ghostly realm and in this last part I want to stress that Ward's use of Creole belief systems supports this trope. With the past and present blurring and Richie's ghost entering the car, a creolisation of the car and the road trip narrative occurs. By becoming a vessel of the more-than-human world, of Richie's ghost, it is opened up to a larger history of cultural creolisation which encompasses racial segregation, structural violence as well as social and environmental injustice. While marked by such violent processes, it is also a history of cultural encounters which led to the combination and transformation of cultures, languages and belief systems whose creolised forms shape the experience of modernity today. The car, then, is in no sense a shiny, slick and self-contained entity; rather, it carries the ghosts of history. These complex connections between the car and the more-than-human world undermine the car's alleged isolating qualities.

This blurring between humans, animals and spirits is based on Native American and Creole belief systems which are being passed down the generations in *Sing*. Embracing these belief systems is arguably what give Kayla and Jojo hope at the end of the novel. While Mam passes on knowledge about the Orishas, often imagined as elemental forces, Pop has learnt from his great-granddaddy that 'there's spirit in everything. In the trees, in the moon, in the sun, in the animals. Said the sun is the most important, gave it a name: Aba' (73). Aba is a term that stems from Choctaw mythology, referring to the 'Great Spirit' (Swanton 2001, 37). Combining and further creolising African American and Native American belief systems, the novel suggests that animist understandings of the world must, in the present moment, also extend beyond the 'natural' elements enlisted by Pop. The environment includes 'unnatural' or hybrid spaces, like the car. There is spirit in the car, as Given and Richie literally occupy the inside of the Chevy. Richie's spirit, a bird, a more-than-human element, significantly transforms the reader's understanding of the car and the road trip and contributes to Jojo's and Kayla's understanding of a haunted world.

The notion that there is spirit in everything may also be what helps Jojo and Kayla come to terms with the world they inhabit. Their experience of the environment is not romanticised or idealist: it does not have redeeming qualities, as early ecocritics suggest with regard to nature's healing, morally conducive properties (Davies 2018, 5). Instead, they are driven through and inhabit a world in which oceans, birds and ghosts carry traces of the oil spill, in which they encounter burnt forests, trees beaten by hurricanes and marked by histories of racialised violence. Nonetheless, the pursuit of a more balanced spirit might help to think of adequate actions. This also speaks to the initial question as to whether road trip narratives are anti-ecological. *Sing* suggests that the road trip can be conducive of understanding the entanglement between human, more-than-human and automobility, rather than rejecting driving as such. Instead, the trip becomes a reckoning with these complexities and ambivalences.

Embracing Pop's and Mam's lessons and their ability to empathise and connect with others, Jojo, though deeply hurt by his mother's decision to leave at the end of the novel, admits that he shares some of Leonie's urge: 'Sometimes, late at night, [. . .] I think I understand Leonie. I think I know something about what she feels. [. . .] I feel it in me, too. [. . .] An unsettling. Deeper' (279). In his curiosity for and closeness to the environment, Jojo takes to walking in the woods as a response to this restlessness, where he encounters the 'tree of ghosts' (283). It is Kayla who now takes care of her brother by telling the ghosts to '[g]o home', singing a 'song of mismatched, half-garbled words' in response to which the ghosts do not return home, as Dillender rightly points out (2020, 144), but at last 'smile with something like relief, something like remembrance, something like ease' (284). It is here that Kayla uses the same hand movements as Leonie did to rub her children's backs. In this final scene of reconciliation and healing, it is Kayla who takes care of her brother – 'like I am the baby and she is the big brother' (285) – allowing past trauma to be somewhat healed by bravely facing it. As Dillender sums up: 'The siblings refuse to avert their gazes from the abruptly terminated lives of their ancestors and instead sing with the ghosts who inhabit their land' (2020, 145). After the road trip has ended, Jojo feels restless and the need to keep moving in a haunted world – though perhaps in different modes than Leonie and Michael. The haunted road trip is arguably a prerequisite for rethinking and coming to terms with Bois Sauvage's history, its present and its uncertain future. Using the genre of the road novel, Ward opens up the space of the car to a history of creolisation that pertains to the characters' everyday life. Ward draws on belief systems rooted in a creolised form of Yoruba culture and Native American belief systems indicative of transcultural entanglements in America's South. Thus, the notion of the car as a cocoon is thoroughly transformed by its cultural and historical embeddedness in the narrative, which is itself testament to cultural changes in the American South. Ward's *Sing* reconfigures the notion of the car as a self-contained, secure and secluded cocoon by representing it as uncomfortable and risky. At the same time, the car is reconstructed as both a part of and a vehicle for engagement with the environment, including the more-than-human world. Ward's *Sing* is exemplary in capturing shifting meanings of automobility in road narratives in the twenty-first century, simultaneously addressing racialised im/mobilities and ecological concerns. *Sing* reworks the road novel so the car accommodates the more-than-human world, dissolving the commonly constructed divisions between car and environment, human and more-than-human, past and present. She thereby revises the road novel genre, previously focused on freedom, individualism and the open road, and captures the ambivalence of the road trip, which nevertheless allows for a more hopeful vision to emerge. While the trip signifies a loss of childhood innocence, it enables Jojo and Kayla to 'unbury' and come to terms with painful, traumatic histories and to accept various hauntings as part of their lives.

Notes

1. In recent years, the term 'environmental justice' has emerged as a lens which 'joins together familiar "environmental" concerns about the degradation of air, water, and land with what are typically considered more "social issues"', such as 'race, gender, and class politics' and 'residential segregation' (Di Chiro 2016, 101).
2. Some examples include John Green's *Paper Towns* (2008), Patrick Flores-Scott's *American Road Trip* (2018) and Sheba Karim's *Mariam Sharma Hits the Road* (2018).
3. This particular aspect of car culture also heavily features in Ward's 2013 memoir *Men We Reaped*.
4. These include Jack Kerouac's *On the Road* (1957), Dennis Hopper's road movie *Easy Rider* (1969) and Hunter S. Thompson's *Fear and Loathing in Las Vegas* (1972). Concerning drug trips in road narratives, Dib notes: 'The drug-fueled road trip, which holds a paradigmatic place in the American imaginary, is premised on the ability to take such a trip in the first place: tripping and traveling become a privilege reliant on the absence of fear that is front and center for people of color. For entitled travelers, drug culture and drug trips are seen as transgressive and countercultural, part of the ethos of escape' (2020, 201).
5. Theriomorphisation 'differs from anthropomorphism in the sense that it specifically relates to animals other than human beings (for example, a "roaring" car engine)' (Bowman 2022, 4).
6 In her article 'The Aesthetics of Petroleum, After *Oil!*' (2012), Stephanie LeMenager briefly discusses the role of gas stations in road novels like Vladimir Nabokov's *Lolita* (1955) and Ed Ruscha's photo essay *Twenty-Six Gasoline Stations* (1963), noting that gas stations are 'crucial switch-points' in the former and symbols of 'decadence' in the latter. Both also hint at rape and sexual abuse, which is a prominent topic in road novels of that time (72). While LeMenager reads these texts in the context of environmental concerns over fossil fuel consumption (71–3), these earlier texts rarely mention oil spills, extractive practices or the impact of exhaust fumes explicitly.

Works Cited

Balmer, Jennifer. 2014. 'Seabird Losses from Deepwater Horizon Oil Spill Estimated at Hundreds of Thousands'. *Science*, October 31. https://www.science.org/content/article/seabird-losses-deepwater-horizon-oil-spill-estimated-hundreds-thousands.

Bowman, Daniel. 2022. 'Horsepower: Animals, Automobiles, and an Ethic of (Car) Care in Early US Road Narratives'. *Journal of American Studies* 56 (4): 613–34. https://doi.org/10.1017/S0021875822000020.

Brunnemer, Kristin Carol. 2009. 'Rewriting the Road: (Auto)Mobility and the Road Narratives of American Writers of Color'. PhD diss. University of California.

Crownshaw, Richard. 2016. 'Agency and Environment in the Work of Jesmyn Ward: Response to Anna Hartnell, "When Cars Become Churches"'. *Journal of American Studies* 50 (1): 225–30.

Davies, Jeremy. 2018. 'Romantic Ecocriticism: History and Prospects'. *Literature Compass* 15 (9): 1–15. https://doi.org/10.1111/lic3.12489.

Dib, Nicole. 2020. 'Haunted Roadscapes in Jesmyn Ward's *Sing, Unburied, Sing*'. *MELUS* 45 (2): 134–53. https://doi.org/10.1093/melus/mlaa011.

Di Chiro, Giovanna. 2016. 'Environmental Justice'. *Keywords for Environmental Studies*, edited by Joni Adamson, William A. Gleason and David N. Pellow, 100–5. New York: New York University Press.

Dillender, Kirsten. 2020. 'Land and Pessimistic Futures in Contemporary African American Speculative Fiction'. *Extrapolation* 61 (1–2): 131–50. https://doi.org/10.3828/extr.2020.9.

Flores-Scott, Patrick. 2018. *American Road Trip*. New York: Henry Holt.

Gilroy, Paul. 2001. 'Driving While Black'. *Car Cultures*, edited by Daniel Miller, 81–104. Oxford and New York: Berg.

Green, John. 2008. *Paper Towns*. New York: Dutton Books.

Hartnell, Anna. 2016. 'When Cars Become Churches: Jesmyn Ward's Disenchanted America. An Interview'. *Journal of American Studies* 50 (1): 205–18.

Hopper, Dennis. 1969. *Easy Rider*. Columbia Pictures.

Ireland, John. 2003. 'American Highways: Recurring Images and Themes of the Road Genre'. *The Journal of American Culture* 26 (4): 474–84.

Jue, Melody. 2019. 'Fluid Cuts: The Anti-Visual Logic of Surfactants after *Deepwater Horizon*'. *Configurations* 27 (4): 525–44.

Karim, Sheba. 2018. *Mariam Sharma Hits the Road*. New York: HarperTeen.

Kerouac, Jack. 1957. *On the Road*. New York: Viking.

Lackey, Kris. 1997. *RoadFrames: The American Highway Narrative*. Lincoln: University of Nebraska Press.

Laderman, David. 2002. *Driving Visions: Exploring the Road Movie*. Austin: University of Texas Press.

LeMenager, Stephanie. 2012. 'The Aesthetics of Petroleum, After *Oil!*'. *American Literary History* 24 (1): 59–86.

Lupton, Deborah. 1999. 'Monsters in Metal Cocoons: "Road Rage" and Cyborg Bodies'. *Body & Society* 5 (1): 57–72.

McKibben, Bill. 1990. *The End of Nature*. London: Viking.

Michlin, Monica. 2012. 'The Haunted House in Contemporary Filmic and Literary Gothic Narratives of Trauma'. *Transatlantica* 1: 1–24. https://doi.org/10.4000/transatlantica.5933.

Mississippi Forestry Commission. n.d. 'Prescribed Burning'. https://www.mfc.ms.gov/burning-info/prescribed-burning/.

Obernesser, Scott M. 2018. 'Road Trippin': Twentieth Century American Road Narratives and Petrocultures from *On the Road* to *The Road*'. PhD diss. University of Mississippi. https://egrove.olemiss.edu/etd/1652.

Pesses, Michael W. 2021. *Ecomobilities: Driving the Anthropocene in Popular Cinema*. Lanham, MD: Lexington Books.

Petrelli, Marco. 2020. 'A Darkness Endemic to Mississippi: Jesmyn Ward's Haunted Places'. *Iperstoria: Journal of American and English Studies* 16: 278–92.

Randell, Richard. 2017. 'The Microsociology of Automobility: The Production of the Automobile Self'. *Mobilities* 12 (5): 663–76. https://doi.org/10.1080/17450101.2016.1176776.

Sayre, Gordon M. 2020. 'The Humanity of the Car: Automobility, Agency, and Autonomy'. *Cultural Critique* 107: 122–47. https://doi.org/10.1353/cul.2020.0017.

Seiler, Cotton. 2008. *Republic of Drivers: A Cultural History of Automobility in America*. Chicago: University of Chicago Press.

Seymour, Nicole. 2016. 'Trans Ecology and the Transgender Road Narrative'. *Oxford Handbook of Ecocriticism*, edited by Greg Garrard, n.p. Oxford: Oxford University Press. https://doi.org/10.1093/oxfordhb/9780199935338.013.152.

Swanton, John. [1931] 2001. *Source Material for the Social and Ceremonial Life of the Choctaw Indians*. Tuscaloosa: University of Alabama Press.

Szeman, Imre. 2017. 'Conjectures on World Energy Literature: Or, What is Petroculture?'. *Journal of Postcolonial Writing* 53 (3): 277–88. https://doi.org/10.1080/17449855.2017.1337672.

Thompson, Hunter S. 1972. *Fear and Loathing in Las Vegas*. New York: Random House.

Urry, John. 2004. 'The "System" of Automobility'. *Theory, Culture & Society* 21 (4–5): 25–39. https://doi.org/10.1177/0263276404046059.

Urry, John, and Kingsley Dennis. 2009. *After the Car*. Cambridge: Polity Press.

Ward, Jesmyn. 2011. *Salvage the Bones*. London and New York: Bloomsbury Circus.

—. 2013. *Men We Reaped*. London: Bloomsbury.

—. 2017. *Sing, Unburied, Sing*. London and New York: Bloomsbury Circus.

Chapter 17

Reclaiming the Ghosts of Trauma's Past: Witnessing and Testimony as Healing in Jesmyn Ward's *Sing, Unburied, Sing*

Apryl Lewis

In a 2017 *NPR* interview, Jesmyn Ward describes her practice of writing about the realities of her region and home town of DeLisle, Mississippi, approximated in her fiction as Bois Sauvage. Ward does not shy away from the harsh realities that the Black community faces, including struggles with drug addiction, generational poverty and systemic racism. On the one hand, Ward appreciates the town and community because of her connections to family. On the other hand, Ward expresses frustration towards people in power who disregard the plights of her community (Briger 2017). In other words, elected representatives and others in power further marginalise poor communities of colour, exacerbating their struggles. These issues plague many of the characters in *Sing, Unburied, Sing* (2017). Ward's novel is about not only traumas on personal and collective levels, but also how the characters battle societal oppression frequently recalled through flashbacks that intersect with and interrupt their present circumstances. An example of such a character is the novel's protagonist Jojo, a thirteen-year-old biracial boy who comes of age in Bois Sauvage. Though still a child, Jojo is compelled to figure out what it means to be a Black man in America, especially in the South. Additionally, by exploring the adversity Jojo's family seeks to overcome, Ward's novel demonstrates how pervasive generational trauma can be within one family and, by extension, within the Black community. I argue that examining the representation of overlaps in traumatic experiences between Black men, women and children can advance the study of African American literature in trauma studies, as well as demonstrate how other forms of trauma and violence such as racism and incarceration stem from white privilege and white supremacy. To advance my argument, I utilise and repurpose canonical trauma theory and primarily, Shoshanna Felman and Dori Laub's

Testimony: Crises of Witnessing in Literature, Psychoanalysis, and History (1992), drawing on their discussions of witnessing and testimony in relation to traumatic experiences in *Sing*. Felman and Laub's text is foundational in trauma studies and widely cited by scholars, though like many early studies of collective trauma it focuses on genocides such as the Holocaust. While such instances of a historical trauma remain critically important as topics of discussion and study, and despite some recent scholarly interventions, most of the content addressing trauma still comes from and focuses on European, white perspectives. Ultimately, the impacts of trauma exist across race, gender, class, socio-economic status and so on. There is room for trauma studies to evolve and allow for continued scholarly conversations about the relationship between African American literature and trauma. Using Felman and Laub's *Testimony* is one way that I bridge the gap between earlier conversations about trauma and African American literature.

The Traumatic Legacy of Parchman Farm

I analyse Ward's novel to explore not only testimony and witnessing, but also historical and recurring traumatic experiences such as slavery, police brutality and wrongful imprisonment. Furthermore, many of the traumas depicted in Ward's novel occur at more metaphorical, ghostly and unconscious levels. The origin point of trauma in Ward's novel is Parchman Farm, also known as the Mississippi State Penitentiary. Part of Ward's research for *Sing* focused on Parchman prison, including a reading of David Oshinsky's *Worse Than Slavery*, which discusses how Black boys as young as twelve and thirteen were charged with small crimes and subsequently sent to Parchman prison. Much like the men in Parchman, Ward points to the fact that children were 'enslaved and suffered and were tortured and sometimes died in Parchman prison, their suffering erased from history' (Briger 2017). However, such mistreatment was justified under the Thirteenth Amendment's provision for criminal labour. In an article for *The Atlantic*, Whitney Benns refers to Section 1 of the Amendment, which states, 'Neither slavery nor involuntary servitude, except as punishment for crime whereof the party shall have been duly convicted, shall exist within the United States, or any place subject to their jurisdiction.' Benns goes on to simplify, 'Incarcerated persons have no constitutional rights in this arena; they can be forced to work as punishment for their crimes' (Benns 2015).

Characters like Pop, his brother Stag, and Richie had no chance to avoid Parchman prison, especially with the increase of prison labour camps and Southern states' insidious tactics to round up Black men on minor offences. However, someone like Michael, a white man, is caught in the cross hairs of incarceration due to drugs and poverty. In Ward's novel, there are four people who, at some point in their lives, become Parchman inmates: Pop, Stag, a twelve-year-old Black boy named Richie, and Jojo and Kayla's white father, Michael. Pop is haunted by memories of Richie, especially of Richie's death. Stag is portrayed as a mentally unstable person who '[stands] in the middle of the street sometimes and [has] whole conversations with Casper, the shaggy black neighborhood dog' (15). Richie remains tethered to the prison even as a ghost. Lastly, Michael goes to prison, leaving Leonie to raise their two children. When Michael is released from prison, he returns to the same prospects: poverty, his racist parents who do not accept Leonie or the children, and access to drugs. Ultimately, Pop and his family members are irreparably altered and traumatised by his time in Parchman, which is evident in Ward's novel.

Witnessing and Testimony in the Wake of Trauma

Pop bears witness to his traumatic experiences from Parchman in relative silence. After Pop's time in Parchman, he and Mam (Philomène) have two children; a son, Given, and a daughter, Leonie. However, at eighteen, Given is killed during a hunting trip by Michael's cousin, which was a pivotal traumatic experience for Leonie and Mam and yet another layer of trauma for Pop to go along with his memories of Parchman. Given's death leaves Pop, Mam and Leonie shaken and grieving for years after. Pop laments that 'When Given died, I thought I'd drown in it. Drove me blind, made me so crazy I couldn't speak. Didn't nothing come close to easing it until [Jojo] came along' (257). In other words, Mam and Pop remain in states of grief and trauma that Jojo and Kayla's presence help to alleviate. A year after Given's death, Michael and Leonie strike up a relationship. Leonie regards Michael as someone who looked past her identity as a Black woman, '[s]aw the walking wound I was and came to be my balm' (54). Leonie thinks Michael does not see her Blackness, but such colour-blindness becomes another form of trauma in the form of micro-aggression. White society certainly sees Leonie's Blackness, and this is reiterated in her interactions with Michael's father and the police officer. In all, Michael's presence is not a solution to Leonie's grief. While pregnant with Kayla, and after Michael is sent to prison, Leonie becomes addicted to drugs and starts seeing a phantom version of Given (34). Overall, the novel begins by providing the reader with a portrait of a family still reeling from grief and a loss that Michael is deeply connected to. According to Felman and Laub, the depiction of grief and loss indicates the reader's role as witnesses to a (fictional) family's tragedy.

Ward's depiction of collective grief through the representation of multiple characters' interior lives allows us to experience, according to Dori Laub, three levels of witnessing: 'the level of being a witness to oneself within the experience; the level of being a witness to the testimonies of others; and the level of being a witness to the process of witnessing itself' (Felman and Laub 1992, 75). While the second level is self-explanatory, the first and third levels need further explanation. The first level involves a character being their own witness within a traumatic experience. Based on Felman and Laub's articulation of witnessing, a character can be a witness to their own trauma, while also having the capacity to testify to their experiences later. In other words, a character can witness and testify, though not always at the same time. The third level coincides with the reader as a witness. In other words, the reader is a witness to a literary character witnessing a traumatic experience. Overall, the three levels of witnessing become a way to methodically address the trauma and traumatic events Ward's characters experience, as well as the way African American literature demands readers engage with depictions of trauma. Like other African American novels that depict traumatic experience from a historical standpoint, such as Toni Morrison's *Beloved* (1987), Octavia Butler's *Kindred* (1979) and Colson Whitehead's *The Underground Railroad* (2016), *Sing* falls into what Anne Whitehead calls 'trauma fiction' (2004, 3). When considering trauma fiction, such works are 'less "fiction about trauma" and more, "reading with trauma in mind"' (Eaglestone 2020, 287). However, this distinction poses a dilemma for the potential of fiction to adequately represent trauma and traumatic experiences. This is because, as Whitehead contends, trauma fiction forces readers and scholars alike to consider the question: 'if trauma comprises an event or experience which overwhelms the individual and resists language or representation, how then can it be narrativised in fiction?' (2004, 3). *Sing* provides one solution to this question with the use of alternating narrators in Jojo, Leonie and Richie. In Jojo's chapters, Pop's memories of Parchman are told in fragments that seemingly have no conclusion until Richie follows Jojo back home from Parchman. In Leonie's chapters, readers can see the extent of her trauma and grief surrounding Given's death. Then in Richie's chapters, his ghostly presence 'represents an appropriate embodiment of the disjunction of temporality, the surfacing of the past in the present' (Whitehead 2004, 6). Put another way, Richie illustrates the unresolved trauma from Pop's incarceration, which is why Richie's narration stops after Pop tells Jojo the truth about his death. Not only does the alternating of narrators represent trauma by 'mimicking its forms and symptoms' (Whitehead 2004, 3), but this approach also portrays generational trauma that starts as early as Pop's enslaved ancestors and trickles down to Pop, Leonie, Jojo and Kayla. Sometimes years pass before an individual can discuss traumas they have suffered; however, that gap between the trauma and the testimony does not make the event less of a reality. Also, the way individuals advance the discussion of trauma can manifest in oral, written and other visual forms. In Ward's novel, testimony is conveyed verbally by the characters and received in written form by the readers. Lastly, witnessing and testimony takes place in the literature and readers are external witnesses to characters' traumas, witnessing and testimonies. To reiterate, Felman and Laub's theories of witnessing and testimony help us understand how the characters in *Sing* attempt to navigate their traumatic experiences and grief.

One scene where many characters bear witness to each other's trauma, along with testimonies that occur thereafter, is when Leonie, Michael, Misty and the children are pulled over by a white police officer after retrieving Michael from Parchman. When Leonie reveals that they are on their way home from Parchman, the officer orders her and Michael out of the car and handcuffs them. Then, the officer orders Jojo to exit the car and get on the ground. When Jojo starts reaching for the gris-gris bag, the officer draws his gun. In this scene, Leonie and Jojo are simultaneous witnesses. Leonie watches and thinks, 'It's easy to forget how young Jojo is until I see him standing next to the police officer. It's easy to look at him, his weedy height, the thick spread of his belly, and think he's grown' (163). In this exchange between the officer, Leonie and Jojo, the mother and son are read as potentially hostile criminals that need to be dealt with. As Marquis Bey notes, '[w]hen the White gaze reads the script of the Black body, it acts on its interpretation of crime and hostility' (2016, 272). This reading of the Black body as violent and criminal is yet another form of trauma. The encounter with the police officer leaves Jojo the most traumatised in the aftermath. Jojo not only witnesses Leonie and Michael being placed in handcuffs but is also the one who gets the officer's gun pointed at him. In this sequence,

Jojo as a Black boy is perceived as more dangerous than a recently incarcerated white man. Jojo narrates how '[t]he cop has his gun out, pointing at me. Kicking me. Yelling at me to get down in the grass. Cuffing me. Asking me, "What you got in your pocket, boy?" as he reaches for Pop's bag' (170). When Kayla jumps on Jojo's back, Jojo worries 'What if he shoot her? I think. What if he shoot both of us?' (170), but only momentarily before he focuses on the gun. After Kayla vomits on the police officer and he lets everyone go without further incident, Jojo recalls, 'The image of the gun stays with me' (170). Jojo goes to describe how '[i]t is a tingle at the back of my skull, an itching on my shoulder . . . I rub the indents in my wrists where the handcuffs squeezed and see the gun' (171). Jojo testifies to his traumatic experience with the officer. Although he does not testify verbally to anyone in the car, Richie is there to bear witness to Jojo's experience.

After Richie joins the group on their way to Bois Sauvage, he is critical of Pop's storytelling regarding their time in Parchman. Richie says, 'The story of me and Parchman, as River told it, is a moth-eaten shirt, nibbled to threads: the shape is right, but the details have been erased' (137). The shirt metaphor is accurate because Jojo recalls, 'Whenever Pop done told me his and Richie's story, he talked in circles. Telling me the beginning over and over again. Circling the end like a big black buzzard angles around dead animals . . .' (248). Pop's talking in traumatic circles when trying to tell Richie's complete story is indicative of history not remaining confined to the distant past. For the longest time, Pop is unable to tell Jojo the painful conclusion about Richie's death. Therefore, Jojo patiently waits for Pop to reach another point in the story that will enable Pop to engage in testifying. The trauma Pop faced as a teenager in Parchman continues into adulthood, further highlighting history's continuity in relation to trauma. Therefore, we receive Pop's testimony through Jojo's narrative. Pop explains how an inmate named Blue raped a female inmate and proceeded to run away from Parchman. Richie stumbled upon Blue during the rape and ran away with Blue not only out of fear, but also 'because [he] was sick of that place. Because [he] wanted to go' (251). Ultimately, Pop was ordered to track Blue and Richie with dogs in tow. While on the run, Blue knocks down a white girl, which incites a mob. In the mob's eyes, according to Pop, 'when it came to Blue and Richie, they wasn't going to tell no difference. They was going to see two niggers, two beasts, who had touched a White woman' (253). After Blue is captured and viciously mutilated, Pop catches up to Richie and assures Richie that 'We gone get you out of this. We gone get you away from here' (255). Not wanting the mob to capture Richie, Pop subsequently stabs and kills Richie. Pop concludes the testimony by explaining how the memory of Richie's death became the traumatic aftermath that continues to haunt them both.

Prior to Pop's testimony, Richie longs for someone to testify to the experiences he cannot remember. Richie also wants to find '[a] song. The place is the song and I'm going to be part of the song' (Ward 2017, 183). However, even when Pop reveals what happened, Richie does not achieve peace and his ghostly spirit persists. Before Mam dies, Jojo asks if Mam will be a ghost. Though Mam will not become a ghost, she does say: '[W]hen someone dies in a bad way, sometimes it's so awful even God can't bear to watch, and then half your spirit stays behind and wanders, wanting peace the way a thirsty man seeks water' (236). Mam's response is indicative of why Richie's ghost is 'caught in a purgatory that prevents him from joining those who die peaceably' (Li 2020, 101) and is unable to leave Parchman until Jojo appears. Therefore, Jojo becomes Richie's last hope for achieving peace and becoming part of 'the song'.

After Mam dies, Richie returns once more, which annoys Jojo. However, Richie can no longer enter the house because '[t]here has to be some need, some lack' (281). Jojo, for the most part, accepts Mam's death and that Mam will not return even as a benevolent ghost. The lack and need that Richie yearns for does not exist. Nevertheless, Richie leads Jojo to a tree filled with ghosts who, like Richie, have a story of their violent fate:

> He raped me and suffocated me until I died I put my hands up and he shot me eight times she locked me in the shed and starved me to death while I listened to my babies playing with her in the yard they came in my cell in the middle of the night and they hung me they found I could read and they dragged me out to the barn and gouged my eyes before they beat me still I was sick and he said was an abomination and Jesus say suffer little children so let her go and he put me under the water and I couldn't breathe. (282–3)

In this moment, Jojo is a witness to the garbled testimonies of all the ghosts in the tree. As Stephanie Li explains, 'By first learning to listen to his grandparents, Jojo becomes able to hear all the voices of his history. Hearing these stories is both his ethical obligation and his familial inheritance' (2020, 102). Although Jojo is present for the ghosts' testimonies, Kayla is the one who enables all the ghosts to find what they desire: a song. Kayla initially tells the ghosts to 'Go home' (284), but when they do not leave, Kayla 'begins to sing, a song of mismatched, half- garbled words' (284). Jojo watches Kayla sing and sees 'the multitude of ghosts lean forward, nodding. They smile with something like relief, something like remembrance, something like ease' (284). Kayla's song soothes the ghosts' traumatised spirits enough so they can finally go 'home' (285). As Richie explains to Jojo, a song is synonymous with the ghosts' final resting place. Kayla's song is a place where these traumatised ghosts, including Richie, can go home and find peace in the aftermath of their traumatic experience. Moreover, Kayla's singing is viewed as a form of witnessing and testimony. Kayla hears the ghosts' testimonies, and her song becomes a testimony to traumatic experiences. Ultimately, Kayla's song becomes a home for the ghosts. Although Jojo and Kayla did not witness the traumatic experiences of the ghosts, their ability to listen and see these ghosts facilitates some semblance of healing.

While *Sing* does not have a happy or healing ending for most of the characters, Mam is able to die on her own terms with Leonie and Given's help. Leonie is confronted with the realisation that Mam is dying. Leonie bears witness to Mam's pain before and after the journey to Parchman. After returning from Parchman, Leonie goes to see Mam, who says, 'If I lay in this bed for much longer, it's going to burn the heart out of me' (214). Mam's suffering is apparent here. Ultimately, Mam asks Leonie to bring on her death by 'constructing an altar of stones', along with cotton, cornmeal and rum, to call upon Maman Brigitte, the mother of the dead (Li 2020, 97). Although Leonie is initially conflicted by Mam's wish, Leonie gives in and gathers all the objects necessary to prepare the altar. As Leonie sees the further diminished physical state Mam is in, smelling of rot and tangled in the bedsheets, Leonie prepares to say the litany that will bring Maman Brigitte. Despite Jojo's begging Leonie to be quiet, Leonie finishes the litany and Given gets in bed and holds Mam while saying, 'I come for you, Mama' (269). Mam follows Given to the afterlife and dies. In this scene, we can see that Leonie 'acted out of mercy as her love led her to a deed that was not "a choice" but a necessity' (Li 2020, 97). Pop reaffirms the sentiment of mercy by explaining to Jojo why Mam finally had to leave them.

Nevertheless, Leonie's actions bring about further traumatisation not only because of witnessing Mam's death, but also because Leonie bears witness to her own traumatic experience. These initial acts of witnessing are ultimately detrimental to Leonie because there is not enough emotional distance from the traumatic circumstances. For instance, Leonie is still in the room holding Mam's nightgown while grieving and processing Mam's death. Still, Leonie is forced to confront a frustrated Jojo, who does not fully understand Leonie's actions. Leonie's emotions shift from grief and sadness to anger and indignation when Jojo demands to know why the litany was spoken, which from his perspective took Mam and Given away (270). However, Leonie explains, '[Jojo] doesn't understand what it means, to have the first thing you ever done right by your mama be to usher in her gods. To let her go' (270). This notion of letting go and acknowledging loss and grief is something that Leonie did not do with Given. Although Mam's final moments were fraught with pain and fear because of Richie's presence, Mam and Given can be reunited in death, which provides them both with peace. However, peace is not extended to Leonie, who reaches a breaking point and repeatedly hits Jojo until Pop pulls Leonie away. This stops Leonie from inflicting further violence on Jojo and, by extension, Kayla. Leonie leaves with Michael so they can eventually go somewhere to get drugs and get away from '[the] death-crowded household' (274) and from responsibility to the family. Due to many traumatic experiences, Leonie inadvertently inflicts trauma on the children. Although Leonie is a source of trauma for Jojo and Kayla, that does not make her trauma less significant to address and analyse. Moreover, Leonie's actions and choices are informed by trauma caused by white privilege and white supremacy in the rural South. White privilege and white supremacy from people such as Michael's father Big Joseph and Leonie's friend and co-worker Misty, exacerbate Leonie's traumatic experiences.

White Privilege and White Supremacy in Relation to Trauma

In the influential essay 'White Privilege: Unpacking the Invisible Knapsack', Peggy McIntosh explains white privilege through metaphor as 'an invisible package of unearned assets' that white people 'can count on cashing in each day' (1998, 148). McIntosh compares white privilege to an 'invisible weightless knapsack of special provisions' (148). Here, McIntosh's main point of emphasis is white privilege's invisibility. We may not see these privileges until the privileges are made overt or obvious. Some examples McIntosh includes in the list include going shopping alone without being followed or harassed, not speaking for all white people, remaining oblivious to the plights of people of colour, and not being pulled over because of race, just to name a few (149). In Ward's novel, Misty tells Leonie to 'take advantage', but this notion of taking advantage comes from a place of privilege that Leonie does not have. As Frances E. Kendall explains in the book *Understanding White Privilege*, 'One of the primary privileges is having greater access to power and resources than people of color do; in other words, purely on the basis of our skin color doors are open to us that are not open to other people' (2012, 62).

Kendall speaks directly to white readers in this instance, though the sentiments reiterate the undercurrent of white privilege for the white characters in Ward's novel. As these scholars ask us to understand, white privilege and white supremacy are historically pervasive and materially relevant to American lives – a point Ward dramatises throughout the novel. White supremacy and white privilege do not occur in a vacuum, meaning that regardless of what century we want to examine American history, we will inevitably find events where white supremacy and privilege prevailed. Kendall provides an array of historical examples of inhuman treatment rooted in white supremacy and privilege:

> [B]reaking apart Black families during slavery . . . removing American Indian children from their homes, taking them far from anything they knew . . . slaughtering tribal people rather than abiding by the treaties that we had entered into with them; using Chinese laborers to build the transcontinental railroad, paying them sixty cents on the dollar that white men were paid, and cutting off their food supply when they went on strike for better wages. (2012, 64)

All these heinous acts yield the same result: oppressing people of colour while upholding white superiority and generating wealth for white people. Systematic discrimination against people of colour exists in 'housing, health care, education, and the judicial systems', as well as 'in the less obvious ways in which people of color are excluded from many white people's day-to-day consciousness' (Kendall 2012, 64). While excluding experiences of people of colour is not always intentionally malicious, the outcome leads to marginalisation of non-white racial groups. The historical track record involving white supremacy and white privilege continues to prolong trauma for the Black community.

To be clear, I consider white supremacy and white privilege to be connected but not the same. White people can benefit from white privilege but not embrace white supremacist ideologies. Definitions of white supremacy highlight the belief that white people are superior in many ways to other races, thereby justifying dominance over other races. Keeanga-Yamahtta Taylor argues that white supremacy 'exist[s] to marginalize Black influence . . . while also obscuring major differences in experience in the social, political, and economic spheres among white people' (2016, 210). Moreover, Frances Lee Ansley refers to white supremacy as:

> A political, economic and cultural system in which whites overwhelmingly control power and material sources, conscious and unconscious ideas of white superiority and entitlement are widespread, and relations of white dominance and non-white subordination are daily reenacted across a broad array of institutions and social settings. (1989, 1024)

White supremacy and white privilege have major implications in the novel and, more broadly, in relation to trauma and traumatic experience. However, most trauma studies scholarship does not call attention to these issues or how pervasive they are in perpetuating trauma. Characters such as Michael and Misty benefit from white privilege, even if their actions and words do not necessarily invoke white supremacy. Then we have Michael's mother Maggie, who uses her privilege to help Leonie get a job at a local bar after Michael goes to prison (32). Lastly, Michael's father Big Joseph is someone who expresses the malice of white supremacist ideology, especially towards Leonie's family, and uses white privilege to minimise punishment that his nephew endured for killing Given.

Leonie's interactions with Big Joseph display the continuity of white supremacy as they invoke earlier centuries of African American history. After they return from Parchman and drop off Misty, Michael and Leonie arrive at Mam and Pop's house, only to find out that they are not home. Michael proposes taking Leonie and the children to visit his parents. Initially nervous about the idea, Leonie eventually relents. The anxiety about being in proximity to Michael's parents, especially Big Joseph, is warranted. After Michael's phone call about his release, Leonie drives to Michael's parents' house to drop off a note for them. However, Big Joseph, on a drivable lawnmower, sees Leonie and accelerates the lawnmower towards her. While trying to start the car, Leonie is terrified and thinks:

> But something about how fast he's gunning that lawn mower, the way he points to that tree, the way that tree, a Spanish oak, reaches up and out and over the road, a multitude of dark green leaves and almost black branches, the way he's coming at me, makes me see violence. (56)

Leonie implies that Big Joseph could lynch Leonie or use the rifle against her as another form of lynching. Big Joseph directs Leonie's attention to a 'No Trespassing' sign 'nailed to a tree feet away from the mailbox' (56). That sign and Leonie's presence is ample enough reason to react with violence. Leonie is close enough to the property and dark enough in skin tone to warrant extermination. Nevertheless, Leonie does escape and is now confronted with the prospect of being inside Big Joseph's home with Michael and the children in tow.

Once they arrive, they are not necessarily welcomed by Big Joseph and his wife Maggie. Although Maggie attempts to be cordial to Leonie and the children, Jojo and Kayla barely speak, which irks Big Joseph. Their silence only fuels Big Joseph's remarks as he says, 'Raised by her, what you'd expect, Maggie?' and then proceeds to say, 'Hell, they half of her. Part of that boy Riv, too. All bad blood. Fuck the skin' (207). Not only does Big Joseph express hatred towards Leonie, but also towards Pop. Referring to Pop as 'boy' verbalises a white supremacist world view. Furthermore, Big Joseph tells Michael, 'I told you they don't belong here. Told you never to sleep with no nigger bitch!' (208). This incenses Michael as he proceeds to headbutt Big Joseph and they end up fighting on the floor in front of everyone else.

Although Leonie removes herself, Jojo and Kayla from Michael's parents' house, Michael and Big Joseph's fight exacerbates the violence Jojo and Kayla have been exposed to in their short lives. Also, the verbal exchange between Michael and Big Joseph reaffirms Leonie's traumatic experiences with racism at large, including previous interactions with Big Joseph. Leonie drives this point further:

> And I can see Big Joseph in my mind's eye, standing over Given, breathing down on him like he's so much roadkill, how he would ignore the perfection of him: the long bow-drawing arm, the high forehead over the dead eyes. (207–8)

Leonie's mental picture of Big Joseph at the scene of Given's death is not far removed from the reality of what happened that fateful night. Michael's cousin killed Given because of a bet that the cousin lost. After Big Joseph goes to the scene and sees Given's lifeless body, the three men return to his house and agree that Given's death should be referred to as a 'hunting accident' (50). This agreement leads to Michael's cousin receiving a sentence of 'three years in Parchman and two years' probation' (50). This chain of events demonstrates how whiteness and white privilege lead to a miscarriage of justice and becomes another traumatic circumstance for Leonie's family. However, the novel's displays of white privilege are not limited to Michael's family, as we can identify scenes where Leonie internalises frustration towards Misty and how that frustration results from Misty repeatedly, though unknowingly, exposing her white privilege.

Leonie's friendship with Misty is problematic because of the awareness of Misty's white privilege. Misty is Leonie's co-worker at a local bar. Misty is first introduced when Leonie goes to the 'cottage [Misty has] had since Hurricane Katrina' (34), courtesy of the Mississippi Emergency Management Agency (MEMA), so they can get high together. The cottage is significant in placing us in the novel's post-2005 time and setting. Many people in states close to the Gulf of Mexico were negatively impacted by Hurricane Katrina, so perhaps Misty's acquisition of this cottage comes as no surprise. However, another implication of the 'pink MEMA cottage' is that Misty did not have to work for her home.

Another example of Leonie's observance of Misty's white privilege occurs after leaving Misty's friends' house. They pass by a billboard advertising a town called Mendenhall, 'Home of Mississippi's Most Beautiful Courthouse' (95). Misty insists on seeing the courthouse, but Leonie refuses. In Misty's mind, the courthouse is likely pretty with 'big columns and everything' (95). However, to Leonie, the courthouse embodies what goes on inside of Parchman according to Michael's letters. Leonie recalls how Michael's letters described 'someone getting jumped in the showers, beaten purple and black', his cellmate and a female guard '[sneaking] around and [having] sex in the jail', and how a guard beat an eighteen-year-old boy and left him to '[bleed] to death like a pig in his cell' (96). Collectively, these instances expose the insidious, violent nature of the American justice system, which runs counter to the 'beautiful' image of a courthouse. Much of this violence remains obscure to the American public, hence Misty's apparent obliviousness to what comes after a trip to court, such as a stint in Parchman. The obliviousness goes back to Kendall's point that white privilege comes with a lack of knowledge about what people of colour, especially Black people, experience. Moreover, the oversight of the relationship racism has with trauma is also suggestive of a blind spot in trauma studies. Again, these examples are meant to convey how relevant and significant African American literature can be in making trauma studies more intersectional.

Conclusion

Incarceration, much like racism, is under-represented in trauma studies scholarship despite the traumatic overtones. If such traumatic aftermath can be captured in Ward's novel, one can imagine the countless stories of incarceration and subsequent trauma associated with imprisonment that are untold. Ward's novel provides a meditation on such untold stories and the traumatic implications that emerge when one carries the burden of bearing witness to their own trauma. To conclude, Given's death, as well as Leonie's personal circumstances with her family, children and Michael, are the result of white privilege and white supremacy from outside influences. While not all the outside influences are malicious, the result is the same: Leonie is ensnared by grief, which later propels the drug addiction. Ultimately, for Jojo and his family, none of them are free from the perils of white supremacy. *Sing* conveys how Black people can succumb, though not willingly, to a society riddled with white supremacist ideologies and white privilege that perpetuates trauma.

Works Cited

Ansley, Frances Lee. 1989. 'Stirring the Ashes: Race, Class and the Future of Civil Rights Scholarship'. *Cornell Law Review* 74 (6): 994–1077. https://scholarship.law.cornell.edu/clr/vol74/iss6/1.

Benns, Whitney. 2015. 'American Slavery, Reinvented'. https://www.theatlantic.com/business/archive/2015/09/prison-labor-in-america/406177/.

Bey, Marquis. 2016. '"Bring Out Your Dead": Understanding the Historical Persistence of the Criminalization of Black Bodies'. *Cultural Studies* 16 (3): 271–7. *SAGE Publications*. https://doi.org/10.1177/1532708616634773.

Briger, Sam. 2017. 'For Jesmyn Ward, Writing Means Telling The 'Truth About The Place That I Live In'. https://www.npr.org/2017/11/28/566933935/for-jesmyn-ward-writing-means-telling-the-truth-about-the-place-that-i-live-in.

Eaglestone, Robert. 2020. 'Trauma and Fiction'. In *The Routledge Companion to Literature and Trauma*, edited by Colin Davis and Hanna Meretoja, 287–95. New York: Routledge.

Felman, Shoshana and Dori Laub. 1992. *Testimony: Crises of Witnessing in Literature, Psychoanalysis, and History*. New York: Routledge.

Kendall, Frances E. 2012. *Understanding White Privilege: Creating Pathways to Authentic Relationships Across Race*. New York: Routledge.

Li, Stephanie. 2020. 'Learning to Listen in Jesmyn Ward's *Sing, Unburied, Sing*'. In *Reading Contemporary Black British and African American Women Writers: Race, Ethics, Narrative Form*, edited by Jean Wyatt and Sheldon George, 88–103. New York: Routledge.

McIntosh, Peggy. 1998. 'White Privilege: Unpacking the Invisible Knapsack'. In *Re-Visioning Family Therapy: Race, Culture, and Gender in Clinical Practice*, edited by Monica McGoldrick, 147–52. New York: Guilford Press.

Taylor, Keeanga-Yamahtta. 2016. *From #BlackLivesMatter to Black Libe-ration*. Chicago: Haymarket Books.
Ward, Jesmyn. 2017. *Sing, Unburied, Sing*. New York: Scribner.
Whitehead, Anne. 2004. *Trauma Fiction*. Edinburgh: Edinburgh University Press.

Chapter 18

Carceral Ecologies: Incarceration and Hydrological Haunting in Jesmyn Ward's *Sing, Unburied, Sing*

Cydney Phillip

The first language the keepers of the hold use on the captives is the language of violence: the language of thirst and hunger and sore and heat, the language of the gun and the gun butt, the foot and the fist, the knife and the throwing overboard. And in the hold, mouths open, say, thirsty.
Christina Sharpe, In the Wake: On Blackness and Being (2016)

'You thirsty?' I ask. 'Yeah,' she whispers.
Jesmyn Ward, Sing, Unburied, Sing (2017)

Parchman prison, a sweltering Southern landscape, and characters perpetually wrestling their own thirst: these are some of the defining elements of Jesmyn Ward's *Sing, Unburied, Sing* (2017), a neo-Gothic odyssey into the barren heart of the Mississippi State Penitentiary. 'I swallow and my throat seems to catch like Velcro', says thirteen-year-old Jojo, the novel's lead protagonist whose incarcerated father's release date prompts the road trip (Ward 2017, 64). 'I think', he continues, 'I know what the parched man felt' (Ward 2017, 64). Jojo's etymological interpretation of Parchman might easily be dismissed as a moment of humour – a reminder of the child narrator's age – but his statement is significant insofar as water deprivation and contamination is an underlying issue at the Mississippi State Penitentiary. Following a 2019 state inspection that exposed an array of environmental health issues festering within the prison, activists took to the Rankin County courthouse in protest. Malaika Canada implored attendees at the rally to '[i]magine [. . .] being dehydrated for days, afraid to drink water that's brown and smells like sewage within pipes filled with rust and mould' (Liu 2019). That the characters comprising *Sing, Unburied, Sing* develop an insuppressible desire for water the closer they get to the penitentiary, teaches Jojo that to fall into the grip of Parchman is to understand what it means to be thirsty.

'Sometimes I wonder who that parched man was, that man dying for water, that they named the town and jail after', says Jojo (Ward 2017, 63). 'Wonder if he looked like Pop, straight up and down, brown skin tinged with red, or me, an in-between color, or Michael, the color of milk. Wonder what that man said before he died of a cracked throat' (Ward 2017, 63). In the July of 2019, almost two years after the publication of *Sing, Unburied, Sing*, a video obtained by the Prison Reform Movement went viral on social media for its exposure of water standards in Parchman prison, affirming the carceral ecologies imagined by Jojo throughout the novel. 'We are dealing with a serious crisis here', an inmate can be heard saying as the camera remains fixed on a bottle of dull, brown water taken from faucets that prisoners are forced to drink from (Prison Reform Movement 2019). Weeks later, Bryan Shaver – then a religious volunteer at Parchman – received information that issues with plumbing persisted in Unit 29. Shaver reported these concerns to the appropriate authorities and had his access to the prison revoked the next day. Such examples were not the first occasions that accounts of the relationship between water and Parchman prison had surfaced. For instance, in 2015, reports emerged regarding 'Parchman's Unit 29, where 1,412 inmates [were] without drinking water from their sinks' for several days (Mitchell 2015). In the scorching heat of midsummer Mississippi – in a facility without air conditioning – inmates were incarcerated in cells without functioning water supplies. The director of the MacArthur Justice Center in Jackson referred it as 'a dangerous situation exacerbated by the fact that it's hot as hell' (Cliff Johnson quoted in Mitchell 2019). These are not isolated incidents. In more than twenty US states, reports identified the presence of arsenic, lead and other toxic substances in the waterways of prisons where 'inmates – including pregnant women – were forced to drink toxic water while prison guards drank filtered water' (Pellow 2017).

Recent trends in American activism have gone a long way in exposing the institutionalised racism that underpins the nation's penal system, but the relationship between mass incarceration and ecological violence remains relatively concealed. In this chapter, I demonstrate how Ward's work serves as a beacon for these kinds of discussions. More specifically, I draw on *Sing, Unburied, Sing* and how it prompts us to engage with the ways in which water is imbricated in the carceral continuum from slavery to mass incarceration. Diana Leong argues that 'slave ships thrived on an ecology of thirst' – as in, 'a set of relations in which humanity is measured through one's relationship to water', with the substance functioning as 'threshold between slave and non-slave [. . .] as the slave's impossibility of relating to water as "sustenance" bars her from the status of the human' (Leong 2017, 805). Land-based prisons of today still pivot around this set of relations. The ongoing control and weaponisation of water forms what I refer to as carceral ecologies, which can be traced back to the Middle Passage.

My engagement with carceral ecologies is guided not by scientific data – of which, unsurprisingly, there is not much –but Black storytelling practices. In her most recent book, *Dear Science and Other Stories* (2021), Katherine McKittrick advocates for methodological practices wherein we think 'analytics as story' (McCittrick 2021, 12), and story as analytics, considering the ways in which Black narratives 'reinvent the terms and stakes of knowledge' (186). Likewise, I turn to Jesmyn Ward's *Sing, Unburied, Sing* to better understand the intersections between prisons and ecological violence. I examine how the novel summons ghosts, water and prisons in order narrate the trajectory of carceral ecologies in the US South. In doing so, the following analysis will examine how, by invoking the history of Parchman prison through Middle Passage symbolism, ghosts and the lead protagonist's grandfather, River, *Sing, Unburied, Sing* provides a lens through which we might begin developing a concept of hydrological haunting in relation to the intersections between prisons and ecological violence, revealing the entanglements between human and aquatic histories, and how they bear on the present. As such, this chapter will merge pelagic and prison studies in its reading of Ward's neo-Southern Gothic, exploring the notion of water as ghostly and shedding new light on issues of incarceration which can be traced back to the slave ship.

Prisons and Water: From Slave Ship to Penitentiary

Critical discussions of incarceration are usually dominated by Foucauldian versions of prison history. Since its publication, Michel Foucault's *Discipline and Punish* (1975) has served as touchstone for knowledge of Western carceral models, tracing the transition from spectacles of punishment to the modern prison system, a disciplinary apparatus built on surveillance and seclusion. Patently absent in Foucauldian conceptualisations of incarceration, however, is an acknowledgement of the carceral infrastructures of colonialism and slavery. As Dennis Childs writes in *Slaves of the State: Black Incarceration from the Chain Gang to the Penitentiary* (2015), 'for the African and those of African descent, the modern prison did not begin with Jeremy Bentham's Panopticon, the Walnut Street Jail, or the Auburn System, but with the coffles, barracoons, slave ships, and slave "pens" of the Middle Passage' (Childs 2015, 29). Childs argues that the carceral model of the Middle Passage – a capitalist system of racialised violence – continues to inform land-based prisons in the age of mass incarceration. His work draws on Dylan Rodríguez's assertion that:

> A genealogy of the contemporary prison regime awakens both the historical memory and the socio-political logic of the Middle Passage. The prison has come to form a hauntingly similar spatial and temporal continuum between social and biological notions of life and death, banal liberal civic freedom and totalizing unfreedom, community and alienation, agency and liquidation, the 'human' and the subhuman/nonhuman. In a reconstruction of the Middle Passage's constitutive logic, the reinvented prison regime is articulating and self-valorizing a commitment to efficient and effect bodily immobilization within the mass-based ontological subjection of human beings. (Rodríguez 2007, 48)

This chapter attempts to move beyond discussions of the spatial synergies between penitentiaries and the slave ship, and towards an understanding of the aqueous violence that underscores America's racialised penal infrastructures, from the Middle Passage to the modern prison system. If, as Leong argues, water-based prisons of the Middle Passage were fortified by an ecology of thirst, it is uncanny, then, that issues of water scarcity and contamination are abundant in the land-based prisons of America today which disproportionately incarcerate African Americans. A 2017 report by *Earth Island Journal* called for a recognition of 'the connections between mass incarceration and environmental issues, that is problems that arise when prisons are sited on or near toxic sites as well as when prisons themselves becomes sources of toxic contamination' (Bernd et al. 2017). They identify crises of unsafe, contaminated drinking water as one of the most pernicious environmental health implications that inmates are vulnerable to. Subjected to soaring temperatures and lack of air conditioning, inmates at the Wallace Pack Unit in 2017, for instance, were advised by the Texas Department of Criminal Justice to drink up to two gallons of water per day to alleviate the extreme heat. 'There was just one problem', write Bernd, Loftus-Farren and Mitra:

> The water at the Unit contained between two-and-a-half to four-and-a-half times the level of arsenic permitted by the EPA. Arsenic is a carcinogen. The prisoners drank thousands of gallons of the arsenic-tainted

water for more than 10 years before a federal judge ordered TDCJ to truck in clean water. (Bernd et al. 2017)

The issue of toxic water is widespread in American prisons. 'In fact, according to the EPA's enforcement database', write Bernd et al., 'federal and state agencies brought 1,149 informal actions and 78 formal actions against regulated prisons, jails, and detention centers during the past five years under the Safe Drinking Water Act, more than under any other federal environmental law' (Bernd et al. 2017).

When exploring the connections between the prison and the slave ship, I am reminded of *Thinking with Water* (Chen et al. 2013) in which the notion of an 'aqueous ecopolitics' is offered, helping us to conceive of water as a political substance that mediates corporeal control (6). 'If we think of the political as the practice of speaking and acting together on matters of common concern, then water may be the most exemplary of political substances' because we 'all have water in common' (Chen et al. 2013, 6). Engaging with the notion of aqueous eco-politics requires us to expand 'the sphere of political "stakeholders," and shift our focus toward those multiple others – human and otherwise, past, present, and future – with whom these watery matters are shared' (Chen et al. 2013, 6). Further, 'given water's capacity to connect and combine, thinking the political with water might help us bring together issues and concerns too often addressed in isolation' (Chen et al. 2013, 6). In this examination, I attempt to do just that by placing environmental degradation, mass incarceration and histories of the Middle Passage in conversation by illuminating how Ward helps us to understand how they are all bound by racialised, water-related systems. Thinking with water in this sense means grappling with the extent to which carceral histories modulate into the present. While I do not provide a complete history of water crises in relation to racialised captivity, the following reading draws on existing research to explore how *Sing, Unburied, Sing* helps us to conceptualise how the water management paradigms that characterise the modern prison system of the US are haunted by histories of the Middle Passage.

The Aqueous Uncanny: Parchman Prison and Middle Passage Symbolism in *Sing, Unburied, Sing*

As Jojo journeys to Parchman prison in *Sing, Unburied, Sing*, memories of the Middle Passage collide with new forms of captivity. Sat in the back seat of a confined vehicle, alongside his motion-sick sibling,

Kayla, Jojo recalls the oral histories his grandfather relayed to him about their ancestors who came 'across the ocean' and were 'kidnapped and sold' (Ward 2017, 69). Stories of the voyage that were passed down their family lineage return to Jojo during the roadtrip: 'everyone knew about the death march to the coast, that word had come down about the ships, about how they packed men and women into them', River told Jojo, 'Some heard it was even worse for those who sailed off, sunk into the far. Because that's what it looked like when the ship crossed the horizon: like the ship sailed off and sunk, bit by bit, into the water' (Ward 2017, 69). Haunting is endured hydrologically in *Sing, Unburied, Sing*, as Ward highlights the role of water in the carceral continuum, reminding us that the watery politics of mass incarceration cannot be neatly separated from older forms of racialised imprisonment. In this chapter, I suggest that hydrological haunting is experienced as what might be understood as the aqueous uncanny, revealing the ways in which the carceral ecologies of the Middle Passage resurface in the penal infrastructures of the present.

Freud defines the uncanny as 'that class of the frightening which leads back to what is known of old and long familiar' (Freud 1955, 220). In other words, 'the uncanny is something which is secretly familiar' but 'has undergone repression and then returned from it' (Freud 1955, 245). I want to think about this concept in relation to the carceral ecologies of Atlantic slavery and mass incarceration, and the ways in which they are remembered and represented in *Sing, Unburied, Sing*. Engaging with representations of water that appear throughout the novel, I suggest that the aqueous uncanny emerges through the ways in which Ward conjures what Édouard Glissant termed the 'abyss' in two of its incarnations – as in, the hold ('the belly of the boat') and the ocean ('the depths of the sea') (Glissant 1997, 5).

In *Sing, Unburied, Sing*, the characters' journey to Parchman prison through a desiccated Southern landscape is haunted by the transatlantic voyages of the Middle Passage. Nicole Dib, in her reading of the novel, argues that Ward deploys the road trip narrative in order to critique the ways in which 'white fantasies of mobility and freedom' are built on the systematic immobilisation of black people (Dib 2020, 135). It is poignant then, that when Jojo and company arrive at the prison to collect his white father, Michael, the ghost of Richie – an African American boy who was incarcerated at Parchman at the same time as Jojo's grandfather – emerges alongside him. The racialised juxtaposition between Michael and Richie is stark.

For while Michael revels in his re-acquired freedom, ready to resume his dysfunctional relationship with Leonie, Richie is never truly able to leave Parchman, as represented in his ghostly, arrested development. 'The roots of African and African American mobility in the United States must be understood in terms that reveal how travel has been contested for black individuals and communities from the start', writes Dib (2020, 139). In what follows, I grapple with the ways in which Ward imagines the imbrications between cars and ships, land and sea, in order to demonstrate how the novel helps us to better understand the racialised, oceanic origins of the carceral state.

In a 2016 interview, Anna Hartnell spoke with Ward regarding *Men We Reaped* and the role that cars play in the memoir 'as vehicles that transport, bridge, and create important spaces' (Hartnell 2016, 214). Ward explains that in *Men We Reaped* cars 'symbolize freedom. But then they also become these places where we're able to be introspective and reflect and connect in certain ways. And so [. . .] it makes me think of the ways the church can function, or has functioned in the past, in the community' (Ward quoted in Hartnell 2016, 214). Car symbolism re-emerges in *Sing, Unburied, Sing*, and while Ward continues to present them as spaces of introspection and reflection, throughout the novel, cars are synonymous with captivity. Despite his wishes to remain at home with his grandparents, Jojo is forced to accompany his mother to collect Michael, his father, from Parchman, cooped in the back of a claustrophobic, overheated space. The car, in many ways, emulates the belly of the ship – a 'nonworld' occupied by both the living and dead (Glissant 1997, 5). '"It's like a snake that sheds its skin"', Ritchie tells Jojo, folded into the space between the back and front seats of the car, '"The outside look different when the scales change, but the inside always the same"' (Ward 2017, 172). From within the interior of an 'electric blue' car, Jojo beholds the spatial dimensions of incarceration and, more specifically, the enduring relationship between confined spaces and dehumanisation, a pairing that stretches back to the Middle Passage and reoccurs in overcrowded penitentiaries of today (Ward 2017, 52). As Stephanie E. Smallwood highlights, 'Because human beings were treated as inanimate objects, the number of bodies stowed aboard a ship was limited only by the physical dimensions and configurations of those bodies' (Smallwood 2007, 68). When examining the ways in which this logic persists, Childs's work on the evolution of captivity is instructive. Childs highlights how the 'dehumanizing and suffocating aspects of [. . .] spaces of racial capitalist terror register the affiliations of the prison architectures of slavery and freedom', arguing that 'land-based' prisons are fundamentally influenced by the 'water-based moving prisons of the Atlantic' (Childs 2015, 43). The ways in which *Sing, Unburied, Sing* alludes to the 'prisons of the Atlantic' through stories of the Middle Passage and the trope of the car as a space of captivity is particularly uncanny in a present in which water-based violence continues to play a role in carceral practices (Childs 2015, 43). As Saidiya Hartman writes, 'The hold continues to shape how we live' (Hartman 2016, 208). The car in *Sing, Unburied, Sing* features as a hybrid carceral space – one that helps us to think about the ways in which the hold modulates into the present by conjuring the entanglements between mobile prisons of the Middle Passage and land-based prisons of today. In this way, the novel symbolises how, to quote Christina Sharpe, 'The hold repeats and repeats and repeats in and into the present [. . .] The details and the deaths accumulate; the ditto ditto fills the archives of a past that is not yet past. The holds multiply.' (Sharpe 2016, 73).

It is worth recognising, however, that Glissant also refers to the constricted space of the hold as the womb abyss. 'This boat is a womb, a womb abyss', he says, 'It generates the clamor of your protests; it also produces all the coming unanimity. Although you are alone in this suffering, you share in the unknown with others whom you have yet to know' (Glissant 1997, 5). The car, transporting its passengers across the South, to and from the penitentiary, haunted by histories of the ship, also becomes a womb abyss – a space in which intergenerational encounters are fostered through the uncanny return of memories of the ocean and different forms of incarceration. To invoke Freud, the car provides a setting in which familiar strangers meet and, throughout the course of the narrative, learn to exist in relation to one another. When the family arrive at Parchman prison to collect Michael's father, and the ghost of Richie also slips into the car, Richie recognises Jojo instantly. 'The boy is River's', he says, 'I know it' (Ward 2017, 135). It is Jojo's eyes, 'dark as swamp bottom', that reveal him to Richie (Ward 2017, 135). In other words, the aqueous uncanny, the strange familiarity evoked by Jojo's connection to water and the spatial dimensions of the vehicle in which they meet, allows Richie to situate himself within a carceral continuum that exceeded his lifetime.

The second abyss, the ocean, is conjured through the motif of drowning. Describing a vision that came to her during a dream, Leonie, Jojo's mother, recalls: 'I am trying to keep everyone above water, even as I struggle to stay afloat. I sink below the waves and push Jojo upward so he can stay above the waves and breathe'

(Ward 2017, 195). She continues, 'I thrust them up toward the surface, to the fractured sky so they can live, but they keep slipping from my hands' (Ward 2017, 195). Leonie's nightmare could be interpreted as a manifestation of her maternal anxieties, but drowning also elicits Middle Passage histories, and it is of no little significance that they emerge in Leonie's subconscious on the night subsequent to her visiting Parchman. Human cargo was regularly overthrown during the crossings of the Middle Passage. William Turner's painting 'Slave Ship (or Slavers Overthrowing the Dead and Dying – Typhoon Coming On)' – which, as Ana Lucia Araujo puts it, depicts 'the bloody pieces of enslaved bodies being eaten by sharks in ocean waters' – is one of the most iconic visual representations of the centrality of drowning to the trauma of Atlantic slavery (Araujo 2014, 78). In many ways, Leonie's dream evokes the image of Turner's painting as she describes being submerged in an ocean that is animated and volatile, 'far out where the fish are bigger than men'; 'there are mantra rays gliding beneath us', she says, 'and sharks jostling us' (Ward 2017, 195). Leonie is at the whelm of the aquatic assemblages depicted in Turner's painting. The motif of drowning, conjured most poignantly following Leonie's encounter with Parchman, thus nods a long trajectory of the weaponisation of water across and within both land and water-based prisons. In doing so, Ward also brings notions of more-than-human agency that contribute to our understanding of how these histories are ecologically archived to the forefront.

Aqueous assemblages and the ways in which they memorialise the drownings of the Middle Passage can be understood in relation to Sharpe's notion of residence time. Invoking the watery deaths endured during the Middle Passage, Sharpe writes: 'the atoms of those people who were thrown overboard are out there in the ocean even today. They were eaten, organisms processed them, and those organisms were in turn eaten and processed, and the cycle continues' (Sharpe 2016, 40). Sharpe outlines residence time – as in, 'The amount of time it takes for a substance to enter the ocean and then leave the ocean' – and scientific indications that human blood 'has a residence time of 260 million years': 'we, Black people', she writes, 'exist in the residence time of the wake' (Sharpe 2016, 40). In the words of Diana Leong, the bodies of the formerly enslaved contribute to 'the saline content of the oceans' (Leong 2017, 812). Their material presence, albeit invisible, signifies the continuities of transatlantic slavery and its durable systems of racialised capitalism and captivity.

Hydrological haunting, therefore, is not just figurative, but a materially uncanny phenomenon, given that water is a medium that both

records violent histories and is used to inflict environmentally mediated violence in the present. The ocean, represented in *Sing, Unburied,
Sing* as being charged with agencies beyond the limits of human control, is both figuratively and materially perfuse with traces of enslaved
Africans who endured the water- based prisons of the past, therefore
rendering it an uncanny space, given that Leonie, too, has been impacted by the carceral continuum. While Leonie may only think water,
ongoing water-management paradigms at Parchman prison evidence
the extent to which those incarcerated in land-based penitentiaries
of today – like those who endured the water-based prisons of the
Middle Passage – are vulnerable to aqueously mediated violence. It is
this strange familiarity, this uncanny encounter with water, perhaps,
that accounts for Leonie's resignation to a watery grave: 'I am failing
them', she says, 'We are all drowning' (Ward 2017, 195).

Hydrological haunting – the ways in which histories of water-based
violence materially and figuratively resurface – is experienced as the
aqueous uncanny, in part, because water is not something that can
be considered distinguishable from the human. As Astrida Neimanis
reminds us, the fact that our bodies are two thirds water invites a
reimagining of 'embodiment from the perspective of our bodies' wet
constitution' – a version that is contrary to 'dominant Western and
humanist understandings of embodiment, where bodies are figured as
discrete and coherent individual subjects, and as fundamentally autonomous' (Neimanis 2017, 1–2). Similarly, in 'States of Suspension:
Trans-corporeality at Sea', Stacy Alaimo reinvokes her concept of
trans-corporeality in relation to water (Alaimo 2012, 476). Alaimo
conceptualises trans-corporeality at sea through the notion of suspension, 'as a sort of buoyancy, a sense that the human is held, but
not held up, by invisible genealogies and a maelstrom of often imperceptible substances that disclose connections between humans and
the sea' (Alaimo 2012, 477–8). It is through this sense of buoyancy
that Leonie experiences the aqueous uncanny:

> I dropped into the feathery dark heart of the water and went all the way
> to the bottom, where the sand was more muddy than grainy and downed
> trees decomposed, slimy and soft at the core. I didn't swim up; the fall
> had stunned my legs, the thunderous slap of the water numbed them. I
> let the water carry me. It was a slow rise: up, up, up toward milky light. I
> remember it clearly because I never did it again, scared by the paralyzing
> ascent. (Ward 2017, 193)

Leonie's plunge is distinct from the patterns of submersion that feature elsewhere in Ward's writings. For example, *Where the Line*

Bleeds opens with twin brothers, Joshua and Christophe, diving into Wolf River. 'The day exploded in color and light and sound around them' when they surfaced, conjuring a euphoric sense of bouyancy (Ward 2008, 4). In *Salvage the Bones* (2011), Esch and friends also spend a lot of time submerged, with the water hole near the Pit serving somewhat as a place of refuge. For Leonie, however, being slowly suspended by invisible forces within the river (that, as Alaimo suggests, indicate the interconnections between aquatic assemblages and the human) evokes horror. Of all of Ward's characters, it is Leonie – who chooses to medicate her anxieties with narcotics – and Michael, Jojo's father, who find the aqueous uncanny most frightening. Resisting the aqueous uncanny, Leonie turns to avoidance as a coping mechanism: '*I can't be a mother right now. I can't be a daughter. I can't remember*' (Ward 2017, 274). Ultimately, Leonie wishes to attain a state of oblivion that, for her, can only be achieved by imposing borders between the human, the aquatic, and their shared histories: thus, she is most at peace when she imagines being alongside Michael in a 'dome of glass' as they 'pretend at forgetting' – 'Our world', she says, 'an aquarium' (Ward 2017, 274).

Jojo's grandmother, Mam, who repeatedly tries to introduce Leonie to the healing capacities of water, also evokes notions of aquatic trans-corporeality. Leonie recalls anxiously telling Mam about her pregnancy, and Mam 'shushing like a stream, like she'd taken all the water pouring on the outside world into her' (Ward 2017, 159). '[S]he was invoking Yemaya', says Leonie, 'the goddess of the ocean and salt water' (Ward 2017, 159). Deriving from the spiritual concepts of Yoruba, stories of Yemaya survived the amnesiac conditions of slavery and the Middle Passage through the oral tradition. In the words of Montré Aza Missouri, Yemaya thus became 'the deity associated with the Middle Passage and the patron of those incarcerated, enslaved and oppressed' (Missouri 2015, 133). In *Sing, Unburied, Sing*, Mam serves as an embodiment of Yemaya – she is, as Richie puts it, 'the saltwater woman' (Ward 2017, 245). As Chen, MacLeod and Neimanis remind us, 'Water does not exist in the abstract. It must take up a body or place [. . .] somewhere, sometime, somehow. All water is situated. Moreover, we are all situated in relation to water' (Chen et al. 2013, 8). Mam's embodiment of Yemaya is a reminder of our watery corporeality, her deteriorating health a representation of the ways in which the waters that comprise our bodies are vulnerable to the flows of the 'economic, political, cultural, scientific' ideologies to which Alaimo refers (Alaimo 2012, 476). Ward's invocation of Yemaya is also, however, an invitation to consider the role of mnemonic storytelling in resisting systems of racialised captivity; just as the story of Yemaya weathered the amnesiac crossings of the Middle Passage, *Sing, Unburied, Sing* demonstrates how stories of water recuperate concealed entanglements between the slave ship and penitentiary in an age of racialised mass incarceration. Before her passing, Mam tells Jojo: 'I hope I fed you enough. While I'm here. So you carry it with you. Like a camel [. . .] Maybe that ain't a good way of putting it. Like a well, Jojo. Pull that water up when you need it' (Ward 2017, 233–4). More than just a work of Gothic fiction, the moments of hydrological haunting that saturate *Sing, Unburied, Sing* affirm that as land-based prisons continue to thrive, we too must 'pull that water up', confronting repressed aquatic histories of racial dominance in order to better understand how the current (both aquatic and temporal) has been shaped by them (Ward 2017, 234).

Towards the end of the novel, Jojo and Kayla encounter a tree, 'full with ghosts [. . .] all the way up to the top, to the feathered leaves' (Ward 2017, 282). Recounting the terror that led to their deaths, the ghosts' eyes speak of being '*hung*', '*dragged*' and drowned (Ward 2017, 282). It is only when Kayla begins to sing, and they are, in the process, acknowledged in relation to 'all water', that the ghosts are able to rest 'with something like relief, something like remembrance, something like ease' (Ward 2017, 284):

> Kayla hums over my shoulder, says 'Shhh' like I am the baby and she is the big brother, says 'Shhh' like she remembers the sound of the water in Leonie's womb, the sound of all water, and now she sings it. *Home,* they say. *Home.* (Ward 2017, 285)

Here, the novel's call for the unburied to sing is realised. Ultimately, it is through the sound of the abyss (both the womb and the marine) that the hung, dragged and drowned ghosts find home. In this way, *Sing, Unburied, Sing* conveys what Glissant refers to as the 'freeing knowledge of Relation within the whole'; when Kayla and Jojo apprehend the carceral continuum in its entirety, the ghosts of the past are at ease (Glissant 1997, 8).

In a rare exchange between Michael and Jojo, following the former's return home from Parchman, the conversation turns to water. Michael, who worked on the rig during the BP oil spill, tells Jojo of how he remains haunted by the event: '*I actually cried*, Michael told the water [. . .] How the dolphins were dying off, how whole pods of them washed up on the beaches in Florida, in Louisiana, in Alabama and Mississippi: *oil* burnt, sick with lesions, hollowed out from the insides' (Ward 2017, 226). Ward's references to the BP oil spill frame the watery politics of mass incarceration in the context of America's broader history of environmental racism. The economic trajectory from plantation to petrochemicals has been highlighted by a range of writers and activists, including Stephanie LeMenager who illuminates 'the trade-off of civil rights for corporate privileges' (LeMenager 2011, 30). St John the Baptist parish, Louisiana, for example, is an area with a concentration of both chemical plants and plantation houses. Approximately 45,000 people reside in the area, predominantly Black and routinely exposed to the toxins emanating from chemical plants – and with air replete with almost fifty poisonous chemicals, the area has the highest rates of cancer in America. This ecological violence has been at the forefront of concerns for activist groups including the Poor People's Campaign and RISE St. James. When Ward nods to these politics in *Sing, Unburied, Sing*, Jojo remarks that he will 'never forget' what Michael said next:

> *Some scientists for BP said this didn't have nothing to do with the oil, that sometimes this is what happens to animals: they die for unexpected reasons. Sometimes a lot of them. Sometimes all at once. [. . .] And when that scientist said that, I thought about humans. Because humans is animals.* (Ward 2017, 226)

The dismissive response offered by officials following the BP spill, remembered by Michael following his release from Parchman, is uncanny because it parallels the resounding silence surrounding the intersections between the prison industry and water degradation, and the ways in which governing bodies have failed to acknowledge the potential for there being causal links between the toxification of water and cancer rates in penitentiaries like Parchman. It is in this absence that the importance of recognising the fact that the present is hydrologically haunted becomes glaringly clear; this is the work performed in *Sing, Unburied, Sing*.

Through uncanny symbolism of the abyss, Ward illuminates how water and land-based prisons are intimately connected. In these entanglements, we are able to read how, in the words of Sharpe, 'Racism, the engine that drives the ship of the state's national and imperial projects [. . .] cuts through all of our lives and deaths inside and outside the nation, in the wake of its purposeful flow' (Sharpe 2016, 3). Though the aqueous uncanny entails engaging with histories of horror, navigating the present in relation to them is crucial to unpacking what Derrida refers to as the non-contemporaneity of the living present (Derrida 1994, xviii). 'And how could I conceive that Parchman was past, present, and future all at once?' asks Richie (Ward 2017, 186). 'That the history and sentiment that carved the place out of the wilderness would show me that time is a vast ocean, and that everything is happening at once?' (Ward 2017, 186). *Sing, Unburied, Sing* casts new perspectives on Parchman prison by illuminating the ecological components of captivity; water materially bears the burden of plantation pasts, the hold constellates into the prison, and carceral ecologies of the past and present merge as we are hydrologically haunted by the abyss – as Sharpe emphasises, quoting Toni Morrison, 'everything is now. It is all now' (Toni Morrison quoted in Sharpe 2016, 41).

Works Cited

Alaimo, Stacy. 2012. 'States of Suspension: Trans-corporeality at Sea'. *ISLE: Interdisciplinary Studies in Literature and Environment* 19, no. 3 (Summer): 476–93. https://www.jstor.org/stable/44087131.

Araujo, Ana Lucia. 2014. *Shadows of the Slave Past: Memory, Heritage, and Slavery.* London: Routledge.

Bernd, Candice, Zoe Loftus-Farren, and Maureen Nandini Mitra. 2017. 'America's Toxic Prisons'. *Earth Island Journal*, 1 June. https://earthisland.org/journal/americas-toxic-prisons/.

Chen, Cecilia, Janine MacLeod and Astrida Neimanis. 2013. *Thinking with Water.* London: McGill-Queen's University Press.

Childs, Dennis. 2015. *Slaves of the State: Black Incarceration from the Chain Gang to the Penitentiary.* Minneapolis: University of Minnesota Press.

Derrida, Jacques. 1994. *Specters of Marx: The State of the Debt, the Work of Mourning, and the New International.* Translated by Peggy Kamuf. New York: Routledge.

Dib, Nicole. 2020. 'Haunted Roadscapes in Jesmyn Ward's *Sing, Unburied, Sing'. MELUS* 45, no. 2 (Summer):134–53. https://doi.org/10.1093/melus/mlaa011.

Foucault, Michel. 1977. *Discipline and Punish: The Birth of the Prison.* Translated by Alan Sheridan. New York: Vintage Books.

Freud, Sigmund. 1955. 'The Uncanny'. *The Standard Edition of the Complete Psychological Works of Sigmund Freud*, edited by James Strachey, 219–53. London: Hogarth Press.

Glissant, Édouard. 1997. *Poetics of Relation.* Translated by Betsy Wing. Ann Arbor: University of Michigan Press.

Hartmann, Saidiya. 2016. 'The Dead Book Revisited'. *History of the Present: A Journal of Critical History* 6, no. 2 (October): 208–15. https://doi.org/10.5406/historypresent.6.2.0208.

Hartnell, Anna. 2016. 'When Cars Become Churches: Jesmyn Ward's Disenchanted America. An Interview'. *Journal of American Studies* 50 (1): 205–18. https://doi.org/10.1017/S0021875815001966.

LeMenager, Stephanie 2011. 'Petro-Melancholia: The BP Blowout and the Arts of Grief'. *Qui Parle: Critical Humanities and Social Sciences* 19 (Spring/Summer): 25–56. https://doi.org/10.5250/quiparle.19.2.0025.

Leong, Diana. 2017. 'The Salt Bones: *Zong!* and an Ecology of Thirst'. *ISLE: Interdisciplinary Studies in Literature and Environment* 23, no. 4 (November): 798–820. https://doi.org/10.1093/isle/isw071.

Liu, Michelle. 2019. 'No water, no lights and broken toilets: Parchman health inspection uncovers hundreds of problems, many repeat violations'. *Mississippi Today*, 5 August 2019.

McKittrick, Katherine. 2021. *Dear Science and Other Stories*. Durham, NC: Duke University Press.

Missouri, Montré Aza. 2015. *Black Magic Woman and Narrative Film: Race, Sex and Afro-Religiosity*. London: Palgrave Macmillan.

Mitchell, Jerry. 2015. 'Well woes leaves Parchman inmates without water'. *Clarion Ledger*, 22 July. https://eu.clarionledger.com/story/news/2015/07/22/woes-leaves-parchman-inmates-without-water/30543441/.

Neimanis, Astrida. 2017. *Bodies of Water: Posthuman Feminist Phenomenology*. London: Bloomsbury.

Pellow, David N. 2017. 'Environmental Inequalities and the U.S. Prison System: An Urgent Research Agenda'. *International Journal of Earth and Environmental Sciences* 2, no. 140 (October). https://doi.org/10.15344/2456-351X/2017/140.

Prison Reform Movement Movement. 2019. 'Water from the faucets at Parchman state prison in Mississippi'. Video, 0:35, 11 July. https://www.facebook.com/search/top/?q=PrisonReformMovement%20parchman%20water&epa=SEARCH_BOX.

Rodríguez, Dylan. 2006. *Forced Passages: Imprisoned Radical Intellectuals and the U.S. Prison Regime*. Minneapolis: University of Minnesota Press.

—. 2007. 'Forced Passages'. In *Warfare in the American Homeland: Policing and Prison in a Penal Democracy*, edited by Joy James, 35–57. Durham, NC: Duke University Press.

Sharpe, Christina. 2016. *In the Wake: On Blackness and Being*. Durham, NC: Duke University Press.

Smallwood, Stephanie E. 2007. *Saltwater Slavery: A Middle Passage from Africa to American Diaspora*. Cambridge, MA: Harvard University Press.

Ward, Jesmyn. 2008. *Where the Line Bleeds*. London: Bloomsbury Publishing.

—. 2011. *Salvage the Bones*. London: Bloomsbury Publishing.

—. 2017. *Sing, Unburied, Sing*. London: Bloomsbury Circus.

Chapter 19

Pilgrimages to the Past in Jesmyn Ward and Toni Morrison

Lara Narcisi

[A recent conversation] captured much of the beauty of my black world . . . And I think I needed this vantage point before I could journey out. I think I needed to know that I was from somewhere, that my home was as beautiful as any other.

Ta-Nehisi Coates, *Between the World and Me* (2015)

In his groundbreaking 1967 book, *Black Skin, White Masks*, Frantz Fanon describes racism as a kind of 'collective catharsis' (1967, 144), and calls attention to the long-standing use of Black men to represent 'the Wolf, the Devil, the Evil Spirit, the Bad Man, the Savage' (1967, 146). He discusses his own realisation of this phenomenon: 'I discovered my blackness, my ethnic characteristics; and I was battered down by tom-toms, cannibalism, intellectual deficiency, fetishism, racial defects, slave-ships' (1967, 112). Half a century later, we see similar acknowledgements of slavery's ineradicable legacy in present-day literary depictions of Black masculinity. Ta-Nehisi Coates titled his memoir *Between the World and Me*, a line he credits to a Richard Wright poem, but which also appears throughout Fanon's book. In the form of a letter to his son, Coates writes of the weight of history on Black men: 'It is so easy to look away, to live with the fruits of our history and to ignore the great evil done in all our names. But you and I have never truly had that luxury' (Coates 2015, 8–9). Claudia Rankine takes a similar perspective in her poetic essay, *Citizen*. She describes the process of writing the sections dealing with Black masculinity in this way: 'I asked a number of my black male friends to tell me a public private story. And in return I gave them nothing. But I did collect the stories' (Rankine 2014, poets.org). This act of collecting is a tribute, a gesture of both respect and preservation, particularly as seen in her many references to murdered

Black males. In an elegy for Trayvon Martin, which, like the works of Fanon and Coates, marks its allegiance to history, Rankine writes:

> Those years of and before me and my brothers, the years of passage, plantation, migration, of Jim Crow segregation, of poverty, inner cities, profiling, of one in three, two jobs, boy, hey boy, each a felony, accumulate into the hours inside our lives where we are all caught hanging, the rope inside us, the tree inside us, its roots our limbs. (Rankine 2014, 89–90)

Rankine's suggestion that Black males always contain the psychological lynching rope within them reiterates that Black masculinity is permanently rooted to the historical brutalities of slavery and its subsequent violence. This argument is taken up in two novels by Black women writers, Toni Morrison's *Song of Solomon* and Jesmyn Ward's *Sing, Unburied, Sing*, both of which use physical journeys to initiate historical journeys for their Black male protagonists who likewise seem to contain both the lethal rope and the more hopeful tree within them. Morrison depicts how her protagonist finds himself on a journey in the South that demonstrates how 'everybody wants the life of a black man' (Morrison 2004, 222). Ward uses an adolescent's pilgrimage to retrieve his incarcerated father to explore poverty, drug addiction and the prison industrial complex, depicting 'the kind of world . . . that makes fools of the living and saints of them once they dead' (Ward 2017, 105). While Christopher Lloyd's chapter in this volume focuses on the corporeal legacies enacted on Black bodies, this chapter analyses the characters' attempts to move beyond themselves and into their pasts, familial and cultural. In both novels, the physical journey is requisite to initiating the historical one, demanding resolution of personal and racial traumas. Both journeys benefit from a transformative balance between masculine and feminine narratives – one born of understandings that alter not only the male protagonists, but also the very homes and families they left behind.

I Propose Nothing Short of the Liberation of the Man of Colour from Himself (Frantz Fanon, *Black Skin White Masks*)

Toni Morrison cites the beginning of her journey writing *Song of Solomon* as the recent death of her beloved father and subsequent desire to understand what the men he knew were 'really like'. She sees the novel as enacting 'a radical shift in imagination from a female locus to a male one', and defines that masculinity in connection to flight, a dominant theme in the novel (Morrison 2004, xii). I would contend, however, that the book presents less of a 'radical shift' from Morrison's gynocentric works and more of an elegant combination of different forms of gendered sojourns. In showing its racial pilgrimages to be intergenerational, collaborative and simultaneously masculine (spatial, airbourne) and feminine (temporal, narrative), it presages Ward's work on similar themes.

The impetus for Milkman Dead's journey is his not-home on Not Doctor Street near No Mercy Hospital, a series of negations that renders him rootless. Milkman's story, as Catherine Carr Lee observes, begins as an inversion of the hero's journey often cited as a framework for this novel:

> Where the classic American initiation story takes the youthful initiate from the bosom of hearth and family, leaving him isolated and alone, Morrison begins with a twentieth-century modern man, alienated and fragmented, and ends with that man's successful connection with a people. (Lee 2003, 60)

The Deads' home stifles them, and even cars, the prototypical postwar American escape metaphor, fail the family; Lena reflects that their vehicle is, like its daughters, a mere showpiece to be used and abused: 'us and the car, the car and us . . . first he displayed us, then he splayed us' (Morrison 2004, 215–16). Young Milkman takes no joy in their car rides either, for looking forward 'he could see only the winged woman careening off the nose of the car', a reminder of the flightlessness that so aggrieves him, and looking backward is 'like flying blind, and not knowing where he was going – just where he had been' (Morrison 2004, 32). Appropriately, it is a car that will bear Milkman back to the past, providing him the recognition of his own history that will enable his forward flight. Despite the ease of his own life Milkman must negotiate the historical trauma of his ancestors because, as Morrison argues, 'when you kill the ancestor, you kill yourself' (Morrison 1984, 344). The novel warns against relinquishing ancestral heritage through its preoccupation with father loss, paralleling the author's own: Macon, Pilate, Ruth, Freddie and Guitar have all lost fathers. Reba and Hagar never know their fathers, an absence initially minimised in their merry malelessness, until Hagar's love-starved self-annihilation implies her longing for a paternal figure. Although the Dead father lives, his disgust over what he deems a necrophiliac oedipal obsession in his wife fragments the couple and leaves the next generation isolated and rootless.

Milkman, however, cannot see the absence of family and history in his life because he is blinded by the illusory comforts, the false home, that his father provides. Macon lectures him on the primacy of possession: 'Let me tell you right now the one important thing you'll ever need to know: Own things. And let the thing you own own other things. Then you'll own yourself and other people too' (Morrison 2004, 55).[1] Driven by avarice to compensate for losses both historical and personal, Macon elides the existence of slavery and the fact that his own father was an owned object. His very name evinces this erasure, a result of his mother, Sing, keeping the mistaken moniker, 'Macon Dead', because 'it was new and would wipe out the past' (Morrison 2004, 54). Yet the past preoccupies him more than he acknowledges, as he spurs Milkman to pursue a lost bag of gold that forces him to unearth long-forgotten history.

In pursuit of his father's obsession, Milkman begins a journey from North to South, reversing the path of the Great Migration. As Catherine Carr Lee points out, Milkman's discovery one day that the people on the street 'are all going the direction he was coming from' (Morrison 2004, 78) foreshadows that fact that 'Milkman will have to move against the tide of black migration north' (Lee 2003, 45–6). In fact, the moving crowds are distressed by the murder of Emmett Till, a Northerner lynched in the South for allegedly whistling at a white woman, while Milkman's glib dismissal of the news: 'Fuck Till. I'm the one in trouble' (Morrison 2004, 88), parallels his father's indifference to racial history. The novel, otherwise meticulous about chronology, misdates Till's death in 1955 to 1953, as though Milkman can manoeuvre the event into the relevant place in his own life story. Milkman's journey parallels Till's as that of a Black Northerner in a confederate state, yet he so quickly forgets Till's murder that in Virginia he 'wondered why black people ever left the South' (Morrison 2004, 260). Milkman's journey must undo this willful ignorance of both the history of slavery and the present of Jim Crow.

Milkman is blind to both past and present due, in part, to his financial privilege. He seems to feel he 'owns' Shalimar much as his father owns houses, and casually peacocks his wealth:

> He was telling them that they weren't men . . . that the lint and tobacco in their pants pockets where dollar bills should have been was the measure. That thin shoes and suits with vests and smooth smooth hands were the measure. (Morrison 2004, 266)

The Southerners respond to this first with a violent assault and then with a ritualistic shaming via hunting expedition, redefining masculinity on their own terms. Yet the reader perceives the men's low status in both their sad scuffle over schoolboy taunts in a run-down convenience store, and the fact that they kill 'coon', a pejorative term used to degrade Black hunters like themselves into the prey they seek. This question of predator and prey haunts the remainder of the novel; Milkman comes to learn that his ideas of individual success often rely on the oppression of others, as when his family's landlord income comes at the literal expense of evicting desperate families like his friend Guitar's. Similarly, Milkman's joy upon learning that his great-grandfather, Solomon, fulfilled his boyhood fantasy of flying fades once he understands the cost of flight. Solomon escaped, but only by abandoning his wife and twenty-one children, as the ghost of his son Jake bemoans: 'You can't just fly off and leave a body' (Morrison 2004, 209). While Solomon, in a continuation of Morrison's inverted migration narrative and in keeping with the 1970s movement, flew 'back to Africa' (Morrison 2004, 328),[2] Jake does not follow. Instead, he marries his sister by adoption, thus keeping things in the family, and, because she is Native American, wedding his roots to his homeland. Morrison elaborates in an interview with Robert Stepto, saying that flight 'is a part of black life, a positive, majestic thing, but there is a price to pay – and the price is the children' (Krumholz 2003, 206).[3] Solomon's name is immortalised in a fabled precipice, but his abandoned wife is the unhappy namesake of 'Ryna's Gulch': an absence, a lack, without even the poetry of 'valley' or 'ravine' to its name.

Milkman continues to learn the costs of male flight when he joyously returns to share his new-found knowledge with Pilate, only to receive a whack in the head and imprisonment in her cellar in a debasing revision of the traditional hero's homecoming. He realises that this is just recompense for his lethal callousness towards Hagar, yet, failing to learn from Solomon, immediately sets off again for another journey.[4] When Pilate takes a bullet intended for Milkman, we see another woman destroyed by a man's quest for self-understanding.

As Pilate dies, Milkman finally revises his dreams of flight, recognising that 'without ever leaving the ground, she could fly' (Morrison 2004, 336). Pilate falls down beside her father and dies as her name flies away with a bird, thus leaving her body with her father on the earth, and her spirit with her mother in the sky. As Morrison later explained, Pilate is 'the best of that which is female and the best of that which is male' (Morrison 1984, 344). Learning from Pilate at last,

Milkman must, as his name implies, reconcile the feminine 'milk' with the 'man': 'Milkman's quest for self-discovery leads him beyond purely patriarchal preoccupations to complicated dual-gendered historical narratives' (Murray 1999, 130). Song and flight, present and history, masculine and feminine, change the home Milkman left behind and the journey he has completed.

Morrison ends the novel not with Pilate's transcendence, but with Milkman's confrontation of his murderous former friend, Guitar. The novel does not clarify 'which one of them would give up his ghost in the killing arms of his brother' (Morrison 2004, 337), though I would agree with Linda Krumholz that the ambiguity of the ending need not be resolved because 'it is more important to consider the ways Morrison has challenged concepts of life and death' (Krumholz 203, 223). Solomon's 'leap' to a new life looks like suicide; Ruth and Pilate share a 'close and supportive posthumous communication with their fathers' (Morrison 2004, 139); and, of course, Milkman's living family is 'already Dead' (Morrison 2004, 89). The ambiguity of life and death fits with Morrison's balancing contrasts; as she writes in 'Unspeakable Things Unspoken', Milkman's leap is 'the marriage of surrender and domination, acceptance and rule, commitment to a group *through* ultimate isolation' (Morrison 2019, 191). In this, perhaps, Milkman is ahead of his time.

Milkman's journey has brought knowledge and connected past to present, merging male and female ancestry. The novel's conclusion thus may seem optimistic, the 'triumphant hope of continuation for an interconnected African American culture and heritage' (Lee 2003, 60). Pilate rising at the very moment Guitar's bullet strikes suggests a problem of timing, however. This lack of synchronicity, in a novel preoccupied with history, suggests that the timing is not yet right for the Black man to come in to his own without sacrificing others in his path. Morrison travels to the past, but also to the future, perhaps anticipating a time when we all can fly without leaving the ground.

My Brothers are Notorious. They have not been to Prison. They have been Imprisoned. The Prison is not a Place you Enter. It is No Place. (Claudia Rankine, *Citizen*)

Forty years later, Jesmyn Ward's *Sing, Unburied, Sing* takes another Black male on a Southern journey into his grandfather's past. Ward acknowledges Morrison as one of her primary influences, describing her first experience reading *Beloved* as transformative: 'I was blinded. Struck dumb. Dust in my lungs. Toni Morrison called me out of my wandering, her words, whole sentences, whole paragraphs, speaking to me as none had ever done so before' (Ward 2019). While *Sing, Unburied, Sing* shares with *Beloved* an interest in the roots of racism and the negotiation of trauma, it most closely resembles *Song of Solomon* in its use of a road trip to trace the development of a male protagonist. Ward is writing in and of a different era, however, and potentially proposes a solution for some of the problems Morrison helped define. Although Jojo's journey is, like Milkman's, instigated by his broken home, he is as mature for his age as Milkman is stunted for his, and his journey will take him through and beyond the past that Milkman can't quite escape.

Jojo, like Milkman, suffers from parental neglect, but one compounded by debilitating poverty rather than careless privilege. While Morrison gives us a psychological understanding of her protagonist's problematic parents, Ward offers a sociological one: Michael and Leonie are victims of, as Greg Chase puts it, 'the criminalization of poverty – an institutional problem that has disproportionally affected communities of color' (Chase 2020, 210). Ward envisions these ills inscribed on male bodies literally and indelibly, as tattoos. Michael tattoos Jojo's name and baby feet on his back, indicative of how he will forever turn his back on his son, leaving him to the mercy of other dangers tattooed there as well (a dragon, scythe and grim reaper). Leonie cannot perceive her father's tattoos, of two cranes of her and her brother Given, as 'a sign of life', but focuses instead on the fact that his crane is 'poised in flight' while hers is 'beak down in the mud' (Ward 2017, 212). This perception recalls Morrison's observation that the men taking flight often leave the women behind; except here, and in Ward's own life, the sisters are abandoned by their brothers' deaths. Beleaguered by resentment, grief and addiction, Leonie can neither provide a home for her son, nor find comfort in the one she and Given were given.

While Morrison's novel spans Milkman's entire life, Ward's centres on Jojo at the crucial age of thirteen, in the process of negotiating his nascent adulthood. Lacking parental guidance, Jojo aspires to emulate his grandfather, River Stone, believing the ability to stomach River's killing of a goat for his thirteenth birthday dinner is the 'measure', as Morrison puts it, of manhood. Over the course of his journey, however, Jojo re-evaluates this standard of masculinity. As he is about to depart for Parchman prison, Jojo embraces River, who tells him 'You a man, you hear?' but also says with his 'pleading eyes' and 'without words: I love you, boy. I love you' (Ward 2017, 61).

Jojo viscerally rejects the goat slaughter because he empathically senses the animal's pain; his manhood, like River's, is built on experiencing and enduring the pain of others. This ability extends backwards through the maternal line, as River describes: 'The dream of [my mother] was the glow of a spent fire on a cold night: warm and welcoming. It was the only way I could untether my spirit from myself, let it fly high as a kite in them fields' (Ward 2017, 23). These lines couple the ideas of flight and home that Milkman desperately attempts to reconcile, and they depict a solid maternal presence unlike that available to any of the three Macon Deads. River is a man because of his mother, and Jojo must become a man in spite of his, but fortified by his grandmother's legacy.

Ward, like Morrison, inverts the traditional road trip narrative; as Nicole Dib points out, the car 'traditionally symbolizes the promise of freedom expressed as free movement for all', yet here creates claustrophobic confinement (Dib 2020, 134). Anna Hartnell expands on this in summarising a 2013 interview with Jesmyn Ward, explaining how cars '"symbolize freedom," and here lies the irony and the paradox, as Ward readily conceded: 'the "freedom" that cars have offered to Americans has, since World War II, led to urban sprawl, the atomization of communities, and the devastation of the environment' (Ward 2016, 205). In this novel, the vehicle is a mobile prison, and the destination is an actual prison; everyone is in chains either literal or metaphorical. Parchman Penitentiary, which forced its inmates, often adolescents, into backbreaking labour under the guise of reformation, haunts River because, 'Parchman the kind of place that fool you into thinking it ain't no prison . . . because ain't no walls' (Ward 2017, 21). Instead of boundaries it is ringed with inmates trained as sharp-shooters, a panopticon forcing the imprisoned to imprison others. In *Worse Than Slavery*, historian David Oshinsky describes Parchman, built on the site of a former plantation, as 'the quintessential penal farm, the closest thing to slavery that survived the Civil War' (Oshinky 1997, 2). In this volume, Cydney Phillip discusses evidence that the 'weaponisation of water' dating back to slave ships continues in Parchman to the present day. In Parchman, as during slavery, mercy and punishment are equally random: River was jailed for letting his brother stay with him ('harbouring a fugitive') and then freed for murder ('capturing a fugitive'). As Greg Chase notes, 'such passages emphasize how Parchman – even more than most Jim Crow-era prisons – replicated the conditions of chattel slavery as they existed in the antebellum South' (Chase 2020, 211). One such condition is the way plantation and prison alike become the only home its victims ever know. The ghost of the slain twelve-year-old Richie reflects: 'I wonder if the reason I couldn't leave Parchman before Jojo came was because it was a sort of home to me: terrible and formative as the iron leash that chains dogs' (Ward 2017, 190–1). Like Rankine's 'rope inside', Parchman internalises enslavement, offering a twisted 'sort of home' that creates a seemingly unbreakable line of intergenerational trauma. Ward knows well how close any young Black man always is to incarceration or worse at the hands of police; as she writes in her memoir, *Men We Reaped*, 'Trouble for the black men of my family meant police. It was easier and harder to be male; men were given more freedom but threatened with less freedom' (Ward 2013, 99). When the reader sees a policeman holding an unarmed Black teenager at gunpoint, and the scared teen reaches towards his pocket, the conclusion seems inevitable. But Ward subverts these expectations when Jojo, seeking the comfort of the gris-gris bag his grandfather gave him for spiritual protection, receives the physical protection of another loved one, Kayla, who vomits on the officer. In so doing she transforms the officer's fear into disgust, and this altered perspective enables him to release the family. Though Jojo escapes, the encounter leaves scars, as he bears the lingering sensation that 'the cuffs cut all the way down to the bone' (Ward 2017, 172). He also realises that his physicality announces itself as a threat, as he reflects when eyed by a store clerk, 'I remember I'm brown, and I move back' (Ward 2017, 175). This will not be something he is likely to have the luxury of forgetting again in his lifetime.

Although Jojo survives, the novel insists we remember other Black men whose encounters with police ended differently. The dying plea of Eric Gardner and George Floyd, 'I can't breathe', appears repeatedly, along with myriad references to troubled breathing and suffocation (Ward 2017, 65, 97, 128, 274). One of the ghosts at the end mourns, like so many Black men, 'I put my hands up and he shot me eight times' (Ward 2017, 282). Jojo's mother loses her beloved brother to gunfire, rather than vehicular homicide as the author describes in her autobiography, *Men We Reaped*. This change gives Given's death a resonance with that of Trayvon Martin, gunned down by a white man who is rapidly exculpated for the crime. Some of the ghosts haunting the family home at the conclusion even wear hoodies like Trayvon's. Racial violence shifts, but never disappears; as Richie says of Parchman, 'it's like a snake that sheds its skin. The outside look different when the scales change, but the inside always the same' (Ward 2017, 172). Just as Parchman is slavery in another form, police violence is merely an updated Parchman. No journey can take Jojo far enough from that reality.

Ward emphasises this painful stagnation through multiple connections to other texts and within her own. As in Faulkner's *As I Lay Dying*, an evident influence for this novel in its Mississippi setting, shifting perspective chapters, and morbid dysfunctional family road trip, the destination is only an unfulfilled promise of forward movement. Faulkner's description of his characters' journey applies equally to Ward's: 'We go on, with a motion so soporific, so dreamlike as to be uninferant of progress, as though time and not space were decreasing between us and it' (Faulkner 1990, 107–8). Ward revises the inertia of Faulkner's plodding, mule-drawn wagon into the drug 'trips' of its characters, which similarly promise progress but result in stagnation. As Greg Chase observes, 'Ward's own work becomes a means not just of supplementing Faulkner's legacy but also of correcting its racial blind spots, offering a kind of redress to the rural Southern communities about which they both have written' (Chase 2020, 201). The novel's two drug houses seem to reference *The Odyssey*, the origin of Faulkner's title, as, like the island of the Lotus Eaters, they entice visitors into lethal stasis. The homes show a contrast between wealthy and impoverished drug dealers but are likened in several ways: both are seductive traps, deterring Jojo's real journey; both are filled with substances yet lack substance; Al appears with a 'cooking spoon', recalling the meth 'cooking' in the lower-class house; both reference dreams of tropical isles; and although Al speaks in elegant lawyer language, we still see his rotting teeth. Most tellingly, Al lovingly refers to his urn full of meth as 'my Baby: my Beloved', which serves both as a nod to Morrison's novel of the same name and to the chilling fact that, to many of the characters, meth is more beloved than their babies (Ward 2017, 148). The parallels between the two drug houses demonstrate how they, like Parchman and the Lotus Eaters, offer only false promises of home, tempting (or forcing) the travellers to stay forever.

Although Jojo successfully returns home, that home is not the same in the end, irrevocably altered by Mam's death. After his pilgrimage to Parchman, however, Jojo is newly able to reassess his family bonds and affirm his grandparents as parents, even posthumously. Michael's surname is erased by remaining unstated in the novel, as Jojo chooses to be a Stone, like his grandparents. In musing that Richie 'could be made of stone', Jojo inducts the lost boy into his found family.[5] The book concludes with Jojo trying to 'be a man' once again with River, this time by feigning stoicism over his grand-mother's death; but eventually he succumbs to tears, a movement towards a different kind of manhood (Ward 2017, 223). Jojo's true rite of passage is his ability to ask for and to absorb River's horrific prison story, understanding that the Stone are not made of stone: 'I hold Pop like I hold Kayla' (Ward 2017, 257). Jojo is not only part River, however, but also part sea, from his grandmother who invokes Yemaya, the ocean goddess in the Yoruba religion. Jojo, learning from each, becomes both a protector and a visionary. It is this dual role that finally allows him to complete his own pilgrimage after his journey has ended, both by releasing Richie's ghost from Parchman, and by releasing River from the haunting memory of it. In this way, as Nicole Dib writes, 'The mold of the return home as a moment of identity creation for a single traveler is broken and replaced with a multivocal meeting' (Dib 2020, 149). As in Morrison, the returned traveller learns more about his community than about himself, and more about connecting his male and female ancestry than about fitting into a predetermined concept of masculinity.

Leonie, like Morrison's Pilate, undergoes less of a transformation than the book's male protagonist; but while Pilate is consistently nurturing and kind, no pilgrimage can make Leonie a positive maternal figure. Jojo describes her as a 'water moccasin' (Ward 2017, 209), a snake also known as a cottonmouth, a literal representation of the effects of chronic meth use on Leonie. Like the snake in the fable Macon recounts to Milkman, Leonie can only poison those she loves; can only be the snake she is (Ward 2017, 54–5). Jojo reflects on his dead pet fish and realises his mother 'ain't never healed nothing or grown nothing in her life . . . Leonie kill things' (Ward 2017, 107–8), and that he must take on the role of protector for the family. In contrast, his grandmother is able to use Leonie's lethality for good, enlisting her daughter to help her die when she is ready: 'Like I drew the veil back so you could walk in this life, you'll help me draw it back so I can walk in the next' (Ward 2017, 216). Assisting her mother's release from cancer is one thing Leonie can do properly and selflessly, changing her destructive nature into a blessing. Afterwards, however, she escapes for her own pilgrimage with Michael, abandoning their children to head back on the road. Leonie reflects, 'the car shrinks the world to this: me and him in this dome of glass' (Ward 2017, 274), which both recalls Jojo's image of his doomed pet fish, and describes the endless drug trip they pursue alone together.

Jojo and Kayla, however, are able to stitch the scraps of nurturing Leonie provided into something whole. In the final transformation of home, the children exorcise the ghosts using the best they have gleaned from their mother. While Jojo can release both River and Richie from the mental imprisonment of Parchman, Richie is purgatorially stuck between here and hereafter. He can no longer enter the Stone home because 'there has to be some need, some lack', and Jojo has 'changed. Ain't no need'; nor can he enter the afterlife and 'Become. The song' until Kayla intervenes (Ward 2017, 281). Throughout the road trip Jojo rubs Kayla's back in circles of eternal comfort; in the conclusion, Kayla disperses the ghosts with those circles, and Jojo grudgingly remembers, 'it's how Leonie rubbed my back, rubbed Kayla's back' (Ward 2017, 284). As she does so, Kayla sings, like Pilate does, a song from her origins: 'like she remembers the sound of the water in Leonie's womb . . . she sings it' (Ward 2017, 285). The Stone children possess both compassion and second sight; they can nurture both humans and ghosts. As Nicole Dib writes:

> The tense journey does not release us from the 'something to be done' that racial haunting puts into the world, but it does put hope in kinship, however fragmented or damaged, that can emerge even between the living and the dead. (Dib 2020, 149)

Though the ghosts do not depart yet – and perhaps some never will – the novel concludes with their final direction: 'Home' (Ward 2017, 285).

Frantz Fanon argues that the weight of history is so heavy that we must try to move beyond it, and that both white and Black people 'must turn their backs on the inhuman voices which were those of their respective ancestors in order that authentic communication be possible' (Fanon 1967, 231). Both Morrison and Ward argue otherwise, demonstrating the importance of returning to the ancestral past through physical journeys that become historical ones. Their different historical positions, however, forty years apart, emphasises how the temporal locus of the novels can shed light on the Black male experience.

Milkman does not return home at the end of the novel; his pilgrimage, though transformative, ends in loss and death. Furthermore, the fact that the Black men in the book can only fly at the price of destroying those they love implies that freedom remained unattainable for a Black man in the 1960s and 1970s. Morrison thus shows the complexity of the obstacles, societal and psychological, confronting Black men in their journey to fulfillment, and then leaves the reader in some doubt as to whether they can be successfully surmounted. Jojo, in contrast, returns home and comes to terms with the merciful brutality of his grandfather's past, releasing the ghosts that have been haunting the Stones. Embodying a new kind of masculinity, Jojo seems poised to break the familial cycle of incarceration. As Ward said in a 2013 interview with Anna Hartnell, 'I do think it's important in fiction to end with hope. Hope equals meaning, and for me there has to be some sense of meaning to any story, to whatever I write' (Ward 2016, 216). Jojo is that hope, and the women in his life help him attain it. Like Milkman, he learns to balance the masculine and the feminine; neither journey would be possible without the help of the women in their lives, and without the ability to learn from and emulate their generosity and compassion. Despite their very different conclusions, both characters progress in wisdom and maturity. Their pilgrimages illuminate not only the distances we have travelled historically, but also the progress yet to be made.

Notes

1. Railroad Tommy offers a disquisition to Milkman and Guitar about all they, as Black men, will never have, including a wide array of comforts, accolades and luxury goods (Morrison 2004, 60). His list has a Lacanian focus on the way that lack shapes the lives of Black men; how the not-having becomes their self-definition. Milkman, however, suffers more from excess than from deprivation.
2. See Olga Idriss Davis (1997) for more contemporary versions of this. Ta-Nehisi Coates also mentions experiencing this desire around the same time period as Milkman: 'Perhaps we should go back . . . Perhaps we should return to ourselves, to our own primordial streets, to our own ruggedness, to our own rude hair. Perhaps we should return to Mecca' (Coates 2015, 39).
3. This conversation continues in separate articles by the two authors. Morrison writes in 'Unspeakable Things Unspoken', 'Whenever characters are cloaked in Western fable, they are in deep trouble; but the African myth is also contaminated' (Morrison 2019, 192). Robert Stepto responds in *A Home Elsewhere* that something is 'a "contaminated" myth if its real and abiding work is to "mythologize desertion"' (Stepto 2010, 70).
4. See Michael Awkward's essay, which 'foregrounds not only Milkman's archeological question, but also Hagar's disintegration' (Awkward 2003, 89).
5. Richie has always seen himself as a Stone, saying of River, 'Him my big brother. Him, my father' (Ward 2017, 135).

Works Cited

Awkward, Michael. 2003. '"Unruly and Let Loose": Myth, Ideology, and Gender in Song of Solomon'. *Toni Morrison's Song of Solomon: A Casebook*, edited by Jan Furman. Oxford: Oxford University Press.

Chase, Greg. 2020. 'Of Trips Taken and Time Served: How Ward's Sing, Unburied, Sing Grapples with Faulkner's Ghosts'. *African American Review* 53, no. 3 (Fall): 201–16.

Coates, Ta-Nehisi. 2015. *Between the World and Me*. New York: Spiegel & Grau.

Davis, Olga Idriss. 1997. 'The Door of No Return: Reclaiming the Past Through the Rhetoric of Pilgrimage'. *The Western Journal of Black Studies* 21 (3): 156–61.

Dib, Nicole. 2020. 'Haunted Roadscapes in Jesmyn Ward's Sing, Unburied, Sing'. *MELUS* 45, no. 2 (June): 134–53.

Fanon, Frantz. 1967. *Black Skin White Masks*. New York: Grove Press.

Faulkner, William. [1930] 1990. *As I Lay Dying*. New York: Vintage International.

Krumholz, Linda. 2003. 'Dead Teachers: Rituals of Manhood and Rituals of Reading in Song of Solomon'. *Toni Morrison's Song of Solomon: A Casebook*, edited by Jan Furman. Oxford: Oxford University Press.

Lee, Catherine Carr. 2003. 'The South in Toni Morrison's Song of Solomon: Initiation, Healing, and Home'. *Toni Morrison's Song of Solomon: A Casebook*, edited by Jan Furman. Oxford: Oxford University Press.

Morrison, Toni. 1984. 'Rootedness: The Ancestor as Foundation'. In *Black Women Writers (1950–1980): A Critical Evaluation*, edited by Mari Evans, 339–45. New York: Anchor-Doubleday.

—. [1977] 2004. *Song of Solomon*. New York: Vintage International.

—. 2019. 'Unspeakable Things Unspoken: The Afro-American Presence in American Literature'. In *The Source of Self-Regard: Selected Essays, Speeches, and Mediations*, 161–97. New York: Alfred A. Knopf.

Murray, Rolland. 1999. 'The Long Strut: Song of Solomon and the Emancipatory Limits of Black Patriarchy'. *Callaloo* 22 (1): 121–33.

Oshinsky, David. 1997. *'Worse Than Slavery': Parchman Farm and the Ordeal of Jim Crow Justice*. New York: Free Press Paperbacks.

Rankine, Claudia. 2014. *Citizen: An American Lyric*. Minneapolis: Graywolf Press.

—. 2014. 'From Citizen, VI [My brothers are notorious]'. Poets.org. https:// poets.org/poem/citizen-vi-my-brothers-are-notorious.

Stepto, Robert. 2010. *A Home Elsewhere: Reading African American Classics in the Age of Obama*. Cambridge, MA: Harvard University Press.

Ward, Jesmyn. 2013. *Men We Reaped*. London: Bloomsbury.

—. 2016. 'When Cars Become Churches: Jesmyn Ward's Disenchanted America. An Interview'. Interview by Anna Hartnell. Cambridge Core, November 2013. https://www.cambridge.org/core/journals/journal-of-american-studies/article/when-cars%09become-churches-jesmyn-wards-disenchanted-america- an%09interview/4A60002FC9B8B006863B9655E08FBE5D/core-reader.

—. 2017. *Sing, Unburied, Sing*. New York: Scribner.

—. 2019. 'I Was Wandering. Toni Morrison Found Me'. *New York Times*, 9 August. https://www.nytimes.com/2019/08/09/opinion/sunday/i-was-wandering-toni-morrison- found-me.html.

Chapter 20

'I need the story to go': *Sing, Unburied, Sing,* Afropessimism and Black Narratives of Redemption

Marco Petrelli

When I discover who I am, I will be free.

Ralph Ellison, *Invisible Man* (1952)

In her memoir *Men We Reaped* (2013) Jesmyn Ward documents an exchange that took place when she was still striving to become a writer. She is back South for the summer from the University of Michigan, having crawfish boil with friends and family in her home town of DeLisle, Mississippi. 'So, what you doing up there?' a friend asks. 'I'm trying to be a writer', she answers while munching on the fish, declaring that she wants to write 'books about home. About the hood.' Her sister chimes in: 'she writing about real shit' (Ward 2013, 69). Fulfilling this resolution, Ward's career has developed to demonstrate a serious involvement with the condition of underprivileged Black people in the South, the will to bring front and centre their everyday struggles for a decent life – or better, for life *tout court* – and to denounce the unrelenting machinery of violence, oppression and discrimination working against them. In the memoir, DeLisle is transfigured into an ephemeral, ravenous being feeding on the lives of young Black men, a ghost wolf made of 'darkness and grief' (Ward 2013, 21) bent on a perennial hunt. As Ward herself writes in the prologue, in telling the stories of her family and her community and how death became the paradigm that defined them both, she hopes to understand the 'epidemic' that befell her home town, 'how the history of racism and economic inequality and lapsed public and personal responsibility festered and turned sour and spread [there]' (Ward 2013, 8).

The urge to narrate is fuelled by the necessity to find meaning in, and deliverance from, the violence that permeates the lives of Black people around her – and, by extension, in America at large. Through her work, Ward gives voice and representation to the African American community, exposing the harrowing conditions in which its people have been forced by neglect, poverty and systemic racism – the effects of which she presents unsparingly. At the same time, her insistence on the salvific powers of kinship and bonds that people establish to counter and redress the destructive, dehumanising impact of institutional violence demonstrates a determination to counter this state of things through the liberation afforded by a community united by love, care and resistance. The desire for redemption reverberates throughout Ward's work, but its outcome is doubtful: attempts at signification are always at risk of being frustrated by the sheer weight of the great darkness bearing down on the precarious lives that populate the author's pages.

The Ghost Story as Social Realism

Ward's first two novels, *Where the Line Bleeds* (2008) and *Salvage the Bones* (2011), are good examples of her often-brutal social realism: a poetics dictated by the hardships and losses she suffered first-hand through the years as a member of a poor Black Southern family and dedicated to reveal, denounce and possibly exorcise the looming spectre of death that haunts Black communities in America. Her vision as a writer might be summarised by a remark she made in an interview about *Salvage the Bones*. 'I couldn't dull the edges and fall in love with my characters and spare them', she said, 'life doesn't spare us' (Ward 2011). But Ward's faithful dedication to the harsh truths of contemporary Black life does not always translate into autobiography or strict realism, as demonstrated by her latest novel, *Sing, Unburied, Sing* (2017), in which, moving further towards the (Southern) Gothic tradition, she deploys an actual ghost, Richie, as one of the protagonists. Far from being a work of pure dark fantasy, the novel blends Ward's sharp focus on actuality with supernatural elements that, on closer inspection, are more an extension of her poetics of realism than a diversion from them. Through Richie and the metaphysical dimensions explored by *Sing, Unburied, Sing*, Ward takes her writing, quite literally, to a higher realm.

This does not mean that her previous works lack sophistication, or depth. Before publishing *Sing, Unburied, Sing*, Ward was a contributor and the editor for *The Fire this Time* (2016), a collection that she describes as an attempt towards the creation of 'an epic wherein Black lives carry worth' (Ward 2016, 11). Here, Ward envisions a future able to reverse the paradigm that stigma and institutional violence dictated upon Black existence, twisting African American life into a 'right to death that sees in death its most essential property' (Marriott 2007 226). The writer longs for such a future, although her mournful words seem to suggest that the present might not hold much room for hope. When death supplants life as the defining element of Blackness, furthering the literary investigation of contemporary African American life to denounce its subjugation also means engaging with the different articulations of necrosis that contribute to its paradigmatic construction. Therefore, combining the attention to the ordinary inequalities that mar Black existence with the semantics of the ghost story, Ward creates a cogent follow-up to *The Fire this Time*, expanding the political implications of her craft as a writer. In doing so, she apparently embraces Jacques Derrida's belief that to engage with a substantial ethical and political dimension one must necessarily speak '*of the* ghost . . . *to the* ghost and *with it*' (Derrida 1993, xviii). Considering how Ward's denunciation is arguably gaining strength book after book, it is indeed possible to understand the move towards the metaphysical represented by *Sing, Unburied, Sing* as a logical step forward in relation to the desire for truth and redemption that connotes all her work.[1]

Ward's latest novel can then be read as a hauntological rumination ripe with the ethical and political implications Derrida ascribes to the discourses on ghosts. The hope in a different future expressed by the introduction to *The Fire this Time* comes into its own through its engagement with the spectral, because without the involvement with actual and metaphorical ghosts, without the responsibility and the desire for justice 'for those others who are no longer', there would be no sense at all in interrogating the future and asking questions such as 'where tomorrow?' 'Whither?' (Derrida 1993, xviii). *Sing, Unburied, Sing* is an attempt to gesture towards the answers to these questions through the speculative dimensions offered by the polysemous figure of the ghost and the Gothic genre. As Avery Gordon reminds us, achieving a deeper understanding of the dialectics of subjection and subjectivity, domination and freedom – a mission that Ward's narrative embraces fully – entails investigating the ghost as the 'dense site' in which the intricacies of social life are revealed (Gordon 2008, 8). The Gothic, for its part, has historically provided access to the 'denied hopes and aspirations of a culture', at the same time demonstrating 'within itself the mechanisms which enforce non-fulfilment'. Because of this, the Gothic is also to be understood as a 'mode of history and a mode of memory' (Punter 2013, 188). As such, African American authors have often appropriated the genre to make it 'a capable and useful vehicle for expressing the terrors and complexities of Black existence in America', using it to 'destabilize and defy any singular projections of their own identity' (Wester 2012, 1–2). *Sing, Unburied, Sing* is firmly set in this tradition.

The supernatural elements of the novel are a symbolic way of dealing with the factuality of contemporary Black life in the deep South and not a detachment from it (see Christopher Lloyd's chapter in this volume). Using a ghost boy as one of the narrators, Ward gives voice to her sombre outlook on the condition of Black people; her desire to chronicle it and to make it visible; and her often frustrated, but never abandoned, desire to redeem African American life through literature. Richie stands as the point of spectral accumulation of the pain, death and grief that have been weighing on the African American community, especially in relation to the perverse action of the prison-industrial complex in the twentieth century. As such, for most of the novel he is a reluctant symbol of unredressed anti-Black violence, a harbinger of doom casting a jet shadow over the other character's fates.

But Ward's representation of the spiritual world that encompasses *Sing, Unburied, Sing* is not limited to the netherworld of darkness synecdochically embodied by Richie. There is another recurring ghost in the novel: that of Given, a member of the family whose story is interwoven with Richie's. Like the young spectre, Given is a victim of Mississippi's long history of anti-Black violence, as he is deliberately shot in cold blood during a hunting trip by a white man humiliated by his superior ability. In this respect, Given's story stands as yet another example of white impunity and senseless Black suffering – the tragic parable of a predestined victim. But, unlike Richie's, his role in the novel isn't only that of a spectral memento of the dreadful impact that systemic racism has on Black lives. After Given's death, his phantom lingers on as a kind of silent but ever-present guardian angel for his little sister Leonie. When she spirals into addiction, Given is there to discourage her drug abuse with his hushed disapproval; and, throughout the plot, he is always there for her, providing an ethereal yet enduring support. He also has a key role when his and Leonie's cancer-ridden mother, Philomène, asks to be led to the other side in order to be delivered from the pain that torments her ailing body.

As for Mam Philomène, it would be a bit of a stretch to consider her together with the other ghosts – the scene of her departure is a moment of heightened spiritual communication between this world and the other, but the character is described as a chiefly corporeal presence throughout the plot. Nonetheless, she contributes to the definition of the novel's metaphysical landscape in great measure. Mam, a medicine woman, practises a syncretic, diasporic religion: she is a devotee of Yemayá, Yoruban patron spirit of water; and Maman Brigitte, a death lwa in Haitian Vodou. Through her teachings and rituals, the story is infused with a distinctively non-Western way of representing the structure of, and the relationship between, the phenomenal world and the hereafter. This foundational spiritual framework produces knowledge able to dismantle racialised institutional and ideological oppression (see Lucy Arnold's chapter in this volume), but its importance also lies at a higher level of abstraction. This overt connection with West African and Black diasporic cultures places *Sing, Unburied, Sing* together with what Heather Russell defines as 'African Atlantic' narratives. As Russell writes, these narratives offer a 'self-conscious resistance' to rhetorical and structural impositions 'that are valued and normalized within Western epistemological and hermeneutical traditions' (Russell 2009, 22). African Atlantic literary works destabilise the hegemonic prescriptions of Western grand narratives; ergo, the discourses on pseudoscientific racism and white supremacy rooted in them. Mam's beliefs, then, represent and intrinsic repudiation of the darkness embodied by Richie, a counterargument that projects a narrative of redemption for Black people.

In the end, the novel's metaphysical dimension is fundamentally ambiguous. The existential pessimism represented by Richie; the melancholic but ultimately hopeful view of the afterlife embodied by Given; and the Black resistance implicit in Mam's spirituality combine to create a multipolar narration in which despair and possibility are inextricably connected in a dialectic whose outcome, again, is uncertain. Still, from a formal point of view Richie is the only ghost in charge of a first-person narration, and thus the pre-eminent character to interrogate when the analysis comes to the novel's uncanny dimension. Richie gives voice to the ineffable, channelling a vision of life after death that would otherwise be left unspoken just like in a séance. Therefore, in the pages that follow I will mainly focus on Richie in an attempt to untangle the conundrum of suffering and redemption that fuels *Sing, Unburied, Sing*'s narrative.

Time and Space in Afropessimistic Narratology

It could be objected that using a ghost as a revealing metaphor for the African American experience also carries with it a representational impasse. On the one hand, following Derrida's claims, a ghost is the threshold through which one can access a more acute way of critiquing the present status quo by disjoining its oppressive power relations and structures of thought. On the other hand, making a protagonist out of a spectre (that is, deploying a non-human or formerly human character) allegedly reiterates how Black life is defined by a paradigm that excludes it from the realm of the living and the human, turning it into a non-living Other – a perspective that can be considered Afropessimistic in essence. *Sing, Unburied, Sing* develops on the thin line that separates the empowering outlook implied by hauntology as defined by Derrida and the utter ontological darkness expressed by contemporary Afropessimist thinkers such as David S. Marriott, Calvin L. Warren and Frank B. Wilderson III.[2]

For the sake of this discussion, I am particularly interested in Wilderson's formulation, because it addresses a specific aspect of Afropessimism's critical framework that proves especially conducive when applied to literary works: the impossibility for Black people (and by extension, for Black characters) to exist in a proper narrative arc – that is, an arc that moves 'from possession to dispossession to (the denouement) the prospect of repossession'; or from equilibrium, to disequilibrium, to equilibrium restored, renewed, and/or reimagined (Wilderson 2020, 199). In short, a narrative that accommodates the possibility for a character to escape their predicaments, and that, providing denouement, affords them redemption. Building on Hortense Spillers's considerations about the enslaved as the 'essence of stillness' (Spillers 1987, 78), Wilderson declares Blackness to be 'coterminous with Slaveness' (Wilderson 2020, 102), affirming that 'Black emplotment is a catastrophe for narrative at a metalevel . . . social death is aporetic with respect to narrative writ large (and, by extension, to redemption writ large)' (Wilderson 2020, 226–7). Wilderson thus transfers the paradigm of social death through which Orlando Patterson describes the condition of the enslaved (Patterson 2018, 38–45) to Black existence in its entirety, with the result of barring Black people from narration itself and from the redemptive qualities implied therein by means of their existential paralysis. The suffering that Blacks have endured throughout modern history offers 'no strategy for redress – no narrative of redemption', writes Wilderson, 'Blackness *is* social death, which is to say that there was never a prior meta-moment of plenitude, never a moment of equilibrium' (Wilderson n.d.). 'The narrative arc of the slave', he adds, 'is *not an arc at all*, but a flat line . . . that moves from disequilibrium, to a moment in the narrative of faux-equilibrium, to disequilibrium restored and/or rearticulated' (Wilderson 2020, 102).

The reciprocity of Blackness and slaveness in terms of positionality assumed by the Afropessimists makes Ward's use of Gothic tropes even more cogent, because, as Teresa Goddu posits, the 'sensationalism' that characterises the Gothic offered nineteenth-century abolitionists a ready-made mode 'through which to express the empirical truths of slavery's horrors' (Goddu 2016, 36). Gothic exaggerations 'documented and made visible the enormity of slavery's crime' (Goddu 2016, 36) and in that they displaced realism as the most effective genre through which the actuality of slavery could be transmitted. When slavery becomes the defining paradigm of Black (non-)life as posited by Afropessimism, the Gothic emerges as a constitutionally germane form of representation. Ward's appeal to the rhetorical strategies of the ghost story is an attempt to verbalise and understand a violence that is otherwise 'beyond the grasp of reason' (Wilderson 2020, 90), giving form to a more nuanced representation of contemporary Black experience.

Still, the fundamental ambiguity of the ghost remains. Gothicism and spectrality can be used as tools to subvert and disjoin the oppressive paradigm denounced by the Afropessimists, but they can also give voice to a bleak hopelessness about Black life that is undeniably nihilistic in the metaphysical dread it expresses. The best way to solve this ambiguity is to test Wilderson's analysis on Ward's novel to see how *Sing, Unburied, Sing* responds to, mirrors, or rewires Afropessimistic understandings of the absence of narrative and the possibility of redemption implied by it. Riffing off Jacques Derrida's words, the question that leads this analysis would be: 'Whither Black narratives of redemption?'

To answer this question, it is necessary to start from the most basic constitutive elements of the novel's storyworld:[3] its space and time. Mikhail Bakhtin's seminal work on the chronotope considers the inextricable intersection of these dimensions to be an essential formal element of literature and of narration at large. According to the critic, spacetime not only determines the genre of a literary work, but it also dictates 'to a significant degree the image of man in literature', with the result that 'the image of man is always intrinsically chronotopic' (Bakhtin 1981, 85). But, according to Afropessimistic narratology, these otherwise crucial categories bear no significance when applied to the storyworld of the enslaved and, by extension, to the representation of the enslaved as characters. Chronotopic representations define the image of human beings in literature, with the result that non-human subjects like the ghost of Richie – and by extension Black people in general, described by Afropessimists '*as* nothing incarnated' (Warren 2018, 9) – are implicitly excluded from narration proper on the basis that a 'highly structured' mesh of space and time is a fundamental prerequisite for a text to be assimilable to, and interpreted as, narrative (Herman 2002, 298). In other words, storytelling needs a thoroughly developed spacetime dimension to classify as narrative proper; but, following Bakhtin, chronotopes are a prerogative of human characters. The paradigmatic representation of Black people as non-human (or worse, as nothingness itself, according to Warren) that Afropessimist thinkers ascribe to modern Western ontology would thus create an insurmountable logical fallacy in the machinery of narration, a 'meta-aporia' that undermines the text's rhetorical structures (Wilderson 2020, 14).

Let's follow Wilderson's line of reasoning for a more in-depth understanding of the supposed incompatibility between Blackness and narrative. The critic declares that 'narrative time is always historical (imbued with historicity)' (2020, 227), an assertion that echoes Bakhtin, for whom the chronotope results from a process of 'assimilating real historical time' in literature (Bakhtin 1981, 84). But the enslaved are barred from the paradigm of the human and from the possibility of experiencing historical actuality because 'for the Slave, historical "time" is not possible' (Wilderson 2020, 227). An actual temporal dimension becomes then a logical predicament for Black narratives on the grounds that narrative time proper 'marks stasis and change *within* the [human] paradigm', but 'it does not mark the time *of* the paradigm, the time of time itself, the time by which the Slave's dramatic clock is set' (Wilderson 2010, 339). 'Time' here is not to be read as an abstract, measurable mathematical quantity, and not even as narratological time *tout court*. Rather, Wilderson's 'time' is an epistemological metadiscourse inextricably connected to Western grand narratives of enlightenment, progress and civilisation – the same grand narratives responsible for conceiving and supporting discourses on racial superiority, slavery and colonialism throughout modernity. In this chronological paradigm, which Wilderson sees as totalising and inescapable, the structural impossibility for Black people to live through Western historical time determines Black literature's failure to artistically appropriate, reflect and process this specific dimension. Modernity as shaped by post-Enlightenment grand narratives ostracises Black storytelling from historical representation, because the subjects it seeks to narrate have been forcibly excluded from the 'ontological and epistemological time of modernity itself, in which Blackness and Slaveness are imbricated *ab initio*' (Wilderson 2010, 340). This does not mean that Black experience cannot be narrated at all, of course. But Wilderson's analysis is useful in understanding how threats to Black existence are entrenched down to the rhetorical foundations of Western thought; and how, at a higher theoretical level, Black narrative is always an act of conflict and resistance.

The substantial absence that characterises historicity as Wilderson defines it also extends to the spatial dimension of Black literature because, according to the critic, 'social death bars the slave from access to narrative at the level of temporality; but it also does so at the level of spatiality' by placing characters in a setting that is but an 'extension of the master's dominion' (Wilderson 2020, 227). In narratological terms, it is possible to say that the 'figure' of the enslaved lacks a proper 'ground' upon which it can articulate its definition and hence its particular existence. As David Herman writes, 'figure-ground relationships are basic to the process of narration. It would be impossible, arguably, to build or reconstruct a storyworld without an articulation of the perceptual field into focused-up participants . . . and a background against which those focused-up entities stand out' (Herman 2002, 275).

According to Afropessimism, modernity has adopted anti-Blackness not only as a series of violent practices like colonialism and segregation, but as a fundamental philosophical orientation. Calvin L. Warren sees modern Western ontology as depending upon anti-Blackness for its articulation, writing that the original Greek meaning of 'being' as 'arising and standing forth' is obliterated in a world that relies on the annihilation of Blackness for its existence (Warren 2018, 12–13). If we translate this consideration in narratological terms with the help of Herman's analysis of the figure-ground relationship, it could be argued that – at least within the limits of modern Western narratives – Black characters can't 'stand out' against their background because the same rhetorical structures that sustain the process of narration also deny them this possibility on the basis of the ontology they proceed from. At a metalevel, then, Western narratives turn Black characters into non-beings exiled in a non-space-time, perpetrating dynamics of exclusion and subjugation in a more abstract but equally violent way. The oppressive matrix of Western narratological normativity strips Black emplotment of the possibility to shape a proper storyworld, turning it into the narrative catastrophe described by Wilderson. The only way out of this deadlock is to break free from the matrix altogether – which is precisely what Richie longs for in his quest for redemption.

The Parchman (non)Storyworld

Richie's placement in the spatial-temporal texture of *Sing, Unburied, Sing* and the character's role in the narrative dynamics of the story seem to confirm Wilderson's claims. First, being a spectre, Richie is inherently unable to cross the line that Afropessimism draws between humans and Black people, that is, a line that differentiates between the 'living and the dead' (Wilderson 2020, 229). Also, as an innocent victim of Jim Crow laws, imprisoned in Parchman Farm for stealing food for his starving brothers and sisters, overworked, lashed and finally killed, Richie epitomises the kind of unredeemable suffering that Afropessimists describe. Still, Richie's story stands out as the strongest centre of gravity of the novel's storyworld, demonstrating Ward's will to accentuate the character's symbolic relevance. In *Sing, Unburied, Sing*, storytelling duty is shared by Jojo (the novel's major focaliser), his mother Leonie and Richie himself. The chronicle of the boy's last days, though, is the subplot that innervates the other stories and the thread that links them all. In addition to being the main mystery that drives the novel, Richie's death also provides a commentary on the post-bellum history of Black people in the South, standing as the ghostly urtext of the other characters' lives. Readers are gradually and indirectly introduced to the boy through the words of a homodiegetic narrator: his old friend and fellow inmate at Mississippi State Penitentiary, River – Leonie's father and Jojo's grandfather.

Wilderson defines Black emplotment as being aporetic with respect to literature at a metalevel, framing Black presence as something of an irresolvable internal contradiction, a logical inconsistency in the machinery of narration that takes place at a level of abstraction higher than the one presented by the story itself. Nonetheless, at the level of diegesis, it is significant that River is not able to tell Richie's story up to its conclusion until very late in the novel: the cruel and violent fate the boy encounters reverberates throughout the years leaving the now-aged man still at loss for words. Forced into an escape attempt by an inmate who assaults a white girl while on the run, Richie is chased by a hounds-led posse composed of wardens, citizens and River himself, who is in charge of looking after the penitentiary's dogs. When the man catches up with the young boy before the lynching gang, he takes his life out of mercy to spare him from being tortured to death by the bloodthirsty mob. The ghost cannot remember what happened in his final moments as a living being and he repeatedly asks for the story to be told, affirming that 'it is the only way [he] can go' (Ward 2017, 230). In Ward's novel,

Wilderson's meta-aporia is transformed into amnesia and aphasia, impairments that sustain the critic's speculation about anti-Black violence being illegible and hence impossible to be effectively grasped and described through words.

Richie's experience of time and space (and thus his chronotopical image) also points to the boy's substantial exile from narrative proper. As far as time is concerned, the ghost is placed in a parallel dimension where the rules of human time (that is, Western historical time) don't apply. By cyclically burrowing into the dirt and sleeping, the spectre can move between past, present and future, freed from the kind of teleological, linear and forward-moving conception of time that belongs to modern Western thought. He describes time as 'a vast ocean . . . [where] everything is happening at once' (Ward 2017, 186), a characterisation that closely resembles the West African conception of Macro-Time, defined by Kenyan theologian John S. Mbiti as 'that ocean of time in which everything becomes absorbed in a reality that is neither after nor before' (Mbiti 1970, 29). As Heather Russell writes, such treatment of time by Black Atlantic authors is to be understood as an act of defiance directed towards the constraining structures of linear Western grand narratives, the same discourses that decreed the institutional dehumanisation of Black people in the first place. 'Such narratives', she writes, 'invoke culturally specific temporal and spatial models that challenge normative narratological structures' (Russell 2009, 13).

In spite of this, when projected upon the character's spatial dimension, Richie's experience of time becomes a subtle entrapment – not a circular time, but an encircling time. After his death, the twelve-year-old ghost finds himself still in Parchman Farm, forever chained to the same place in which he was imprisoned towards the end of his short life. He says:

> How could I know that after I died, Parchman would pull me from the sky? How could I imagine Parchman would pull me to it and refuse to let go? And how could I conceive that Parchman was past, present, and future all at once? (Ward 2017, 186)

Although capable of slipping back and forth in time, the ghost is nonetheless unable to escape from the prison's premises, to make the leap from being freed from captivity (as dramatic and final as this act is, in his case) to being set at liberty. His spatial articulation is but another plantation that holds him down even in the afterlife. Even if he is not bound by time, space still functions as a prison for him, frustrating his attempts at transcendence and characterising his fluid experiencing of temporality as a suffocating loop rather than a non-linear, liberating experience. Richie's chronotope is a meta-physical ensnarement, an otherworldly Gothic labyrinth from which escape is not possible.

Parchman Farm is the traumatic centre of the novel, a space upon which the trajectories of the protagonists converge and where the mundane and the spectral intersect. Balancing the novel around this place, Ward is calling attention to the racist history of the US South and its impact on the present by stressing the racialised dynamics that characterise the prison-industrial complex, of which the Mississippi State Penitentiary is a particularly apt example. As David Oshinsky reports, Parchman was an enormously lucrative operation, generating profits of almost a million dollars a year well into the 1950s (Oshinsky 1997, 224), approximately when River and Richie meet in the prison's fields. Until the *Gates v. Collier* case would denounce the blatant abuses perpetrated on its inmates, Parchman was also 'something familiar', and 'a powerful link to the past': a contemporary, state-managed antebellum plantation disguised as a penitentiary 'where blacks in striped clothing worked the cotton fields for the enrichment of others' (Oshinsky 1997, 155). Time is out of joint in Parchman because the past – in typical Southern Gothic fashion – irrupts into the present to destroy it; or better, it lingers in the present thanks to the institutional will to preserve the relational dynamics of slavery, dispossessing people like Richie from their selfhood and their humanity. Ward frames the story of the ghost and Parchman within a fluid, ambiguous temporality in which past and present are not neatly separated to emphasise how African Americans are still haunted by the spectre of slavery – contemporary Mississippi and even the afterlife are but an extension of the Old Southern plantation. 'Sometimes I think it done changed', Richie says, 'then I sleep and I wake up, and it ain't changed none' (Ward 2017, 171); an affirmation that, although directed towards Parchman, sounds like an evaluation of American history writ large. Even if Richie is not totally 'fixed in time and space', he is still forced into the kind of 'undynamic [non-]human state' that Hortense Spillers associates with the condition of being enslaved (Spillers 1987, 78).

Saidiya Hartman defines the 'afterlife of slavery' as the 'skewed life chances, limited access to health and education, premature death, incarceration, and impoverishment' that still largely define the lives of Black people in America (Hartman 2007, 6). The ghost character is a clear example of the endurance of this paradigm of suffering, one that has a crucial role in Ward's plots and is revealed and investigated in each of her novels. But *Sing, Unburied, Sing* does more than suggesting how the legacy of slavery is alive and well through the tragic stories of its protagonists. By showing us a version of the great beyond that isn't different in substance and dynamics from an actual prison (or plantation), Ward is claiming that slavery has the power to define Black people even after their death: in the world of the novel, the afterlife of slavery also brings about an afterlife of enslavement. Bryan Wagner posits that Afropessimism is an attempt to formulate an account of Black suffering 'without recourse to the consolation of transcendence' (Wagner 2009, 2), but Ward seems to deny Richie even this relief when she describes his inability to step forward into the blissful heaven that appears before his eyes towards the end of the novel (Ward 2017, 241).

Time, Love and Home

Still, *Sing, Unburied, Sing* tries at least to suggest a way out of the radical dispossession represented by the young Black ghost. In a couple of passages (Ward 2017, 182–4; 186–91), Richie insists upon three concepts that have taken a completely different meaning to him thanks to his ordeal: time, love and home. As far as time is concerned – and as discussed above – the spectre demonstrates an ambiguous relationship with temporality. Time is a dimension potentially able to free him from the entanglement of systemic anti-Black violence, but it ultimately fails to stand as a redeeming force because of its association with space in the creation of Parchman's storyworld. Richie is unable to reconstruct a meaningful narrative out of his experience because of the spacetime that defines him: his chronotopic image is one of inherent enslavement and impossible redemption.

'Love', unlike 'time', is explicitly connoted in *Sing, Unburied, Sing*. Affirming that '[t]here's more' to love than what is usually associated with the word (Ward 2017, 183), Richie goes on to suggest that love is to be intended as a fraternal bond established between the oppressed, a different relational dynamic aimed at creating a community of care among Black people within the walls of the endless prison of modernity. Thinking about a prostitute who services the Black men of Parchman, Richie says:

> [W]hen I thought about the way Riv admonished Sunshine Woman, how he stepped away from her to protect me, I began to understand love. I began to understand that what Riv and Sunshine Woman did wasn't an expression of love, but Riv's standing in the sun for me was. (Ward 2017, 189–90)

The key to escape, or at least to counter, the irredeemable history of anti-Black violence is found in the construction of a collectivity of resistance, of which River and Richie are a small but significant fragment.

'Home' seems again to be an ambiguous concept for Richie. When he is finally able to leave Parchman and follow Jojo down to the Mississippi coast to reunite with River, the spectre ruminates about his previous entrapment within the prison's limits, concluding that his difficulty in breaking free from the farm for more than half a century might have been related to the fact that the penitentiary was indeed a kind of 'terrible' home for him (Ward 2017, 191). His experience stands as an answer to Wilderson's rhetorical question about the status of Black people and their ubiquitous enslavement: 'Where is the line between prison and home?' (Wilderson 2020, 104), the critic asks. In an apparent perversion that is nonetheless coherent with an Afropessimistic framework, Richie belongs to Parchman just like he belongs anywhere else – in a world united by anti-Blackness, the prison-plantation and home become coterminous. There is no place for home in this world for Richie because '[t]here is no world without Blacks, yet there are no Blacks who are in the world' (Wilderson 2020, 42). Still, Richie's quest for a place he can call home is integral to his desire to be released, so much that his deliverance seems to rely entirely upon the prospect of breaking the chains that fetter him to this world and moving to a place able to afford deliverance. Again, this drive seems to dovetail Wilderson's speculations on the relationship between Blackness, narrative and redemption when he writes 'there is no place . . . to which Slaves can return as Human Beings. When this happens, Blackness will be redeemed' (Wilderson n.d.).

The attention towards time, love and home demonstrates the ghost's desire to find a storyworld and a narrative able to grant him the ontological value he has been denied both in life and in death, a different story that could allow him to be in the world and of the world. Richie's insistence on love and the necessity to 'get home' in order to be healed from his condition echoes Hartman's words on Black people's dispossession and the painful search for a place to really be home:

> The transience of the slave's existence still leaves its traces in how black people imagine home . . . It's why we never tire of dreaming of a place that we can call home, a place better than here, wherever here might be . . . This sense of not belonging and of being an extraneous element is at the heart of slavery. Love has nothing to do with it; love has everything to do with it. (Hartman 2007, 87–8)

Place and love are joined together by Hartman in the creation of a whole finally able to redeem Black people from their substantial alienation. But the right kind of love is needed. Hartman connects the etymological origins of the word *odonkor* (the closest term to 'slave' in Akan language) to *odo*, 'love', revealing a subtle ambiguity able to reverse the meaning of the term, neutralising its empowering potential as suggested by Richie. At the end of her intellectual journey in the history of the slave trade, Hartman is eventually able to overcome such polysemic impasse through a different understanding of love. She finally finds a way to feel at home through a kind of love that is the product of a community tied together by a history of suffering, resistance and '*the possibility of solidarity*', a '*we who become together*' (Hartman 2007, 231).

But this is not the case with Richie. The ghost boy's enhanced understanding of time, home and love and the fact that his story is finally told until its terrible end by River is not enough to set him free. He is still looking for its place, a storyworld that, in an allusive, elliptic way that once again seems to stress how narrative fails to properly serve the expressive needs of Black people, is also defined as a 'song'. 'The place is the song and I am going to be part of the song', Richie says (Ward 2017, 183). As a matter of fact, in the final act of the novel Richie and a number of other spirits (African American spirits victims of racist violence, judging by the sparse details provided) are possibly freed from this world by a 'song of mismatched, half-garbled words' sung by Kayla, Jojo's infant sister (Ward 2017, 284). It is interesting to notice how Hartman's closure too is achieved through a song whose words she cannot understand, the 'song of the lost tribe' (Hartman 2007, 235), a connection that points to some liberating power inherent in sound, rather than in words.

If River's story is unable to release and restore Richie because of its intrinsic participation in Western narrative paradigms, the only solution is to change the paradigm entirely: the switch to a code that represents an abrupt formal departure from Euro-American logocentricity and its ensnarement. In accordance with African Atlantic narratology as described by Heather Russell, Ward demonstrates a will to break free from Western narratives by interrogating, disrupting and reformulating '[t]he very logocentricity of these systems' (Russell 2009, 3). The song, as a place, stands as an aural equivalent of a chronotope able to neutralise the paradigm of enslavement, close the gap between the living and the dead and lead the spirits to a place in which their humanity can be redeemed. The song is a sonic vessel leading 'home', wherever it might be.

'Home', the last word of the novel, seems to suggest that, despite Wilderson's claim about the absence of a spacetime in which the enslaved can be redeemed, through the restoration of humanity granted by the dissolution of a state of stillness there is indeed a place where the enslaved can return and be liberated. However, Richie and Given's stories also suggest that redemption is once again a consolation granted by transcendence, a culmination whose prerequisite is corporeal death, and thus not something achievable in this world. The only character who seems to somewhat repudiate this rule is Philomène. In her final moments, she asks Leonie to evoke Maman Brigitte and be ushered away to eternity, freeing her soul and leaving her ravaged, agonising body behind. Given's ghost is also released in the process, and the two step into eternity together. Philomène is in full control of her destiny: in the ability to weave her own story up to its willing denouement lies the possibility to disrupt Western narrative impositions and to stand forth as a full-blown character who inhabits a proper narrative arc. Once again, though, redemption is synonymous with death. Mam and Given find their peace in the afterlife instead of being trapped in a purgatory like Richie, but their deliverance becomes possible only in the transcendent.

As her penchant for open endings demonstrates, Ward herself seems to be in two minds about the possibility of earthly restoration. She can only 'burn . . . and hope' (Ward 2016, 11) for a world in which Black life is redeemed, and the unfailing devotion she writes into the relationship between Jojo and Kayla demonstrates her will to project a future of salvation for the Black community, an epic wherein Black lives carry worth. Songs of home, time and love like *Sing, Unburied, Sing* can help imagining and prefiguring such a future, but the question of its immanence remains open-ended. Still, Ward's latest writing to date, 'On Witness and Respair', suggests that there is time for hope no matter the darkness that shrouds this world.

Notes

1. This intuition seems to be confirmed by the sparse details about her upcoming novel that Ward gives in an article published in *Vanity Fair*, 'On Witness and Respair: A Personal Tragedy Followed by a Pandemic,' in which she describes the protagonist as a 'woman who speaks with spirits' (Ward 2020).
2. It is not my will to present an analysis of Afropessimism (quite a contested theoretical framework), nor to back up or confute the claims of

its practitioners – an exercise that far exceeds the (strictly literary) limits of this chapter. I refer to some Afropessimist tenets (mainly through Wilderson's formulation) exclusively in their theoretical implications for Black narratology.

3. Although Wilderson mentions the term 'story world' (2020, 227), drawing it from H. Porter Abbott's *The Cambridge Introduction to Narrative*, he doesn't provide further discussion of this conceptualisation in light of his claims on Black narrative. My understanding of the storyworld derive from Abbott's *Introduction* and David Herman's *Story Logic*, in which the critics use it to move the focus from diegesis (strictly defined: the act of narrating) to the narrative world (a spacetime complex) that is created by this act (Abbott 2008, chap. 12; Herman 2002, 13–17).

Works Cited

Abbott, Porter H. 2008. *The Cambridge Introduction to Narrative*. 2nd ed. Cambridge: Cambridge University Press. EPUB.

Bakhtin, Mikhail. 1981. 'Forms of Time and of the Chronotope in the Novel'. In *The Dialogic Imagination: Four Essays*, edited by Michael Holquist, 84–258. Austin: University of Texas Press.

Derrida, Jacques. 1993. *Specters of Marx*. New York: Routledge.

Gordon, Avery. *Ghostly Matters: Haunting and the Sociological Imagination*. Minneapolis: University of Minnesota Press.

Goddu, Teresa A. 2016. 'U.S. Antislavery Tracts and the Literary Imagination'. In *The Cambridge Companion to Slavery in American Literature*, edited by Ezra Tawil, 32–54. Cambridge: Cambridge University Press.

Hartman, Saidiya. 2007. *Lose Your Mother: A Journey Along the Atlantic Slave Route*. New York: Farrar, Straus & Giroux.

Herman, David. 2002. *Story Logic: Problems and Possibilities of Narrative*. Lincoln: University of Nebraska Press.

Marriott, David. 2007. *Haunted Life: Visual Culture and Black Modernity*. New Brunswick, NJ: Rutgers University Press.

Mbiti, John S. 1970. *African Religions and Philosophy*. New York: Anchor Books.

Oshinsky, David. 1997. *Worse than Slavery: Parchman Farm and the Ordeal of Jim Crow Justice*. New York: Free Press.

Patterson, Orlando. 2018. *Slavery and Social Death: A Comparative Study*. Cambridge, MA: Harvard University Press.

Punter, David. 2013. *The Literature of Terror: A History of Gothic Fictions from 1765 to the Present Day*. Vol. 2, *The Modern Gothic*. London and New York: Routledge.

Russell, Heather. 2009. *Legba's Crossing: Narratology in the African Atlantic*. Athens: The University of Georgia Press.

Spillers, Hortense. 1987. 'Mama's Baby, Papa's Maybe: An American Grammar Book'. *Diacritics* 17, no. 2 (Summer): 64–81.

Wagner, Bryan. 2009. *Disturbing the Peace: Black Culture and the Police Power After Slavery*. Cambridge, MA: Harvard University Press.

Ward, Jesmyn. 2011. 'Jesmyn Ward on *Salvage the Bones*'. By Elizabeth Hoover. *The Paris Review*, 30 August. https://www.theparisreview.org/blog/2011/08/30/jesmyn-ward-on- salvage-the-bones/.

——. 2013. *Men We Reaped*. New York: Bloomsbury.

——, ed. 2016. *The Fire this Time*. New York: Simon & Schuster.

——. 2017. *Sing, Unburied, Sing*. New York: Scribner.

——. 2020. 'On Witness and Respair: A Personal Tragedy Followed by a Pandemic' *Vanity Fair*, 1 September. https://www.vanityfair.com/culture/2020/08/jesmyn-ward-on-husbands-death-and-grief-during-covid.

Warren, Calvin L. 2018. *Ontological Terror: Blackness, Nihilism, and Emancipation*. Durham, NC: Duke University Press.

Wester, Maisha L. 2012. *African American Gothic: Screams from Shadowed Places*. New York: Palgrave Macmillan.

Wilderson, Frank B. III, n.d. 'Afropessimism and the End of Redemption'. *Humanities Futures*. https://humanitiesfutures.org/papers/afro-pessimism-end-redemption/.

——. 2010. *Red, White and Black: Cinema and the Structure of U.S. Antagonism*. Durham, NC: Duke University Press.

——. 2020. *Afropessimism*. New York: Liveright.

'The most beautiful song': Jesmyn Ward and Diasporic Recognition

Sheri-Marie Harrison

I woke to Minneapolis burning. I woke to protests in America's heartland, Black people blocking the highways. I woke to people doing the haka in New Zealand. I woke to hoodie-wearing teens, to John Boyega raising a fist in the air in London, even as he was afraid he would sink his career, but still, he raised his fist. I woke to droves of people, masses of people in Paris, sidewalk to sidewalk, moving like a river down the boulevards. I knew the Mississippi. I knew the plantations on its shores, the movement of enslaved and cotton up and down its eddies. The people marched, and I had never known that there could be rivers such as this, and as protesters chanted and stomped, as they grimaced and shouted and groaned, tears burned my eyes. (Ward 2020)

Jesmyn Ward's recognition that grief and rage at Black death are felt and shared globally is among the striking but unsurprising things about her account of witnessing global Black Lives Matter protests in the wake of her husband's death from COVID-19 and George Floyd's murder in 2020. Her grief-filled encounter with 'the revelation that Black Americans were not alone in this' – something she knew all her life but had never experienced in this way – is also about the power of witnessing. 'They witness our fight too', she says, 'see our hearts lurch to beat again in our art and music and work and joy. How revelatory that others witness our battles and stand up. They go out in the middle of a pandemic, and they march.' Echoed here are the contradictory experiences of struggle, loss, hope and resilience amidst systemic discrimination and violence that are central to Ward's work overall. The final words of Ward's essay are 'we here', an African American vernacular declaration of solidarity through presence and a homonymic affirmation of hearing/listening.

In *Sing Unburied, Sing*, Ward uses the ghost Richie to imagine the opposite: the inability to access the land 'across the face of the water', where the people sing 'the most beautiful song'. Richie 'can't understand a word' of this song though, and recognising that he has no access to 'that golden isle', he tells us, 'Absence. Isolation. I keen' (Ward 2017, 242). Here, and in 'On Witness and Respair', Ward gestures to the importance of recognition and solidarity from spaces beyond the ground of African American experiences in the United States. Even as this volume explores the various contours of nature and climate, history and memory, community and family, and intertextuality in Ward's writing, the chapters focus, in large part, on Ward's writing within the localised context of the United States. While this specificity is vital to understanding her work, and indeed among the strengths of the pieces included here, moments of mutual recognition such as the one Ward describes in her essay demonstrate the imperative of also attending to how Ward's work is connected to larger conversations – in particular, ones about the afterlives of slavery beyond the boundaries of the United States.

The idea of slavery's afterlives, as it has been taken up by Saidiya Hartman, Christina Sharpe and Yogita Goyal, is characterised by the localised experience of a globally shared phenomenon. For Hartman, slavery's afterlives in the US include 'skewed life chances, limited access to health and education, premature death, incarceration, and impoverishment' (Hartman 2008, 6). Sharpe frames the afterlives of slavery more figuratively and in terms of the challenges of representation: 'transatlantic slavery' she tells us, 'was and *is* the disaster . . . The disaster and the writing of the disaster are never present, are always present' (Sharpe 2016, 5). Goyal, meanwhile, is concerned with the appearance of slavery in writing as a 'frame' for 'a range of contemporary phenomena across the globe: from human trafficking to illegal immigration, from conscription in war as a child soldier to forced marriage from debt and bondage, to domestic servitude' (Goyal 2019, 2). This brief afterword closes the collection with the charge of attending to the local *and* the global – and perhaps even more importantly, their interrelationships – in Ward's work, considering how slavery's afterlives continue to define connection across the Black world.

Though slavery itself is not represented in Ward's writing, the precarity that hounds the lives of the denizens of Bois Sauvage across her fiction functions within Goyal's sense of a frame 'as the defining template through which current forms of human rights abuses are understood in order to rethink race in a global frame' (Goyal 2019, 2).

Michelle Alexander's sense of a 'new global economy' in which young Black men are 'deemed disposable' is apparent in Ward's first novel, *Where the Line Bleeds* (Alexander 2020, 18). The novel's newly graduated eighteen-year-old twins, Joshua and Christopher DeLisle, are faced with depleted employment options in a Gulf Coast where there is no industry because of the outsourcing of blue-collar jobs, and low-salaried service positions or drug dealing are among the few choices for economic viability that remain. As Martyn Bone suggests in this volume, even as *Where the Line Bleeds*, like Ward's other novels, takes place almost entirely in the US South, 'over the course of the novel, the twins' experiences anatomise the formation of this world by both a regional history of racialised labour and the contemporary global expansion of neoliberalism' (p. 63). Transatlantic slavery is not the only origin point of this global formation, but it is certainly among the key factors at its roots.

The reality of the incomplete abolition of slavery in the United States and beyond requires us to think about American and global literature in relation, or to think more fully about the global presence in American literature. Indeed, the ways this incomplete abolition manifests in contemporary literature demonstrates how we have not yet figured out how to reckon with – or, more accurately, have in fact repressed – global histories of violence. The afterlives of slavery are present in scenes like *Sing Unburied Sing*'s iconic image of a tree filled with transhistorical ghosts who refuse to leave, intoning instead, 'home'. It is also present in the racist criminal justice system that persists in the experiences of Ward's family and her characters' families, across three generations. It is in Ward's treatment of ghosts and haunting, via the Gothic and its own historical imbrications with the transatlantic slave trade, that we can begin to trace the global connections in Ward's work. As Maria ElenaTorres-Quevado notes in her discussion of *Men We Reaped*, Ward 'has not merely inherited the Gothic; she has conscientiously deployed its generic features to make her own intervention into the broader narrative of the Black rural South' (p. 183).

The Gothic appears in Ward's work under the sign of temporal collapse. This term delineates how traumatic and destructive aspects of the past continue to erupt in the present. In *Sing, Unburied, Sing*, among the most pronounced images of temporal collapse is the tree of ghosts where Richie eventually finds home, ghosts who 'speak with their eyes' a litany of suffering: '*she locked me in the shed and starved me to death while I listened to my babies playing with her in the yard they came in my cell in the middle of the night and they hung me they found I could read and they dragged me to barn and gouged my eyes out before they beat me still . . .'* (Ward 2017, 282). The reader is alerted to the temporal differences of these horrors through the clothes the ghosts wear: 'rags and breeches, T-shirts and tignons, fedoras and hoodies' (283). The absence of punctuation makes one experience run into the other, effecting in the process a continuity in collective experiences of racialised violence and suffering that are uninterrupted from one individual to the next, one event from another event, one time period to the rest. Here, the violent vestiges of slavery continue to reverberate across time among ghosts who all exist together in the present of the novel.

When the toddler Kayla faces this tree of ghosts and tells them to '[g]o home', the ghosts 'shudder, but they do not leave' at her command. As if recognising their need for comfort, she 'raises one arm in the air, palm up, like she is trying to soothe [. . .] but the ghosts don't still, don't rise, don't ascend and disappear. They stay' (Ward 2017, 284). Kayla's next effort in comforting or ushering the ghosts home is to begin singing 'a song of mismatches, half garble words' that her brother, Jojo, cannot understand, though the melody is familiar (284). This song contrasts the one from the land across the sea – 'the most beautiful song' – that Richie hears but cannot understand (241). As she sings, the ghosts 'smile with something like relief, something like remembrance, something like ease'. While they seem soothed by her song, they still do not vacate their perch. They remain there in the trees, still saying 'home', affirming in Kayla's song that, like Richie, they are home. In this way, Ward defamiliarises the concept of home, not as a place of refuge and comfort, but, for ghosts like Richie, an endless limbo. Ironically, it is from the ghost narrator Richie's perspective that we see the desirability and respite of the land across the water, from which he is barred. Here, for a moment, Ward's use of haunting becomes less a metaphor for past trauma than an embodiment of a very real, concrete state experienced by many in the contemporary world. It is a vision that is less about national belonging than perpetual migrancy.

Goyal suggests that 'the embrace of the gothic' in contemporary literature 'enables a different sense of the relation between the audience and the figure of the victim, as well as a fuller appreciation of the itineraries of terror, rooted in colonial history that have led us to this moment' (Goyal 2019, 68). In attending to the afterlives of slavery in Ward's work, we can also attend to the ways the history of slavery and its legacies in the United States are connected to a larger, longer, and shared colonial history. In its resolution, *Sing, Unburied,*

Sing does not offer safe passage home for the ghosts of the past who have suffered racial violence across centuries. The novel also does not offer correctives or hope for a brighter future, nor does it exorcise the ghosts from past brutality. It instead lays bare the realities of our time and their roots in systems that depend on the criminalisation and disenfranchisement of Black people. Even more striking, however, is the way in which the needs of Ward's ghosts are understood by Black children, like Kayla. If Richie is cut off from understanding the song of the golden isle, Kayla's song affirms and soothes the presence of the violently dead among us. 'Home, they say. Home' are the last words of the novel. As this example of Ward's attention to the Gothic shows then, home is where horror lives alongside us.

With this in mind, genre too is another crucial aspect of Ward's work that could receive more critical attention. Each of Ward's novels have distinct formal features and genre identifications. Her first novel, *Where the Line Bleeds* (2008), is a coming-of-age story about twin brothers raised by their blind grandmother. As the boys graduate high school and enter adulthood, the severely limited opportunities available to them for employment and economic mobility put pressure on their young lives and their paths diverge. *Salvage the Bones* is, using Susan Fraiman's and Kristin J. Jacobson's definitions, a 'domestic' novel, about the lives of teenage siblings surviving and supporting each other in the face of both everyday precarity and the imminent landfall of Hurricane Katrina. *Sing, Unburied, Sing* (2017) is a road novel that also reworks Gothic traditions. A fourth novel, *Let Us Descend* (October 2023), is a historical narrative set in the mid-nineteenth century, about an 'enslaved woman whose mother is stolen and sold south to New Orleans, whose lover is stolen from and her and sold south, who herself is sold south and descends into the hell of chattel slavery' (Ward 2020, 104). In addition to these three published novels, the forthcoming novel, and a memoir, Ward has also edited a collection of essays, *The Fire This Time* (2015), and has recently published a commencement speech she made at Tulane in 2018 as *Navigate Your Stars* (2020). Broadly then, we might classify these works in terms of form, genre or hybrid genre: a *Bildungsroman*, domestic/disaster narrative, road novel/ghost story, historical novel, memoir, essay collection and personal narrative. Contemporary conceptions of genre – particularly those presented by Lauren Berlant and Theodore Martin, with their emphasis on unfixedness – provide useful ways to approach Ward's work and how it enables thinking about race in a global frame. One account of genre that might provoke particularly rich readings of Ward's work is Theodore Martin's description of the 'drag of genre' which operates in relation to the 'drift' of the contemporary (Martin 2019, 6). Martin argues that genres 'lead distinctly double lives, with one foot in the past and the other in the present; they contain the entire abridged history of an aesthetic form while also staking a claim to the form's contemporary relevance' (Martin 2019, 6). It is easy to see how this notion might apply to Ward's writing, and many scholars, including those in this volume, have discussed Ward's work in relation to its intertextualities, allusions, genre histories she has worked in – each of which has a specific set of ideological attachments. The Gothic again is a central example, to the extent that it deploys horror to register social and political critiques.

Ward's restless movement through different formal strategies and perennial interest in precarity also lends itself to Lauren Berlant's sense of genre flailing, a movement across genres employed as 'a mode of crisis management that arises after an object, or object world, becomes disturbed in a way that intrudes on one's confidence about how to move in it' (Berlant 2018). Accordingly, 'we genre flail so that we don't fall through the cracks of heightened affective noise into despair, suicide, or psychosis. We improvise like crazy, where 'like crazy' is a little too non-metaphorical.' (Berlant 2018). We might usefully locate Ward's work alongside Berlant's genre flail – not because it operates in the new 'genres of the precarity' that Berlant identifies in *Cruel Optimism*, like the 'situation tragedy', but because it is so attentive to the expectations and ideological attachments of the genres Ward writes in. Returning one final time to *Sing*'s tree of ghosts, it is important that the traumatised ghosts from a past that extends back to slavery are not exorcised at the end of the novel, as say Beloved is in Toni Morrison's novel, but remain at home with the novel's children. In this way, Ward's writing often articulates the slippages between precarious lives and the expectations these genres set up.

It is here, too, that it becomes imperative to think about Ward as among a larger cohort of Black diaspora authors whose writing enacts the kinds of slippages that disrupt the predictability and familiarity of genres, illuminating common concern with the obvious and sublimated ways race continues to constrain and marginalise Black life across the world. This cohort includes among others, Helen Oyeyemi, a Black British author of Nigerian descent. Oyeyemi writes, in *The Icarus Girl* (2005) and *White is for Witching* (2009), about impish child ghosts and haunted houses in a manner that demonstrates the indeterminate nature of many of the elements we have come to see as fixed, even within discourses that thematise the hybrid, alienating and dispossessing nature of diasporic realities. Marlon James, meanwhile, is a Jamaican writer whose novel *The Book of Night Women* (2009) is a neoslave narrative that does not end in the death, maiming or formal freedom of its protagonist, thereby disrupting one of the most formulaic genres that shape the definition of freedom in our present: the slave narrative. And Trinidadian Ayanna Lloyd Banwo's novel *When We Were Birds* (2022) focuses on the family of women whose duty since slavery has been maintaining the delicate balance between the living and the dead. In a narrative tradition that often centres the Queen's Park Savannah as the primary site of national identity and struggle – this is where Eric Williams gave anti-colonial speeches, where Black Power protests and even carnival culminate – Lloyd Banwo instead positions Lapeyrouse Cemetery, and thus death, at the centre of the novel about nationalism's legacies in the present.

Jesmyn Ward shares with these other writers a project of exploring Black life by attending to the afterlives of slavery in the present, charting their genre flailing relationship to the literary forms and genres that underwrite how freedom is imagined and articulated.

Even as this collection serves to affirm Ward's work as of critical importance in contemporary literature, it does not do so with completist aspirations. There remains so much more to be said about Ward's writing, the interrelations discussed above, the forms of mutual recognition across contemporary Black diasporic writing, and the regenerative power of global collective witnessing. It is our hope that this collection serves as an initial provocation that productively enables the further study of Ward's work in these and other directions.

Works Cited

Alexander, Michelle. 2020. *The New Jim Crow: Mass Incarceration in the Age of Colorblindness*. 10th anniversary ed. New York and London: The New Press.

Berlant, Lauren. 2018. 'Genre Flailing'. *Capacious: Journal for Emerging Affect Inquiry* 1, no. 2. http://capaciousjournal.com/article/genre-flailing/.

Fraiman, Susan. 2017. *Extreme Domesticity: A View from the Margins*. Illustrated ed. New York: Columbia University Press.

Goyal, Yogita. 2019. *Runaway Genres: The Global Afterlives of Slavery*. New York: NYU Press.

Hartman, Saidiya. 2008. *Lose Your Mother: A Journey Along the Atlantic Slave Route*. 1st ed. New York: Farrar, Straus & Giroux.

Jacobson, Kristin J. 2010. *Neodomestic American Fiction*. Columbus: Ohio State University Press.

Martin, Theodore. 2019. *Contemporary Drift: Genre, Historicism, and the Problem of the Present*. Repr. New York: Columbia University Press.

Sharpe, Christina. 2016. *In the Wake: On Blackness and Being*. Illustrated ed. Durham, NC: Duke University Press.

Ward, Jesmyn. 2017. *Sing, Unburied, Sing*. New York: Scribner.

—. 2018. *Where the Line Bleeds*. New York: Scribner.

—. 2020. 'On Witness and Respair: A Personal Tragedy Followed by a Pandemic'. *Vanity Fair*, 1 September. https://www.vanityfair.com/culture/2020/08/jesmyn-ward-on-husbands-death-and-grief-during-covid.

Index

EU representative:
Easy Access System Europe
Mustamäe tee 50, 10621 Tallinn, Estonia
Gpsr.requests@easproject.com

www.ingramcontent.com/pod-product-compliance
Lightning Source LLC
Chambersburg PA
CBHW051059030726
47504CB00006B/1695